The high scout shifted his aim to the last fire giant and fired. The enchanted shaft took its target high in the breastbone. Tavis uttered the command word. The brute's head disappeared in a blue flash, then his body collapsed in a clanging heap of steel and flesh.

The high scout turned to face Queen Brianna and found her lying in the bottom of her sleigh, clutching her abdomen. Avner was kneeling by her side holding her head. When he looked up to meet Tavis's gaze, his eyes were wide with alarm.

"I think your baby likes the fighting!" he yelled. "He's coming!"

## NOVELS BY TROY DENNING

**RETURN OF THE ARCHWIZARDS**
The Summoning
The Siege
The Sorcerer

**THE AVATAR SERIES**
Waterdeep
Crucible: the Trial of Cyric the Mad

**LOST EMPIRES**
Faces of Deception

**THE TWILIGHT GIANTS**
The Ogre's Pact
The Giant Among Us
The Titan of Twilight

**THE CORMYR SAGA**
Beyond the High Road
Death of the Dragon
(with Ed Greenwood)

FORGOTTEN REALMS®

# THE TITAN OF TWILIGHT

### THE TWILIGHT GIANTS

### BOOK III

## TROY DENNING

WIZARDS OF THE COAST™

The Twilight Giants, Book III
# THE TITAN OF TWILIGHT

Cover art by Duane O. Myers
First Printing: September 1995
This Edition First Printing: October 2005
Library of Congress Catalog Card Number: 2004116923

9 8 7 6 5 4 3 2 1

ISBN-10: 0-7869-3798-X
ISBN-13: 978-0-7869-3798-1
620-96991740-001-EN

U.S., CANADA,
ASIA, PACIFIC, & LATIN AMERICA
Wizards of the Coast, Inc.
P.O. Box 707
Renton, WA  98057-0707
+1-800-324-6496

EUROPEAN HEADQUARTERS
Hasbro UK Ltd
Caswell Way
Newport, Gwent NP9 0YH
GREAT BRITAIN
Please keep this address for your records

Visit our web site at **www.wizards.com**

For my mother

## Acknowledgments

I would also like to thank the following people for their contributions to the Twilight Giants Trilogy in general and The Titan of Twilight in particular: my editor, Rob, for his forbearance, unwavering support, and many insightful suggestions; my friend Degar and my instructor Lloyd of the AKF Martial Arts Academy in Janesville, WI, for their thoughts on titanic combat; Pat H., for sharing her expertise with difficult deliveries; Jim W., for his early enthusiasm and valuable suggestions; and most especially Andria, just because.

# Prologue

Through the still winds I sweep, silent as death. Below, the Vale: a crooked gorge of rock and snow forever clad in dusk's ashen winter livery. One beat of my umbral wings, and I sail half its immense length. The forlorn halls of Bleak Palace pass beneath my breast, a grim memorial to my ancient hubris. Two beats, and a craggy wall looms ahead. An insufferable yearning as cold as it is deep shudders through my tenebrous body. I long to soar over the cliff top, to fly into blue midnight and let slip this eternal eventide.

Instead, I dip a wing and bank. I circle back the way I came, as I have done a thousand times more than there are stones upon the land, and I listen to your voices. For an immeasurable eternity, they have poured through my head in an endless, ghastly rain—all the profane things you whisper when no one is listening, no one but me:

*"Of course, you don't have to, my dear! But if you like this shiny necklace . . ."*

*". . . where the lady stores her jewels—and if you want the key, I need my money. . . ."*

*". . . tonight, my love. Strangle her while she sleeps, and we'll always be . . ."*

Does it surprise you to know I am listening? It shouldn't. Your sinister whisperings come to me from all the black corners of your dark, distant world; at times they fill my head with such a profane, raucous rustling

1

that I cannot hear my own thoughts.

And even I—I, Lanaxis, the Titan of Twilight; mother-murderer and eternal prisoner of shadow; founder of Ostoria, Empire of Giants—even I cannot silence your voices. The gods have proclaimed that I must listen, and I dare not defy them. They are trying to tell me something—something momentous, I am sure.

*Unbalanced? Demented?* Will you call me mad?

Listen.

Aren't my words ringing inside *your* head?

Yes, yes! Now you understand. We're *all* mad, each of us. The voices make us that way; deranged and maniacal, quite possibly dangerous—but you more than me. I am, after all, chosen of the gods.

And suddenly I, Lanaxis the Chosen One, am sitting alone upon the crumbling steps of my palace, staring, as is my habit, into the eternal dusk above. Where the moon should hang is an enormous green eye. For a moment I am bewildered; then I realize what has happened: I have slipped free of the moment and settled in the past, sometime during the Time of Troubles, when the gods walked the land and chaos ruled Toril. It is, as always, impossible to know the date more exactly.

And truly, it doesn't matter. Time has lost its meaning. Since long before the first human kingdoms arose in the south lands, twilight has hung in this vale. The dusk is as perpetual and still as the heavens themselves. Never does night fall, nor the sun rise to herald a new dawn. There are no days by which to tally the tenday; no tendays to track the months. In this valley, the season never changes. The years pass without notice; they blur into decades; the decades into centuries; the centuries into decades of centuries. Life has become an endless series of moments that add up to nothing.

It is no wonder that I have slipped the currents of time, that I flit in and out of the eternal river like a dipping gull.

A bird's shadow appears on the snowy ground ahead. I look up and see a roc, as large as a cloud, soaring across the vale. Well do I remember the flavor of the raptor's meat—lean and wild, with a spicy tang that tickles the roof of the mouth.

I leap up and hurl a splintered pillar at the bird. As swift as a lightning bolt, the shaft flashes across the sky to bury itself in the raptor's breast. The creature screeches and reels. It dives, talons extended to exact revenge, but even a roc is no match for a titan's spear. The life seeps from its wings, and it rolls over to plummet toward me in a limp bundle of feathers.

But the gods would deny me even this simple feast. As the bird's shadow sweeps across my head, the great carcass dissolves into glimmering golden twinkles. A cold, tingling energy seeps into my body. Black, incorporeal feathers sprout along the edges of my arms, and my feet change into the talons of a great, shadowy raptor. Overwhelmed by the urge to launch myself into the sky, I beat the air with my umbral wings and rise into the purple twilight.

Thus is the *shadowroc* born, and still I have not decided whether it is the gift of the gods or their curse. How I long to flee this valley! How I yearn to soar over distant lands and see what has become of the world my brothers and I ruled!

Now I am with them again: Nicias and Masud, dynast of cloud giants and khan of fire giants, and also Vilmos, paramount of storm giants, Ottar, jarl of frost giants, and others too numerous to name. We stand beside the bubbling waters of the Well of Health, in the longest and most majestic colonnade of Bleak Palace, the largest and most exalted of the citadels of the Sons of Annam.

I have slipped far into the past, to that fateful moment I live again and again, to the moment I have already endured a thousand times and am doomed to suffer ten thousand times more. My brothers will not meet my gaze, and I know it falls to me alone to save Ostoria from our mother's faithless treachery. I feel the Mother Queen's rumbling approach, and the poison is quick from my hand to the well.

Othea arrives, her shadow plunging the entire colonnade into twilight. She is as large as a mountain, with hips like hillocks and a bosom of craggy buttresses. Her eyes are black, like caves, and her white hair billows off her head like a plume of snow.

I bid my two-headed servant, the ettin, to carry a chalice of water to Othea, but she will not drink. Her craggy mouth twitches at the corners, and she declares my brothers will drink with her. My mind fills with a white haze, thoughts sailing through it like wind-driven snow. A warning to my brothers would be a warning to Othea. Perhaps she knows what I have done? Is she testing me, to see if I will sacrifice my brothers to poison her?

I must. I will play this game to the end. Othea is the wife who cuckolds her husband, who loves her paramours' bastard races more than she loves us, who would give our empire to the children of her lovers.

I command my servant to bring chalices for my guests, and with my own hand I fill each cup. The tray shakes in the ettin's grasp. The ettin knows what I have poured into the well, but neither head speaks. They carry the goblets to my guests. I watch my brothers drink.

Yes, Othea drank too. I have slipped the moment again. I am once more the shadowroc, flying back and forth in the Vale, a lump of ice where my heart should be. The sensation is very clear to me, even thousands of years later; as my brothers fell dead, the blood in my veins turned to half-frozen slush. I began to shiver uncontrollably, my skin grew icy and numb, and the tears rolling down my cheeks stung like windblown sleet. I thought I had saved Ostoria.

Of course, I was wrong. Othea had already laid her curse on me, as she told me with her last, rattling breaths: her shadow will lie over Bleak Palace forever, filling me with a cold, sick regret for what I have done. I am free to leave, but when I do—this is the true treachery—when I do, I will become mortal. I will grow old and infirm; eventually I will die. The choice is mine: to spend eternity in cold twilight, or to sacrifice my immortality.

I have endured longer than Mother expected, I am sure.

It has not been easy. I have sat paralyzed for whole centuries, staring at a single stone between my feet, caught in the grip of a despair so profound that I remained in Othea's shadow only because I lacked the will to flee. But I *did* endure, and now I know I was never truly alone. The gods were watching over me; it was they who kept my feet rooted to the stones when I could think of no reason to remain. They have decreed a special destiny for me, and the time is close when I will fulfill their purpose.

I can tell, for they are speaking to me again. Your voices are ringing in my head, and the message is growing clear:

*"Please, whatever you desire—but I beg you, spare them. Save my little ones. . . ."*

*". . . you understand what we want. . . ."*

Yes, I understand. The world is full of evil—evil that has arisen from the destruction of Ostoria. The task the gods have set before me is clear: I must save Toril. I must reestablish the Empire of Giants and restore harmony to the world.

But I cannot rule this empire myself. After my mistake—I did not hesitate to poison my brothers, but it *was* a mistake—I am not fit. The king must be someone destined to rule, in whose veins flows the divine right of dominion. It is my duty to ensure that he is born.

I know who the mother is to be.

"Bring princess here?" The question comes from Goboka, a foolish ogre who has come to my vale seeking the powers of a shaman. "What princess?"

Goboka stands before me: a tiny, loutish figure lost in the vastness of my audience hall. I sit upon my throne, cloaked in a magic mantle of purple shadow. I have forgotten why I started concealing myself from mortal visitors—perhaps it was shame over my fall—but the habit has served me well. The giants have come to think of me as a sort of sacred spirit, and they do my bidding as if by divine command.

"The princess will . . . be born next . . . year," I explain, barely forcing the words out. I have managed to slip through time to the exact moment of Goboka's visit, and I must strain to explain what I want. Time builds a certain momentum as it rushes forward, and changing its course—even when the moment is recent—is no easy matter. "You must . . . bring her here no later than . . . her nineteenth birthday."

Again, your voices:

*"Why us? What have we done . . . ?"*

*". . . she's a beautiful filly, but for that price . . ."*

*"There are plenty of women who would . . ."*

No! Only her. Only Brianna of Hartwick may bear the child! She is descended of Annam's last son, who was ordained by the All Father to become king of giants and rule Ostoria with wisdom and justice. True, Othea robbed the child of his birthright—but she did not kill the seed. The seed lives on, awaiting but a wisp of divine breath to bring it to life again.

I will be that wisp.

"I beg your pardon," says Julien, the ettin's handsome

head.

We are standing together, my servant and I, in the moments before they are to leave Twilight forever. Beside us bubble the black waters that once we called the Well of Health, but have since named the Pool of Despair. Goboka has failed—through the eyes of my eagle familiar, I have seen Brianna's bloody axe and watched his headless body sink beneath a mountain mire—and I have just told my servant what I expect of them.

"You can't ask that of us!" Julien insists. "Othea cursed us, too. If we go after the princess, we'll die!"

I nod my head sadly. "Someday—but not until you grow old." I give the ettin a suit of magical armor I have forged for their misshapen body, and also a vial of powder I have mixed to ensure their success. "The armor will disguise you as a handsome human prince, and the powder will make Brianna fall in love with you."

"Why we need magic powder for that?" demands Arno, the ettin's ugly head. "Any woman love us!"

Love.

Is it not love that licenses treachery? This is so, and for me more than others. Do you think it is for my own sake that I poisoned the Mother Queen? Or for myself that I abide this murky prison? I endure for the sons and daughters of my dead brothers.

The mother-murderer suffers for the good of Toril.

Lanaxis the Chosen perseveres so that the giants may set the world to rights—and the time is nigh when they shall. True, the ettin died, but it would be wrong to say that he failed. He did better than Brianna knows; better, even, than I should have expected.

Now I stand on my palace balcony, my vacant gaze fixed on the icy wastes beyond the balustrade. But it is not the dusk-stained snows I see, nor the wind's cold hiss to which I listen. In the window of Brianna's throne room—the princess has become queen, but it would be foolish to ask me when—in the window perches my pet, his keen eyes and sharp ears serving me as his talons never could.

The queen's belly is swollen with child. Before her looms a milky-eyed firbolg with a mane of flyaway hair and a pelt of white beard.

"I have dreamed your birthing," he says. "You will bear two sons, one handsome and one ugly. It would be better for the Ice Spires if the ugly one never has a name."

Brianna's knuckles whiten. The change is almost imperceptible, but the eyes of my familiar are too keen to miss it. "I am to kill my child—on your word?"

"Majesty, I am sorry. If the ugly one grows to manhood, the giants will fill the Clearwhirl with the blood of 'kin and men."

"I, too, have dreamed." Brianna's voice is sharp with anger. Good. "But not of twins and wars. I have dreamed of a land ruled by children—"

"But Majesty, you're no seer! Your dream has no meaning!"

The queen rises, glaring. "In Hartsvale, my dreams are the *only* ones that have meaning!"

Your dreams and mine, Brianna. Your dreams and mine.

# ❖1❖
# Gorge of the Silver Wyrm

Tavis Burdun felt the detonation before he heard it: a faint quiver in the soles of his feet, followed instantly by a feeble shock wave breaking against his back. A muffled *karumph* rolled up the gorge from someplace far behind him, sweeping last night's snowfall off the craggy precipices, and he smelled whiffs of some mordant, caustic fume. There was a slight lull, then a deafening crack as an enormous ice curtain broke free of its cliff and crashed down on the far side of Wyrm River.

"Halt the Company of the Royal Snow Bear!" Tavis boomed, addressing the long column of warriors ahead. Even without the roar of shattering ice, he would have had to yell. A fierce boreal wind had been howling down the gorge since dawn, filling the canyon with a whistling keen as eerie and cold as a banshee's wail. "Halt the horse lancers! Halt the footmen and front riders!"

As the company sergeants relayed the commands forward, Tavis turned and looked back down the canyon, raising his hand to halt the elegant sleighs coming toward him. He saw nothing unusual, only the icy, rutted road that the queen's entourage had followed into the dusky Gorge of the Silver Wyrm. To one side of the route lay the broad ribbon of Wyrm River's frozen surface, with a sheer granite cliff looming above the far bank. To the other side rose a steep, craggy slope flecked with the stumps of a felled pine forest. A web of precarious footpaths laced the barren hillside, stringing together the rock heaps that spilled from the mouths of the canyon's fabled silver mines. Atop a few of the mine dumps stood a handful of tiny figures, weary miners who had crawled from their dank holes to watch the queen's procession. If they felt any concern over the muffled blast, their motionless forms did not betray it.

The royal sleigh, the first in the procession, continued to come toward Tavis. It was drawn by the queen's favorite horse, Blizzard, a white-flecked mare with a snowy mane and a disposition as fierce and unpredictable as her namesake. The beast did not halt until she reached Tavis's side, where she cast an angry glare into his eyes and snorted sour-smelling steam into his face. He grabbed the horse's bridle and pushed her head away, then fixed his attention on the sleigh's fur-swaddled driver. The young man was a lanky border scout with a yellow beard, twinkling gray eyes, and a touch of larceny in his ready smile.

"Avner, keep a taut rein on the Queen's Beast," Tavis advised, calling the petulant mare by his favorite nickname. "I don't like her look."

Before the young scout could reply, a muffled voice sounded behind the fleece curtain that enclosed the sleigh's passenger compartment. "Tavis? What was that horrible crash?"

"Falling ice, milady."

A mittened hand drew the curtain aside, revealing the striking form of Tavis's wife, Queen Brianna. She was a tall, big-boned woman with robust features and a chin as strong as a man's. Even her white fur cloak could not conceal the fact that she was enormously pregnant. She filled three-quarters of the booth, with a belly so swollen she could barely close her coat. There were dark circles under her eyes, for her condition made sleep difficult, and her cheeks were puffy and red from the bitter cold—but Tavis hardly noticed these flaws. He saw only her maternal radiance, the most ravishing of any beauty.

"Falling ice?" Brianna asked. "It sounded more like a falling mountain, Lord Scout."

Tavis pointed at the enormous ice blocks scattered along the far bank of Wyrm River. "There was some sort of blast behind us. It shook an ice curtain off the canyon wall." He nearly had to yell to make himself heard over the wind. "The road's not blocked, but we shouldn't go on until I know what happened."

"In that case, we may continue." The speaker rode into view and stopped his gray stallion on the far side of Brianna's sleigh. He was the earl of the Storming Gorge, Radborne Wynn, a stout old man wrapped in a cloak of silver ermine. With a tuft of ice-caked beard and a long mane of gray hair, he looked as august and feral as the mountain goats that roamed the canyons of his wind-blasted barony. "A tunnel wizard's spell caused the blast."

"You told me there would be no mining magic while Brianna is in the canyon!" Tavis barked. "Didn't you issue the command?"

Radborne responded with an icy glare. "The wizard responsible will be severely punished, Lord High Scout," he said. "I assure you, there is no need to speak to me in such tones."

The high scout clamped his jaw shut and looked away, running his eyes over the craggy slopes as though he had not heard the comment. He had learned not to apologize to nobles—such overtures were interpreted as signs of weakness—but the earl had a point. Tavis had been anxious and short-tempered the entire journey—

though with good reason, he thought.

The earl's miners had struck a rich new vein deep in the gorge, and with the royal reserves bled dry by three years of war against the giants, the treasury needed the extra silver. Unfortunately, the deposit could not be mined until Brianna blessed it. An ancient tradition held that Skoraeus Stonebones would swallow anyone who took ore from an unconsecrated vein, and tunnel wizards considered their calling dangerous enough without incurring the wrath of the stone giant god. So despite her delicate condition, Brianna had undertaken a difficult winter journey that would bring her within eight leagues of a fire giant stronghold at the canyon's far end. As the lord high scout of Hartsvale and the first defender of her majesty the queen, Tavis would have been remiss in his duties if he were not worried.

The high scout tried to steady his nerves by reminding himself that he had taken every possible precaution. The fifteen horse lancers of the Royal Snow Bear Company sat fifty paces up the canyon, in front of a roadside mine portal, their white chargers snorting steam and the pennon flags of their posted lances snapping in the wind. Ahead of the riders stood a hundred pikemen armored in frost-rimed breastplates. In front of the footmen, there was a contingent of swift, lightly armored front riders. A rearguard of six lancers and twenty footmen followed behind the royal entourage, while several bands of border scouts patrolled ahead, behind, and to both sides of the procession.

Tavis could do nothing more to ensure his wife's safety, but still he was plagued by the incessant sensation that he had overlooked some lurking danger.

Perhaps he was worried about the firbolg seer, Galgadayle. The old prophet had not bothered the queen since last spring, but Tavis doubted that had been the end of the matter. The fellow's dreams were never wrong, and everyone in the Ice Spires knew it. Twice, Galgadayle's prophecies had saved entire tribes, once when he foresaw a landslide that engulfed a verbeeg village, and another time when he predicted a flood that deluged a fomorian cave. If the seer claimed that one of the queen's twins would grow up to lead the giants against the northlands, there would be no shortage of people trying to put the babe to death. It did not even matter that the queen's own priest had divined the contents of her womb and discovered that she had only one child inside. Given the choice of believing Galgadayle or the imperious Simon of Stronmaus, most people would choose the beloved seer.

Even Tavis had his doubts. Like a knelling bell, Galgadayle's prophecy echoed through his dreams at night, woke him at dawn, and tolled through his mind all day long. Firbolgs could not lie. If the seer claimed to have dreamed ill about the royal offspring, then he had. But why had he seen twins, while the queen's priest divined but a single child?

After a few moments of being ignored, Earl Wynn grew impatient. "If we hurry, we can still reach the Silver Citadel before twilight." He cast a nervous eye at the crooked sliver of winter sky hanging over the canyon. Although it was barely two hours past noon, dusk was already beginning to darken the gray clouds. "I'm sure her majesty will appreciate a hot meal and a warm hearth this even—"

An enormous subterranean boom cut the sentence short. The road bucked, and Blizzard whinnied, her voice as shrill as the wind. The big mare reared against her harness rods, lifting the front of the royal sleigh high into the air. Tavis leapt past her slashing hooves and grabbed her bridle. He jerked the startled creature back to all fours, already casting an angry glance in Rad-

13

borne's direction.

"Earl, do *any* of your tunnel wizards heed your commands? One miscreant is bad enough, but two are—"

A deafening roar erupted behind the high scout, drowning out his complaint. The ground trembled beneath his feet, and a blast of hot wind scorched his neck. The same mordant fumes that he had sniffed earlier filled the canyon with a caustic, acrid stench. Tavis spun around and saw an immense tongue of flame lashing from the mine portal beside the road. Inside the inferno he glimpsed the writhing, wraithlike shapes of rearing chargers and flailing riders, then he was half-blinded by the glare and had to look away. Over the horrible crackling of the fire came the squeal of burning horses and the howls of dying men.

Blizzard neighed wildly and shied away from the blast. Only Tavis's grip on her bridle kept the mare from spinning away and toppling the royal sleigh. She reared, jerking the high scout off his feet. He came down hard on the icy road, then lay on his back, struggling to hang on to the bridle as Blizzard whipped her head to and fro. He twisted his hand into the leather and pulled. Although a runt by the standards of his race, Tavis was still a firbolg. His strapping arms were more than strong enough to manhandle a creature as small as a horse.

Tavis pulled Blizzard's nose to within reach of his free hand, then pinched her nostrils shut. The mare's eyes flared, but she quieted instantly. The high scout returned to his feet and looked back toward the sleigh, where Avner sat blanched and wild-eyed, cursing the Queen's Beast under his breath. Brianna sat far back in the passenger compartment, gripping the hand rails so tightly that her knuckles were white. Her complexion had turned pale, and the shadow of a grimace lingered on her face.

"Milady, are you injured?" Tavis asked. "Did that jolt—"

"I'm pregnant, not feeble." Brianna glanced over the scout's head, then hissed, "Hiatea have mercy!"

For the first time, Tavis noticed that the deafening roar behind him had been replaced by the hiss and pop of melting ice. The searing heat had yielded to the flesh-numbing cold of deep winter, and the acrid stench of the explosion had been swept down the canyon by the fierce boreal gale. A few of the wounded had raised their voices to shriek in eerie harmony with the wailing wind, but most were too stunned to do more than groan.

The three closest horse lancers had already struggled to their feet and were calling to their mounts, which were clambering up the steep hillside as fast their hooves could climb. More riders lay scattered across the road, their flesh as black as their scorched armor. Despite their terrible burns, several men were crawling over the hissing ice to their charred horses, already drawing the daggers that would put the loyal beasts out of misery. A huge plume of yellow smoke was billowing from the mine portal beside the road. The fumes were so thick that Tavis could not see the coughing, confused footmen on the other side of the cloud.

Behind Tavis, Avner gasped, "Milady, no! You're the queen!"

"I'm also Hiatea's high priestess." Tavis turned to see his wife climbing out of her sleigh, her gaze fixed on the groaning soldiers ahead. "And those men are suff—"

Brianna's eyes rolled back in their sockets, then she groaned sharply. She clenched her teeth and grabbed her abdomen with both hands.

Tavis bolted to her side, catching her in his arms. "The baby!"

He lifted Brianna back into the sleigh, then cast a

wary eye toward the yellow smoke boiling out of the mine ahead. He did not relish the thought of his pregnant wife passing through those caustic fumes, but he cared less for the idea of watching her give birth in the open. Turning around was out of the question. It would be dark before they could clear the courtiers' sleighs off the narrow road behind them.

"Avner, close the curtain," Tavis ordered. "We've got to get the queen to the Silver Citadel, now!"

"There's . . . no rush," Brianna gasped. "It's nothing . . . I've had these pains before."

"What?"

The queen let out a slow breath, then sat up. "They probably don't mean anything, Tavis." Her face no longer appeared anguished, but her cheeks remained pale, and the pain was slow in fading from her eyes. "I've been having them now and again."

"And you didn't tell me?" Tavis growled. "When we left Castle Hartwick, you must have known your time was near!"

"I knew no such thing—and I still don't," Brianna retorted. "It could be another year before I give birth— we really have no way to tell, do we?"

The high scout could not argue. The queen had been pregnant more than three years already, since just after the war broke out. Tavis had not worried for the first two years, since firbolg women carried their offspring that long, but he had grown steadily more concerned over the last year. The blood of Brianna's divine ancestors still ran strong in her veins, and Tavis secretly feared that the three racial stocks of their progeny had combined in some terrible way to prevent the birth—or to make the infant the hideous monster of Galgadayle's dream.

A low, grating rumble sounded from someplace inside the mine tunnel, then Radborne's shocked voice echoed off the canyon wall. "F-Fire giants!"

Tavis looked toward the mine, where the large, boulderlike shape of a giant's head protruded from the smoking portal. The brute's ebony face was surrounded by a halo of orange beard and scarlet hair, but the high scout could see little more through the billowing yellow fumes.

Tavis took his bow off his shoulder. At eight feet long, the weapon was not quite as large as the legendary Bear Driller, which had been destroyed three years earlier in a battle against an ancient ettin. The new bow, however, was easily a match for Bear Driller, as it was strung with woven steel and reinforced with the rune-etched ribs of a glacier bear.

"Be ready, Avner." Tavis pulled an arrow from his quiver. It was thicker than most, with red fletching, a stone tip, and runes carved along the shaft. "I'll clear the way."

The high scout was surprised to hear a nervous edge in his voice. Usually, he felt coldly tranquil at the beginning of a battle, unconcerned about anything except maneuvers and tactics. But today his thoughts were a boiling cataract of fear and doubt. Images of his pregnant wife kept appearing in the churning froth inside his head, like a swimmer being swept downstream.

The fire giant squirmed forward until his lanky shoulders came into view, then he thrust his powerful arms out of the mine and dug his fingers into the tunnel's stone collar. He began to pull his torso out of the hole. The ice hissed and turned to steam beneath his breastplate, as though the heat of the forge still lingered within his black armor.

Tavis nocked his arrow and pointed the stone tip into the fuming portal, not even bothering to search for a gap in the giant's black armor. The high scout drew his bow, at the same time hissing, "taergsilisaB!" A ruby gleam flared from one of the runes etched into his weapon, then flashed out of existence. He released the bowstring. A sharp clap echoed off the canyon walls, and the arrow flashed away, leaving a blinding streak of crimson between the bow and the tunnel mouth. The shaft flew into the mine, then pierced its target's thick armor with a muffled clang.

The fire giant did not drop dead, for even an arrow driven by the lord high scout's magic bow was not powerful enough to fell such a foe in a single strike. The mighty warrior merely grunted in surprise, then instinctively reached for his wound.

"esiwsilisaB!" Tavis cried, speaking the command word that would activate the runearrow's magic.

From inside the mine came a glimmering blue flash and a mighty boom. The fire giant's torso shot out of the portal and plummeted over the steep bank of Wyrm River, trailing a spray of crimson blood from the truncated waist. Blizzard whinnied in alarm, and Tavis grabbed her reins. A muffled crack reverberated deep within the mountain.

There was no opportunity to cry out or to cringe in fear, and even the queen's mare did not have time to rear. The hillside simply folded inward over the tunnel. At the top of the ravine, a frozen buttress of stone lost its hold on the canyon wall and came rumbling down the slope. Tavis and Blizzard barely managed to retreat half a dozen steps before the avalanche roared over the mine portal and swallowed the fallen lancers of the Royal Snow Bear Company. The churning mass spread up the road, then spilled over Wyrm River's steep bank and rumbled across the broad ribbon of ice, engulfing the fire giant's truncated corpse and finally crashing against the far side of the canyon.

For a moment, Tavis could do nothing except stare at the mountainous jumble before him, listening to the dying thunder of the avalanche echo down the crooked gorge. He felt himself shivering in the cold wind and realized that he had broken into a nervous sweat. The landslide had come so close to swallowing his wife's sleigh, and him with it, that he could have reached out with his bow and touched a frost-rimed boulder as large as himself. Even Blizzard seemed stunned by the close call. She stood stiff and motionless at his side, the muscles of her powerful shoulders trembling with fear.

Brianna was the first to speak. "It seems we finally have a name for your new bow, Tavis," she said. "I hereby dub it Mountain Crusher."

"Hear, hear! The giants will need Surtr's own help to dig out of there." Radborne's eyes were fixed on the hillock of stone and ice ahead. The heap rose thirty feet above the mine portal, and the choking yellow plume that had been pouring from the tunnel a moment earlier had now been reduced to a few scattered wisps. "Well done!"

From the other side of the rubble heap came a sergeant's terrified voice: "Your Majesty? Lord Scout?"

"The queen is well!" Tavis yelled back. "What of the footmen?"

"Mostly able. The slide buried a dozen of us," he replied. "What would you have us do?"

"Climb over here," Tavis called. "We're going to need you to carry the queen's sleigh over the avalanche."

The high scout did not even consider abandoning the sleighs to retreat up the canyon. Even if Brianna had been in any condition to ride, they would only find more fire giants coming down the road. The fumes he had sniffed after the first, distant explosion smelled the same as the mordant smoke that had been pouring from the mine ahead. Unless the magic of Radborne's tunnel wizards bore the same odor as fire giant alchemy, it seemed likely that their ambushers had planned to trap the queen between two war parties.

The footmen began to cross the landslide, their armor clanging loudly as they clambered and slipped over the ice-rimed boulders. Tavis relayed orders to the front riders to dismount and wait on the other side of the avalanche in case the queen's party needed to borrow the mounts. While the high scout arranged his wife's escape, Avner unhitched Blizzard and set her free. The trails that laced the canyon walls were too narrow and precarious for sleighs, but the stubborn mare had followed her beloved mistress over paths far more perilous.

Tavis was about to send word for the courtiers to abandon their sleighs when a familiar, sharp odor came to him on the wind. He heard a soft crackling, as of a distant fire, then a cry of alarm rose from the back of the column. The high scout turned to see the first of his enemies rounding a bend, about three hundred yards beyond the entourage's rearguard.

The fire giant was a lanky, dark figure that loomed thrice the height of a man. Like the one Tavis had killed a few moments earlier, this brute was armored in steaming black plate. He also wore a massive helmet upon his head and a buckler as large as a table strapped to one forearm. In his other hand, he carried a flaming sword longer than Tavis was tall.

The high scout drew another runearrow from his quiver, but did not nock it. Over the long line of courtier sleighs, he could see that the rearguard's six lancers were already charging the brute. If he used the arrow now, he would catch them in the blast.

The fire giant bellowed his war cry and stomped forward to meet the attack, lowering his buckler to protect his groin from his foes' upturned lances. Behind him, another giant was already stepping around the bend.

The first giant's fiery sword descended on the leading

pair of horsemen. The huge blade struck with a blinding white flare. When the flash faded, the cleaved bodies of horses and riders were tumbling toward their killer's feet in a tangled ball of smoke and blood. The wind grew heavy with the stench of charred flesh.

The surviving riders leapt their horses over the mess, angling their weapons at their enemy's hips. The leading pair splintered their lances against the giant's steel shield, then crashed into his thick legs with a clamorous boom. Even a fire giant could not stand against two chargers at full gallop. The impact knocked the brute's legs from beneath him, and he dropped to the road face first, crushing the horsemen and their mounts beneath his heavy body.

Before the fire giant could recover, the last pair of riders arrived, their weapons pointed at the soft, unarmored flesh at the base of his neck. The momentum of the charge drove their lances deep into the giant's torso, eliciting a scream as thunderous as it was brief, then their mounts crashed into his shoulders. The horsemen flew from their saddles and tumbled down the length of their foe's spine, their armor chiming against his until they skidded off his flanks.

As they struggled to their knees, the next fire giant stepped around the bend and carefully crushed each man beneath his foot. Behind the brute, Tavis could see at least two more giants, and he suspected there was a long line behind them.

The high scout nocked his runearrow.

The palace courtiers began to leap from their sleighs and scurry down the road. Swaddled as they were in thick cloaks of combed fur, they looked like a herd of frightened wolf pups fleeing the slavering jaws of a snow dragon. Their abandoned draft horses also panicked, turning the road into a churning mass of hysterical beast and man. Sleighs began to plummet over the riverbank and topple along the edge of the road, and such a tumult of terrified shrieking filled the air that it was impossible to separate the human voices from those of the horses.

Tavis aimed at the chest of the leading fire giant, more than three hundred yards away, and hissed the command word that would trigger his bow's magic. A rune flared red and vanished from sight. The high scout released Mountain Crusher's bowstring, and the arrow streaked away, leaving a trail of crimson light above the jumble of abandoned sleighs.

The runearrow pierced the black armor as though it were leather instead of steel. The giant peered down at the fletching that had sprouted in his breastplate, and Tavis could imagine the brute's face scowling in fear and confusion. Fire giant armor was as thick as a dungeon door, hammered from special steel forged only in the fires of their volcano homes. For anything less than a storm giant's spear to pierce it was unthinkable—at least without magic. The fellow reached up to pinch the arrow between his thumb and finger.

"Blast him now!" urged Radborne. "Say the word!"

Tavis remained silent. When the giant tried to extract the runearrow, the butt of the shaft broke off. The warrior's face paled to an ashy charcoal. He turned to face his comrades, pointing at the pinhole in his armor. The second giant in line leaned down to inspect the wound, with a third peering over his shoulder.

"esiwsilisaB!" Tavis cried.

A sapphire light reflected off the slope beside the three giants, then a thunderous boom shook the canyon. The wounded brute dropped where he was, a smoking hole in his chest. The second giant's head simply vanished in a ball of blue flame. The third survived long enough to cover his mangled face and turn away, then fell over the riverbank and crashed through the ice.

Four more giants stomped around the bend. The foot-men of the rearguard formed two wedges and started down the road.

The palace courtiers began to gather around the queen's sleigh, assaulting both Brianna and Tavis with a din of questions and suggestions. The scout quickly found himself trying to keep the frightened crowd at bay as well as watch the giants ahead. He did not notice the arrival of the rest of the Royal Snow Bear Company until a sergeant clanged to a stop at his side.

Tavis turned to the man, a grizzled veteran with a gray beard and bushy black eyebrows. "Get these worthy gentlemen and ladies out of the way," the high scout ordered. "Send the rest of your footmen to reinforce the rearguard."

As the sergeant and his men began to herd courtiers toward the landslide, Tavis took an inventory of his quiver and bow. He had plenty of black-feathered runearrows left, and four runes still remained on Mountain Crusher's lower limb. Unfortunately, those sigils were of little use at the moment. The runes on the upper limb were the ones that made his shafts pierce the fire giants' thick armor, and only two of those remained.

The high scout looked up the canyon. The four fire giants were scuttling down the narrow road, hunched over so that he could barely see their heads and shoul-ders above the abandoned sleighs. The brutes were hid-ing behind their bucklers, with the surfaces angled to deflect arrows. They had been careful to space them-selves so that Tavis's blasts could not kill more than one at a time.

The rearguard was still a hundred yards from the leader.

Tavis nocked another runearrow. As the main body of the Royal Snow Bear Company pushed through the tangle of abandoned sleighs, the high scout fired at the second of the approaching giants. The magic shaft streaked away, penetrating both buckler and armor with a single loud clang. The high scout spoke his second command word. The blast sent the huge warrior's buckler twirling high into the air, with the arm that had been holding it still attached.

The leading giant cast a nervous glance over his shoulder. He grimaced at the sight of his comrade's mangled carcass, then rose to his full height and charged. Tavis nocked another runearrow, but held his fire. The rearguard's first wedge was already rushing to meet the attack. The three point men brandished battle-axes, and everyone else held long pikes.

The giant closed the distance in three crashing steps. The men in the middle row angled their pikes toward his midsection. He brought his buckler down instantly, sweeping the sharp points aside, and swung his fiery sword into the wedge. A chorus of agonized screams echoed off the cliffs, and the wind was suddenly heavy with the stench of charred flesh. Four severed bodies dropped in midstride.

The wedge continued its charge, the weapons of the rear echelon now rising toward the fire giant's vulnerable loins. Too late, the brute realized his mistake and stepped away, trying in vain to bring his shield back into position. The pikes struck home, and a loud crackle echoed off the walls as several shafts snapped against his steel armor. The giant bellowed in pain and stumbled back, the splintered ends of two wooden poles protruding from the seams in his armor. The axemen went to work, hacking at his ankles as though felling a tree. The huge warrior toppled to the icy road, crushing three more humans before the survivors swarmed him.

The rearguard's second wedge began its charge, rushing forward to meet the last pair of fire giants. Hoping to spare them the trouble of felling both brutes, Tavis pulled another runearrow and turned Mountain Crusher back down the canyon. The pair had wisely decided not to hide behind their bucklers and were rushing up the road at a full sprint. The high scout drew his bowstring back and aimed at the one in front.

Before he could fire, a bolt of lightning arced away from the queen's sleigh. It struck the leading fire giant with a thunderous bang, burning a terrific hole through his breastplate and the chest it protected. The bolt blasted through the brute's backplate and crackled halfway to the next giant before finally fading.

The high scout shifted his aim to the last fire giant and fired. The shaft took its target high in the breastbone. Tavis uttered the command word. The brute's head disappeared in a blue flash, then his body collapsed in a clanging heap of steel and flesh.

"Well done!" exclaimed Radborne. "You saved my mines!"

"That's a good thing, I suppose," Tavis allowed. "But I was more concerned with the queen's safety."

The high scout turned to face Brianna and found her lying in the bottom of her sleigh, clutching her abdomen. Avner was kneeling by her side holding her head. When he looked up to meet Tavis's gaze, his eyes were wide with alarm.

"I think your baby likes the fighting!" he yelled. "He's coming!"

The high scout slung his bow over his shoulder and went to his wife. "Sergeant! I want men here!" he bellowed. "We must carry the queen's sleigh over that landslide!"

The sergeant arrived almost instantly. "Begging your

pardon, Lord Scout," he said. "But I don't think we'll be having time for that."

Tavis looked up and saw the sergeant pointing down the canyon. Another fire giant was peering around the bend.

# ❖ 2 ❖
## Winter Battle

The crushing agony receded as it had come, smoothly and swiftly, and Brianna felt like a door was being lifted off her abdomen. Her broken waters were already growing cool against her thighs, but the effort of breathing still sent torrents of liquid fire tumbling through her body. Something was wrong. The royal midwife had said there would be no pain when the womb unleashed its flood, yet the queen had not suffered such pain since the ogre Goboka had punched her in the stomach. She felt herself flush with fear, tiny pearls of sweat popping out on her brow and lip. In the bitter cold, the beads froze almost as quickly as they formed.

"Brianna?"

The queen opened her eyes to find Tavis peering at her. His rugged firbolg features were tense with concern, and his eyes were fixed on her lap, where her cloak had opened to reveal a half-frozen stain of thin, milky fluid. Blizzard, now free of her harness, had hooked her chin over the edge of the sleigh to stare at her mistress. Only Radborne, still sitting on his silver stallion, had averted his gaze.

Brianna tugged her coat closed, then, with Avner's help, pulled herself onto her seat. "The baby's coming."

Tavis cringed. "He has a bad sense of timing."

"*She,*" the queen quipped, hoping the banter would relax her husband. She had never seen Tavis panic, but he looked nervous today—and today, of all days, she needed him calm. "The child is a girl—by royal decree."

Tavis grinned, but the smile quickly vanished as a fire giant's angry bellow dropped out of the wind. The death screams of several men echoed off the canyon wall, and the reek of charred flesh filled Brianna's nose: a sick, rancid odor that made her jaws ache with the urge to vomit. Then came the clatter of snapping pikes, more yelling, and the booming crash of a collapsing giant. The Royal Snow Bear Company had felled its next foe.

Blizzard snorted anxiously and stomped her foot, no doubt urging the queen to take flight before it was too late. Tavis stepped onto the sleigh's running board, his ruddy complexion now as white as Brianna's cloak, and reached for her.

"No. See to the battle." It was the hardest command the queen had ever given. All her maternal instincts howled for her to find a quiet and safe place to give birth—but there was no safe place, not with the fire giants' attacking. She pushed Tavis away. "Go and stop our enemies."

"I'm the first defender," Tavis objected. "My duty is to see you to safety, if I can."

"Then you mean to abandon my mines?" Radborne's voice was indignant.

Tavis gave the earl a cold glare. "Your silver mines mean nothing to me."

"But they mean everything to Hartsvale—and I want you to save them," Brianna said. She switched her gaze to Radborne. "Earl, you will fetch my midwife, then assemble an escort in case I must flee the battle."

Radborne scowled. "These *are* my mines," he objected. "My place is—"

"Gentlemen, I am not asking your opinions." Brianna cast admonishing glances at both Radborne and Tavis. "I am issuing commands."

Tavis raised his brow, then set his jaw and took a runearrow from his quiver. To Avner, he said, "Promise me this, Scout: no matter what happens to me, you won't let the giants have Brianna or the baby."

Avner nodded grimly. "On my honor."

"Tavis, nothing's going to happen to you." Brianna tried to sound confident. "That is *my* promise."

"In battle, even a queen cannot guarantee such a thing," Tavis replied. He kissed Brianna, then turned to face Radborne. "Earl, we have our orders."

With that, the high scout turned away and rushed off. He crossed the road and angled up the mountainside, then traversed the slope above the main body of the Royal Snow Bear Company. Now that Brianna had persuaded him to concentrate on the battle at hand, the firbolg seemed completely in his element. He ran along the frost-rimed slope with bow in hand, vaulting ice-draped boulders and sidestepping snow-capped stumps without taking his eyes off the fire giants. Tavis was known as the Lion of Hartwick for his great size and hunting prowess, but Brianna thought of him more as a sleek, noble bighorn ram. He was powerful, swift, and agile without being bloodthirsty or cruel, and he possessed a certain feral dignity rare in human men. If something happened to her husband today—the queen stopped herself, for there was no use even considering that possibility. Tavis Burdun would never fall, not in this battle, nor any other.

As the high scout moved up the canyon, a steady war din started to build: screaming footmen, bellowing giants, the crackle of flaming swords and snapping pikes, steel clanging against steel. Other smells merged with the sick stench of burning warriors: coppery blood, throat-scorching brimstone, the fetor of spilled entrails. Brianna's stomach grew hollow and queasy. She forced herself to breathe through her mouth. She climbed out of her sleigh, holding on to Blizzard's snowy mane while she peered up the canyon.

Two hundred yards away, the road was becoming a river of pain and death as a long line of fire giants waded into a swirling current of knee-high soldiers. The queen could see her footmen swarming around the first three foes, hacking with gleaming battle-axes at huge ankles, or jabbing pikes into the seams between thick plates of ebony armor. The giants were fighting back viciously, clearing broad swaths of road with every swing of their fiery swords. Brianna counted a dozen more brutes coming down the canyon to join the battle, and she could not even see the end of their line.

Tavis was already a hundred yards up the canyon, above a jumble of courtier sleighs lying abandoned along the roadside. He was less than twenty paces from the leading fire giants, easily within bow range; from that distance, he could sink an arrow into each of a giant's eyes before the dead body hit the ground. Nevertheless, the high scout continued forward, traversing the slope well above the reach of his enemies. The queen saw one giant try to climb after him, but a thicket of pikes instantly drove up beneath the warrior's loin apron. The brute thundered in pain and collapsed into the battle swarm.

Brianna felt her hand drifting toward her sleigh, where the satchel containing her spell components lay on the bench. She allowed herself to pick up the bag, but restrained the urge to reach inside. Through long experience, the queen had learned the wisdom of saving her magic for critical moments, when a rain of fiery hail or a well-placed lightning bolt could turn the tide of a battle.

Tavis finally stopped and nocked his runearrow. He fired down the hill. The queen waited for the shaft to detonate, but the blue flash and sharp crack never came. Apparently, the arrow had bounced off the target's thick armor—it was inconceivable that the lord high scout had actually missed. He drew another runearrow and fitted it onto Mountain Crusher's bowstring.

On the hillside below Tavis appeared two fire giants, crouching behind their bucklers and scrambling up the slope. One brute's breastplate was striped by a long runnel of blood, bright and red against the ebony steel. From his collarbone protruded a tiny, feathery stub: the high scout's first runearrow.

Tavis ignored the pair and fired at the road again. Brianna felt a growing tension low in her abdomen and knew another labor pain was coming. The two giants lowered their bucklers and charged up the slope, raising their huge swords to strike.

"What's that firbolg doing?" Brianna demanded of no one in particular. "Say the command word!"

She would have said it herself, but that was not possible. Three years ago, Tavis had nearly died when a spy learned how to discharge his runearrows and detonated one in his face. Now, the command words had to be spoken backward, and even then, they worked only if spoken by the person who had nocked the shaft.

By the time his foes reached striking range, Tavis had pulled another runearrow from his quiver. Brianna did not see what good it would do him, for he would never have the opportunity to nock it. The fire giants' huge swords dropped, tracing fiery arches against the hillside. Tavis gathered himself to leap, then the giants' flaming blades came together in a brilliant flash.

The hillside erupted into a fiery ball, spraying

scorched rock and blazing stumps into the air as high as the giants' heads. The looming warriors raised their swords and struck again, hewing great, smoking furrows deep into the mountainside. They did not stop swinging until they had churned the ground into a blackened mound of stone and earth. Even then they continued to jab the tips of their blades into the heap, like a pair of nervous hunters trying to spear a wolverine before it scurried from its den and chewed their legs off.

The giants were doomed to fail. Brianna saw Tavis more than twenty paces down the slope, rising to a knee, the runearrow in one hand and Mountain Crusher in the other. His cloak was badly tattered from catching on stones and stumps, and he looked rather unsteady on his feet. Despite his condition, he quickly nocked his arrow and fired.

The shaft streaked up the slope and planted itself behind a giant's knee. If the fellow cried out, his voice was lost in the battle din, but he suddenly hunched over to slap at the wound. He said something to the brute with the runearrow lodged near the collarbone, and they both turned to face Tavis. In the same instant, the enormous, bearded face of a third fire giant appeared behind the scout.

Brianna's hand slipped into her satchel. Before she could withdraw the spell component, her husband abruptly rushed across the slope toward a nearby crag. Behind him, sapphire lights flashed beneath the armor of his foes, and a trio of loud, sharp booms shook the canyon. All three giants collapsed, one with nothing below his loin apron, one with nothing above his breastplate, and the third with nothing between his chin and his belt. With the impact of their crashing bodies, Brianna's swollen stomach reverberated like a drum.

The baby noticed the rumble, too. The queen's belly

suddenly began to jump and dance above the child's kicking feet. A tiny fist pressed against her kidney, sending a fiery pang of anguish through her lower back. Almost instantly, the pain faded to a dull ache, but it also slid forward and encircled her abdomen. The coil slowly tightened, and the crushing agony of a labor pain gripped her.

The queen gritted her teeth and kept her gaze fixed up the canyon. One of the giants had fallen onto the road, but the other two were still tumbling down the slope, descending upon the road in a fiery avalanche of blood, bone, and steel. They came to rest atop the third giant, forming a hillock of black armor and flesh.

The death of the three fire giants caused no eerie silences or temporary lulls in the battle; the fighting continued. The Royal Snow Bears pressed their attack with renewed vigor. One giant fell when he looked over his shoulder at his dead comrades, the next when he slipped and dropped to a knee. Brianna's pikemen swarmed up the gorge, leaving the road behind them strewn with bodies large and small. The roar of combat faded to a drone, and the rancid battle-smell grew so thick the howling wind could not sweep it from the canyon.

The Snow Bears' advance came to a rumbling halt thirty paces later, when they crashed into a long line of charging fire giants. As the battle din returned to its former roar, four giants at the rear of the column climbed the hillside into Brianna's view. Unlike their comrades on the road below, they had no bucklers strapped to their arms. They carried their swords, dark and cold, in their scabbards. The four spread out and cautiously started across the barren slope toward Tavis, bobbing and dodging to make themselves difficult targets.

Doing her best to ignore her growing pain, Brianna reached into her satchel, considering which of her spells would best aid her husband.

As her fingers closed around a small glass rod, Avner cried, "Majesty, look!"

The young scout was standing on his bench, pointing up Wyrm River. Brianna looked over the top of her sleigh and saw several fire giants near the bend in the canyon, belly-crawling down the river's icy surface. They were not hiding—even the thought was absurd—but trying to distribute their weight across the ice so they did not fall through. They would soon outflank the Royal Snow Bears, for the company no longer had enough men to spread their lines across the frozen river.

Brianna glanced back toward Tavis. When she saw him standing beneath his crag with another runearrow in hand, the queen took a pinch of powdered brimstone from her satchel and turned her attention to Wyrm River. She removed her goddess's golden talisman from her neck and pointed it up the canyon.

"Valorous Hiatea," she said, "I call upon you to aid these brave and noble warriors in their just cause, that they may prevail against our enemies and ever serve your will."

The amulet, shaped like a blazing spear, began to glow, the golden fire dancing as though the metal had truly burst into flame. Brianna tossed her brimstone into the air, at the same time uttering her spell. A river of acrid amber fumes shot from the talisman and streaked up the canyon. When the yellow smoke reached its targets, it coalesced into a huge, roiling cloud that hung in the wind like a boulder in a cataract. The fire giants craned their necks at the billowing vapors, and the queen hissed the mystical word that would unleash the spell's fury.

With a thunderous crack, the yellow cloud burst, spilling a shower of sizzling, popping fire pellets onto the frozen river. The giants bellowed in surprise and leapt to their feet, the tiny balls of flame bouncing like hailstones off their black plate armor. Although Brianna could see that her blazing storm was hardly incinerating the fire giants, the brutes were nevertheless frightened—and with good reason. They had taken no more than three steps before a series of long, sharp crackles rang through the canyon. A hissing, impenetrable steam cloud rose about their legs. Almost as one, the entire group dropped through the thawing ice, filling the canyon with an eerie chorus of chattering and gurgling as their heavy armor dragged them beneath Wyrm River's frigid waters.

The agony in Brianna's abdomen had grown worse. She felt as if someone were standing on her stomach, grinding hobnailed boots into her womb. Her knees were trembling, and the pain deepened with every breath. The queen grabbed a handful of Blizzard's mane and cursed Radborne for taking so long to return with her midwife, then looked toward her husband.

Tavis's four attackers had discovered they could not dodge the firbolg's deadly aim. Now they were rushing across the slope, pulling boulders out of the ground as they ran. Brianna could see stripes of blood streaking the armor of two giants, and the high scout was just drawing his bowstring to fire another runearrow. He would have plenty of time to plant his deadly shafts in the remaining foes long before they reached him.

But even Tavis Burdun was not infallible. As he loosed Mountain Crusher's bowstring, his target suddenly pulled a boulder out of the ground and stood upright. The shaft bounced off the giant's armor and ricocheted down the mountain, disappearing into the midst of the melee. The high scout's shoulders slumped. He could not detonate any of his runearrows without obliterating what remained of the Royal Snow Bears.

The fire giants hurled their boulders. Tavis threw himself down the mountain to escape the barrage, and his foes sprinted forward.

Brianna pulled a small stick of purple glass from her satchel. Her hands were trembling—whether from crushing pain or naked terror, she did not know. She pointed the glass rod at the giants and, squeezing the words up from deep within her pain-racked body, beseeched Hiatea's blessing.

As Brianna spoke, Tavis rolled to his feet holding the long, thin shaft of a normal arrow. He nocked and fired in one smooth motion. The queen did not even see the missile streak through the air. Her husband simply released Mountain Crusher's bowstring, then a giant slapped a hand over his eye and dropped to a knee.

The flames on Brianna's golden amulet began to dance. The queen summoned the spell to mind, then groaned aloud as her anguish deepened. It felt as if the inexorable power of her abdominal muscles were grinding her pelvis bone to powder. She forced herself to exhale, twice, trying to breathe away her agony. The pain only grew worse.

Brianna fixed her eyes on her husband. He was racing down the hillside, reaching for his quiver with stones and stumps flying past his head, dodging fire giant boots as they kicked the ground around him into a froth. The queen opened her mouth, forcing her tongue to curl and trill as she shaped the arcane syllables that would save her husband's life.

An unbearable surge of pain gripped her. She heard herself scream and felt her knees buckle, and her half-finished spell misfired. The glass rod dissolved in her hand, becoming a twinkling beam of purple luminescence that shot out of the canyon and hung high in the sky, fluttering and hissing and popping like the boreal lights gone mad.

A fire giant's boot slammed into her husband and sent

his limp body tumbling across the mountainside. Then Brianna felt the stinging bite of ice beneath her body and realized she had collapsed. A moment later, she heard the cold thunder of boulders raining down on the frozen road, and the voices of her loyal footmen rising together in a long, mournful wail: the death shriek of the Royal Snow Bear Company.

# ❖3❖
## Oin Meadowhome

Brianna lay doubled over in an icy rut—for minutes, it seemed—her ears ringing with the screams of the Royal Snow Bear Company. She felt the road shuddering beneath her body, the wind rasping across her cheek, even her own voice burning like bile as her screams boiled up from her womb. But she heard nothing—nothing save the cries of her loyal soldiers, perishing beneath the thundering torrent of granite.

The seeping mists of despair filled the queen's mind, and through this darkening haze swarmed a bevy of somber thoughts. The giants had won, and more than the battle. They had captured the gorge, and with it the silver that kept Hartsvale's armies strong; they had felled her husband, and with him the pillar of her strength; soon, they would take Brianna herself, and with her the infant so desperately fighting to reach a bloody and uncertain future.

Brianna did not know what to do when—if—her enemies captured her. They would present her to their mysterious guardian, the Twilight Spirit, so he could use his magic to get a giant king on her. To prevent that, the queen had vowed to die before allowing any giant to take her alive—but she had made that pledge before her

38

pregnancy. Now, she worried that she lacked the strength, perhaps even the right, to make the same choice for her child.

Brianna opened her eyes and exhaled long and hard, then rolled to her knees.

A pair of hands grasped her beneath the arms. "Wait a minute," said Avner. "I'll help you up."

Avner pulled backward, rocking Brianna into a kneeling position—and filling her belly with fiery pain.

"Avner!" she barked. "What *are* you doing?"

"We've got to go."

The young scout pointed up the canyon to where the abandoned sleighs of the courtiers sat beside the road. A single fire giant was already walking by the tangle, casually kicking to death panicked draft horses as he passed. The brute was little more than a hundred yards away, close enough to see his flashing bronze eyes and foul green teeth.

Brianna clenched the young scout's arm. "Avner, I can't run," she gasped. "Not now!"

Avner reached into his cloak and withdrew a purple flask sealed with a cork. Inside was one of the thick, frothy healing potions that Brianna's high priest had given to Avner and Tavis. "Maybe if you drink this."

Brianna pushed the vial away. "I'm not wounded; I'm giving birth," she said. "Simon's elixirs won't help me. I need Gerda."

The young scout paled. "Radborne hasn't returned." He studied her with a growing expression of horror. Brianna was a foot and a half taller than him, and weighed a hundred and fifty pounds more. There was no question of his carrying her. "Maybe the Beast—"

The queen shook her head. "Even if Blizzard could climb the landslide, I can't ride." The mere thought of sitting on a horse filled her with an unbelievable ache. "You go for help."

Avner cast a nervous glance up the canyon, and Brianna followed his gaze. The leading fire giant was passing the last of the courtiers' sleighs. Fifty yards behind him, several of his companions were slowly coming up the road, stopping now and then to grind what remained of the Royal Snow Bear Company into the ground.

Avner unsheathed his sword. "I can't leave your side," he said. "I promised Tavis."

"You will do as I order! It's our only chance." Brianna grabbed his arm and pulled herself up. Although her pain was receding, she clenched her teeth at the effort. "And hand me my spell satchel before you leave."

The young scout started to argue, but abruptly stopped when a loud clatter erupted from the landslide behind them. Brianna turned around to see Radborne Wynn and six front riders escorting a pair of twelve-foot strangers down the jumbled boulder heap. Long pelts of ice-crusted beard hung from the jaws of both newcomers. They wore their brown-furred parkas drawn tight against the howling wind, so that they resembled the fabled bear-men reputed to inhabit certain remote valleys of the Ice Spires.

"Firbolgs!" Avner slipped his sword back into its scabbard. "We're saved!"

"I wish we were," Brianna muttered. Like everyone else in court, Avner had apparently heard of the firbolgs' recent alliance offer—but not the price they asked in exchange. "They're no friends of ours."

Avner scowled and started to draw his sword again, but Brianna motioned for him to leave the weapon sheathed.

"I don't know what to expect," she whispered. Perhaps the firbolgs had decided to offer their help without demanding the life of her unborn child. "Just follow my lead."

From behind Brianna came the fire giant's booming

voice, bellowing for his companions to hurry. The firbolgs lumbered down the slide at their best pace, easily outdistancing their human escorts. One was as brawny and broad shouldered as a bull moose, with pale eyes the color of blue tourmaline. The other was spindly enough to be a verbeeg; his eyes were more like alabaster, white and milky and deep: Galgadayle.

Blizzard neighed spitefully at the newcomers. She stepped in front of Brianna, positioning her white-flecked torso between the queen and the hairy strangers. The firbolgs stepped off the landslide and stopped a single pace away. Though the mare was as large as any charger in the kingdom, her shoulders rose barely as high as their waists.

"I am Raeyadfourne, ur Meadowhome," the burly one stated. He bowed, then gestured at the gaunt seer. "I'm sure you remember Galgadayle, oin Meadowhome."

Brianna understood just enough of the firbolg tongue to recognize the appellations as titles, rather than names. Galgadayle translated roughly as "The One who Dreams for Us," while Raeyadfourne was "Broad Shoulders that Bear Our Burdens." "Oin" simply meant "lies in," identifying Galgadayle as a resident of Meadowhome, while "ur" meant "watches over," identifying Raeyadfourne as its chief.

"What are you doing here?" Brianna demanded.

Galgadayle glanced down the canyon, where the crashing footsteps of a sprinting fire giant echoed off the cliffs. "I should think you'd be happy to see us," he said. "We came to save you."

The seer pushed Blizzard aside as though she were a house pet. The big mare stumbled into Avner and knocked him to the ground, then Galgadayle scooped Brianna up in a single arm. This drew a scowl from Raeyadfourne, for snatching strangers up without permission bordered on lawlessness, but the chieftain did not voice

41

any objections. He merely pulled a six-foot battle-axe from its sheath and stepped toward the fire giant.

"I'll hew the orange beard," Raeyadfourne said. "Galgadayle will carry you to safety, Queen."

"Safety?" Brianna scoffed. "This is abduction!"

"The elders have discussed your reluctance to heed Galgadayle." Raeyadfourne did not look at Brianna as he spoke. "The first law is to defend the clan, so they have decided to take you under protection until the twins are born."

With that, the chieftain turned to meet the fire giant. Galgadayle started up the landslide, cradling Brianna in one arm. Avner snatched the queen's satchel off the ground and followed, lagging behind as he clambered over boulders that the seer stepped across in a single stride. Blizzard did not even try to follow. She cast a wary look at the jumble of huge rocks, then bounded up the mountainside toward one of the precarious mining trails.

A sonorous battle cry rang off the canyon walls, followed by the thunderous clang of a huge axe striking thick steel. Brianna looked past Galgadayle's shoulder and saw Raeyadfourne duck as the fire giant's sword swept over his back. The chieftain drew himself to his full height—which put his head at his foe's midriff—and swung his axe. The giant twisted away and counter-attacked, and the two warriors fell into a vicious, clamorous dance of death.

Avner scrambled to the seer's side, then caught Brianna's eye and cocked an eyebrow.

"There's no need for violence, young man," warned Galgadayle. "I mean no harm to either your queen or Tavis's son. It's the other twin, the one fathered by the ettin, I want."

Avner tripped in astonishment and fell to his knees. Brianna hardly noticed, for she felt as though the seer had punched her in the stomach. The ettin was the magical imposter whom the Twilight Spirit had sent to court her. His powerful love potion had befuddled her for days at a time. She did not remember being seduced by the spy, and she could not recall much of what had happened during the dreamlike haze.

Brianna twisted in her captor's arms and saw Avner slowly rising to his feet. His expression was more hurt than suspicious, for he knew as well as anyone that the firbolg seer could not lie about this matter—or any other.

"Avner, Galgadayle's mistaken!" Brianna cried. The queen wanted the young scout to know the truth, and not only because he was her best hope of escape. Avner was like a son to her and Tavis; to lose the youth's trust would be to lose all that remained of her family. "You were there when Simon divined my womb! I'm carrying only one child!"

Galgadayle nearly dropped Brianna onto the sharp rocks. "That can't be!" He tipped his head to look down at her. Brianna could barely see his white eyes above the ice-crusted curtain of his long beard. "Who is this Simon?"

"A high priest of Stronmaus," Brianna explained. "He said you were wrong."

Galgadayle considered Brianna's words for a moment, then shook his head. "You're lying. My dreams are never wrong."

Brianna glanced back and saw that Avner had started up the landslide again. His expression was thoughtful and enigmatic, but his eyes would not meet the queen's.

On the road beyond Avner, Raeyadfourne was slowly giving ground to the fire giant. One side of the giant's steel apron hung bloody and askew, while half a dozen glancing blows had left the firbolg's parka seared and smoking. The rest of the fire giants were only thirty paces from the battle, and one was already climbing the hillside to flank Raeyadfourne.

Brianna's six front riders came scrambling down the slide, the frozen links in their mail coats rattling like bones. They carried their lances at port arms across their chests and did not slow as they approached the queen, obviously intending to help Raeyadfourne with the fire giants. Earl Wynn was ten steps behind the men, clambering over the boulders as best he could in his plate armor.

"Wait!" Brianna ordered. "I need you men here."

The front riders clattered to a stop several paces from Galgadayle, politely leaving space for the firbolg to continue up the slide. Brianna and her captor were now so close to the summit that she could see the next bend in the gorge.

"Stop this firbolg!" Brianna commanded. "He's abducting me!"

Most of the front riders merely scowled in confusion, but two men instinctively obeyed the queen's command. The seer did not stop until the tips of their weapons were pressed against his belly. Then, as the other front riders moved to surround him, Galgadayle tightened his lips and let out a whistle as loud and piercing as the cry of an eagle.

Brianna expected some strange spell to render her men unconscious or helpless, but that is not what happened.

Instead, Earl Radborne demanded, "Majesty, what are you doing?" He had stopped behind the front riders and was pointing down the slide, to where Raeyadfourne was diving over the riverbank to avoid being trampled by fire giants. "There are more giants coming!"

"Let them!" Brianna snarled. She let her eyes drift toward the crest of the landslide, then asked, "Where's Gerda? I need my midwife."

"We have taken her into our troop's protection," Galgadayle answered. "We have done the same for all your courtiers."

Brianna felt her abdomen tighten, though she could not tell whether it was another labor pain or a sign of her growing apprehension. She looked at Galgadayle's face. "Put me down, or I'll order my men to attack."

The seer squeezed her tightly in the cradlelike crook of his elbow. "That will do you no good. I have already summoned our warriors," he said. "Even if you kill me, you have no hope of escaping."

"I'll take my chances," Brianna replied. When the firbolg made no move to put her down, she looked to her front riders. "Kill—"

Galgadayle flexed the biceps of his enormous arm, forcing the air from her lungs and preventing her from finishing her command. The front riders braced themselves, but Brianna could see by their eyes they were reluctant to attack for fear of causing her death.

Radborne pushed his way forward to Galgadayle. "You heard the queen! Release Her Majesty." He raised his arms over his head and still could not reach Brianna. "Hand her down!"

Galgadayle shook his head. "That I cannot—arrghhHH!"

The seer's muscles went limp. Brianna plummeted into Radborne's arms, and they crashed to the ground in a clamorous heap of steel armor and fur coat. A dull, throbbing ache blossomed deep within her belly. Suddenly, she seemed to smell every vile and sour thing in the gorge: the brimstone stench of fire giant swords, the coppery blood and steaming entrails covering the road below, even the sour frozen sweat beneath the armor of her own front riders. Her gorge rose, and a dry, rasping sound came from her throat. She saw Galgadayle's feet stomping in a circle beside her.

From somewhere above came Avner's scream, "Save

the queen! Take her and run!"

Brianna looked up to see Avner dangling from his sword, which was planted to half the depth of the blade in Galgadayle's back. The young scout was trying to brace his feet on his victim's hip so he could widen the wound, but the anguished seer was shaking and twisting so violently Avner could not get a foothold.

Two front riders grasped Brianna beneath her armpits and pulled her off Radborne. Her belly filled with pain, and she screamed aloud. Her rescuers paid the cries no heed and dragged her up a hut-sized boulder, safely away from Galgadayle's writhing figure. She saw Radborne try to rise, then one of the seer's heavy feet came down squarely on the earl's breastplate. The steel buckled like tin, and the noble's death rattle left his lips with the sound of a trembling tambourine.

Brianna tried to rise, but made it only as far as her knees before she doubled over, howling in pain. Her womb had tightened again, and she felt something inside as hot and fiery as lava. She glanced down the slope and saw the leading fire giant already climbing toward her. From other side of the landslide came the muffled clatter of the firbolg troop.

The queen clutched at the arms of her rescuers. "I can't run!" she gasped. "Get me out of here!"

The front riders pulled her cloak off her arms and tied the empty sleeves across her chest, then rolled the lapels to make a makeshift stretcher. By the time they finished, their fellows had scrambled up the boulder to help. Together, the six men hoisted the queen into the air and started up the landslide, each using his free hand to brace his spear butt on the treacherous ground.

Brianna was facing downslope, where Avner still clung to Galgadayle's thrashing form. Finally, the young scout managed to plant his feet squarely on his victim's hip. He jerked on his sword, and the blade snapped with a loud ping. Avner sailed backward through the air and vanished between two boulders. The firbolg collapsed to his knees, growling like a beast and twisting an arm around to claw at the steel sliver in his back.

Brianna glanced down the landslide and saw that the leading fire giant had already climbed halfway up the slope. Another pair followed close behind, while the last two in line were spreading out to prevent the queen's party from doubling back toward the road.

From between the boulders where Avner had fallen came the young scout's voice, "ythgimsilisaB!"

The familiar crack of a rune spell echoed up the slide. A black streak flashed into existence, pointing at the fire giants below. A piercing clang echoed off the leader's armor. The brute's arms flew up, and he sailed backward through the air as though a catapult boulder had caught him in the chest. He slammed into the warrior behind him. They both crashed to the ground in a clamorous heap of black armor, then the leader's body went limp and his bronze eyes turned the color of dried blood.

Avner climbed out of his hiding place. In one hand, he held a simple leather sling, in the other a shiny steel ball. The missile, Brianna knew, was one of three her runecaster had given the young scout.

"Avner, no!" Brianna called. It hurt to yell, but if Avner stayed to fight, he would be trapped between two enemies when the firbolgs crested the hill. "Come here!"

Avner shook his head and fit the steel ball into his sling. "The giants—"

"Young man . . . to my side!" Brianna forced the words out, trying to assume the tone of an angry mother. She had not used that voice with him in more than two years, since before he had sworn the oaths of the Border Scouts and taken his place in the war against the giants. "Now!"

Avner scowled and cast an anxious glance at the fire

47

giants, then reluctantly put his weapon away and bounded up the slide. The giants began to climb again, and Brianna breathed a sigh of relief. She had taken control of events, and that fact alone gave her hope.

Brianna craned her head up the hill and saw that her litter bearers had almost reached the canyon wall. They were angling toward the edge of the landslide, where Blizzard waited to meet them at the broken end of a mining trail. The slide itself became a narrow plume of dirt and rock as it ascended the mountainside toward the mile-long furrow from which it had spilled.

"Not . . . the . . . trail," Brianna gasped. Despite her increasing optimism, her pain had grown so severe that she found it difficult to speak. Her womb was contracting rapidly and severely now, and she felt a growing hollowness in her lower abdomen, as though a great, empty bubble were forming inside. "Up . . . the slide."

The front riders stopped in their tracks. Brianna could hear the tremendous clatter of the fire giants climbing after them, and she could smell the sharp fumes of their flaming swords. On the other side of the landslide, the firbolgs were so close that she could hear their deep voices booming commands to each other.

"Majesty?" asked one of the front riders. "The trail is our only chance of outrunning—"

"Do as the queen says." It was Avner's voice. In spite of the loose ground, the young scout had approached them as quietly as always. "She knows what she's doing."

Avner laid Brianna's satchel next to her, then stepped to the front of the litter and grabbed hold. The party had barely gone fifteen yards before three fire giants reached the bottom of the plume, their coppery eyes sparkling with bloodlust and their swarthy lips twisted into green-toothed snarls. Each time the brutes exhaled, wisps of yellow vapor poured from their nostrils, and Brianna smelled the bitter stench of brimstone.

The leader leveled his sword at the queen's litter-bearers and opened his mouth to speak—then a roaring clamor rose at his back. A wall of hairy firbolgs poured over the crest of the slide, their long beards streaming in the wind and their huge axes whirling above their heads. The eyes of the giants turned as yellow as their flaming swords, and they spun around to find a tide of fur-clad warriors swirling about their hips.

The battle did not begin so much as erupt. The fire giants lashed out wildly with their swords, slicing off burly arms and slashing into thick chests, filling the air with the charnel-house stench of spilled entrails and scorched flesh. The firbolgs countered with a flurry of axes, and soon the knelling of their weapons against the giants' black armor overwhelmed even the thunderous bellows of the wounded and the dying.

Avner led the queen's party to the edge of the slide, then released his hold on her litter and pulled his sling from inside his cloak. Brianna did not have to ask what he was doing, for a single fire giant had escaped the battle and was angling up the canyon wall to cut them off. Nevertheless, she caught the young scout's sleeve before he could go.

"Avner . . ."

Brianna could barely hear her own voice above the battle clamor, but she did not have the strength to speak louder. She was shaking uncontrollably—from the pain, not the cold—and her body felt entirely too weak and achy for the strenuous business of delivering a baby. She pulled Avner close to her mouth.

"Avner . . . thank you, for believing me . . . not Galgadayle."

Avner gently pulled his sleeve from her grasp. "I'm just keeping my promise to Tavis," he said. "I'm not really sure what to believe."

As Avner spoke, the baby shifted and slowly began to drop toward Brianna's pelvis. The horrible pain in her stomach subsided almost instantly, and everything below her waist suddenly felt loose and open.

"You'd better go kill that giant," the queen said. "And find someplace for us to hide—we'll know soon enough who to believe."

# → 4 ←

# The Silver Duchess

The queen's cry broke from the tunnel, as shrill and piercing as the shriek of a striking wyvern. Avner cringed and prayed that the keening wind would swallow the sound before it reached the ears of their enemies. He crawled on his belly to the edge of the rock dump and peered into the darkening canyon, where he saw a swarm of firbolgs on the trails far below. The entire troop had stopped climbing and tipped their heads back. They were too distant to tell if any of the warriors were looking toward the Silver Duchess, the mine where the queen's party had taken refuge, but the young scout was careful to keep his chin close to the ground.

Avner counted thirty burly silhouettes spread across the bottom of the slope. That was many fewer firbolgs than before the battle with the fire giants, but it was far more than the queen's small party could hope to turn back. After killing the last fire giant, Avner had only one magic runebullet left for his sling. The front riders had no missile weapons at all.

The young scout cast a longing glance over his shoulder. Less than a hundred yards above, the gorge's crooked lip hung silhouetted against the purple twilight sky. He had hoped to make it over that crest and join the border scouts patrolling the canyon rims, but the party had been forced to hide in the Silver Duchess so Brianna could deliver her baby. The birth was taking much longer than Avner had expected. He tried to stay calm, telling himself that the battle's thunderous clamor had certainly alerted the patrols to the trouble in the canyon. He did not understand why a company of his fellows wasn't running down the slope now.

"Tavisssss, you baaaarrggh!"

Brianna's curse became an incoherent, grating wail that made Avner's teeth ache. He looked back into the canyon and saw firbolgs pointing up the slope every which way. A few fingers were aimed in the direction of the Silver Duchess. The young scout pushed himself back across the rock dump into the shelter of the tunnel mouth, then stood up. A faint draft wafted out of the dark hole, so gentle it was almost imperceptible, save for the stale heat and dank granite smell on its musty breath. Five front riders sat just inside the portal, looking out over the canyon and self-consciously trying not to seem too interested in what was happening deeper in the mine.

Fifteen paces beyond them, at the creeping black edge of the mine's gloom-cloaked throat, the queen was squatting over her fur cloak. She was naked, save for the flaming spear talisman hanging around her neck. There were baggy, dark circles beneath her violet eyes, which had themselves grown almost black with pain. Her skin was as pale as snow, her mouth twisted into a hideous, gaping grimace by the anguish racking her body. Runnels of tears and sweat streamed off her face to dribble on her blue-veined breasts, while her swollen belly throbbed with spasms so rapid and severe they made Avner wince and swear he would never be so cruel as to father a child.

The sixth front rider was kneeling in front of Brianna, holding his outstretched hands beneath the queen's trembling hips. Although Gryffitt was an old married man, his face had a green tint visible even in the dim light. He kept averting his gaze, as though he could not quite bear what he was seeing. Only Blizzard, who stood nearly invisible in the murk beyond the queen, seemed at all easy with what was happening. The mare kept up a reassuring nicker, and once in while her snout appeared out of the darkness to give Brianna a comforting nuzzle.

Avner envied the horse's unquestioning loyalty and compassion. He kept hearing Galgadayle's warning about the twins and could not help feeling angry with Brianna. Love potion or not, if she had remained true to Tavis and sent the imposter away in the first place, there would be no question now of whose baby it was.

Brianna's belly stopped throbbing, then several bands of muscle tightened around it like a belt. The queen's eyes rolled back in her head and her mouth yawned open. Avner rushed to her side, at the same time pulling his frozen mitten off his hand.

"Majesty, don't yell!" He slipped the edge of his mitten between her teeth, then said, "Bite down on this."

Brianna turned her head and looked at him with a wild, bug-eyed glare. The mitten flew from her mouth, then a deafening shriek filled the dark passage. Avner had heard such a cry only once before, as a frost giant's axe cleaved a warrior through at the hips, but that man had been fortunate enough to die a moment later. There was no telling when the queen's agony would end.

Avner slipped one arm around Brianna's shoulders and clamped his free hand over her mouth. The sound vibrated through his fingers and continued to reverberate off the dank walls, only slightly muted by his grasp.

"Milady, the firbolgs are coming!" Avner hissed.

Brianna glared into the young scout's eyes. She

clutched his wrist and used it to support herself. She felt as though she were slowly exploding from the inside out; her lower back ached with such a fiery, crushing pain that she wondered if her kidneys had been smashed. Her intestines had turned into writhing, searing snakes of anguish. The worst agony of all was her pelvis. She could feel her womb pushing the baby against the inner edge of the cavity, trying to force the infant out and managing only to drive barbed spikes of pain deep into her bones.

It would have been easier to squeeze a boulder through a keyhole. For several minutes now, Brianna had not felt the baby descend any farther, and she was growing weak. Her midwife had said that would not happen. Gerda had told her that Hiatea gave every mother the strength she needed to deliver her child, but the queen could feel her vigor fleeing her body on the wail she was breathing into Avner's hand. Her infant was stuck.

"Majesty, the firbolgs will hear you," Avner pleaded. "Please, you must be quiet!"

Brianna ripped Avner's hand from her face. "Surtr . . . take the firbolgs!" she said, half groaning and half growling. She was surprised to find she could talk at all; a moment ago, she could force nothing out but wails of agony. "Do something useful . . . kill them!"

"There are at least thirty, Majesty," replied Avner. "We can't possibly—"

"Don't bother me with . . . with this!" Brianna snarled. She heard a clatter from the front of the tunnel as the nervous front riders rose to obey her orders; then she regretted her words. She wasn't going to save her child by issuing impossible orders. "Wait, you men! Don't listen to me. Can't you see I'm giving—" She paused to groan. "That I've got other things on my mind?"

The soldiers glanced at each other and studiously

avoided looking toward the back of the tunnel. They hovered just inside the portal and did not seem to know what to do. Brianna dropped to her knees, then fixed her gaze on Gryffitt's slack-skinned face. She had seen fog giants with better color.

"What do you think, Gryffitt?" the queen asked. She could still feel the baby against her pelvis, but the pressure from her womb was slackening. She hoped that meant her body was resting, not that it had given up. "The delivery isn't going well, is it?"

Gryffitt's baggy eyes flicked away. "I'm not much of a midwife, Majesty."

"But you *are* a father six times over," Brianna countered. "Surely, you learned something."

Gryffitt rubbed his beard-stubbled chin. "I've never heard such yelling, milady," he said. "Even with number three, and he was breech."

Brianna's heart sank. "That's what this feels like." She looked to Avner and asked, "What about Gerda?"

The young scout shook his head. "There are thirty firbolgs between us and the road," he said. "And even if we could get past them, there are twenty more with the courtiers."

Brianna nodded. "Then you and I must turn the baby."

Avner swallowed. "But Gryffitt—"

"Will keep a watch on the firbolgs," the queen interrupted. She did not want the front rider with her, even if he was a six-time father. The last person she needed nearby was someone more terrified than she. "Gryffitt understands what a woman in labor might say. He'll know better than to obey if I start shouting crazy commands."

"I'll do my best, Majesty."

Gryffitt turned toward the tunnel mouth, the strain already draining from his face. Brianna shook her head, unable to understand the peculiar male fear that made it easier to battle a troop of grim firbolgs than to help a woman give birth.

Avner cast an envious glance after the front rider. "And Gryffitt, keep one eye on the canyon rim," he said. "When our border scouts finally show up, we don't want them thinking the firbolgs are on our side."

"I'll let 'em know who the enemy is." Gryffitt fastened his parka against the chill wind outside, then dropped to his belly to crawl out on the rock dump. "Don't worry about that."

"Avner, I need your help now," Brianna said.

The young scout reluctantly turned around. "Of course, Majesty," he said. "What can I do?"

Brianna almost told him that he could start by speaking to her more warmly and trustfully, but stopped herself. Even a queen could not command her subjects to feel certain emotions, especially not subjects she cared about deeply. Besides, he would see soon enough that Galgadayle was wrong.

"I'm going to cast a spell," Brianna explained. "But you'll have to be the one to use it."

As she spoke, the queen sat down on her cloak and pulled her satchel to her side. She withdrew a small, ragged book of mica, then peeled off a single silver sheet. The leaf was almost as clear as glass, save that the color of the mineral cast a gray sheen over everything behind it, and the grain caused a faint blurring. Brianna placed the sheaf on the underside of her swollen belly, directly over her womb, then took her goddess's talisman from around her neck.

"Valorous Hiatea, patron of families and nature, always have I served your cause well and kept your creed close to my heart," Brianna whispered. "I call upon your magic now, that I may safely bring my own child into the world and abide in the true light of your glory."

The amulet's silver flames glowed to life, then suddenly flickered and began to crackle and dance. Brianna touched the talisman to the mica on her belly, then took a moment to gather her concentration and lock her pain safely away in one corner of her mind. Once she felt sure she could ignore any sudden surges of agony, she slowly and confidently uttered the mystical syllables of her spell.

A silver aura flashed around Hiatea's spear talisman, and the flames stopped dancing. A shimmering, pearly light passed from the amulet into the mica, which vanished in a puff of sparkling white smoke. Brianna felt a scorching heat against her belly. The pain spread deeper and outward, until her whole stomach burned as though someone had spilled boiling water on it. Her skin began to glow with a brilliant sheen. The queen felt her baby kicking and clawing inside her womb, as though it, too, could feel Hiatea's searing magic.

Though it was not apparent to her, Brianna knew that her flesh was growing silvery and pellucid. She often used this spell on desperately ill or injured people to look inside and see what was wrong. In Hiatea's wisdom, however, patients could not look inside their own bodies—as much, the queen suspected, to preserve life's mystery as to prevent sufferers from seeing their own grotesque injuries and growths. Brianna wished that just this once, the spell would work differently. More than anything, she wanted to see the child in her womb, to confirm for herself what Simon had told her: that Galgadayle's dream was quite mistaken.

Avner's eyes, growing wider and more uneasy as the glow brightened, remained fixed on her belly. Finally, when the queen's shining stomach illuminated the tunnel with a flickering gray light, the young scout's jaw dropped, and Blizzard nickered in astonishment. The mare lowered her nose to the queen's abdomen and sniffed the skin; her ears pricked forward and her black eyes grew huge with astonishment.

Avner pushed the mare's head aside and, amazingly enough, did not get bitten. "I can see the baby!"

Along with several layers of muscle, membrane, and intestinal walls, the queen's skin had become as transparent and brittle-looking as the mica she had laid on it earlier. Through the silvery window, Avner could see into the queen's womb, where a bluish infant lay squeezed into a pocket of pink, fibrous flesh. The baby was reclining with its legs tucked in front of its belly and its head pointed down toward the birth canal. Its face was turned away, showing a mane of surprisingly thick and black hair on the back of its head. A pulsing blue cord ran over its flank to a sack of turbid liquids at the top of the womb.

Although its eyes were certainly still closed, the infant was craning its neck back, as though trying to peer through its mother's pelvis into the outside world. Both hands were stretched down toward the birth canal and gently clawing at the walls of the soft prison, but Avner could see the child would never escape. The baby's skull was as big around as a catapult stone, much too wide to fit through the cramped opening of the queen's pelvic cavity.

"Avner, what's wrong?" Brianna asked, her voice edged with pain. "Simon *was* right, wasn't he? It's not twins?"

The young scout took a deep breath. He looked up, trying to keep his face relaxed so Brianna would not see how frightened he was. "No. There's only one."

The queen sighed in relief, then gave him a condescending, if weak, smile. "Do you believe me now?" she asked. "Firbolgs may not lie, but they're not always right, either."

Avner did not know how to reply. Although Galgadayle had clearly been wrong about the twins, the infant's full head of silky black hair was distressing. Tavis's hair was full, and Brianna's was silky—but only the ettin's had been black.

A front rider approached from the tunnel mouth. The man, Thatcher Warton, knelt at Avner's side, being careful not to look toward his naked queen. "The firbolgs are moving toward the trails that lead up here," he murmured. "If you don't hurry, they'll trap us here."

His whisper was not quiet enough to escape the queen's ears. "Hurry? How should I hurry?"

The front rider flushed and did not answer.

"Perhaps Blizzard could sit on my stomach?" Brianna growled. "That would squeeze the child out in short order, would it not?"

Thatcher only looked at the ground. His face showed no sign of ire or indignation, and Avner suspected Gryffitt had warned him that the queen might seem unreasonably cross.

Brianna glared at the front rider for a moment, then closed her eyes and hissed between clenched teeth. Avner looked down and saw the infant's small fist pushing deep into the wall of her womb. The pain seemed to help the queen focus. She let out two deep breaths, then fixed her gaze on Avner.

"Maybe it doesn't matter if they catch us," Brianna said. "Firbolgs are a scrupulous people. Once they see that I'm carrying only one child, they'll realize Galgadayle was wrong. They'll never hurt—"

"It's better not to take that chance, Majesty." Avner glanced at the infant's black hair. "They lost more than a dozen warriors against the fire giants. They won't be in a reasonable mood."

"What does their mood matter?" As Brianna spoke, the fibrous flesh of her womb rippled, then folded around the baby like a glove. "They're looking for the ettin's child. Once they see that I don't have him, they'll release Gerda."

The queen's voice sounded more desperate than certain, and Avner realized she was dangerously close to pinning her hopes of salvation on the very enemies who had driven her into this hole.

Brianna groaned, then braced her hands against the floor to push herself into a sitting position. "I need my midwife, Avner."

"You can't put your faith in the firbolgs," he said. "Even if you show them what's in your womb, they might kill it."

Brianna scowled. "I don't . . . understand," she gasped. "What are you saying?"

Avner did not want to tell the queen about her child's hair. She was already having a difficult time with labor, and any suggestion that the child wasn't Tavis's might dishearten her to the point of giving up.

"Firbolgs don't trust anyone who can lie." Avner was thinking fast. "They'll think you're trying to trick them."

Brianna's face fell. Her eyes rolled back in her head, and she let out a short cry. Avner glanced down at her belly and saw the infant's head pressed hard against her pelvic bone. Her womb walls quivered with the effort of trying to force him through the pelvic cavity.

"I'm . . . too . . . weak." Brianna clutched Avner's arm, and seemed to be trying to pull herself into a kneeling position. "I can't do this . . . not alone."

"Majesty, you're not alone." Avner slipped his hand under her arm, then looked up. Thatcher was still staring at the wall. "Thatcher, help me with the queen. I think she wants to kneel."

"Of course, with Her Majesty's permission." The front rider reluctantly turned to obey. "Please pardon my cold—in the name of Stronmaus!"

The man's eyes had fallen on Brianna's transparent

womb and remained locked there. His jaw hung slack, and his brows were arched.

"What's wrong?" Brianna slumped onto her back, sweat streaming from her brow as she struggled to peer down at her swollen belly. "What. . .is it?" she gasped. "Deform . . . ities? Is it a monster?"

"No, not at all," Avner replied. He pushed the staring front rider toward the front of the mine, whispering, "Go back to the portal. Tell Gryffitt to keep me informed, and to keep an eye out for those scouting parties. They should be here by now."

The front rider had barely left before the scout felt Brianna's fingers digging into his arm.

"Avner, tell me!"

Before answering, the scout tried to free his arm, fearing Brianna would break it when she heard what he had to say. Like all Hartwicks, the strength of her giant ancestors still ran in the queen's blood. Even in her weakened condition, her grip was powerful enough to crush bone.

The queen's fingers only dug deeper into his flesh. "The baby's in . . . trouble."

Her eyes were once again glassy with pain, and they drifted away from his face. "It's not . . . dead?"

Avner took Brianna by her shoulders. "From what I can see, your baby's alive and healthy."

This seemed to calm the queen. "It's . . . it's breech?"

Avner took a breath, then shook is head. "The child looks as if it might have been fathered by Stronmaus," he said. "It's large."

"Large?"

"Maybe thirty pounds. It looks like a two-year-old," Avner clarified. "It can't fit through your pelvis."

Brianna scowled. "That . . . just . . . can't be," she objected. "Gerda said . . . she said no bab—iiiaaaargh!"

The queen's yell was so loud that Blizzard flinched

61

and clattered a step back into the darkness. Brianna's womb had closed around the infant like a fist. It was pushing the child against her pelvis so hard that the baby had nearly doubled in two. The young scout placed his hands on Brianna's transparent belly, directly over the crumpled infant, and pushed against her womb.

Brianna howled more loudly and beat her hands against the floor. Blizzard came out of the shadows, nickering at Avner. He ignored the petulant mare and kept his eyes fixed on the queen's anguished face.

"I'm sorry, Majesty," he said. "Your own belly's going to kill him. I don't know what else to do."

The queen's fist came down again, and a small piece of granite broke in two.

"The firbolgs have found us for sure." Gryffitt did not bother speaking quietly. "They're bunching up!"

"How long before they get here?" Avner asked. He could not imagine moving the queen, but neither could he imagine letting the firbolgs catch her here. "Do we have time to finish the delivery?"

"We have a while," Gryffitt replied. "Maybe ten minutes, fifteen if we go kill the one in front."

"You stay here," Avner ordered. "What about the canyon rim? Is there any sign of our patrol?"

It was a moment before Gryffitt replied. "I see something, just a few silhouettes." He paused, then added, "But they're too big to be humans, and they're all— Stronmaus save us! I think they're fomorians!"

"Look across the canyon," added Thatcher. "Verbeegs!"

Avner felt his body go weak, and his muscles began to tremble. Fomorians and verbeegs were giant-kin, like firbolgs, and he knew it was no coincidence that they had appeared instead of the border scouts he was expecting. The entire giant-kin brood had united against the birth of Brianna's child.

"Av . . . ner!"

Avner looked back to the queen, who had managed to prop herself on one elbow. Her other hand was rummaging for something inside the satchel where she kept her spell components.

"Yes, Majesty?"

"Do you . . . still have . . . Simon's healing . . ."

The queen did not have to finish her question. Avner took one hand away from her belly and reached into his cloak. He withdrew the small purple flask and offered it to her.

Brianna shook her head. "Not yet." She pulled her dagger from her satchel and turned the hilt toward Avner. "Baby might . . . need it."

The young scout stared at the weapon, uncomprehending.

"You can see . . . the baby," Brianna said. "It's the only . . . way."

Avner was too terrified to reply. He could only shake his head and stare at the knife's gleaming blade.

"Take it!" Brianna thrust the weapon toward him, then collapsed onto her back. "Cut my child free . . . I command it!"

\* \* \* \* \*

Since dawn has my eagle battled the cold boreal wind, that I might witness the debacle below. Through his eyes have I watched the Sons of Masud fall like trees to the axes of men, and through his nostrils have I smelled their acrid blood heavy in the air. I have heard dying fire giants call my name, adjuring me to guide their spirits safely to Surtr's fiery palace, and I have seen their warm corpses sinking into the ice. I have tasted the sour sapor of defeat, and it has filled my throat with the burning bile of despair.

My plan, of course, was not perfect—I am no god—but it *was* sound. The fire giants were too slow to implement it; too slow, and too faint of heart.

*Cowards?* Perhaps. They faltered. They faltered, and so the firbolgs will carry the day.

I am watching them now, the firbolgs clambering toward Brianna's dank hiding place. In grim silence they climb, thirty warriors no larger than bears, weary of gait and pale with their barbarous intent. Their compassion makes softlings of them all; worse, it makes them liars. What honest warrior would shirk at murder to save his people? Not I; I killed, and willingly.

My eagle beats its wings, rising high above their heads and flying straight on toward the tunnel where Brianna hides. By the flickering torchlight inside, I see the queen's guards pinning her to the floor, one with a knife poised above her womb. Foolish woman. If she had come to me, I would have removed the infant with my magic. Now, she must trust the child's life to an unwieldy dagger and a trembling boy.

My pet reaches the tunnel mouth and wheels along the mountainside. He dives deep into the canyon, down half the length of the slope, and swoops low over the first firbolg. Talons as sharp as needles rake his quarry's face. The warrior screams and falls, his hands reaching for an empty eye socket. My eagle banks away, a volley of shouts chasing him over the dusky gorge.

This small reprieve is all I have to offer the unborn emperor. It is little enough, I know, but Annam's children have fallen farther than I thought. In Ostoria's absence, the giants have grown as weak and stupid as all the races of Toril.

"... and we know who did that, Charles."

"... now you must leave, my darling ..."

"Don't be afraid. One foot after the other ..."

Be silent, I pray you!

I know what the gods demand of me, yet I would tarry here a while longer. Even I cannot reach the mine ahead of the firbolgs, and I am loathe to leave the Vale before I must. For a mortal to relinquish himself is no great sacrifice; his life is a fleeting and uncertain thing, and it will end soon enough.

I surrender eternity itself.

From the queen's hiding place erupts a shriek as piercing and shrill as a wyvern song. The voice, of course, is Brianna's, and in her scream there is more hope than anguish. The eagle raises his head toward the mine, his predator's mouth watering at the sound of her distress, but I command him to fold his wings and dive. The emperor is coming, and I must find a better way to guard the child than scratching at firbolgs' eyes.

# ◦ 5 ◦
# Into the Darkness

The scream caught Tavis as a rope catches a hanged man, at the end of a long, lonely fall. The high scout found himself dangling in cold, bleak darkness, numb and queasy and thick-headed, with no idea of how long he had been plummeting through the icy murk. The flesh on one side of his body felt soft and pulpy where the fire giant's boot had caught him, and a huge goose egg had risen where his skull had slammed into a boulder, but these injuries did not actually hurt. He was merely aware of them, as he was aware of the black, frozen emptiness into which he had sunk, and the anguished cry that had rent its desolate tranquility.

Tavis would have heard that scream anywhere. Had he been at home in Castle Hartwick, he would have heard it ringing inside the keep's thick granite walls; had he been fighting frost giants in the bleak northern plains, he would have heard it rolling across the white wastes of the Endless Ice Sea; and even in this lonely dark place, the cry had cleaved the frozen gloom like the almighty axe of Annam the All Father. Brianna was hurt.

The first defender opened his eyes, and his mind turned inside out. The blackness through which he had been falling was suddenly inside his head, and Brianna's voice yielded to the wailing wind. A crooked chasm of purple twilight took shape before the high scout's eyes. He came to realize that he was lying head-down on a steep slope, staring up into the dusk sky. Save for the icy throbbing deep in his battered bones, his body had gone numb from cold, and the gorge felt as empty and deserted as the dark place from which he had come.

Tavis dug his boot heels into the frozen hillside and slowly pushed his feet around, so that he would no longer be lying upside-down. The effort sent swells of frigid agony slushing through his body, and he began to form an idea of his injuries. His right flank hurt from his hip to his armpit. Each breath filled him with anguish, a sure sign that some of his ribs had snapped beneath the giant's kick. One shoulder seemed strangely weak, as though the blow had momentarily popped it out of joint. His head hurt most of all. A swirling brown fog had seeped up from some rank place to fill it with caustic fetor and raw, aching pain.

The high scout was injured, and badly. With each breath, the sharp point of a broken rib might be slashing his vital organs to shreds—the possibility seemed more likely every time he inhaled. He had certainly suffered a skull concussion, perhaps even a fracture. It would be some time before his thoughts came rapidly and clearly; more importantly, his reflexes would be slow, his judgment suspect. There was also the danger that his pummeled brain would let him slip away in a blissful sleep.

Groaning, Tavis propped himself up. A short distance away stood a black spire eagle, no doubt here to feast on the battle carrion. The high scout brandished an aching arm, but the bird merely hissed and continued to watch.

Fifty paces below Tavis, a belt of purple-shadowed ice ran alongside Wyrm River: the road. The surface was strewn with dark boulders and frozen, contorted bodies, both human and giant. Other than the high scout himself, there were no wounded. Unlike firbolgs, neither humans nor fire giants could tolerate bitter cold; their wounded were doomed to quick, frigid deaths.

Farther up the canyon, the courtiers' sleighs lay shoved and shattered to the side of the road, many with the twisted carcasses of draft horses still in the harnesses. Down the canyon, Tavis could barely make out a mangled heap of debris that had once been the royal sleigh. Nearby lay a few dark blotches, the corpses of men and horses that had died in the queen's defense. Beyond the sleigh, the landslide's jumbled slope was distant and dark. In the purple shadows near the crest lay the huge silhouettes of several fire giants. Save for a single pennon flag snapping in the wind, nothing moved, and no one cried for help.

Tavis grew cold and queasy. His arms began to tremble, and such a wave of weariness washed over him that he nearly collapsed. Brianna was gone. He had heard her scream with his heart, not with his ears. The fire giants had carried her into their cavern—how long ago he could only guess—and her voice had traveled to him not through frigid air or dense granite, but through the mystical bond between husband and wife. To reach him across such a medium, the cry must have been as much spiritual as it was physical, and only one thing could cause his wife such grief: the giants had murdered their child.

A croak of despair, all the sound he could voice, tumbled from Tavis's mouth. His arms folded beneath his weight, and he felt the cold ground beneath his back. Above the gorge's opposite rim hung a blue star with a blurry white aura. The silvery halo began to dance like the boreal lights, and a female voice sang in a high, lilting pitch. A cold numbness fell over Tavis's body. His eyelids began to close. He fought to keep his eyes open, but his grief, deeper than any pain tormenting his body, kept pulling them closed. He had failed his queen and his child. Something frightened and weak inside him wanted nothing more than to die and forget.

The throb of fluttering wings sounded over Tavis's head, then a hard beak pecked his brow. The high scout's eyes opened to find the eagle standing over him, its head cocked to one side.

"Wait till I die," Tavis muttered. He raised his hands to push the bird away.

The eagle hopped aside, then opened its beak and screeched. The sound was deafening, as sharp and piercing as the shriek that had awakened him. Brianna's scream. Whether Tavis had heard her with his ears or his heart, the queen had screamed. She needed him, perhaps now more than ever.

Tavis slipped a frostbitten hand into his cloak, his numb fingers searching for one of Simon's healing potions.

\*     \*     \*     \*     \*

Avner's hands were slick and warm with blood, and the baby's skull was so large that he could barely hold it in both palms. When he tried to pull the infant through the incision in Brianna's womb, the head slipped from his grasp and dropped back into the slick red pocket from which it had come. Although the queen's belly was no longer transparent—the spell had faded when he began to cut—one of the front riders had lit a makeshift torch, and the young scout could now see the child's profile. Even from the side, the infant looked as ugly as a troll, with a round heavy face, pug nose, and a wild mane of matted black hair.

"Get that baby out of me—now!" Brianna shrieked. She lay in front of Avner on her outspread cloak, her arms, legs, and head pinned to the floor by front riders. Although she was doing her best to hold still, she had been unable to keep from jerking and twisting as Avner opened her womb, and the struggle to restrain her had left the five front riders almost as exhausted as she. "Take it out, you clumsy oaf!"

An angry whinny sounded from deeper in the tunnel, where Blizzard had been tied to a rough-hewn mining timber. The mare's hooves scraped a warning across the stone floor. Avner ignored the beast and pushed his hands back into the warmth of the queen's stomach. He slipped his fingers under the baby's jawline, then pulled slowly and steadily. The head and shoulders came out of the womb with a loud sucking sound. The child smelled coppery and sour, like a concoction of blood and curdled milk. It was wet with its mother's blood, and covered by a thin coating of something that felt like wax. The infant was so large that Avner had to move his hands beneath the armpits before he could extract the hips and feet.

"By Stronmaus!" gasped Gryffitt, who was holding his belt over the queen's forehead. "That boy's as big as my two-year-old!"

"Tavis . . . was right? A boy?" Brianna croaked. Without awaiting an answer, she ordered, "Avner, clear . . . clear his—"

"I remember," Avner replied. The queen had given him explicit instructions about every phase of the birth. "This is the one part I couldn't forget."

Avner turned the infant around and placed his mouth over the child's nose and lips, then sucked the mucus plugs from the airways and spat the membranes onto the tunnel floor. They left a coating of sour-tasting slime in his mouth, but the young scout hardly noticed. The baby was as blue as a robin's egg and just as still. His dull russet eyes were open, and he was staring at Avner with a vacuous, unblinking gaze.

"He's not breathing," Avner said. He looked to Brianna. "What am I supposed to do?"

"Make sure his passages are clear," she replied. "Then wait a moment."

Before the queen finished speaking, the child snuffled, then yawned, blinked, and glanced around the tunnel. When his gaze returned to Avner, the young scout could not help gasping. The newborn's eyes had changed to a blue as pale and sparkling as glacier ice. With each breath the baby took, his complexion darkened and became more ruddy. His double chin vanished, his jowls tightened into a firm jawline, and his face grew thinner and more handsome. The infant's stubby nose lengthened into a straight, bladelike appendage, and even his black hair seemed to be lightening to bronze.

"Iallanis save us!" cried the torch holder. "That child's—"

"Breathing, you fool." Avner cast a reproving glance at the man, who was the only other person who could have seen the transformation. "His color's changing, that's all."

"Let . . . me see." Brianna tried to raise her head, but even without Gryffitt's belt holding it in place, she would have been too feeble to manage.

"Of course, Majesty." Avner held the child up, deliberately keeping the face turned away from the queen. Although the incision across her abdomen wasn't as gruesome as some belly wounds he had seen, Brianna had already lost enough blood to weaken even a Hartwick. The young scout feared the shock of seeing her child's appearance change before her eyes would kill her. "He's a handsome boy."

"Give me," Brianna commanded.

Although her eyes remained glazed, the queen's smile was radiant, and Avner knew the worst of her pain was

71

past. He held the child a moment longer, until he was certain the boy's face had undergone the last of its mysterious changes, then nodded to Thatcher. The front rider released the queen's arm, then took the infant and passed him to Brianna. She laid the baby on her chest, and he began to suckle immediately, clinging to her with a grasp as secure as a yearling's.

"Now finish," Brianna ordered. "Not much time before the firbolgs . . . And, Avner—"

"Yes, Majesty?"

The queen smiled beatifically, then said, "Thank you."

With that, she returned her arm to Thatcher's grasp and allowed the front riders to pin her to the ground once more. Avner slid a hand into Brianna's belly and grabbed the umbilical cord—still blue and pulsing— then pulled gently. The queen gasped, more in surprise than pain. A small, membranous sack filled with pink-tinged fluid slipped from her womb. The young scout laid the pouch aside, then, as Brianna had instructed him, reached inside to make certain no part of the membrane had torn off.

Once the womb was completely empty, Avner untied a skin of blessed water that the queen had prepared and poured it over her incisions. Dark bubbles frothed up from the cuts, covering Brianna's stomach with a thick, brown-streaked foam. The scout sat back and waited for the lather to do its cleansing work, happy he would soon be closing her up. It was disconcerting enough to see the queen naked, but after actually reaching inside her body to extract the child, he would never again look at her without being at once awestruck and embarrassed.

Avner felt almost in love with Brianna. He had become connected to her and the child on some spiritual level more profound than he could understand; when he looked at them, an alien warmth rose from deep within his heart, and he felt bound to the pair by a force far too powerful to resist. It was not an attraction the young scout welcomed. Such feelings seemed a betrayal of Tavis's friendship, as though some part of him wanted to usurp his mentor's place.

"Great," he muttered to himself. "I'll need a posting in the Eternal Blizzard to get past this."

"What?" Brianna asked.

"I wish Tavis were here."

"You're . . . doing fine," she said. "Tavis would be . . . proud."

The dark bubbles on Brianna's abdomen turned clear and drained off her body in pink-tinged runnels. Avner took a needle and thread from the torch holder, then began to sew the queen's womb shut. Like all Border Scouts, one of the first things he had learned was how to mend both his comrades' wounds and his own winter clothing, so he was no stranger to the art of stitchery. Despite his patient's groans and a steady flow of blood seeping from the incision, he worked quickly and efficiently, pinching the wound closed with one hand and hooking the curved needle through its edges with the other.

Avner had almost finished closing the womb when Blizzard neighed madly, then began to scrape at the ground and jerk against her reins. He glanced at the mare. Her eyes were fixed on the tunnel mouth, where the enormous silhouette of a firbolg was blocking the entire portal. Although the 'kin was kneeling on one leg, he was so large he had to stoop down and turn his head sideways to peer into the mine. His shoulders were as broad as the passage was wide. With pale blue eyes gleaming from a tangled wreath of windblown hair, his shadow-cloaked face resembled some fierce woodland spirit.

Several front riders released Brianna to reach for their weapons, and the queen herself cried out in alarm.

"Don't worry about him!" Avner gestured the front riders back to Brianna. "We've got to finish here."

"But he—"

"Do as I say!" Avner pulled a stitch tight. "We've plenty of time."

Avner had learned the value of cramped spaces as a child, when he had often eluded the town guard by crawling into sewers or ducking through culverts. In narrow confines, the advantage belonged to the runt. The firbolg would need to squeeze into the tunnel on his hands and knees, making it easy for the queen's party to flee deeper into the mine and find another exit—or to turn and fight, if it came to that.

Avner hooked the needle through the womb. Brianna flinched so violently that one leg slipped the grasp of an inattentive front rider, tightening a set of abdominal muscles that the young scout had carefully separated. The fibers slipped back into place, causing him to drag the sharp needle across the queen's womb. Brianna screamed, her head jerking forward. Gryffitt's belt held her in place, and the front riders once again pinned her securely to the ground.

"I see the queen's birthing has been a difficult one," said the firbolg. Avner recognized the rumbling voice as Raeyadfourne's. "Give us the ugly child, and Munairoe will heal the mother."

"Fine. Go fetch him." Avner had no intention of letting any firbolg near Brianna, but it couldn't hurt to buy time—especially if the needle had caused more injury to the womb. The young scout glared at the man who had allowed the leg to slip, then hissed, "Pay attention. You're more dangerous to the queen than the firbolgs."

Avner returned his attention to his patient and carefully pushed the stringy muscles away from the incision, then examined the small cut his needle had made. The tip had scratched the womb, but hadn't pierced it. He glanced toward the front of the tunnel. Raeyadfourne was still watching and waiting for his fellows to arrive. The young scout did not like the chieftain's patience. It suggested that he had someone who could offset the disadvantage of the cramped tunnel, perhaps a shaman or runecaster.

Blizzard continued to jerk at her reins and neigh at the firbolg, and Avner continued to sew, working as fast as he could without being careless. He was just putting in the last stitch when Raeyadfourne spoke again.

"Munairoe is coming up the trail now." The firbolg was still kneeling at the front of the mine. His head was pushed just inside the collar, with the crown of his skull pressed against the roof of the tunnel. "Bring out the queen and her twins."

It was the queen herself who replied. "I have only . . . one child, and he is handsome . . . as handsome as his father." Brianna's eyes shifted to Thatcher. "Show him."

Avner nodded his permission, then opened one of Simon's healing potions. He poured half the contents directly over the seam he had sewn in Brianna's womb. The blood immediately ceased seeping from the closure. The edges fused together, leaving an ugly red scar in the incision's place, but the queen was not ready to move. Before his task was complete, the young scout still had to close a layer of membrane and another of flesh.

As Avner worked, Thatcher released the queen's arm and lifted the baby into the torchlight.

Raeyadfourne snorted in disgust. "That child? Kaedlaw?" he scoffed, using the firbolg word for 'handsome as the father.' "A name will not disguise a hideous face. Bring him out, and our shaman will help you survive to raise the princely one."

"But I have . . . only one child!" Brianna protested. "And he . . . he is Kaedlaw."

The queen's brow was furrowed in confusion, as

though she could not imagine why Raeyadfourne insisted on calling her child ugly. Avner feared he knew the reason. The firbolg did not see the same face as Brianna; he saw the visage that had been upon the child's face at the moment of birth. The young scout glanced at the torch holder. The man was gazing toward the tunnel mouth, his eyes tense with the strain of keeping secret the transformation he had witnessed.

"Pay attention," Avner hissed. "Hold that light down here, where I can see."

Raeyadfourne's rumbling voice filled the tunnel. "Galgadayle's dreams have never been wrong. You must give us K-Kaed—uh—law." The firbolg's voice cracked with the strain of speaking a name that was a lie to his eyes. "We demand this for the good of Hartsvale, as well as our own."

"We'll give you nothing," Gryffitt growled. "And if you want to take this handsome boy from the queen, you'll have to do it from the sharp end of a lance."

As Gryffitt made his declaration, Avner was carefully moving into place the edges of the translucent membrane he had cut to reach Brianna's womb. He allowed her abdominal muscles to slip back where they belonged, then poured the remaining healing potion over the area. Normally, the patient was supposed to drink the elixir, but the queen had said her insides would mend faster if the tonic was poured directly onto them.

From outside came the heavy footsteps of a second firbolg. Raeyadfourne turned away from the tunnel mouth to converse with his fellow. Avner motioned the front riders to their weapons.

"Gather your things quietly," he whispered. "We'll be leaving shortly."

"Where we going, if you don't mind my asking?" asked Gryffitt. "Getting ourselves trapped in the back of a mine seems no better than fighting it out here."

"Earl Wynn said the veins in this mountain cross each other like a tangle of worms—and the tunnels follow veins," Avner explained. "With any luck, we'll connect to another mine and sneak out that way."

As the front riders gathered their parkas and weapons, Avner began to close the cut on the exterior of Brianna's abdomen. Without the front riders to pin her down, she flinched and jerked whenever the needle pierced her skin, but her motions caused him little trouble. The movements were not as severe as when he had been closing her womb, and even if his hand slipped, he was not likely to cause serious injury. He worked as fast as he could, spacing the stitches just tightly enough to close the wound. If the edges overlapped in places, he did not worry. There would be time to tidy up later.

Avner was only half finished when Raeyadfourne spoke again. "Running will do you no good," the firbolg said. "Even if you escape us, the fomorians and verbeegs will be waiting at the other exits."

"I never thought to see the day when firbolgs consorted with the likes of those scum," commented Gryf-fitt. He and the other front riders had already slipped back into their parkas and gathered their weapons. "Have you taken a sudden liking to thieves and murderers?"

Raeyadfourne shrugged, and it seemed to Avner that the firbolg had changed somehow. The chieftain's silhouette appeared somehow more feral and threatening.

"The verbeegs and fomorians are our brothers," Raeyadfourne explained. "If you surrender the ugly child, you have nothing to fear from them."

"Let me heal the queen, and give us the second child," boomed a second firbolg, Munairoe. "He will not suffer at our hands."

Avner saw a pair of green eyes peering around Raeyadfourne and realized what had changed. The chieftain's beard now hung clear down to his belly. His hair had become a long, wild mane, and, most importantly, his huge shoulders no longer covered the tunnel mouth completely.

"He's shrinking!" Avner gasped.

A guttural curse erupted from deep within Raeyadfourne's throat. He threw off his bearskin cloak and pulled a four-foot hand axe from his belt, then scuttled into the tunnel. Although the chieftain still had to squat on his haunches, he was now small enough that his hands remained free to fight.

Blizzard went wild, filling the passage with earsplitting shrieks. She whipped her head violently against her reins, drawing an ominous creak from the thick mining timber to which she was tied, and her hooves hammered the stone floor. The front riders ignored the angry mare and leveled their lances, moving forward to attack the chieftain.

"You men, wait!" Avner yelled. If the front riders attacked Raeyadfourne now, they would still be fighting when the rest of the firbolgs reached the portal. "Come back here!"

Avner pulled his hand axe from its sheath and hurled it at the post to which the Queen's Beast was tied. The weapon tumbled straight to the timber and sliced cleanly through Blizzard's leather reins. The angry mare hardly paused to gather her feet before springing up the passage. She bounded over Brianna and knocked the front riders aside as she barreled past to attack Raeyadfourne.

The firbolg's hand axe rose and came down, burying itself deep into the mare's flank. The wet snap of shattering bone echoed through the tunnel. Blizzard continued forward, bowling Raeyadfourne over and burying her teeth into his neck. She landed astride the chieftain, as a wolf might a man, and ripped a mouthful of flesh from his throat. Raeyadfourne bellowed in pain, a spray of blood erupting from the wound. He pulled his axe free and raised it to strike again. Blizzard lowered her muzzle to bite, and the vicious fight erupted into a bloody melee from which neither beast nor firbolg would emerge whole.

Gryffitt and the rest of the front riders returned to the queen's side. Avner motioned for them to lift Brianna, then pinched together the unsewn edges of her incision.

"Let's go." The young scout used his chin to point deeper into the mine. "And someone grab my axe."

The torch holder led the way, his light casting a flickering yellow glow over the craggy walls. The rest of the front riders followed close behind, carrying Brianna and Kaedlaw upon her cloak. Avner brought up the rear, with the queen's knees locked around his waist and the edges of her incision squeezed between his fingers. His view of the tunnel floor was blocked by his patient's makeshift litter, and he kept stumbling over loose stones and jagged knobs of rock.

The awkward procession had barely gone ten steps before a panicked whinny sounded from the portal. Avner glanced over his shoulder. Two firbolg warriors were dragging the queen's mangled horse out of the mine. The beards of both warriors were extremely long, hanging almost to their waists, and neither of them looked much larger than Tavis. They passed Blizzard to someone outside, and the mare let out a shriek that sounded almost human.

The two firbolgs reached into the mine and grabbed their groaning chieftain beneath the armpits. Raeyadfourne was covered in blood from his jawline to his belly, and his body remained limp as the warriors pulled him through the portal. The pair passed their injured fellow to the green-eyed shaman, then entered the tunnel themselves. To fit into the passage, they only had to stoop over.

"Faster!" Avner said. "Run!"

The torch holder broke into a trot, as did the men carrying Brianna. Their feet moved almost in unison, filling the tunnel with the martial cadence of tramping boots. Several times, Avner tripped and nearly fell into Brianna's lap, and she soon volunteered to hold her own wound closed. For the first time, little murmuring sounds came from Kaedlaw's mouth. He did not seem to be crying or groaning so much as calling the count.

The passage followed the crooked, winding course of a silver vein, and Avner quickly lost his bearings. They seemed to be traveling ever deeper into the mountain, but the young scout knew better than to trust his surface dweller's instincts. For all he knew, the tunnel could be less than a dozen feet underground.

Avner soon found himself thinking in terms only of the area illuminated by the flickering torchlight; there was the murk ahead, warm and still and thick with the smell of musty stone and moldering wood; there was the floor beneath his feet, sometimes sloping up and sometimes down, often slick with mud and always strewn with loose debris and potholes; there were the walls around him, craggy and colorless, supported at regular intervals by crudely shaped arches of mud-crusted mining timbers; and most of all, there were the firbolgs coming up behind, clattering and cursing through the darkness, stumbling along without a torch, yet slowly and steadily closing the distance to their prey.

Avner waited until they rounded a sharp curve, then stopped and pulled his sling from inside his cloak. "Keep going," he said. "I'll buy us some time."

"Avner, no!" Brianna sounded as exhausted as she did pained. "You're all I have . . . left."

"I'll be along," he promised. "Nothing's going to happen."

The young scout slipped behind one of the thick posts that supported the ceiling, then fit his last runebullet into the pocket of his sling. As the queen's party moved off, he took advantage of the fading torchlight to eye the decaying timbers above his head. Although his runebullet was hardly as powerful as one of Tavis's runearrows, he suspected it could still bring the roof down on their enemies. Unfortunately, the heavy bracing suggested that the rock above was very unstable. The rumble of even a small cave-in could start a chain reaction that would bury him—and perhaps the queen—along with their pursuers.

Avner looked down the tunnel toward the fleeing front riders. He could still see Brianna and her bearers, illuminated in the torch glow. If he stepped into the passage too early, the firbolgs would see his silhouette against the light.

The young scout waited, simultaneously keeping his eyes fixed on the receding torch and listening to his enemies' approach. Their gaits were sporadic and heavy, punctuated by dull thuds, resonant clatters, and a constant rumble of angry curses. By the time the flickering torch had vanished from sight, the firbolgs were so close that Avner could hear their parkas rubbing against the walls and smell their sweat in the damp air. He stepped from behind his post, whirling his sling over his head. An eerie whistle echoed through the mine.

"What's that?" The firbolg's cry seemed to come from the roof, directly above Avner's head.

The young scout flung his missile at the voice, at the same time crying out, "ythgimsilisaB!"

There was an ear-splitting crack and a brilliant white flash. A firbolg shouted in terrible pain. In the same instant, Avner glimpsed the faces of the two warriors—one astonished, the other disbelieving—less than three paces away. The light vanished as quickly as it had appeared, leaving the scout with nothing but swimming white spots before his eyes. The rich smell of blood filled the tunnel and something warm splashed across his face. Avner barely leapt away before the injured warrior crashed down where he had been standing.

"Ethelhard?" called the second firbolg.

Avner did not hear whether Ethelhard answered, for he was already rushing down the tunnel. Unlike his enemies, he moved almost silently, his knees rising high to lift his boots over unseen debris, his feet coming down toe-first so he could dance away when he happened to land on unsteady footing. As he ran, he kept one hand pressed against the wall to give him some idea of the passage's course. Although Ethelhard's comrade had fallen silent, no doubt fearing another attack such as the one that had killed his companion, the young scout took no pleasure in his triumph. Now that his pursuers were quiet, he could hear the muffled din of more firbolgs coming down the tunnel. Judging by the steady reverberations of their boots, these warriors were moving swiftly and confidently. They had torches, and they fit into the cramped mine as well as the pair Avner had just stopped.

The young scout continued forward at his best run, expecting to see the flickering yellow glow of his companions' torch at any moment. He felt the tunnel make several sharp turns, and the floor began to rise and fall at steep angles. Once, a breeze wafted over his shoulders as he ran through a curtain of cool air flowing down from someplace outside, and another time he passed through a humid stretch of passage that stank fiercely of stagnant water and bitter minerals.

But it was not until Avner felt a gust of hot air from the opposite side of the cavern that he stopped running. With his heart pounding like a double-jack against drill steel, he turned toward the tunnel's other wall. He put out his hands and took one step forward, and two, then three. The breeze blew steadily into his face. With his next step, the floor seemed to vanish beneath his boot. He almost fell, then found solid stone a foot below where it should have been. He turned again, and that was when he felt it: a craggy, rounded corner where a side-passage opened off the one he was following.

Avner retreated back into the main tunnel—at least, what he hoped was the main tunnel. He had rounded dozens of sharp bends. How many of those had actually been junctions, like the one across the way? By following only one wall of the passage, he could have turned off the main pathway any number of times. Each curve might have been a fork in the tunnel, or it might have been just another bend in the mine. Somewhere back there, probably not far from where Ethelhard had fallen, the front riders had made a different choice than Avner, and with them had gone the queen.

# ⇒ 6 ⇐
# The Drifts

Night had fallen; though the boreal lights bathed the canyon's ice-draped rim in a rainbow curtain of dancing reflections, their ghostly rays could not pierce the abyssal gloom deeper in the gorge. The landslide at the bottom was cloaked in a mantle of dark, swarthy purple, and Tavis could hardly see the rocks beneath his feet. He had to climb by feel, testing each step carefully before trusting his weight to the slick stones, and even then he often braced himself on his bow to keep from falling.

Everything hurt. His shoulder ached so much he could hardly move it; each breath filled his chest with a swell of dull pain. His frozen feet burned with the dubious blessing of renewed circulation. The constant throbbing in his head felt no worse than having a battle drum pressed to his ear, and he could not string two thoughts together without a conscious act of will. In his belly, he felt the warmth of Simon's healing elixir working its magic—but that was little comfort now. Tavis found his fist inside his cloak, grasping his second healing potion. He forced himself to withdraw his hand empty. It would be foolish to use the second vial before the first had finished its work.

As Tavis climbed the landslide, he remained alert for

clues as to where his foes had taken Brianna. The fallen fire giants above were mere silhouettes, barely distinguishable from the huge boulders heaped along the crest of the slide. Beside some of the bodies flickered the orange glow of guttering fire swords, suggesting that the battle had ended less than an hour ago. The high scout saw no human corpses at all.

Tavis's heart began to hammer. If the fire giants had left their dead in the canyon, perhaps Brianna had escaped after all.

About halfway to the crest, Tavis heard rocks clattering nearby, then an anguished cry too deep and resonant to be human. He dropped into a crouch, then crept toward the sound. A short distance ahead, a bushy-maned profile rose above a big rock. Though the head was little larger than the high scout's, it had the wild mane of hair and beard typical of firbolgs. The figure groaned again, then pushed an arm over the boulder and clutched at the cold stone. It turned a pair of milky white eyes toward Tavis.

"Over . . . here." Strained as it was, the deep voice sounded chillingly familiar. "Help me!"

Tavis neither showed himself, nor drew his weapon. "Galgadayle?"

The seer looked toward Tavis's voice, then groaned in disappointment. "You?" He slipped lower behind his boulder. "Tavis . . . Burdun?"

"What are you doing here?"

"They didn't . . . find . . . after battle," the seer croaked. "Couldn't yell . . . too much . . . pain."

Suddenly, Tavis understood why the fire giants had left their dead behind. They had lost the battle. "The Meadowhome Clan is here?" he asked. "You killed the fire giants?"

"We . . . had to come," the seer replied. "Must protect the tribe. The law . . . demands it."

Galgadayle lost his grip on the boulder and slipped out of sight. Tavis crept up the slide, confident he was not being lured into a trap. The pain in the seer's voice had been genuine, but more importantly, firbolgs were incapable of such treachery. They might wait in ambush or sneak up on a foe, but the same instinct that made it impossible for them to lie also prevented them from enticing an enemy to his death.

Tavis slipped around the boulder to find Galgadayle sitting in a hollow between several stones. The air was heavy with the reek of urine and fresh blood. The seer held one arm twisted behind him, pressing his hand against the small of his back. He was only about two-thirds as large as when he had visited Castle Hartwick.

The size change did not surprise Tavis as much as it might have. His mentor, Runolf Saemon, had once known an entire tribe of firbolgs to grow two feet in a single day. For a time, Tavis had pleaded with every firbolg he met to show him the trick, but they had all refused. The scout had finally given up, concluding that their law forbade sharing the secret with an outcast.

Tavis knelt at Galgadayle's side and reached out to move the seer's hand. "You're smaller than I remember."

"I've lost blood." Galgadayle pushed Tavis's arm away. "Finish me quickly . . . nothing to gain with torture."

Tavis half-smiled at the attempt to change the subject. The seer was more afraid of breaking the law than of dying.

"I won't torture you—or kill you." The high scout did not blame Galgadayle for trying to capture Brianna. The seer was acting on his conscience. As wrong as he might be, that did not make him evil, and Tavis was not in the habit of killing people for their mistakes. "I'd rather help you, if you'll allow me."

Galgadayle glared at him with one white eye. "I have brought harm to your . . . family," he said. "Why show me mercy?"

"Because you're no longer a threat," Tavis replied. "Killing you would make me a murderer."

"Perhaps," Galgadayle groaned. "But the law does not require . . . nowhere is it decreed you must help an enemy."

Tavis shrugged. "I have learned a different kind of law with the humans," he said. "It comes more from inside than out, and it can be as nebulous and shifting as a cloud, but I must obey it nonetheless."

Galgadayle considered this, then took his hand away, revealing a large, mangle-edged hole in his cloak. Though it was too dark to see more, Tavis smelled fresh blood. It was heavy with the scent of urine, a sure sign the seer would die without help.

"You'll have to lie down so I can reach the wound." Tavis gently guided Galgadayle onto his stomach.

"This changes nothing." Despite Galgadayle's words, there was a note of gratitude in his strained voice. "When the child is born . . . Raeyadfourne must still— aarghh!"

Tavis began to probe the wound, bringing Galgadayle's sentence to a harsh end.

"What happened to my wife?" Tavis continued to work. His fingers came across the stub of sword blade that had been broken off just below Galgadayle's kidney. "Who has her?"

The seer shook his head. "That I will . . . not tell you," he groaned. "Leave me, if you wish. I'll probably die anyway."

"No, you won't," Tavis said. "I have a healing elixir."

Galgadayle craned his neck to glance up at Tavis, his eyes flashing with a brief hope that quickly vanished behind dark clouds of despair. The seer gave Tavis a wry smile, then shook his head. "Keep your potion," he said. "The cost is too dear."

"I'm not trying to buy your knowledge." Tavis had watched Brianna deal with her earls often enough to know there were more effective ways than bribery to learn a person's secrets. "The potion is yours, but it won't do any good unless I pull that broken blade out of your back. To do that I'll need light."

"All—all I have is a sparking steel." Galgadayle sounded forlorn. During the time it took to start a fire and make a torch, the seer could well bleed to death.

"I have a magical light," Tavis said. "But I don't want to attract fire giants."

Galgadayle sighed in relief, and when he spoke, he sounded like a dead man to whom the gods had given a second life. "You won't," he said. "There's no need to worry about that."

"How do you know?" Now that the seer's thoughts were on saving his own life, Tavis could try to draw out the information he needed. "If a straggler attacks while I'm pulling out the steel, there won't be much I can do."

"There . . . aren't any . . . stragglers." Galgadayle sounded as though the frustration of trying to reassure Tavis would kill him long before he bled to death. "Our warriors . . . killed them . . . all of them."

The high scout's stomach felt queasy and heavy. If the fire giants were dead, Brianna was with the firbolgs. "In that case, maybe I should fetch your shaman," Tavis suggested. "It would be safer if he removed the blade."

"No!" Galgadayle objected. "I won't live . . . long enough."

"They couldn't have gone far."

The seer started to reply, then thought better of it and glared at Tavis. "You're as devious . . . as a human," he said. "Can you lie, too?"

"I would if I could," Tavis said truthfully. "I've sworn to protect the queen, and I'd do anything to keep that vow."

With that, the scout took Mountain Crusher in both

hands and whispered, "tnaillirbsilisaB." A rune flared with sapphire light, then the entire bow radiated a pale blue glow. Tavis leaned the weapon where it would illuminate the injury. He pulled his dagger and cut Galgadayle's fur cloak away from the wound. The scout had little trouble finding the end of the steel shard, for it protruded from a short crescent of severed sinew and sliced meat. Whoever had planted the blade had deliberately tried to work it back and forth, a vicious killing technique more commonly employed by assassins and thieves than by honorable soldiers. Tavis knew instantly who had done this to the seer.

"You're lucky, Galgadayle." Tavis pulled a wad of soft, clean cloth from his satchel and laid it on a stone beside the seer. "Avner usually strikes truer than this."

"Who?"

"The one who stabbed you in the back." Tavis pinched the stub of the broken sword between his fingers and jostled it, lightly, to see how securely the blade was lodged. "I hope you didn't kill him."

Galgadayle shook his head. "The coward got away," he hissed. "But if I—"

"Got away?" Tavis interrupted. If Avner had escaped, so had Brianna. The youth's ethics were certainly questionable, but not his loyalty. "Your warriors didn't capture him?"

Galgadayle's head pivoted toward the mountainside, then he realized his mistake and looked away. "I'm feeling weak."

Tavis glanced up the gloom-shrouded slope. He saw only a purple, inky darkness as deep as the Abyss itself, but he was smiling when he looked back to his patient. "Avner has taken my wife into the mines, hasn't he?"

Galgadayle's eyes widened. "I don't . . . I didn't say that."

"You didn't have to."

Before his distracted patient realized what was happening, Tavis pulled the shard from Galgadayle's back. The steel slipped out of the wound like a dagger from its sheath, and it was removed before the seer could open his mouth to scream. The fragment was about two feet long and covered with a dark coating of slime and blood.

"You . . . tricked me!" Galgadayle seemed more surprised than angered.

"You have nothing to complain about." Tavis tossed the bloody shard aside. "The blade came out in one piece, didn't it?"

He used the cloth he had set aside earlier to stanch the heavy flow of blood, then guided Galgadayle's hand to the wound. Once he knew his patient was strong enough to hold the dressing in place, he helped the seer sit up. Tavis took his healing potion from his cloak and uncorked the purple flask.

"Drink this." He placed the elixir in Galgadayle's free hand. "And when you feel well enough to move, find someplace warm to spend the night."

The seer did not lift the flask to his lips. "You will not . . . you *cannot* save the child," he said. "There are many . . . many miles of tunnel up there."

"I'll find my way." Tavis stood and grabbed his rune-etched bow. "Now drink up. I'd hate to see you spill the last of Simon's elixir."

The seer lifted the potion to his lips and downed it in a single gulp. When he finished, he raised the empty flask to Tavis.

"I thank you for my life." He still sounded weak, but the anxious edge had slipped from his voice. "And I would repay your favor with . . . with a warning."

"I'm listening," Tavis said. "But if this is about the child—"

Galgadayle shook his head. "Watch out for the . . .

verbeegs . . . and the fomorians," he said. "And pray . . . pray that Raeyadfourne finds your wife . . . before they do."

\* \* \* \* \*

Brianna's litter-bearers were exhausted. Their efficient double-time trot had degenerated into a disorderly jog occasionally punctuated by the thud of tripping feet. The sound of their labored breathing echoed through the tunnel like the wheezing of a punctured forge bellows.

The party was passing through a labyrinth of winding passages that the tunnel wizards called "the drifts," where the narrow corridors crossed and recrossed each other as they followed the meandering "drift" of the silver veins. The queen did not dare call a rest. Even suspended on her cloak, she felt the stone floor rumbling beneath the heavy boots of her pursuers, and she heard their distant voices echoing louder at each fork in the tunnel.

Brianna did not know what had become of Avner, but it seemed apparent the young scout's plan had failed. She had heard the crack of his runebullet and, for a short time thereafter, the sounds of pursuit had fallen silent. The queen and her bearers had slowed their pace so he could catch up, but he had never arrived. Then a distant rumble had begun to build behind them and resolved too soon into the tramping boots of a firbolg troop. The front riders had been running hard since, and Brianna had knotted her stomach into a snarl worrying about her young friend.

Kaedlaw stopped suckling, then fixed his handsome blue eyes on Brianna and opened his mouth wide to cry. The noise that came out sounded nothing like a sob; it was more of a long, gurgling growl. Several of the queen's exhausted bearers cast nervous looks over their shoulders, peering not at the infant, but down the dark passage behind them.

"Carry on," Brianna said. "It's only Kaedlaw—commanding to be burped, I imagine."

"Strangest sound I ever heard a baby make, Majesty," huffed the torch holder. "Sounds more like a—"

"Marwick, you'd do well to save your wind." Brianna started to ask the young front rider if he expected a half-firbolg prince to sound the same as his own peasant runt, but she caught herself and said instead, "If you have that much breath left, you can change places with Thatcher."

A crimson flush crept over Marwick's face. His green eyes flashed briefly to Kaedlaw, then he fell back and traded his torch for Thatcher's place at her cloak.

The queen was still using one hand to keep her incision closed, so she balanced her son on her chest and used her free hand to gently pat his back. Kaedlaw's growl only became louder. She covered him with her shift, thinking he might be cold, but that also failed to silence him.

"Don't worry, Majesty," wheezed Gryffitt. "He's just tired. It's a rough way to come into the world."

"Yes, it is," Brianna agreed.

The queen felt as exhausted as Kaedlaw, and that worried her. She had already lost so much blood that she was cold, sleepy, and dizzy, and blood continued to seep from the incision. A dark curtain had begun to descend inside her mind. When it fell completely, her son would be left an orphan, with nothing more than half-a-dozen exhausted guards to defend him from the firbolgs.

The front riders carried Brianna deeper into the drifts. Always, they strived to follow the largest passage, on the theory that it was the least likely to come to a sudden end. Kaedlaw's growls gradually abated to mere murmurs, and the clamor of their pursuers grew steadily louder. It was not long before the queen could make out some of what the firbolgs were shouting:

". . . clear here."

"This . . . empty."

"Not in here."

The cries kindled a glimmer of hope in Brianna's breast. She propped herself on her elbow, then watched the gray walls and mineral-crusted timbers slip past. At the next fork, she ordered her litter-bearers to carry her down the smaller of the two passages.

Thirty paces later, the queen almost missed what she had been looking for. A small drift branched off the main corridor; its entrance was so narrow and ragged that it looked like a shadow. The passage itself was barely as wide as a man's shoulders, with the walls lying at a cock-eyed angle and the floor sloping down toward the heart of the mountain.

"Wait!" Brianna ordered. "Stop here!"

The front riders stumbled to a halt, then Gryffitt cast a nervous glance back toward the fork. "Milady, the firbolgs are closing," he panted. "We may not have time to backtrack."

"We're not backtracking, we're hiding—in there." Brianna pointed at the narrow drift, then added, "And I need a volunteer to lure the firbolgs away. Someone fast."

All eyes turned to Marwick.

"Take the torch back to the fork and go a little way up the passage," Brianna ordered. "Stay ahead of the firbolgs, but let them catch a glimpse of the light now and then, and don't go too fast. We don't want to make it obvious you're alone."

"As you wish, milady." Marwick reluctantly reached for the torch.

Thatcher did not yield the brand. "Majesty, perhaps I should go instead," he suggested. "Marwick has a family."

93

"There's nothing to worry about," Gryffitt growled. "Those aren't fomorians back there. All Marwick has to do is surrender when he runs out of tunnel. If he doesn't fight, the firbolgs won't hurt him."

Gryffitt and another front rider carried Brianna into the cock-eyed drift, tipping her sideways to prevent her broad shoulders from becoming lodged in the narrow confines. The warm stench of sulfur filled the passage, causing Kaedlaw to start murmuring again. The other front riders crammed themselves in behind the queen's litter; then Marwick took the torch and left, plunging the drift into a darkness as thick as sap. Already, Brianna heard firbolg axes clanging against the walls of nearby tunnels.

Kaedlaw began to complain more loudly, filling the drift with a deep, rumbling growl. Brianna turned his face toward her breast, hoping he would start to suckle again. That only made him angrier. She laid her hand across his cheek to muffle the noise. He still sounded as loud as a snoring bear.

A chorus of shouts erupted from the fork as the firbolgs spotted Marwick's light. They rushed after him, the fury of their pounding boots shaking the drift walls. The thunder continued for minutes. Kaedlaw's growls grew ever more ferocious. He kept twisting his head away from Brianna's hand, determined to make himself heard. The queen found herself holding her breath, as though that would quiet her indignant son. She prayed to Hiatea that the din would continue until he wore himself out.

But Kaedlaw was a strong boy. The thunder gradually began to diminish, and the newborn's complaints seemed that much louder. Brianna tried to reassure herself with the thought that her pursuers could not possibly hear the child over the hammering of their own boots.

She was finally beginning to believe herself when a hand shook her ankle.

"Thatcher says a firbolg's coming down the tunnel," whispered a front rider. "He wants to know if he should attack."

Brianna appreciated the young man's diplomacy. He was really hinting that she should find a way to quiet Kaedlaw, but he was too wise to suggest the queen's child might be placing the party in danger.

"Tell him to be ready, but to hold fast unless I call the order." Brianna would battle her pursuers to the death, but she was under no illusions that it would save her child. If it came to bloodshed, the rest of the firbolgs would quickly realize they had been tricked. "I'll do what I can to spare us a fight."

The queen pressed Kaedlaw more tightly to her breast. She pulled the edge of her cloak over him, but even the heavy fur could not smother his cries. The thunder of the firbolg boots continued to diminish, and she saw the first dim glow of torch light flickering outside the drift. It was growing steadily brighter, as though the warrior were walking carelessly down the passage, not really expecting to be ambushed.

"Kaedlaw, forgive me," Brianna whispered.

The queen slipped her hand over her son's face and covered his mouth. He began to struggle, beating and kicking at her chest and trying to twist out of her grasp. Although her fingers muffled his cries, he still had enough air to continue his protests. He sounded more like a fox kit than an infant, but Brianna knew better than to think their pursuer would be fooled. She tightened her grip until she felt her palm pressing into Kaedlaw's jaw bone, then pinched his nostrils shut and started to count. If the firbolg was still here when she reached a hundred, she would order Thatcher to attack.

A firbolg's deep voice rang down the corridor outside

their hiding place. "It's no use hiding, Queen," he called. "We're going to find you."

Brianna felt her men tense and heard hand axes swishing from their sheaths.

"Not yet," she whispered.

The firbolg was trying to draw them out. If he really knew they were here, he would be calling his fellows back, not yelling threats into the dark—that was what Brianna hoped.

The queen's count reached twenty-five. Kaedlaw finally ran out of breath and fell silent, but he continued to struggle against the smothering hand. Outside the drift, the thunder of the main troop suddenly grew quieter, as though they had rounded a corner in some distant tunnel, and Brianna heard the rustle of heavy boots scuffing across the stone floor outside.

"What's that bitter scent?" the firbolg called. "Is that giant spawn I smell?"

Brianna counted fifty, and she bit her tongue to keep from answering the insult with an attack order. The affront was the worst a firbolg could offer, for the enmity between 'kin and their true giant brethren dated back to the birth of their races.

The rumble of the firbolgs' main troop had grown so muted that Brianna heard other voices in nearby passages. Like the pursuer in the drift outside, they were attempting to lure her from hiding by hurling taunts into the darkness. The queen counted seventy-five, and Kaedlaw stopped struggling in her arms.

An icy fist closed around Brianna's heart, but she did not dare remove her hand from the child's face. She could see her men's heads silhouetted against the light of the firbolg's flickering torch. The warrior would certainly hear the slightest gurgle. She already feared that her own throbbing pulse was loud enough to give the party away, and she smelled her own sweat growing heavy beneath the sulfurous stench of the drift. It would not be much longer, she knew, before the odor grew thick enough to reach the warrior outside.

"Think about what you're doing, Queen," the firbolg called. "The wicked twin will slay his brother to assure ascension to your throne. A strong queen—a good mother—would protect both her kingdom and her worthy child. She would give the giant spawn to us."

Brianna counted eighty-five. She slipped her fingertips under Kaedlaw's jaw and searched for a pulse. She could not find one, and the infant remained as still as death. The queen silently called upon Hiatea to protect her child. In reply, she heard the dark, angry voice of another god, one who promised that if the firbolgs forced her to smother her own child, her vengeance would be as terrible as her grief.

Brianna shuddered. She did not want vengeance; she wanted to escape with her child.

At ninety-five, the queen heard Raeyadfourne's weak, raspy voice call out from the fork. "Let's go, Claegborne," he said. "We'll have trouble enough catching the others."

The warrior did not reply. The tunnel fell so quiet that Brianna could hear Claegborne's torch hissing and sputtering. The firbolg had to be within two or three paces of her hiding place. A strange, muted rumble sounded inside her skull, and the queen realized she was grinding her teeth. She stopped, fearing her pursuer had already heard the noise.

The count reached a hundred.

"Stop wasting my time," Raeyadfourne ordered. "If you've found something, say so."

A pair of heavy steps sounded from the fork as Raeyadfourne started down the passage. Brianna opened her mouth to order the attack, then the torchlight outside suddenly dimmed.

"Don't trouble yourself." Claegborne started back toward Raeyadfourne. "I smelled something, but it was just brimstone blowing up the passage. This tunnel must connect to the bottom of the mine."

The icy fist inside Brianna's chest clamped down, squeezing so hard that she feared her heart would burst. Kaedlaw had already been without air for nearly two minutes, but she forced herself to keep her palm over his face as she listened to the firbolg withdraw. The thought that she might be smothering her own child left the queen shivering and queasy, but she would feel no better if the firbolgs returned to murder him before her eyes.

Finally, the heavy steps of the two firbolgs abruptly faded to muted thumps as they reached the fork and started up the opposite tunnel. Brianna pulled her hand from Kaedlaw's face, ready to slap it back at the slightest hint of a grumble. When the child made no sound, she wet her fingers and held them before his nostrils, alert for the faintest stir of breath.

The queen felt nothing but the drift's sulfurous breeze.

"Someone strike me a light," Brianna commanded. "Thatcher, go to the fork and keep a watch for our enemies."

A noisy rustling filled the cramped darkness as the front riders scurried to obey. Brianna placed her lips over Kaedlaw's nose and mouth and blew a slow, gentle breath into his lungs. When he did not cry out, she pressed lightly on his abdomen to push the air back out, then repeated the process. As she worked, she heard the sharp crack of someone breaking a lance, then the shrill rip of cloth. A cork popped as it was pulled from a flask, then the pungent reek of torch oil filled the passage. Brianna silently begged her son to breathe, but he did not cry out or gasp.

A front rider scratched a flint across a striking steel,

filling the tunnel outside with brief sparkles of white light. Forgetting about her own wound, the queen used both hands to raise her son's chest to her ear. She heard a single, feeble thump, then nothing.

"I need that light!"

The queen cradled her son in the crook of her elbow, then blew another gentle breath into his lungs. A tiny orange light flickered at the end of the passage. It gradually grew bright enough to reveal the form of a man squatting in the tunnel outside, blowing gently on a small pile of burning tinder. It took only a moment for the flame to grow steady enough for a second man to light the head of a makeshift torch. He passed the brand into the cockeyed drift, handing it to the front rider at Brianna's feet.

As the torchlight fell over her son, the queen cried out in alarm. Kaedlaw's handsome face was gone. In its place was an ugly round visage with brown eyes, a pug nose, and puffy cheeks. The infant's lips had suddenly become meaty and bluish. He had a mouthful of snaggle-teeth and a rolling double chin, and he looked as cold as a statue.

"What is it, Majesty?" asked Gryffitt. "He isn't dead?"

"I don't know yet."

The queen looked up and realized that she was the only one who could see her son's new face. Gryffitt was standing on the low ground behind her, and the man at her feet had to reach across his chest to hold the torch for her. He could not look in her direction without staring directly into the flame.

Brianna placed her thumbs over her son's sternum and began to press down in the rhythm of her own heart. Kaedlaw opened his mouth, unleashing a belch as deep and foul as an ogre's growl. A blue sparkle appeared in his brown eyes, his meaty lips pursed out to suck a lungful of air, then, all at once, his heavy jowls disappeared, his teeth straightened, his nose length-ened, and once more he was her handsome young son.

The change puzzled Brianna only briefly, for she quickly decided what she had seen was an illusion. Those who lost too much blood often became disori-ented and confused. The transformation had been no more than a hallucination of her blood-starved brain. The queen was sure of that.

"Majesty, what of the child?" Gryffitt asked. "Is he well?"

"He's going to be fine," Brianna answered.

All the front riders sighed in relief.

"Then perhaps we should see to you, Majesty," Gryf-fitt suggested. "Unless we finish Avner's work, I fear . . ."

The front rider let his sentence trail off, apparently thinking better of what he had almost said.

"It's okay, Gryffitt. I'm no more anxious to make an orphan of Kaedlaw than you are. Take me into the tun-nel." Brianna clutched her son more tightly to her breast, then added, "And Hiatea have mercy on the fir-bolg that makes me cover my son's mouth again."

*     *     *     *     *

Tavis stood at the tunnel wall, peering into the black throat of a crooked, craggy-sided chimney that yawned overhead like the serpentine gullet of a famished wyvern. Mountain Crusher's recurved tip pointed up the gloomy shaft at a slight angle. Only the high scout's firm grip kept the weapon, still glowing with magical blue light, from flying up the hole of its own accord. Brianna was up there somewhere, at least if the bow's seeking rune was to be trusted.

Unfortunately, that knowledge did not mean Tavis could actually reach his wife. The rune merely pointed in her direction, without indicating whether the route was passable. The chimney, which the miners called a *raise*, might end a dozen yards overhead. It might wander within a foot of the queen, only to turn in the opposite direction and leave the high scout farther from her than before. Or, it might lead straight to Brianna. The only way to find out was to climb.

Tavis tied his quiver to his hip and slipped Mountain Crusher over his chest. The tip of the bow swung around so that it pointed up the shaft. The weapon would have floated free if the string had not caught in the high scout's armpit. Tavis gulped down a lungful of the tunnel's sulfur-reeking air, then reached into the chimney and hauled himself up.

He barely fit. Though the raise was more than eight feet wide, it was not much thicker than Tavis's torso. To pull himself into the cramped space, he had to wedge his back against one wall and press his palms against the other, keeping his elbows tucked tight at his sides. It was strenuous work, and the high scout still felt weak and dizzy from his injuries. By the time he had pulled himself up far enough to use his knees and feet, his muscles were burning with fatigue. The sulfur stench from the tunnel below made matters worse, filling his lungs and throat with such a scorching stink that he could hardly breathe.

Tavis forced himself to gulp down more air, then clenched his teeth and pushed himself up another few inches. It would be slow going, but he had few alternatives. Shortly after leaving Galgadayle, a group of firbolgs had seen his glowing bow and started rolling boulders down the slope at him. The high scout had been forced to duck into this tunnel, trusting Mountain Crusher's magic to help him find his wife before her pursuers.

Nor were the Meadowhome warriors Tavis's greatest worry. He had yet to spy any verbeegs or fomorians, but the high scout knew better than to doubt Galgadayle's word.

Both groups were formidable foes.

The verbeegs were as organized as they were cunning. They would move quickly to seal every exit from the mountain, then begin a search of the entire warren—no doubt aided by the magic of their shamans and ingenious runecasters. If they captured Brianna before the virtuous firbolgs, they would not content themselves with killing her child. Almost certainly, they would also demand an impossible ransom for her release.

The fomorians posed an even greater danger. Although they were the largest and least intelligent of the giant-kin races, they were born to darkness. They could squeeze their peculiar, deformed bodies through holes half their size, and they walked through pitch blackness in utter silence, with the patient, slow movements of spiders on the stalk. When their hunt was successful, nothing delighted them quite so much as twisting their live prey into grotesque parodies of their own malformed bodies.

Brianna *had* to be at the end of this raise; Tavis could not bear to think of what might happen if she was not. Unfortunately, the farther he climbed, the more Mountain Crusher pointed at the wall instead of straight up. He began to fear that soon the tip would be leveled at an impassable wall of solid granite.

Tavis came to a rocky choke point too narrow for his thick torso. He blew out his breath and tried to pull past, but succeeded only in lodging himself between two craggy ridges of granite. He tried to push back down, thinking he could traverse sideways and climb through at another angle. He could not descend.

Tavis attempted to break free through sheer force, trying to move up, down, sideways, and all directions between. He succeeded only in exhausting his battered body. His weary muscles began to shake uncontrollably, and the granite grew damp and slick beneath his palms. His boots trembled free of their nubby footholds, leaving him suspended in the crevice like a thief stuck in the palace chimney. For each breath, he had to struggle against a crushing glove of stone.

Tavis's own odor, as musky and bitter as minkwort, overpowered the sulfurous stench from below. The firbolg could see nothing but the stone before his eyes, glowing eerily blue in his bow's magic light. The darkness around him grew heavy and smothering, as though the immense weight of the mountain itself had poured into the absolute blackness of the raise. Nothing existed below his feet save the impenetrable murk, and nothing above him, nor around him, but more of the same. The high scout had a vision of himself: a tiny, buglike creature trapped in a minor crevice lost deep within the mountain's immense, cloying gloom.

Tavis's pulse sounded in his ears. With each beat, he felt the cold stone grating against his ribs, sending sharp pangs of agony through his battered torso. He tried to squirm sideways. The pain only worsened, and he grew more convinced that he had lodged himself forever. He heard his own voice groaning and snarling, as though someone might actually hear him through all those immeasurable tons of granite.

The high scout forced himself to stop struggling, to close his eyes and mouth and simply feel his situation. He was caught beneath his chest. Somehow, he managed to push the largest part of his body—his breast and shoulders—past the choke point. After a moment's reflection, he realized he had been trying to pull himself through the constriction, which meant his arms had been raised above his head.

Tavis unfastened the ties on his scout's cloak, then blew out his breath and raised his arms. The pressure on his ribs abated, and he slid down a few inches. He let his body go slack and fell out of his coat. Mountain Crusher slipped over his shoulder and started to float up the raise, and the high scout fell into the darkness below.

Tavis thrust his feet and hands against the chimney wall, bringing himself to a quick halt—then almost lost his hold as his heavy scout's cloak landed on his head. He pulled the coat off, then realized that the raise was still illuminated by Mountain Crusher's blue light. He looked up and saw his glowing bow a dozen feet above the choke point, where the raise gradually bent over and became a narrow corridor with cockeyed walls. The weapon was scraping along the ceiling, slowly floating into the drift.

Tavis folded his cloak over his quiver and climbed back to the choke point. This time, he slipped through with only a minimum of grunting and cursing. He scrambled up the raise and caught his bow a few steps inside the drift. The cockeyed passage sloped upward at a gradually decreasing angle for about fifty paces. There, dancing on the wall of a junction with another corridor, he saw the orange glow of torch light.

Tavis felt he would find Brianna near the torch, but he had no idea who would be with her. He wrapped Mountain Crusher inside his cloak, then crept up the drift as silently as a fox on the stalk. His heart was pounding so hard that he did not hear the strange, gurgling growl until he had almost reached the junction. He stopped and quietly eased his sword from its scabbard.

A woman hissed, then groaned in pain—Brianna!

With visions of cruel, malformed fomorians dancing through his head, Tavis threw his cloak into the passage to distract his wife's captors. He followed with his sword raised, then heard several voices cry out in surprise. He found himself stooped over in a small tunnel, staring down at his wife's fur-swaddled form. One man was holding a torch over her, while another knelt on the floor, hunched over her bare midsection. There were no giant-kin—fomorians or otherwise—anywhere near the queen.

Tavis lowered his guard.

Someone behind him hissed, "Firbolg!"

"Wait, it's me!"

Tavis was spinning even as he spoke, bringing his sword around to deflect the misguided assault. A sharp crack rang off the tunnel walls as his blade sliced through a well-aimed lance, but even the lord high scout of Hartsvale was not fast enough to counter the thrust of the second front rider. The point of a lance sliced across his flank, opening a long gash above his hip.

Tavis grabbed the lance and jerked it from the man's hands. "Is this the proper way to greet me?"

"Lord High Scout!" The men uttered the exclamation together, then one continued, "But you—Avner said you fell to the fire giants!"

"I did." Tavis returned the lance he had taken, then pressed his hand over his bleeding wound. "But—"

"But Tavis Burdun always honors his duty," interrupted Brianna. Her voice was hardly more than a whisper. "Even if he must cheat death to do it."

"Firbolgs can't cheat, milady," he replied. "You know that."

Tavis sheathed his sword and faced his wife. She had a pearly grin upon her lips and a violet sparkle in her eyes, but her joy could not hide how hard the last hours had been for her. She looked haggard and weak. Her golden hair was sweat-plastered to her head, and her complexion was more pale than alabaster. Her pain showed in the lines etched into her brow and around her mouth, and her cheeks were as sunken and hollow as a corpse's. Although her belly was no longer swollen in pregnancy, Front Rider Gryffitt was carefully sewing shut a long incision that someone had cut across the lower part of her abdomen.

Tavis could hardly bring himself to look away from the wound. If he had not seen the joy in her eyes, he would have assumed that one of their enemies had cut the child from her womb.

Tavis knelt at his wife's side. "What happened?" he asked. "How badly are you hurt?"

"I'm fine." Brianna's voice was as serene as moonlit snow. "And Tavis—I have something to show you."

The queen opened her cloak. There, suckling at her breast, was the most hideous infant Tavis had ever seen. The baby was the size of a two-year-old, with stubby limbs and pudgy red fingers that pinched at its mother's flesh like talons. It had dull brown eyes as ravenous as they were vacant, a short pug nose, bloated cheeks, and blood-red lips. Sparse tufts of wiry black hair covered its fat, round head, and the thing resembled a goblin more than a child.

"Well, Tavis?" Brianna asked. "Don't you think he looks like you?"

# ❖ 7 ❖
# The Drainage Tunnel

The muggy underground air suddenly felt cool and crisp, a sure sign that Tavis and his companions were finally nearing an exit. They were deep down in the mine system, wading through the turbid orange waters of a drainage tunnel as long as it was straight. The walls babbled with the constant echo of dripping water, and the ceiling was so lofty that even the high scout could stand upright. Dozens of side tunnels opened off the main passage, all filled with streams of cloudy, auric water that stank of iron and copper and a dozen other minerals too obscure to name. But it was the heavy smell of brimstone—sharp and acrid and fresh—that concerned Tavis. The queen's party could not be far from where the fire giants had broken into the mine warrens.

"Thatcher, hold up a minute." Tavis was carrying the queen and her child in his arms, for the tunnel waters were so deep that only he could keep them dry. "Do you feel that cold air?"

The front rider stopped and nodded. "It's coming from there." He gestured forward with Tavis's glowing bow, which had become the party's only light source when their torch guttered out. "We must be near an exit."

"Thanks be to Stronmaus," whispered Gryffitt. "I was

beginning to think we'd never get out of this labyrinth."

"We haven't yet," Tavis cautioned. "Our enemies are sure to be watching the portals."

"Then let us hope they missed one," Brianna said. "If we keep stumbling around in the dark, sooner or later we'll run into Raeyadfourne's warriors—or something worse."

The queen was looking much healthier now. After Gryffitt had finished sewing her up, she had used her healing magic to mend both her own wounds and some of those Tavis had suffered. Unfortunately, she had been unable to do anything about her fatigue. She was still so weak she could hardly stand.

Tavis nodded to Thatcher. "Lead on," he said. "But keep a watchful eye, and you other men hold your weapons ready."

The other front riders arranged themselves on Thatcher's flanks, two carrying hand axes and two bearing lances cut short for use inside the mine. The party continued down the tunnel. The foul waters grew deeper, the interval between support timbers shorter. Twice as they passed side passages, Tavis heard the distant rumble of firbolg voices.

The air became cooler. They passed a drift in which the waters sat stagnant, with no sign of any current flowing from the other end. Deep within the passage echoed the sucking sounds of draining water, and Tavis smelled the mordant reek of brimstone hanging heavily about the entrance.

A dozen steps later, the main tunnel intersected another flooded corridor. The two passages joined and angled off together. The cold breeze became a frigid wind. The water was up to Tavis's navel now, and he could feel the current pressing against the front of his thighs—the opposite direction he had expected.

Thatcher stopped in the intersection. "The wind's

coming from up there."

He was not pointing down the joined passages, but up the opposite arm of the intersection. This tunnel was even more heavily braced than the one in which the queen's party stood. It looked as though it had been driven through wood instead of granite.

"And down the main tunnel?" Tavis asked.

Thatcher waded around the angle. He came back a few moments later. "I think it's the tunnel you blew up with your runearrow," he reported. "The passage is filled with rocks, and the support timbers have burned away. I saw a boot sticking out of the rubble. It had to be as large as my chest."

The report did not please Tavis. The main body of the firbolg troop had been hiding just up the canyon from the site of the fire giants' ambush.

"What are we waiting for?" Brianna asked. "The choice is obvious enough. Let's walk into the wind."

Tavis shook his head. "Not without scouting ahead." He pointed at Thatcher and one other front rider. "You two take a look."

Thatcher and his companion waded up the opposite fork of the mine, holding Tavis's bow and their own weapons above the swirling orange currents. Mountain Crusher's blue glow reflected off the water and danced across the timber-lined ceiling, filling the tunnel with a half-moon halo that steadily dwindled away. The darkness grew as smothering as a cave-in, and Kaedlaw began to growl.

"Maybe I should cast my light spell," Brianna suggested.

"I'd rather you saved it," Tavis replied.

Thatcher and the other front rider were bait. If there were firbolgs hiding outside, Mountain Crusher's light would draw them out. The resulting commotion would serve as an alarm, and the queen's party could slip away during the turmoil.

Kaedlaw's growl became a fierce, echoing howl.

"Is there any way to keep him quiet?" Tavis asked.

"What do you want me to do, smother him?" Brianna snapped. "If the firbolgs hear him, you'll just have to kill them."

Tavis clamped his jaw shut and tried to listen past Kaedlaw's howling.

"I didn't mean to snap, Tavis," Brianna apologized. "But he nearly died the last time I tried to keep him quiet."

Tavis felt her tug on the cloak he had laid over her legs, then she tucked it around Kaedlaw. The child's howling quickly abated, leaving the tunnel to the relative silence of dripping water.

"That's better, isn't it?" Brianna whispered to the infant. "But when we're outside, you'll have to give your father's cloak back to him."

Tavis was thankful for the darkness, for it prevented the queen from seeing the grimace that creased his face. How could his wife and the front riders think he had sired the hideous infant—or even call the child by a name suggesting it resembled him? Galgadayle's prophecy was at least partially correct; the brutish child was not Tavis's offspring, but that of the Twilight Spirit's imposter prince.

"Maybe we'll let the front riders carry me," Brianna said, still talking as though she were speaking to Kaedlaw. "And your father can wrap you inside his cloak so you both stay warm."

"He'll be warmer with his mother," Tavis said. "And you can keep my cloak to be sure. I'll be fine."

Brianna stiffened in his arms. She was silent for a long time, then said, "Lord Scout, if I didn't know better, I'd think you were reluctant to hold your son."

Tavis's mouth went dry. "I-I'm holding both you and

K-Kaedlaw now."

"That's not what I mean. You haven't actually *touched* him since you found us," Brianna said. "In fact, you've hardly looked at him. What's wrong?"

Tavis wanted to turn the question back on his wife—to demand how she could possibly think he had sired the hideous thing, to ask whether she was blind or took him for a fool—but he fought back the urge. Despite the baby's grotesque appearance, Brianna was convinced he had fathered the child. Now was hardly time to tell her otherwise. Besides, it would take more than a half-reliable prophecy to make him betray the oaths he had sworn to the queen.

"Well, Tavis?" Brianna pressed.

"We—uh—should—uh—"

A pair of anguished wails reverberated out of the opposite drainage tunnel, sparing Tavis the necessity of saying more. The screams did not end, but continued to echo through the darkness, randomly changing pitch and volume, as though the bodies from which they came were being played like living instruments. The gruesome music carried a steady undertone of crackling and splashing, and the basal throb of deep-throated chortling.

"Hiatea have mercy!" Brianna gasped. "What's happening in there?"

"I don't know, Majesty," said Gryffitt. "But we'll put an end to it soon enough." He started to splash toward the tunnel, with the other two front riders close behind.

"No!" Tavis ordered. "Stay with the queen."

"Begging your pardon, Lord Scout," said Gryffitt. "But if that was me up there, I'd want some help."

"If we try to help them, we'll join them." The two front riders had walked into an ambush, as Tavis had half-expected, but it hadn't been firbolgs. "You men take the queen and start back up the tunnel. I'll hold them here."

"Them?" Brianna demanded.

"Fomorians," Tavis answered. "Galgadayle told me to watch out for fomorians and verbeegs."

The wails continued unabated.

"*Galgadayle* told you?" Brianna sounded stunned.

"I pulled Avner's sword out of his back," Tavis admitted. "He won't be doing us any more harm."

"He has done more than enough already," Brianna growled. "How—"

"If the fomorians catch you, they'll do more!" Tavis thrust Brianna toward Gryffitt. "Take her and go."

Several pairs of hands reached up to take the queen. "We'll wait at the drift where we heard the water draining," said Gryffitt.

"Don't wait," Tavis replied. "And if you must stop to hide, do it well. Fomorians see in the dark better than we see in daylight."

As the front riders waded away, Tavis started toward the opposite drainage tunnel. He stopped when he heard Brianna uttering a spell. A pale silver light flared behind him. He turned to see his wife lying on the shoulders of her three bearers, a glowing dagger in her upraised hand.

"I thought we should see as well as the fomorians," she explained. "And Tavis, try to come back. I'd rather Kaedlaw grew up knowing his father."

"I'll do what's in my power, milady."

The tortured screams of the two front riders finally died. Tavis waded into the darkness ahead and slowly made his way to the wall. He placed himself between a pair of rough-hewn support timbers, chimneyed up the side of the tunnel, and braced himself between the ceiling arches. He freed one hand long enough to draw his sword, then settled in to wait.

As the last sloshing echoes of Brianna's departure faded away, Tavis saw a familiar blue glow flickering across the turbid waters below. Mountain Crusher. He grasped his sword more tightly and tried not to think of the fatigue burning in his thighs and shoulders. The magical light grew brighter, illuminating bands of blood swirling in the orange river. The weapon itself floated into view atop the water, spinning in the current and sweeping the walls with its cold, shimmering light.

The bow remained in one piece, with Thatcher's hand still gripping the handle. The wrist was cocked at an impossible angle. The arm jigged and jagged in three different directions, then came to an abrupt end at the mangled elbow.

Two foul-smelling mangles of flesh and bone drifted into view. They had been twisted into grotesque parodies of human bodies, their limbs bent against the joints or torn off entirely. Organs that should have been safely tucked inside the torsos now hung outside. Tavis looked away, fighting the urge to retch.

Mountain Crusher brushed against a timber, then spun into the opposite wall and caught its string on a rock spur. The two bodies slowly bobbed past, lingering beneath Tavis so long that it almost seemed the spirits of the two front riders were torturing him for sending their bodies to such hideous deaths.

The crest of a gentle wave rolled down the tunnel, carrying the corpses away. A sweet, musky scent rose off the water, mixing with the smell of sulfur and musty wood.

A stubby, gray-skinned hand came into view. It had only three gnarled fingers, each ending in a sharp, broken nail that protruded from the tip like a muskrat's claw. The appendage itself was as large as a human torso, its ashen hide mottled with black warts and crimson boils. The twisted thing advanced at a glacier's pace, reaching out to dislodge the glowing bow. Tavis heard no sloshing water, no wheezing breath, no sound at all.

At length, a fomorian's warty, pear-shaped head came into view. Like all of his kind, the hunter was hideously and uniquely deformed. One eye hung in the center of his forehead, and the other rested atop his pate. From one side of his head dangled a pair of drooping ears. His broad nose ended in a single cavernous nostril, and an ivory curtain of crooked teeth jutted over his thick lower lip. Though the brute was squatting on his haunches, he was so large that the wiry hair on his back brushed the ceiling in front of Tavis.

The fomorian's two eyes worked independently as he advanced, one searching the tunnel ahead, the other scanning the walls and ceiling. One of the dark pupils swept past Tavis's hiding place, then stopped midway down the wall and started to rise again.

The high scout leapt from his corner, aiming his sword at the eye atop the fomorian's head.

The hunter flinched and turned away. Tavis's blade drove straight through the thick skull. A torpid shudder of death ran down the brute's crooked spine. The misshapen body went slack and slumped into the murky waters, filling three-quarters of the passage even lying on its belly.

A puff of hot, rancid air wafted over Tavis's shoulders. Without pausing to dislodge his sword, he jumped off the corpse, angling toward the rock spur where Mountain Crusher had snagged. From the darkness behind the dead fomorian came the boulderlike fist of a second hunter. The blow caught Tavis in midleap and sent him hurtling down the passage into a timber post. He heard the muffled snap of cracking ribs, then lost his breath and dropped into the water.

A shower of rock dust, pebbles, and splintered wood splashed down around his shoulders. Tavis looked up. Above his head, the end of a rotten beam was sagging beneath a ton of broken, growling stone. A frustrated hiss sounded behind the dead fomorian as the second hunter tried to shove aside his companion's bulky corpse. The high scout pushed himself away from the tunnel wall, less concerned with his angry pursuer than the drooping beam overhead.

The ceiling did not come crashing down, but continued to pour into the water in a steady stream of stone and dust. Suddenly, Tavis saw the mountain above him not as a solid mass of granite, but as a colossal heap of pulverized stone being slowly ground to dust beneath its own immense weight. Keeping one eye on the drooping beam, he reached out and lifted Mountain Crusher off the rock that had snagged its string.

A growl of rage sounded upstream. Tavis spun around, already pulling a wet arrow from his quiver.

A pair of silver eyes were glaring over the dead fomorian's back. The orbs were as large as bucklers, and set so close that the edges almost touched. Tavis could barely see the rest of his foe, a creeping black silhouette slipping across the corpse's humped back. To fit through the narrow space, the hunter had flattened out his body as though he were a mouse crawling beneath a door.

Tavis nocked his arrow and pointed the tip between the two gleaming eyes. The dark shape of a huge webbed hand interposed itself between the arrow and its target. The high scout drew his bowstring back, groaned at the pain in his cracked ribs, and loosed the shaft.

The arrow tore through the shielding hand with a sound like ripping leather, then crackled into the narrow band of cartilage between the fomorian's eyes. A deafening screech echoed through the tunnel. Tavis nearly gagged on the rancid odor of the hunter's death rattle.

The fomorian's eyes, now dull and glazed with death, continued to move as another hunter tried to work the body out of the cranny.

Tavis retreated to the fork and waded up the tunnel, each step a struggle against the pain in his ribs. This time, there would be no quick cures for his anguish. He had given the last of Simon's healing potion to Galgadayle, and Brianna had no more mending spells left. The high scout clenched his teeth and reminded himself that his agony was nothing compared to the torture Thatcher and the other front rider had suffered.

Soon, Tavis saw the silvery glow of Brianna's magical light spilling from a passage ahead. He waded up to the tunnel and found Gryffitt crouching in the entrance. The corridor was scorched and rubble-strewn, with the jagged tips of boulders jutting out of the opaque waters. Loose stones dangled from the ceiling like stalactites. About twenty paces behind the front rider, the queen and her escorts were crouching in ankle-deep water at the edge of a gaping hole.

"I told you not to wait," Tavis chided. "There are more fomorians behind me."

"And we heard firbolgs up ahead," Brianna countered. "Now come here, before they see that glowing bow of yours."

Tavis slipped past Gryffitt and clambered over the submerged rocks toward the queen. The passage was clearly the route through which the fire giants had entered the mine system, for the walls were coated with fresh soot. The pit where Brianna had stopped was easily ten paces across. A steady flow of water poured into the hole, splashing off stones somewhere far below and filling the battered passage with the eerie sounds of a subterranean cascade.

"Do you have any runearrows left?" Brianna asked.

Tavis nodded. "About half a dozen."

"Good." She gestured at the disintegrating ceiling. "Nock three and stick them in the roof."

From the mouth of the drift, Gryffitt called, "There's a

torch coming down the tunnel."

Tavis glanced across the pit, and his heart sank. The hole was too wide to jump, and it would not be long before the fomorians cleared the opposite fork of the drainage tunnel. He looked back to his wife.

"If you're thinking of bringing the ceiling down on us—"

"I'm not." Brianna tossed her glowing dagger into the pit, revealing a huge tunnel about fifteen feet below. The passage was more than ten feet in diameter, with smooth, soot-coated walls. "We're going out the back way—and you're going to close the door behind us."

\* \* \* \* \*

Avner stood well back in the drift, spying upon several giant-kin and their captive, Marwick. The young scout held his throwing dagger in his hand, and his eyes were locked on the prisoner's terrified face.

The throw would be a difficult one. Marwick was kneeling about twenty paces away, in the center of a large, irregular cavity where a tangle of drifts merged from above and below and every other direction. The front rider's captors sat around him, crammed into the mouths of the nearest passages like bears into badger holes. Two of the 'kin might have squeezed into the hollow with their prisoner, but the cavern was too small to hold all five.

Avner could silence Marwick easily enough, but escaping so many 'kin would be difficult. The three firbolgs—Raeyadfourne, Munairoe, and Galgadayle—had shrunken to a size not much larger than Tavis. Despite the cramped drifts, they would not have much trouble running him down.

The two verbeegs were another matter. Even squatting on their haunches, they had to tuck their chins to fit into the passages. Unfortunately, they each carried a big crossbow and a quiver full of barbed, nasty-looking quarrels. To make matters worse, they had also put together a crude sketch-map of the mine. Their knowledge of the terrain would give them a sure advantage.

"Human, I warn you not to lie," Munairoe said, speaking to Marwick. "If I must call the wind spirit into this dank place, she will not take pity on a scofflaw."

"I told you, the queen bore only one child," Marwick insisted. "Your seer was wrong."

"Galgadayle's dreams are as right as a firbolg's tongue," insisted Munairoe. "It is humans who lie."

"Not this time." Marwick kept his gaze fixed on the floor. "One child. I saw Avner take him from her womb."

"Raeyadfourne, enough of this!" hissed a verbeeg. He was a slender, gray-haired male with features as sharp as spearheads. "Make us a gift of your prisoner, and we shall know the truth soon enough."

Raeyadfourne glowered at the verbeeg. "Torture is a breach of the law, Horatio."

Horatio's lip curled into a contemptuous sneer. "Your law."

Raeyadfourne scowled. "Must I remind you—"

The verbeeg raised his hand. "I know, I know." There was an air of resignation in his voice. "We agreed to obey your law. Carry on."

Horatio pulled a parchment map from inside his cloak and unrolled it on the floor. He began to examine the document as though the interrogation no longer interested him.

Raeyadfourne looked back to Marwick. "If the queen bore only one child, was it handsome or ugly?"

Marwick's eyes flickered from the ground to the chieftain's face, then back again.

Avner prayed the man to remain quiet. When the firbolgs captured Brianna and found only one infant, there was still a chance they would think their seer had made a mistake. But if Marwick told them about the child's transformation, Raeyadfourne would realize, as Avner did, that the twins had entered the world in a single body.

When Marwick did not answer, the second verbeeg's hand shot out and covered the captive's face. Avner grimaced, for the huge arm blocked his shot at both the front rider's heart and throat. A quick kill was no longer possible.

"Since you have no use for this jaw, you won't mind if I crush it," growled the verbeeg. He was much younger than Horatio and, save for his harelip, too handsome for his race. "Speak!"

Raeyadfourne grabbed the verbeeg's arm, but could not pull it away. "You're perilously close to a breach of the law, Jerome," the firbolg warned. "And harming the prisoner will not guarantee his honesty."

"There are ways to learn the truth even from liars." Jerome started to the pull the front rider toward him. "And I promise not to break any of your darling laws."

Avner considered throwing his dagger into Marwick's stomach, but that would not silence the front rider for long. The shaman Munairoe would simply heal the prisoner, as he had already healed the wounds of both Raeyadfourne and Galgadayle.

Raeyadfourne grabbed Jerome's arm with both hands, refusing to let the verbeeg drag Marwick any farther. "You do not know the law, Jerome," the chieftain said. "How can you promise not to breach it?"

Avner saw that a narrow angle was opening to Marwick's throat. The throw would be difficult, through the crook of Jerome's elbow and perhaps under Raeyadfourne's forearms, but it was his only chance. The young scout raised his arm and waited.

A series of muffled steps sounded from the drift

behind Raeyadfourne. "We've found them!" yelled a booming voice. "Tavis Burdun is with them!"

Raeyadfourne and the verbeeg both released Marwick. Avner lowered his dagger, biting his cheeks to keep from crying out in joy. He had never truly believed Tavis was dead—it would take more than a fire giant's boot to keep the lord high scout from fulfilling his oath to Brianna—and now Avner knew everything would be fine. Tavis had found his way back to the queen, and as long as he was with her, no harm would come to either her or Kaedlaw.

Raeyadfourne crawled out of his drift and turned around to face the messenger, nearly crushing Marwick against the wall. "Found them?" the chieftain demanded. "Where?"

"Down low in the mine. Quillorn and Romney heard a fomorian screaming and followed the sound into a flooded tunnel." The messenger did not come forward far enough for Avner to see. "They glimpsed a light shining from a side tunnel, and heard a woman's voice."

As the messenger reported, Avner saw Horatio's finger drop to one corner of his sketch-map.

The messenger continued, "They waded down to the passage, but they weren't fast enough to stop the humans."

"Stop them?" demanded Raeyadfourne.

"When they looked into the passage, they saw blue light shining up from a big hole in the floor, and there were some of Tavis Burdun's exploding arrows in the ceiling," the messenger reported. "They heard his voice call out a magic word, then ducked around the corner. The whole tunnel collapsed on the pit."

"Karontor's wolves! They've dropped into the fire giant tunnel!" Horatio's fingers flew back and forth over his map for a moment longer, then he looked up at Raeyadfourne. "We may as well go home and prepare for war! They're going out the other end!"

Raeyadfourne frowned. "The other end?"

"The fire giants tried to trap the humans between two groups," Horatio explained. "Their tunnel had two portals."

"Then let's go!" Raeyadfourne started into a drift. "We'll cut them off."

"Where?" Horatio demanded. "The only thing we know about the second portal is that it's someplace down the canyon. The fire giant tunnel will run straight to it, while we must wind our way out of this mine and up the gorge—"

"Enough!" Raeyadfourne's eyes had grown angry as a blizzard. "We can't give up now. For all we know, the fire giant tunnel could be blocked. I'll gather my warriors and the fomorians, then start digging. You take the verbeegs and try to find that exit."

"We'll never reach it before the humans," Horatio warned.

"But you *will* try." Raeyadfourne motioned to Galgadayle and Munairoe, then started into the drift with the messenger.

"Wait!" barked Jerome, starting after the firbolgs. "Do you take us for fools? If the tunnel is blocked, you'll capture the queen and we'll be left outside. I'm going with you."

Horatio caught the younger verbeeg by the arm. "Jerome, what difference does it make who captures the queen?" His voice was strangely calm. "The important thing is to kill the child, and we can trust the firbolgs to do that."

Jerome scowled at his fellow. "You want me to go with you?"

"Exactly." Horatio smiled at Raeyadfourne, then placed a hand on Marwick's trembling shoulder. "And since we are going outside anyway, we'll put the captive

**121**

with the others your tribe is holding."

Raeyadfourne frowned. "There's no use torturing him," the firbolg warned. "He knows nothing that will help us capture the queen."

Horatio nodded. "On my word, we will not harm him."

"My thanks, then," the chieftain replied. "And I shall look in on his condition later."

Raeyadfourne turned and led his two fellows into the tunnel. Marwick's fear showed so brightly that his eyes were almost glowing. The front rider stared after the firbolg torches until they had faded into darkness, then darted for the drift next to Avner's.

Jerome was expecting the maneuver. The verbeeg's arm shot out quick as lightning and plucked the front rider off his feet. "Now, midget, you will tell us what you know."

"Of course," Marwick gasped. "You don't have to hurt me. I won't hide anything."

Avner raised his dagger, but had to hold his throw when Horatio snatched Marwick from the younger verbeeg.

"Jerome, we have no time for that."

Horatio snapped the front rider's spine as casually as a man would wring a chicken's neck, then threw the lifeless body down the black maw of narrow shaft. The corpse bounced down the passage with a series of slowly fading thuds.

Jerome peered down the hole. "Why did you do that?"

Horatio planted a finger on his map. "Because of this pit," he explained. "Unless I miss my guess, the fire giants cut through it with their tunnel. If we hurry, we'll be waiting when Queen Brianna goes by."

Jerome's harelip twisted into an greedy smile. "And then she'll be *our* prisoner," he said. "We can demand all the ransom we want."

\* \* \* \* \*

The tunnel was as smooth and straight as the halls of Castle Hartwick, and so dark that the soot-covered walls swallowed light as a river swallows snowflakes. The queen's party was moving along at a trot, with Gryffitt running thirty paces ahead, holding the queen's dagger to illuminate his path. Brianna was holding Mountain Crusher to light the way for Tavis and his fellow litter bearers.

Despite the pain in his ribs, Tavis easily kept pace with the others. There was nothing to see in this passage and little to worry about, other than a few boulders hanging loose in the ceiling and the slick footing of the wet floor. With any luck at all, they would be out of the mountain shortly.

"I think we're going to be safe, milady," Tavis reported. "We should reach Wynn Castle by sunrise."

"You've done well, Lord Scout," Brianna replied. "But I must admit I won't feel safe even after we return to our own castle. The war with the giants has been bad enough. I don't know if we can defeat a 'kin alliance as well."

"Let's not worry about the 'kin now," Tavis suggested. "Perhaps the light of day will show us a way to put to rest our trouble with them."

"What could possibly change between now and tomorrow?"

Tavis hesitated before answering, and it was a mistake.

"Well?" Brianna asked. "What will daylight show us, save more trouble?"

"Perhaps we can strike a compromise with the firbolgs," Tavis replied. "After all, Galgadayle's dream was not entirely correct."

"*Entirely?*" Brianna sat up, twisting around to look at

Tavis and consequently shielding her nursing child from his view. "Exactly *what* do you think was correct about Galgadayle's prophecy?"

Tavis did not want to answer. Lying was out of the question, of course, but so was telling Brianna that her child's face bore the worst features of both the ettin's heads. "Let's discuss this tomorrow, after we've had more rest."

"No. I want to know now," Brianna insisted. "You don't think Kaedlaw is your son, do you?"

The two men carrying the forward half of the litter stumbled and nearly fell.

"Brianna, this is not the time to discuss what I think," Tavis said. "You're still weak, I'm exhausted and sore, and the only important thing is to reach the protection of Wynn Castle."

"Answer me!" Brianna yelled. "I command it as your queen."

"We'd better slow down," Tavis said. Once his fellow litter bearers had obeyed, he took a deep breath and met his wife's gaze. "Kaedlaw was fathered by the imposter. He's too ugly to be mine."

The two front riders glanced over their shoulders, one with an arched brow and the other a slack jaw.

Brianna shrieked, "Ugly?"

Tavis nodded, his eyes fixed on Kaedlaw's piggish face. "That round head," he said. "That pug nose and double chin . . . what made you think he was my child?"

Tears streamed from Brianna's eyes. "Tavis, how could you?"

Tavis wanted to reach out and embrace his wife, but he could not free his hands without dropping her litter. "You were beguiled."

"You're the one who's beguiled!" Brianna shouted. "What spell did Galgadayle cast on you—or have you betrayed me of your own accord?"

"I haven't betrayed you," Tavis insisted. "But you must admit that the child doesn't resemble me. Just look at his eyes: mine are blue and yours are violet, but his are brown. And whose eyes were brown? The imposter's!"

Brianna's expression went blank, then her eyes began to widen in terror. At the same time, the two front riders abruptly stopped walking and turned around.

"Lord Scout, what are you talking about?" asked one. "The child's eyes are as blue as ice!"

Tavis scowled at the man. "What's wrong with you?" He looked from the front rider to Brianna, who now had a distant expression on her face, then back again. "Did the queen order you to say that?"

The second front rider shook his head. "She ordered nothing of the sort. The child looks just like you!" The man looked toward the queen with an expression so tender he might have been her husband, then added, "Not that you deserve a royal son!"

Brianna threw her legs over the edge of the litter and, still holding Tavis's bow, stumbled around behind the two front riders. There was a mad, terrified light in her violet eyes.

"Gryffitt!" She did not look away from the high scout as she yelled.

Far up the passage, Tavis saw the front rider's distant figure stop. "Yes, Majesty?"

"Come back here," Brianna commanded. "You shall carry my litter, and we shall send this—this firbolg—to scout ahead."

"That's not necessary, Brianna," Tavis said. "There's something strange happening here. I'm seeing one thing, and everyone else another."

"Silence, firbolg!" Brianna snapped. Something clattered far up the tunnel, in the darkness beyond Gryffitt, but the queen paid it no heed. "You will do as I command, or I'll have you executed for treason."

From behind Gryffitt came the echo of flat feet slapping against the wet floor. The front rider pulled his hand axe and spun to face the noise.

Tavis dropped his end of the litter and held a hand out to Brianna. He heard another clatter up the tunnel, and then a loud thump.

"Your Majesty, my bow—please!"

Brianna pulled away, still oblivious to what was happening behind her. "Stay back, traitor!"

Gryffitt's distant figure hefted his axe and stepped forward. A sharp twang echoed off the tunnel walls. The front rider dropped his axe and Brianna's glowing dagger, then pitched over backward. He landed flat on his back, a huge crossbow bolt protruding from his chest.

A slender, gray-haired verbeeg stepped into the light of Brianna's dagger. In his hands, he held a large crossbow with an iron quarrel nocked in the groove. The tip was pointed straight at Brianna.

Tavis reached for his bow, but stopped when the newcomer raised the crossbow menacingly.

"Don't be foolish. These bolts are poisoned." The verbeeg backed away from the glowing dagger, once more cloaking himself in darkness. "We would prefer to keep the queen alive, but we will forego the ransom if we must. Now drop your weapons."

"What do we have here, Tavis?" Brianna asked. She glared up the tunnel and refused to set Mountain Crusher aside. "More of your allies?"

"Of course not, milady." The high scout slowly unbuckled his scabbard belt and motioned for the front riders to do the same. "But I would advise you—"

The verbeeg suddenly gave a strangled, gurgling cry. His crossbow clattered to the tunnel floor, releasing its bolt to ricochet harmlessly off a sooty wall. The verbeeg himself appeared an instant later, falling face-first into the light of the glowing dagger. There was blood cascading down his chest and a scrawny human form clinging to his back.

"Avner?" Tavis gasped.

The young scout leapt off the verbeeg's back and grabbed Brianna's glowing dagger, then started down the passage.

"Nothing to worry about," he called. "There were only two."

"Avner, I'm so happy to see you!" Brianna walked forward and pushed Mountain Crusher into the youth's hands. "Keep a close eye on Tavis. He seems to be acting like just another firbolg."

# ◆ 8 ◆
# Wynn Castle

With five armored escorts following close behind, Tavis clambered up the stair turret and stepped onto the roof of Wynn Castle's arsenal tower. At the parapets across the way stood Basil of Lyndusfarne, Royal Librarian and Runecaster to Her Majesty the Queen. The ancient verbeeg held his spindly hands clasped behind his back and wore a cloak of matted wolf-fur over his stooped shoulders. The tips of his big ears were crimson with cold, and his white hair was so thin that it barely concealed his gray, scaly scalp. He seemed as oblivious to the high scout's arrival as he did to the muttered conversation of his own guards.

Tavis stopped at the verbeeg's side, but said nothing. Basil's milky blue eyes were focused far across the snowy plain, where the sun had kindled a twilight blaze in the clouds behind the glacier-clad peaks of the Ice Spires South. The runecaster looked almost blissful. His bushy eyebrows were arched in nearly sacred awe and his thick lips upturned in rapturous joy, but his expression did not conceal entirely the toll taken on him by the last three years. The circles under his eyes were as deep and black as canyons, and his cheeks were sunken with fatigue.

"Hello, Basil," Tavis said. "You're the last person I expected to find at Wynn Castle."

"I wouldn't have missed this for anything." Basil did not take his eyes off the clouds.

Tavis felt sure his friend meant the sunset, not the hundreds of giant-kin scattered across the shadow-streaked snows outside. The first party of firbolgs had arrived at the castle that morning, less than two hours after the queen's battered entourage. Since then, a constant stream of 'kin had been pouring from the Gorge of the Silver Wyrm. They were already building a siege tower and ram shed so they could storm the walls, perhaps as soon as tomorrow. Their leaders were no fools; no doubt, they realized that Brianna had immediately sent for reinforcements. If they did not capture the queen before her reserves arrived, they never would.

The giant-kin had a difficult task ahead of them. Wynn Castle guarded the southern passes through which Hartsvale traded with the outside world, and only Castle Hartwick, the queen's permanent residence, was stronger. More than once, Wynn Castle had withstood barrages of flame and stone cast by whole companies of fire giants. If the citadel had held against those assaults, it would likely survive anything hurled at it by the giant-kin.

Basil continued to stare at the sunset, completely lost in its beauty. The absentminded verbeeg often seemed to forget his surroundings—he sometimes went days without remembering to eat—but seldom was he absorbed by something so mundane as twilight.

"You didn't come all this way to watch the sun go down," Tavis said.

The high scout took Basil's elbow and gently turned him around. The verbeeg's gaze remained fixed on the blazing clouds, his body swiveling beneath his head until his neck could crane no farther. As his eyes were torn from the mesmerizing sight, the bliss drained from his face like water.

"What are you doing here?" Tavis asked. In case Basil had forgotten where 'here' was, he added, "Why did you come to Wynn Castle?"

Basil shrugged. "I've never seen this castle. Now seemed as good a time as any."

"You haven't set foot outside Castle Hartwick in three years," Tavis countered. "In fact, you've barely left the Royal Library."

The verbeeg knitted his gray brows and tugged at his wispy beard. Then his eyes glimmered. "I have news for you! And for Brianna, too, when you can arrange an audience." Basil glanced toward the center of the castle, where the four ice-draped towers of Wynn Keep loomed above the inner curtain. "The guards seem to have forgotten who I am. I can't get past the keep gate."

"You're doing better than I am," Tavis replied. "They won't even let me into the ward."

"But you're her husband!" Basil winced as soon as he spoke, then looked down at Tavis with an apologetic expression. "Aren't you?"

The high scout spread his hands. "Who knows?" he asked. "I was yesterday."

Basil's face fell, and he looked away shaking his head. "This is terrible," he said. "It could make things difficult."

"You think it hasn't already?" Tavis growled.

Basil did not seem to notice the scout's foul humor. "What did you do?"

"What makes you think *I* did something?" Tavis snapped. "I didn't do anything—except save her from the fire giants and the giant-kin and guide her out of Earl Wynn's mines."

"*Something* must have happened," Basil pressed. "And I must say, it couldn't have occurred at a worse time. Tell me what you've been doing since you left Castle Hartwick."

Tavis nodded, then glanced around the ramparts. Counting his five armored escorts and the guards watching over Basil, there were nearly a dozen men on the roof of the small tower.

"You men go down inside and warm up," he suggested. "I think we're safe enough here."

Tavis's escorts and Basil's guards exchanged nervous glances. Neither group made any move to leave.

"What's wrong?" Tavis demanded. "Do as I say."

"I'm sorry, milord," said the sergeant. "But the queen gave orders. We're to keep a watch on all the 'kin in the castle—especially you."

Tavis's stomach balled into an aching knot. He found himself stepping toward the sergeant, and he saw his own hands rising to shove the man into the stair turret. The soldier and his fellows all went pale, but they stood their ground and reached for their swords.

Basil's long fingers dug into Tavis's shoulder. "There's no need for violence," said the runecaster. "I can arrange our privacy, if that's what you want."

Tavis allowed himself to be stopped, then took a deep breath and addressed the guards. "I didn't realize what your orders were. Please carry on—and I'm sorry for my reaction."

"No offense taken, milord," said the sergeant. "If my wife ordered a guard on me, I'd be . . . er . . . surprised, too."

In spite of his words, the soldier did not remove his hand from his sword hilt, and neither did the guards with him.

Tavis retreated to the ice-capped merlon where Basil was already kneeling on the roof, using a small runebrush to trace a circle around their feet. Though the tip had not been dipped in paint or ink, a sparkling green pigment flowed from beneath the bristles. When the runecaster finished drawing the boundary, he slowly and carefully traced a complicated tangle of sticklike lines in the heart of the ring.

The rooftop fell instantly silent. Tavis could see the soldiers a few paces away, shifting uneasily and discussing the spell among themselves, but he could not hear them.

"As long as we don't break the circle, they won't hear our words." Basil tucked the runebrush back into his cloak. "Now, I suppose you'd better tell me exactly what happened in the Gorge of the Silver Wyrm."

"I'm not sure I know—exactly." Tavis rested his elbows on the icy merlon and looked out over the darkening plain.

Despite the deepening shadows, the giant-kin were still at work. Firbolg sawyers were dragging logs across the snowy plain to verbeeg carpenters, who were busy lashing the timbers into huge siege machines. Even the fomorians were helping, skinning hundreds of deer, elk, and moose for the hides that would defend their towers against flaming arrows.

"Tavis, you're behaving like a human," Basil observed. "If I didn't know better, I'd say you were ashamed of something."

"Not ashamed, but I should have handled things better," Tavis admitted. "We were only five leagues from the Silver Citadel when the trouble started. . . ."

The high scout recounted everything that had happened the previous day, from the onset of the fire giant attack through the arrival of the queen's party at Wynn Castle, when Brianna had locked herself in Wynn Keep and ordered Tavis to remain in the outer bailey. By the time his story was done, twilight had fallen completely. The 'kin out on the plain were no more than shadows moving in the moonlike glow of the snow.

"I don't blame Brianna for being upset about K-Kae—er, her son," Tavis concluded. "So am I, but what can I do? I saw what I saw, and I can't claim that child as my own. Brianna has no right to be angry with me."

Basil slapped his brow. "Firbolgs! The problem is Galgadayle, you oaf!"

Tavis frowned. "The seer?"

"Why you had to spare him is beyond me, but to tell Brianna what you did was madness!" The verbeeg shook his head. "No wonder she doesn't trust us. You've certainly ruined any chance that she'll believe what I have to say. We'll be lucky if she doesn't execute us both, much less grant me an audience."

"Why should she execute us?" Tavis was genuinely confused. "I did what was right."

" 'Right' is a relative thing," Basil countered. "I don't see how saving the person who convinced three tribes of giant-kin to murder your wife's baby is right—and more importantly, neither does Brianna."

"But the law—"

"Your wife *is* the law," Basil said. "And in her eyes, you've sided with your own race against her."

"But it makes no difference that the child isn't mine! I haven't abandoned my oath!"

"Haven't you?" Basil asked. "Then you believe Galgadayle was lying? Or perhaps you're willing to sacrifice the northlands to the giants?"

Tavis slammed his fist on the merlon, shattering the ice cap and sending a silvery cascade of shards clattering down the tower wall. He watched the fragments disappear into the snow drifts atop the frozen moat, then shook his head.

"You know as well as I that Galgadayle can't lie," Tavis said. "But maybe he's mistaken. He was wrong about the twins."

"Not really. If humans see the face of your child, and

firbolgs see the face of the imposter, then perhaps she did bear twins," Basil said. "And that makes your decision even more difficult."

The runecaster did not have to clarify what he meant. If both children had been born in the same body, then the imposter's spawn could not be destroyed without killing Tavis's son as well. A queasy feeling filled the high scout's stomach. He was torn between two intolerable prospects: allowing the ettin's offspring to mature and lead the giants against the northlands, or helping the 'kin murder his own child.

Tavis's oath as lord high scout allowed only one choice. He had promised to protect Brianna's kingdom and defend her person against Hartsvale's enemies, even if it meant taking her life to prevent them from capturing her. If Basil was right, the only way he could keep his vow was to slay not the queen, but her child—and his child as well.

Tavis's hands started to tremble, then his knees grew weak and he had to brace himself on the icy merlon. He was beginning to understand why Brianna did not want him near her baby.

"If that child truly looks like me to Brianna, I can't imagine how she feels."

"That's what I've been trying to tell you."

Tavis looked into his friend's ancient eyes. "Basil, we must find out exactly who K-Kaedlaw is," he said. "And I'm afraid the burden must lie with you."

"Why?"

"Because Brianna's not going to let me anywhere near that baby, and I don't blame her," Tavis replied. "Besides, we already know what *I* see. Maybe your vision will prove truer than mine, especially with the aid of your runes."

"At the moment, I suspect the queen would not look kindly upon me—or any giant-kin—painting runes on her child's forehead," Basil replied. "Besides, Kaedlaw's parentage is hardly important."

"Of course it is!" Tavis growled. "There's more at stake here than my pride—much more."

Basil shook his gaunt head. "That's what I came to tell you," he said. "It doesn't matter if Galgadayle's dream is right."

"How can that be?"

The verbeeg twisted his thick lips into a cunning smile. "Because we have the power to prevent the prophecy from coming true—and it wouldn't matter if Kaedlaw's father was Memnor himself!"

Tavis grimaced. "Are you saying what I think?"

Basil's eyes twinkled like stars in the purple twilight sky. "I found Annam's axe," the verbeeg confirmed. "I know where Sky Cleaver is, and *you* can recover it."

Tavis backed away. He would have stepped outside Basil's rune circle had the verbeeg not stopped him.

"You know what I think of this," Tavis said. "Mortals were not meant to wield such weapons."

Basil's grin only widened. "I know," he said. "The giants will have no choice except to bow to you. As for Galgadayle and the 'kin armies—well, they can join us, or fall beneath our might."

Tavis shook his head, more in disbelief than opposition. "Basil, listen to yourself! You don't even have the axe, and already you're talking as though you rule the world."

The verbeeg nodded. "I know," he said. "That's why *I* mustn't be the one. But your heart is pure, Tavis. You can wield the axe for all of us."

"My heart may not be as pure as you think," Tavis replied. He would never be able to look at Kaedlaw without feeling a very private anger. "And even if I were as pure and noble as you believe, what happens to the weapon when I die?"

Basil rolled his eyes. "Tavis, you aren't going to die for a long time—not with Sky Cleaver in your hand!"

"Everyone dies sooner or later, Basil," Tavis said. "But a weapon like that endures forever. Even if I have the strength to control it, the next owner may not—and I won't be responsible for what happens to the world then."

"So, put it back before you die!" Basil snapped. "But Sky Cleaver would give you the power to keep your oath to Brianna. You must wield it—or break your word."

The verbeeg folded his arms across his chest and stared down his cob nose.

"That might be so—if I could control the axe," Tavis said. "But you're hardly power-mad, Basil, and the mere thought of Sky Cleaver fills your head with visions of conquering giants and forcing the 'kin tribes to bow at our feet. How can I hope to resist the weapon's lure when I actually hold it in my hands?"

"That's—that comparison's ridiculous!" Basil sputtered. "I'm a verbeeg. I don't have any morals!"

"My point exactly," Tavis replied. "Once I recover the weapon, you will stop at nothing to steal it away."

"There would be no need to steal it," Basil answered. "I have no interest in becoming any sort of emperor."

"Then what do you get?"

A hungry light flickered to life in Basil's eyes. "Knowledge," he answered. "Sky Cleaver has the power to cut to the heart of any matter."

"I should have known," Tavis snorted. "Never, Basil. Not if the giants were pouring through the gates and I was the last warrior alive to defend the queen."

"Really?" The verbeeg's lip curled into an oddly affable sneer. "It may be the only way to learn Kaedlaw's true paternity."

Tavis stepped forward until he was standing chin-to-chest with the verbeeg. "Basil, you should know better than to try extorting me," he warned. "You may be a friend, but even you cannot stand between me and my sworn duty."

The runecaster's sneer vanished. He looked over the parapets and fixed his eyes on the white plain, where the purple twilight shadows were inexorably sliding toward Wynn Castle. "I had to try. You know that."

"No, I don't, Basil," Tavis replied. "Some things are unpardonable, even for verbeegs."

Tavis stepped back and rubbed his boot sole across the floor, wiping away a small swatch of Basil's privacy rune. The entire circle evaporated, as did the symbol at its heart.

Tavis heard his guards crying out in astonishment. He scowled, unable to imagine that a vanishing rune would cause such a reaction, and turned to find the soldiers standing on the opposite side of the tower. They were pointing toward the inner ward, where an eagle-shaped cloud of purple gloom was spiraling down from the twilight sky.

"What is it?" The sergeant glanced back at Tavis. "Is Hiatea herself coming to see the queen's child?"

"I doubt it." Tavis started across the roof. "Sound the alarm—and get your men to the keep!"

The sergeant shoved his warriors into the stair turret.

The murky eagle lowered a pair of great, taloned feet and swept low over Wynn Keep, beating its huge wings to bring itself to a halt. A tremendous wind buffeted the inner ward, raising a thunderous clatter as cobblestones and other debris sailed into the walls. The bird settled to the ground, concealing its lower body behind the high ramparts of the inner curtain. It stretched its wings to its sides, and the feathers curled back upon themselves to create a pair of armlike limbs. The raptor's deep breast broadened into a wide, manlike chest, and the feathers on its neck became a fringe of long dark hair.

"Diancastra watch over us!" Basil hissed, his flat feet slapping the roof behind Tavis. "And may Hiatea save the queen, for we never will!"

The last of the shadow bird's feathers vanished, then a pair of ears sprouted behind its temples. The hooked beak retracted into a long aquiline nose, and the murky creature was suddenly an impossibly huge giant. The colossus stood taller than Wynn Keep itself. His shoulders were as broad as the corner towers, and his biceps larger than their stair turrets. He wore a cloak of purple twilight, with a sash of starlight shimmering across one shoulder. Upon his head sat a crown of black silver beset with rubies and sapphires darker than the night.

The giant's face was as swarthy as his attire, with teeth the hue of robin eggs, gleaming damson eyes, and skin so richly purple it was almost black. Save for the silhouette of his square-cropped beard and a sliver of moonlight glinting off his brow, little else could be seen of the intruder's features. The colossus seemed more an apparition of the dusk than a living, breathing being, and Tavis knew that his wife's true enemy had shown himself at last: the Titan of Twilight.

# ☙ 9 ❧
# Wynn Keep

On the head of the spear danced a silver flame, a flame fueled not by burning oil or blazing pitch, but by the queen's ardent devotion. When she felt the cold floor shudder beneath her knees, that flame sputtered and dwindled to a cinereal flicker. Through the shuttered window came the muffled and distant voices of shouting men. The floor trembled again. The spear shaft rattled in its sconce, and the pearly faith flame winked out altogether. The queen's thoughts reeled inside her mind. She found herself plummeting through a vast, abyssal void. She continued to fall, her head spinning ever faster, until Kaedlaw growled in the darkness.

The rumble caught Brianna like a rope. Her thoughts stopped swirling, and she was suddenly, completely *there*, kneeling in the small cold temple, listening to her son grumble on the altar before her. The queen reached out, blindly feeling her way along the stone platform until she located her fur-swaddled child. She pulled him out of his wrappings and tucked him beneath her cloak, then called for Avner.

A squeal rang off the stone walls as the door's iron hinges grated open. The young scout stepped into the doorway, filling the small chamber with the shimmering

139

yellow glow of his candle.

"Yes, Brianna?" He reached her side with a single step. "What did you learn?"

"Nothing. I was interrupted." The queen held her hand out to him. Even kneeling, her arm was at the height of Avner's chest. "But it doesn't matter. *I* know who fathered my child. Tavis is the one who can't see straight."

A troubled look flashed across Avner's face. "Milady, I should . . ." He hesitated, then slipped an arm beneath her elbow. "Well, you should know Tavis isn't the only one."

Brianna did not rise. "What do you mean by that? Surely, you haven't betrayed me as well?"

"Of course not, Majesty!" The young scout's jaw dropped in a show of indignation. "I was speaking of Raeyadfourne. He didn't find the prince handsome, either."

Brianna studied Avner's face. The young scout's difficult childhood had made a master liar of him, and she found it more difficult to read his hidden feelings than those of her most devious earls. Had he really been thinking of the chieftain, or had he also seen the strange face she had glimpsed in the mines?

"I fail to see what Raeyadfourne's reaction has to do with my husband's." Through the closed window came the muffled trumpet of an alarm horn. The 'kin were attacking sooner than expected, but Brianna was far from concerned. Reinforcements would arrive long before her enemies could breach Wynn Castle's thick walls. "Raeyadfourne is my enemy. Tavis is the father of my child—whether he admits to it or not."

"I know—but you shouldn't be so hard on the lord scout," Avner said. "Firbolgs see Kaedlaw differently than humans."

"My point exactly." Brianna rose to her feet, relieved

that the young scout was only trying to defend Tavis. She had already ascribed the incident in the mine to a delusion and had no wish to second-guess herself now. "People see what they expect. If Tavis sees a monster in his child's face, it is because he trusts the firbolg seer more than he trusts me. I have not decided whether that is treason to his queen, but it is certainly betrayal to his wife."

Through the temple door echoed the tramp of boots, stomping up the curving stairwell that connected the tiny chamber to the rest of the keep. From outside the small window came the snap of firing crossbows and the sound of shouting voices.

Avner frowned. "That sounds like it's coming from the inner curtain." He set his candle on the altar, then stepped to the shuttered window. "I'd better see what's happening."

"It can't be the firbolgs," Brianna said. "We would've heard the siege—"

"Don't open the shutter!" The soldier's voice came from the stairwell. "He'll grab the queen!"

Brianna spun around to find a fully armored garrison guard clambering into view. In his hands, he held a cocked and loaded crossbow, which he was pointing across the temple at the small window.

"Who will grab me?" Brianna lifted her spell satchel off the altar. "We're thirty feet off the ground! Even storm giants aren't that tall."

"The fiend is!" The guard climbed into the doorway. Behind him followed a long line of his fellow warriors. "The giants must've called him. He's walking 'round the keep, looking in—"

A sharp crack sounded from the window, followed by a blast of icy wind. Avner cried out, and Brianna looked over her shoulder. The shutter was gone. Avner was staring gape-mouthed through the casement, his eyes fixed on a buckler hovering outside. The shield had a peculiar design, with a black, platter-sized disk set in a damson circle.

"Stand aside!"

The garrison guard rushed into the temple, raising his crossbow to his shoulder. Avner backed away from the window, and the weapon clacked, sending a bolt of black iron through the casement. In the same instant, a purple lid slid down to cover the buckler outside.

An eye!

The quarrel passed through the lid without tearing the skin or drawing blood; it simply disappeared as though it had entered a bank of fog.

"Hiatea help us!" Brianna clutched Kaedlaw more tightly to her breast. "No giant is that big!"

The lid rose, once again revealing the huge eye. The pupil was as black and deep as Memnor's cold heart. A low, rumbling thunder reverberated through the temple walls. So sonorous was the sound that it took Brianna a moment to recognize it as a voice.

". . . the child," it growled. "Come to the window."

Another clack sounded from the door, sending a second quarrel past Brianna's shoulder. This time, the eye didn't blink. The bolt simply sailed into the black pupil and vanished.

Avner grabbed Brianna's arm and pulled her toward the stairwell. The narrow passage was crammed with soldiers, each holding a loaded crossbow and struggling to see past the warrior ahead.

"Stand aside, you men!" Avner yelled. "Let the queen pass!"

The young scout forced his way into the stairwell, shoving two men aside so Brianna could squeeze in after him. Though the soldiers were pressed flat against the wall, the corridor was so tiny she could barely force her way past their armored bulk. From behind her came the sound of clanging steel; the men who had already entered the temple were attacking with their swords.

A tremendous crash shook the chamber. A gray cloud of dust billowed into the stairwell, filling Brianna's mouth with the caustic bite of powdered rock and mortar. A pair of screams sounded from the temple. The guards at the top of the stairs fired their crossbows, then pulled their hand axes and rushed into the room. The next sound was the shrill grate of crumpling armor. One of the soldiers fell instantly silent. The other began to wail. It was not the cry of someone who would die quickly, but the spastic gurgle of a man drowning in his own blood.

The queen and Avner had barely pushed past the next guard before this man also fired and charged. His scream was mercifully short, then a deafening clatter sounded from the top of the stairs. Brianna glanced over her shoulder and saw a purple hand tearing away the curved wall behind her. The appendage was the size of a double door, with knuckles as large as boulders and fingers the length of battle-axes.

The fist withdrew to discard the rubble in its grasp. A pair of guards hefted hand axes and shoved past the queen. The appendage returned to the cramped corridor, and the two men began hacking at the wrist. Their blades sank through the purple flesh as though it were mist. The hand pushed past them and reached for Brianna.

"Go, Avner!"

The youth flung himself headlong down the passage, shoving the guards over backward. Brianna sprang after the young scout—then felt something cold and ethereal slipping around her waist. She tried to break free but managed only to crush her tender abdomen against her captor's hand. Searing pain boiled up through her stomach, filling her with such agony that she screamed and nearly dropped Kaedlaw. She was entwined from the

waist down by four dark fingers, each as large as a firbolg's arm.

Avner gathered his feet and spun around, drawing his
sword. Brianna pulled Kaedlaw from inside her cloak.

Avner's face went pale. "No, Majesty!"

"Take him!"

Brianna thrust the infant into Avner's free arm, then
lost sight of the pair as she was dragged up the devas-
tated stairwell. She tried to twist free, but her captor's
grip was secure. She clutched at the wall and succeeded
only in bloodying her fingertips.

The fiend pulled her into the rubble-strewn temple,
where the odor of blood hung so thick the air smelled
like liquid copper. Heaps of mangled armor lay every-
where, often with the groaning remnant of a shattered
body still twitching inside. One man lay upon the broken
altar, the crimson head of the queen's faith spear protruding from his punctured breastplate.

Brianna stretched her fingertips toward the spear.
"My goddess, help me!"

"The gods won't answer, child. It is by their will that I
have come for you," rumbled her captor. "Now you must
be quiet and save your strength. You have suffered
much, and it is a long journey to my Vale."

"Twilight!" Brianna gasped. "No!"

A wave of cold air rolled down the queen's back as the
Twilight Spirit pulled her through the shattered window
casement. The keep walls spun out of sight, and Brianna
found herself staring into a purple face as large and
murky as the darkening sky. Seen from a distance of a
mile or two, the titan's square features and even proportions might have been handsome, but from so close, the
visage was hideous in its very hugeness. His shadowy
brow overhung his eyes like a parapet hoarding, his
nose jutted out like a cliff buttress, and from his cavernous mouth wafted a breeze as cold and stale as a

tomb's breath.

"Where is your child?" The titan's angry voice shook Brianna to the core, setting her ears to ringing and her stomach to quivering. "What have you done with my nephew?"

* * * * *

Another tremendous crash sounded inside the ward, shaking the gateway so violently Tavis nearly lost his footing. He took the clamor to be a good sign. If the titan already had what he wanted, he would not be tearing Wynn Keep apart handful by handful. The high scout reached the end of the vaulted passage, and, with Basil close behind, followed their escorts through the wicket door at the base of the iron-clad gates.

When Tavis entered the ward, his heart sank into his stomach. The keep roof lay scattered across the cobblestones, crumpled into twisted heaps of lead and rafter. Inside the fortress itself, several fires were burning out of control, casting streaks of dancing orange light through the slender arrow loops and pouring huge plumes of black smoke into the sky.

The titan stood at the front of Wynn Keep, a looming figure cloaked in purple gloom, barely distinguishable from the fading dusk light. He was straddling the dry moat that guarded the approach to the entry gate, ripping the upper story off the temple tower with one hand and holding Brianna in the other. A semicircle of garrison soldiers stood at his feet, firing a constant stream of crossbow quarrels into his body. The bolts simply passed through the colossus and bounced off the walls behind him, drawing no attention whatsoever from their target. Perhaps a dozen men lay wounded at the feet of the colossus, their open mouths voicing screams that could not be heard above the din of demolition.

The sergeant who had been guarding Tavis pulled a hand axe, then turned to his small company of men. "Ready yourselves!" he yelled. "We'll save the queen!"

"How?" Tavis asked. "What makes you think your axes will have more effect than those crossbows?"

The sergeant spun on the high scout, frowning at his presence in the inner ward. "Milord, the queen barred you—" The objection came to an abrupt end as the titan dropped another handful of rubble to the ground. A sheepish look fell over the sergeant's face, and he glanced back toward the keep. "Never mind—but we've got to do something!"

The titan lowered his head to peer into one corner of the tower. He plunged his free hand deep into the building and began to feel around, like a man trying to pull a weasel from its hole. Since he already had Brianna, the colossus could only be searching for Kaedlaw.

Tavis pointed to one of his escorts. "You, fetch my bow and quiver from my chamber." As the man left to obey, the high scout turned to Basil. "We need your help."

The verbeeg was already holding his runebrush. "Show me your blades, all of you," he ordered. "And keep them steady!"

The high scout drew his sword and braced it over his arm. Basil touched his brush to the weapon and painted, tracing a moon-shaped pattern of turquoise light upon the metal. A rich blue stain crept outward from the glowing sigil, turning the entire blade the color of sapphire. The steel began to shimmer like starlight, then became dusk-purple and vanished from sight, save for the rune itself and a gleaming line of cobalt along the weapon's edge.

Basil nodded his approval, then moved to the sergeant's hand axe. "These runes will help your steel find purchase in Lanaxis's armor," he said, using the titan's ancient name. "But don't swing your weapons about unnecessarily."

"Why?" The sergeant scowled at the glimmering stain spreading across his axe blade.

"My runes haven't had time to dry." Basil was already working on the next soldier's weapon, and he did not even look up as he spoke. "The night air will rub them off."

Across the ward, Lanaxis had moved to the back end of the keep and was peering into the red tower. He reached inside, came up empty-handed, then grunted in anger and slapped his palm against the spire. The third story came loose and crashed to the ground with a deafening boom.

Tavis shouted an order, but realized his ears were ringing so hard that even he couldn't hear his own voice. He motioned for the sergeant to join him, then started across the ward at his best sprint. The others would have sense enough to follow when their weapons were ready.

By the time Tavis dodged past the rubble heaps and reached the temple tower, his hearing had returned to normal. He found a dozen stunned crossbowmen waiting for him, their faces shocked and hopeless.

"It's no use, milord," said the leader. "He's a phantom. Nothing will touch him!"

"These will!" Tavis raised his sword and, without slowing his pace, pointed to the glowing rune. "Come along, and when someone falls, arm yourselves with his weapon."

Fifty paces away, at the other end of the keep, the titan pulled a struggling body from the red tower. Tavis's stomach turned queasy with fear that it might be Avner, who was the most likely person to whom Brianna would have entrusted Kaedlaw. A steel gleam flashed between Lanaxis's dark fingers, and the high scout breathed easier.

His young friend never wore armor.

The titan opened his hand and let the steel-clad figure drop. The man screamed briefly, then crashed to the ground twenty paces ahead of Tavis. Lanaxis stooped over and pushed his arm back into the red tower, allowing the high scout a brief glimpse of Brianna. Her eyes were fixed on the interior of the building, her mouth hanging open in a terrified expression that left no doubt who Lanaxis would pull from the tower next.

From inside came the rumble of collapsing walls, followed by the muffled screams of dying men and the clack of firing crossbows. A flurry of black quarrels streaked from the keep's arrow loops and sailed harmlessly through the titan's body.

Then Tavis was upon his foe.

The high scout found himself at eye-level with a murky shin so large he could not have stretched his arms around it. There was no time to slip behind the leg to attack the heel tendon. Tavis drew his weapon back and chopped at the front of the ankle, hurling his full weight into the blow.

It was like trying fell a mature spruce with a single axe-strike. The impact numbed Tavis's arms to the shoulders, and his stinging hands lost their grasp on the hilt. A deafening roar boomed down from the sky, then he found himself stumbling across the cobblestones. The high scout braced his feet and managed to regain his balance. The ground heaved beneath his feet as the titan shifted his immense weight, jerking his injured foot into the air. The fetid smell of stale blood filled Tavis's nostrils, and a cascade of warm brown fluid rained down on his head.

The high scout did not look up. He simply dived away and hit the cobblestones rolling.

Lanaxis's heel came down behind him, cratering the ground and bouncing him into the air. Tavis slammed down on his back, tumbled onto his feet, hopped twice as he regained his balance, then spun toward his attacker. His sword was still lodged in his foe's ankle, the blade buried at least ten inches into the joint, but that did not stop Lanaxis from drawing his leg back to kick.

Tavis bent his knees, gathering himself to leap away. Lanaxis's foot reached the zenith of its arc, nearly ten yards away, and started back down.

Three soldiers charged past to meet Lanaxis's gloom-booted foot. They hit with a mighty crash and flew off in three separate directions, leaving their rune-scribed axes buried in the titan's instep. The foot continued to sweep forward.

The high scout leapt aside and grabbed for his weapon, deftly jerking it free. Lanaxis's leg reversed direction and came swinging back like a pendulum. The foot was upon Tavis so fast that he barely had time to bring his sword around. The heel impaled itself on the tip, then drove straight down the rune-scribed blade and slammed into his shoulder.

Tavis felt the bone snap beneath his biceps, then his feet left the ground. He flew through the air for what felt like a dozen seconds. Finally, he crashed onto the cobblestones and started rolling, each somersault more painful than the last. He did not stop until he slammed into the jagged stones of the inner curtain.

Tavis slumped in a battered heap to the ground, a venomous haze of pain poisoning his mind with thoughts of surrender. Every fiber of his pain-racked body demanded that he relinquish himself to the numbing mists of oblivion. But something outside him kept urging him not to give up, to keep his eyes open and hold on. It was a voice, a woman's voice, and she was screaming his name.

Tavis looked toward the center of the ward and

glimpsed his wife, still gripped in Lanaxis's hand and staring in his direction. He tried to wave to her, but his broken arm would not rise. The titan turned to face a small company of guards assailing him with Basil's rune-scribed axes, and the high scout lost sight of Brianna's terrified face.

A *whoosh* sounded through the ward, and Lanaxis's shoulders rose. He tipped his head forward to look at the men clustered about his shins. A keening wail filled the air, then a blustering cloud of purple murk spewed from the titan's mouth and gushed over his attackers. Voices screamed and armor clanged, and the men went tumbling across the cobblestones to slam into the stone walls of the inner curtain.

Lanaxis continued to exhale for minutes. Soon, his purple breath was rolling into every corner of the ward, carrying with it such biting cold that Tavis's flesh went numb. The scout gathered his strength and pushed himself to a seated position. When the pain filled his head with turbid swirls of oblivion, he took several deep breaths and fought to stay alert.

The wail of Lanaxis's storming breath finally died away, leaving the ward immersed beneath a frigid blanket of murk. The high scout gritted his teeth and slowly, painfully, pushed himself to his feet. He suffered several moments of blurred vision, then found himself staring across the top of a purple fog. The titan had already returned to his search and was burrowing into the red tower like a badger after chipmunks.

On the far side of the ward, Basil stood in the gate and held Tavis's bow and quiver in hand. The runecaster started across the ward, giving wide berth to the keep. The high scout staggered forward to meet his friend, watching the titan tear into the foundation of the red tower. Lanaxis would not find his prey there, at least if Avner still had the baby. Any border scout knew better than to let himself be trapped in a dead-end hole.

By the time the two giant-kin reached each other, Lanaxis was on his knees, pulling the last stones from the tower dungeon. Dusk had given way to a moonlit night. The titan's murky breath had settled into the cobblestones, leaving a host of frozen human corpses scattered across the ward. From the outer curtain came the distant booming of Raeyadfourne's battering ram. The 'kin army was the least of Tavis's worries. Even if they broke down the gates of the outer curtain, they would still have to smash through the gates protecting the inner ward. By the time they succeeded, Lanaxis would have Kaedlaw and be long gone.

Basil took one look at Tavis's broken arm. "I can see you won't be needing your bow." The verbeeg slipped the weapon over his own shoulder. "And I suppose you still think it's wrong to use Sky Cleaver?"

Tavis glared up at the runecaster. "What I think doesn't matter—unless you already have the weapon?"

Basil shook his head. "I was only asking."

A mighty clatter echoed across the ward as the frustrated titan hurled a handful of rubble against the inner curtain. He peered one last time into the foundation of the red tower, then rose to his feet and lurched toward the flag tower.

"At least he's limping," Tavis muttered. The pounding at the front gates increased in tempo, but the scout heard nothing to suggest the beams were ready to give way. "And we did buy Avner some time."

"True, but even our adept young friend can't hide forever," Basil said. "And you're in no condition to help him—or Brianna. What are we going to do?"

Tavis thought for a moment, then looked toward the front of the castle. "There's only thing we *can* do: let Galgadayle and his bunch at the titan," he said. "If we're lucky, we'll be the ones who survive to pick up the pieces."

*  *  *  *  *

From the front of the keep rang the clamorous din of chains rattling off their spools, a sure sign that someone had knocked out the gate's winch stops. A loud, shrill squeal echoed through the inner ward as the drawbridge, slowed by the friction of the immense chains, began its fall. The titan, who was kneeling over the long gallery that ran from the demolished red tower to the flag tower, stood and turned toward the sound.

Brianna cursed, for she had finally reached the tiny glass rod with which she hoped to escape. It had been a difficult process, and not only because her captor's grip was like steel. It had required both patience and tenacity not to alarm him as she worked her hand over to the strap of her spell satchel, then pulled the sack around to where she could reach inside. Now, when she finally had the component in her grasp, Lanaxis was once again holding her three stories off the ground. There was a time when she would have taken the plunge gladly to escape him, but no longer. The titan wanted Kaedlaw, and she would not save her son by dying.

No sooner had the keep's drawbridge boomed into place than a rumbling clatter erupted inside the entryway. The titan limped over to the flag tower, and Brianna saw a small, mule-drawn cart racing across the ward. An armored guard sat in the driver's seat, madly lashing the terrified beast in the harness. In the bed of the small wagon sat Avner, so tightly wrapped inside his heavy scout's cloak that Brianna could see little more than his sandy beard. In his arms, he held her squirming son, snugly bundled inside a cocoon of furs. Kaedlaw clearly did not appreciate the rough ride, for he was struggling so hard that the young scout could barely hold him.

Ahead of the cart, the path was unobstructed clear into the outer bailey. Tavis and Basil had departed just a few minutes earlier, pausing at the inner curtain to open the ironclad gates. At the time, the act had puzzled Brianna as much as the withdrawal itself, but now she suspected her husband had been trying to create an escape route for Avner. Border scouts were trained to anticipate each other's needs, and no pair had ever worked together better than Tavis and Avner.

Lanaxis limped around the flag tower, closing a quarter of the distance to the cart in two lurching strides. The queen silently beseeched her goddess's blessing, at the same time pulling the glass rod from her spell satchel. Avner and her child were less than thirty paces from the gate. Lanaxis took another step and began to stoop over; in another stride he would have them. Brianna pushed her arms over the titan's index finger. She pointed both hands at his face and uttered the mystic syllables of her spell.

The glass rod evaporated in a flash of silver light. A crackling thunderbolt shot from Brianna's fingertips and struck the side of Lanaxis's face. The air filled with musty blue smoke. The titan dropped to a knee, raising his hands to cover his eyes.

Brianna slipped from his grasp and plummeted a dozen feet to his lap. She heard herself grunt as the breath left her lungs, then a dull ache filled her chest. She slid down an enormous thigh and dropped onto the ward's icy cobblestones.

"Foolish girl!" Lanaxis's hissing voice was as loud as a blustering wind. "There's no need to fear me!"

The titan pulled his hands from his face. A milky blue haze now covered one eye. The lightning had burned the purple murk from one side of his head, exposing a pale layer of raw, wrinkled skin. Even his robe had been affected by the brilliant flash, for it was now streaked by long stripes of gray and tattered linen. "The gods have such plans for your son!"

"They should've . . . told me." The queen could barely choke the words out, but she was leaping to her feet as she said them. "I have plans . . . of my own."

Brianna ran for the gate. The mule cart was less than twenty paces ahead, just entering the vaulted passage beneath the gatehouse.

The heft of a huge axe suddenly fell across the far end, blocking the tunnel's exit. The mule smashed headlong into the handle and came to an instant halt, braying loudly as its legs buckled beneath its body. The cart rocked forward on its harness rods. One of the shafts snapped and the small wagon toppled onto its side, spilling the passengers out. Kaedlaw flew from Avner's arms.

The child shed his swaddling rags in midair, revealing a long wrinkled snout at one end and a tiny curled tail at the other. He hit the ground on all four hooves and ran, squealing wildly. The young scout came down a few paces behind the piglet, his armor clanging like an alarm bell, and Brianna realized Avner had not been in the cart at all.

In the next instant, a line of screaming firbolgs erupted from the tunnel. The warriors, or at least those in the lead, carried rune-scribed blades with gleaming edges of cobalt. Brianna suddenly knew where Basil and her husband had gone after leaving the ward, and why they had paused to open the gate.

"Traitors!"

The queen spun and ran toward the keep, her gaze fixed on the citadel's rear corner. There, the queen's tower stood more or less intact, missing only its roof and small portions of the third-story walls. Brianna could not see the back side of the spire, but she suspected Avner and her child would be there, climbing down a ladder from a hidden sally port on the second floor. The secret door had been designed for just such urgent departures, and, aside from the drawbridge, it was the keep's only exit.

Lanaxis stepped over Brianna, covering half the distance to the keep in a single stride. Her heart sank. It would take Avner more than fifty paces to carry her child across the inner ward; the titan would be upon him in five. The queen could only pray that Avner would hear his pursuer's booming footfalls in time to return to the tower.

A loud grunt sounded behind Brianna. A rune-scribed axe tumbled over her head and arced down into Lanaxis's calf. The titan stopped at the front corner of the keep and braced himself on the battered temple tower, then glared at the long column of firbolgs charging toward him. He uttered a syllable in some arcane language, then stepped forward and smashed his purple boot onto the ground.

A resounding bang shook the entire castle, then a fan of dark rifts sprang from under the titan's heel. A fissure shot beneath Brianna's feet, and she barely leapt over before it widened into a chasm thirty feet across. She crashed down on the far side and rolled several times, then came up on her knees, looking back toward the inner curtain. A web of abyssal crevices separated her from the main body of the firbolg troop, but she could see three huge warriors clinging to the rims of a nearby chasm.

Brianna rose to her feet and resumed her sprint toward the keep gate. Lanaxis was already upon the queen's tower. He did not step past to pluck Avner off the open ward, nor did he start tearing the spire apart as he had the others. Instead, he squatted down and wrapped his arms around the entire tower.

The queen reached the drawbridge. The keep's battered walls obscured her view of Lanaxis, but she could feel the entire building shaking. She rushed into the foyer, where she found a dozen frightened soldiers blocking the corridor. They immediately swarmed toward Brianna, hurling questions at her like ballista arrows. Firbolg boots began to boom across the drawbridge behind her, and a loud crack sounded from the queen's tower.

"Out of my way!" Brianna grabbed two men and shoved them toward the drawbridge. "Stop those firbolgs!"

The rest of the guards leapt aside to let her pass, then rushed forward to meet the firbolgs. Brianna turned down a smoke-filled gallery that led to the queen's tower. A tremendous clamor echoed through the passage behind her, followed by the agonized screams of both men and firbolgs.

The queen raced blindly through the corridor, coughing and choking on the acrid smoke that seemed to flow from every opening. A sharp crack reverberated through the keep, and the gallery floor bucked beneath her feet. She reached the stair turret of the queen's tower and threw open the oaken door.

It was dark inside, and she heard no echoes to suggest Avner was descending the cramped stairwell. She could not be sure he was trapped inside the tower, but she suspected Lanaxis would not be uprooting the spire if there was any chance the young scout had escaped with her son.

A deep-throated cough rumbled down the gallery. The queen looked back and saw a firbolg's hulking silhouette in the smoky corridor. She stepped into the stair turret, then slammed the door, dropped the crossbar, and rushed up the spiraling stairs. Like all well-fortified towers, this one could not be accessed from the first floor. Brianna would have to reach the second story landing before she could enter the building.

A tremendous rumble sounded from the tower foundations. The stair turret shuddered so violently that she lost her footing and fell. A crash sounded from the barred door below, then the wooden stairs groaned beneath her pursuer's weight. The smell of firbolg sweat filled the passage.

Brianna turned onto her back and drew her knee to her chest. When she heard the firbolg's heavy breath coming around the bend, she thrust her foot down into the darkness. Her heel caught the warrior square in the brow. His head snapped back, slamming the back of his skull into the wall, and the warrior slumped onto the stairs without crying out.

The stone walls shuddered, then the stairwell began to shake in steady rhythm. Brianna scrambled up the stairs and came to the second story, where the turret ended five feet short of the dark entrance to the queen's tower. The ironclad door hung open, swinging on its hinges as the entire spire rocked back and forth. To her right, the queen saw one of the titan's huge hands grasping the side of the building.

"Avner?" Brianna called. "Answer me!"

Lanaxis gave a mighty grunt. There was a loud bang in the foundations, and a billowing cloud of dust rolled up from void below. The tower tipped away from the stair turret. Brianna swung her arms back and sprang across the broadening chasm, then tumbled into the second-story foyer of the queen's tower.

# ✦ 10 ✦
# The Queen's Tower

Brianna could not stop shaking. She sat in the listing angle where the pine floor met the chamber wall, swaddled in her own fur cloak and the woolen capes of five men-at-arms, but even that heavy armor was no defense against the insidious cold. It hung within the tower's stone walls like the memory of dead kings, its chill poison seeping through all her layers to spread its biting salve over the soft flesh of her back. It came whispering through the arrow loops on gusts of frigid air, driving darts of icy numbness deep into her frozen bones. Even Kaedlaw's breath, wet and heavy against her skin, seemed to sink deep into her breast, filling her with such a cool, dull ache that she feared her milk would turn to slush.

The queen knew she should find a way to warm the dark room, for Kaedlaw's sake if not her own, but she could see no way to do it safely. Even if the hearth did not lie on the high side of the floor, it would have been impossible to keep the burning logs from flying all over the chamber. The whole building was swaying in time to the titan's limping stride. To keep her from being battered to death, Avner had moved all the furniture into the foyer, where it had promptly fallen out of the yawning hole that had once connected the tower's second story to its stair turret.

Nor could she cast a spell. It required all her concentration to keep her feet braced against the floor and her back pressed firmly against the cold wall, and she could hardly let go of Kaedlaw long enough to make the necessary gestures.

Besides, Brianna suspected warming the room would do little to stop her shivering. She was caught in the grip of a despair colder than the stones at her back, more biting than the icy winds gusting through the arrow loops; with every beat of her heart she felt the fingers of her grief squeeze tighter, filling her breast with a chill lethargy as difficult to battle as the titan. Lanaxis had been born of the gods themselves; he was as old as Toril, and his power was second only to that of his almighty parents. If such a being wanted her son, what could a mere queen do to save the child? There was only one thing, and Brianna was loathe even to think of it.

A muffled groan sounded from the fireplace, and Brianna knew Avner was coming down the chimney—the only route to the third story without a stair turret. The young scout dropped into the empty firebox, then tumbled down the listing floor and came to a rest against the stone wall.

The tower swung as the titan took another huge step. Avner careened into the far wall, and a moment later came rolling back to collide with Brianna. He grabbed her leg and held on, then braced himself and sat up. By the pale slivers of moonlight that spilled through the arrow loops, she could see him rubbing his shoulder.

"What news?"

"None good, I'm afraid," Avner replied. "Did you hear that crackling a few minutes ago?"

"I thought the tower was coming apart."

"We're not that lucky," Avner said. "We signaled a

troop of horse lancers. Lanaxis called a fire blizzard down as soon as they turned toward us. The company was incinerated to the last man."

"So there won't be any messengers riding ahead to call for help."

Brianna's legs began to shake so severely that her boots started to slide across the pine boards. Her body swayed in time to Lanaxis's stride, and her frozen back slipped across the stone wall. The queen pulled her feet back into place and redoubled the pressure against them.

In the dim light, Avner apparently failed to notice her struggle. "Even if a messenger had gotten away, it wouldn't have made any difference," the youth replied. "No horse alive can outrun Lanaxis."

"Blizzard could have. She would have found a way." Brianna allowed herself a moment of silence, then asked, "Can you tell where we're going yet?"

"He's seems to be following the Clearwhirl north," Avner reported. "We see glimpses of the river every now and then."

"And where are we now?"

Avner swallowed. "We passed River Citadel a little while ago. We could see the turret pennants snapping in the moonlight."

The cold hand around Brianna's heart clamped down until it seemed the aching muscle would stop beating. The titan had already carried them across an eighth of her kingdom.

"How long until dawn?" The hour candles had gone out when Lanaxis pulled the tower from the ground, and to Brianna, sitting alone in the darkness, every minute since had seemed an hour. "I think he'll have to stop then."

Avner grimaced. "The Bleeding Circle has barely risen above the horizon. We'll be in the Bleak Plain by dawn." There was an uneasy pause, then the young scout continued, "We have to slow him down, or Tavis will never catch up."

"Don't you think we have troubles enough?" Brianna scoffed.

"Tavis wouldn't betray you."

"Then why did he save Galgadayle's life?" the queen demanded. "And open the gates for the 'kin army?"

"*I* would have opened the gates." The quickness of Avner's reply suggested he had thought of his answer long before coming down the chimney. "Can you think of a better way to get rid of the 'kin than to let them attack Lanaxis?"

"Avner, you'll have to do better than that. We both know that wasn't what he had in mind."

"We don't know what he was thinking," Avner countered. "We only know what you saw, and there could be dozens of explanations."

"The most likely being that he believes Galgadayle," Brianna said. "He thinks Kaedlaw is the ettin's child. He admitted that much."

Avner remained silent, a sure sign he was struggling against the urge to blurt something out. Brianna could almost feel the words straining at his lips.

"Avner, what is it? You have something to tell me."

"No, Majesty."

Brianna cocked an eyebrow. "Don't lie to me, Avner," she warned. "You're the first defender now, not a street orphan."

Avner sighed heavily. "As you wish, then. I won't lie— but I respectfully decline to say more. Call it treason if you like."

"Perhaps I will!"

"I'll carry the execution order to Dexter myself," Avner replied. "And that'll be the last thing your first defender ever says."

Brianna fell silent, considering the young scout's bluff. She knew he would not carry the command to the guards on the third floor, as surely as he knew she would never issue it, but Avner preferred subtlety and subterfuge to grand gestures. The queen could think of only one sentiment that would compel the youth to make such a statement.

"Avner, you'll only make things worse by trying to protect Tavis."

"Tavis loves you!" Avner hissed. "He could never violate the oath he swore!"

The young scout's boots scraped against the floorboards as he scrambled up to the fireplace, and Brianna realized that the icy hand grasping her heart had finally squeezed too hard. She felt more than despair; she felt alone and utterly without hope. Avner was right: Tavis *did* love her, had always loved her and always would—and that was the very thing that made him so dangerous. Tears began to stream down her face, leaving freezing trails of stinging water on her cheeks.

"Avner, why do you think I'm so scared?" Brianna called. "I know Tavis loves me—but that won't stop him from keeping his oath. If he believes Galgadayle's prophecy—and he must, or he'd recognize his own child—then I *know* he'll kill Kaedlaw. His oath requires it."

The scraping of Avner's boots stopped, and Brianna heard his heavy breath up near the fireplace. "What if *you* saw the ettin's face when you looked at Kaedlaw?" he asked. "Wouldn't the oath you swore as queen of Hartsvale demand the same thing?"

"But I *don't* see the ettin," Brianna countered. "I see Kaedlaw's father. I see Tavis!"

Avner fell silent for a moment, then he asked, "Do you really believe Tavis Burdun would kill *your* son on sight?" The youth's voice was brusque and scornful.

"Give him time. Eventually, Tavis will see what you see."

"And if he doesn't?"

"Trust that he will," Avner replied. "It's your only hope, because I doubt anyone else can save you—or Kaedlaw."

Brianna heard the young scout's clothes rustling as he climbed into the chimney. If she let him go now, she would have nothing left but a hollow, achy feeling as empty and cold as the dark chamber in which she sat.

"Avner, wait!" Brianna ordered. "I know how to delay the titan—but you'd better be right about Tavis!"

\* \* \* \* \*

An occasional tremor shook the ravaged castle, as though deep in its foundations the citadel still felt the distant strides of its debaucher. A haze of moonlit steam rose from the crater where once had stood the queen's tower, and a cold wind moaned through the rents in the northern curtains, where Lanaxis had kicked his way through the castle walls. Packs of verbeegs and fomorians rummaged through the ruins of the inner ward, searching for treasure and food, while the Meadowhome firbolgs stood by with scowls of uneasy disdain on their bearded faces.

Tavis studied the scene with growing anger. He sat in the shadow of the dilapidated flag tower, listening to Galgadayle and Raeyadfourne argue with the chieftains of the verbeeg and fomorian tribes about the conduct of their warriors. In the meantime, the looting continued unabated while the cries of the human wounded—as scattered and weak as they were—went unanswered. The high scout had already tried to aid the men himself, but each time his captors reminded him that he was a prisoner of honor and forbade him to leave his seat.

From around the corner of the flag tower came a

grinding, crunching sound, like a wolf gnawing on the bones of a felled moose. Tavis stood. His head reeled as the blood rushed toward his feet. His vision narrowed, and he would have fallen had Basil not steadied him.

"Sit down," ordered Munairoe, the firbolg shaman. He had packed a layer of mud around Tavis's broken arm and cast a healing spell on the limb. The bone felt as if it were cooking from the marrow outward. "The spirits have not finished mending your arm, and there is still the matter of your honor."

"I have no intention of breaking my word," Tavis retorted. "But I have seen enough of your allies' debauchery!"

Tavis stepped past the shaman and hobbled around the flag tower, clenching his teeth at his pain. He felt bloated and hot inside, as though someone had gorged him with boiling oil, while every breath of the chill air filled his lungs with a keen, biting numbness. He found a fomorian hunter standing in the corner where the tower abutted the battered keep.

The brute had thrust his head and arms through a breach in the second-story wall, so that only his hairy, pear-shaped back was visible. The gnawing sound came from inside the building. At the fomorian's feet lay a suit of mangled armor splashed with blood so fresh it was still steaming in the cold night air.

A fiery, seething rage boiled up within Tavis, filling him with a fury almost too great for his battered body to withstand. The color drained from his vision, his ears started to ring, and a sour, acrid taste burned the tip of his tongue. He pulled a broken length of floor joist from a nearby rubble pile and stepped over to the fomorian, raising the board in his good hand.

"What are you doing?" gasped Munairoe, coming around the flag tower. "Need I remind you—"

Tavis swung the timber as hard as he could, smashing

it into the back of the fomorian's legs. A strangled shriek reverberated inside the gallery. The hunter's knees buckled, then dropped to the rubble-strewn ground with a tremendous clatter. His head popped out of the breach in the wall, his loose jowls shaking and the mangled thigh of a human warrior dangling over his blubbery lip. He spit the leg against the keep and roared in pain, then turned toward his assailant. When he saw who had assaulted him, the look of astonishment and hurt in his eye changed to resentment.

"Why hit Awn, you?" The fomorian raised his fist. "Awn smash, yes him should!"

Tavis could barely hear the words over the ringing in his ears, and the marrow in his bones had changed into something like molten lava. He stepped forward and smashed his club into Awn's ribs, then slipped away to avoid a counterblow. The astonished hunter doubled over, holding his ribs and grunting for breath.

"Maybe this . . . will . . . teach Awn not to . . . eat the dead!" The acrid taste in Tavis's mouth had so dried his tongue that the words seemed to stick to his teeth.

The high scout raised his club again. Before he could strike, Raeyadfourne came pounding around the flag tower and jerked it from his hand. Awn spun toward Tavis, his own hand raised.

"Now Awn mad!"

Raeyadfourne reached over Tavis's head and pushed Awn into the wall, then quickly interposed himself between the two combatants.

"This is a firbolg prisoner," the chieftain warned. "He's under my protection."

"Not when him hurt Awn, no." The fomorian pointed to a red welt where Tavis had smashed the floor joist across his knees. "That hurt plenty—and him do it for fun!"

Raeyadfourne glared at Tavis. "You promised to

behave as a prisoner of honor."

"I am." Tavis pointed at the mutilated remains in the corner. His vision faded, and the bloody scene appeared to him in shades of gray and black. "He was eating the dead."

"So, what that matter?" The fomorian chieftain, Ror, stepped around the tower. He was nearly twice Tavis's height, with slender, sticklike legs that hardly look capable of supporting the huge belly above them. "Awn gots to feed."

"It's cannibalism!" Tavis objected.

"To you, perhaps—but then, you *are* a traitor to your own race." Orisino, the horse-faced chieftain of the verbeegs, followed Ror around the tower. His gray lips were curled into a sneer that showed two rows of vile yellow teeth filed to sharp points. "Who are you to say fomorians shouldn't eat humans? The gods have seen fit to let wolves eat foxes."

"It's not the same thing." Tavis kept his attention fixed on Raeyadfourne.

The chieftain did not meet Tavis's gaze. "We have discussed the matter at length," he sighed. "It's not cannibalism, and there's no law against foraging for food during time of war—however disgusting that food may be."

"The spoils go to the victor," added Orisino.

"You're hardly victors," Tavis snarled. "I opened the gate!"

"*After* we hit it with our ram," the verbeeg countered. "As I understand firbolg law, that means you surrendered the castle."

Tavis stepped toward Orisino, his hands knotted into balls. "I surrendered noth—"

The high scout's jaw clamped shut, preventing him from finishing, and the taste in his mouth grew so bitter he wanted to spit out his tongue. The ringing in his ears became a clanging, then his eyes rolled back in their sockets and he fell. When the back of his skull smashed into the ground, every muscle in his body clamped on his bones. He began not just to tremble, but to quake and buck as though he had been struck by lightning.

Tavis had no way to tell how long his paroxysm continued. His entire body ached from terrible exertion as though from feverish illness, and he could feel several sets of large hands gripping his arms and legs. Basil's voice broke through the clamor in his ears, shouting for him to open his mouth, but the scout could not obey. Someone pushed a pair of fingers into his mouth and jerked his jaw down, then someone else thrust an axe handle between his teeth.

Slowly, Tavis's muscles released their bone-crushing grip. The harsh taste in his mouth was replaced by the more familiar flavor of his own blood, and the deafening clamor in his head gave way to the concerned voices of Basil and the Meadowhome firbolgs. The back of his skull was resting on a huge, immensely sore lump. When he tried to turn his head, he found it was held securely in place by a firbolg hand.

"Let me go." Tavis's speech was thick and painful, for he had nearly bitten off the tip of his tongue. "I'm better."

When the hands released him, the high scout turned his head off the painful lump. His vision cleared. He found himself surrounded by a ring of 'kin: Galgadayle, Raeyadfourne, Munairoe, Basil, Orisino, Ror, and even Awn. Tavis still saw their faces in tones of gray, and he heard a deep, low buzzing beneath the murmur of their concerned voices.

Munairoe knelt at Tavis's side. "How are you feeling?" He began to remove the mud cast on the high scout's arm. "I didn't expect this. I was only trying to mend your broken bone."

Tavis flexed his broken arm and discovered that it felt

better. It was the only part of his body that didn't hurt. "You succeeded in that much at least," he said. "But what didn't you expect? What happened to me?"

Munairoe ran his eyes over Tavis's bruised and battered body. "Just how many times *have* you been healed since yesterday?"

Tavis shrugged. "I could have been dead three times over."

Munairoe's lips tightened. "No wonder you went into convulsions! All that magic—your system is in shock."

"Is that why he's gone gray?" Basil squinted at Tavis's head.

The high scout ran his fingers through his hair, as though he could feel the color change. "My hair's turned gray?"

"Don't worry," Basil replied. "It's just a streak—really quite handsome, if you ask me."

"Nobody has." Munairoe frowned at the ancient runecaster, then looked back to Tavis. "How do you feel?"

"My ears are buzzing," he said. "And I can't see colors."

The shaman pursed his lips. He exchanged knowing glances with Galgadayle and motioned the seer to Tavis's other arm.

"I'm sorry, Tavis." Galgadayle stooped over to slip a hand beneath the scout's arm. "I had hoped Munairoe could repay the kindness you showed me in the Gorge of the Silver Wyrm. I didn't expect this."

A cold knot formed in Tavis's stomach. Before he could ask what the seer meant, Basil pushed his way to Munairoe's side.

"Expect what?" the runecaster demanded. "You haven't killed him?"

"No, of course not," replied the shaman. "But I'm afraid he won't be going after the titan as he had planned."

"How unfortunate," sneered Orisino. "And I was so looking forward to seeing him flattened."

Tavis pulled his arms free. "What trick is this?" he growled. Before he had opened the gates for the firbolgs, he had made Raeyadfourne swear that he and the other citizens of Hartsvale would be released when the 'kin army left the castle. Apparently, the shaman and seer had found a way to prevent the high scout from interfering with their plans. "The firbolgs of Meadowhome have spent too much time in the company of verbeegs and fomorians."

"This is no trick," said Munairoe. "Your injuries are too serious for travel, and I cannot use magic to heal them without causing permanent damage to you."

Tavis listened carefully for any sign of a lie, but the shaman's voice remained steady and true. "Could I still fight?"

Munairoe nodded reluctantly. "But the price would be years of your life. Your whole system would be weakened. It would be more difficult for you to heal naturally, and—"

"Heal me anyway."

"You don't understand," the shaman objected. "This is not something that *might* happen—it *would*. Without a potion or spell, even small cuts would take weeks to mend, and one day your heart would simply stop beating—"

"If I leave Brianna to the titan, it will stop beating now," Tavis said. "There's nothing in our agreement that says you must heal me, but I am asking you to do this before you leave."

Galgadayle nodded. "If that is what you wish."

"*If* you are willing to pay our price." Orisino's beady eyes were barely visible, peering around Munairoe's broad shoulders. "There is always a price, you know."

"That's for me to decide," growled Munairoe. "It is my magic—"

"But *our* quest." Orisino looked to Raeyadfourne. "When we joined forces, we agreed that the Council of Three would make all the decisions, as long as those decisions did not violate the law—did we not?"

"Yes, but—"

"Then I say we place a price on our help, just as Tavis placed a price on his before opening the gate." Orisino cocked an eyebrow at Ror. "What say you?"

The fomorian shrugged noncommittally.

"Then it's decided," said Orisino.

"And what would this price be?" Tavis asked. "I warn you, I will not promise to slay the queen's child."

"Why not? Kill fomorians!" grumbled Ror. "Kill plenty fomorians, you."

"Only when they threaten the citizens of Hartsvale."

"This child is a greater threat than all the fomorians— even to your humans," said Galgadayle. "In joining us, you would be serving the greater good."

"I don't know that," Tavis replied. "Your dream could be mistaken."

Raeyadfourne and Munairoe rolled their eyes, and Galgadayle did not even grace the argument with a rebuttal. The seer placed a comforting hand on Tavis's shoulder.

"I know this is difficult for you, my friend," said Galgadayle. "History will not blame you if you don't join us."

"There is nothing to decide," Tavis replied. "I swore an oath to Brianna, and I will keep it—whether or not you are right."

"Then you will not object to the price we ask for Munairoe's help," said Orisino. "It will benefit you as well. After all, we must all fight the titan, whether or not we wish to kill the queen's bastard."

Tavis glared at the chieftain, his anger droning like a bee in his ears. "What's your price?"

Orisino stepped from behind Munairoe. He raised his

hand, holding his thumb and forefinger close together. "A small thing," he said. "You will guide us through Hartsvale, and order any human companies we meet to let us pass in peace."

"And that is all?"

"Yes," Orisino replied. "In return, we will help you catch the titan."

Tavis considered the verbeeg's offer. "I'll do it—on one condition."

Orisino nodded, as though he had been expecting the counteroffer. "We're listening."

"That no one will slay the child except me," he replied. "It will be my decision whether or not to kill Kaedlaw."

"No!" Munairoe and Galgadayle boomed the word at the same time.

"You know we cannot allow that," added Raeyadfourne.

Orisino gave Raeyadfourne a disapproving scowl. "It seems to me that you're forgetting the terms of our alliance again," he said. "I, for one, find Tavis's condition perfectly acceptable."

"Because you have no intention—"

"Nevertheless, this is a decision for the Council of Three," Orisino interrupted. "I favor promising what Tavis asks—and I'm quite sure Ror does as well."

Ror scowled. "Huh? What if Tavis say don't kill—"

"Ror, Tavis *is* a firbolg," Orisino said. "If you can't trust a firbolg, who can you trust?"

A glimmer of understanding flashed in the fomorian's eye, then his lips curled into a larcenous smile. "Oh, yeah," he snickered. "Ror trust *Tavis,* sure thing!"

\* \* \* \* \*

Across the moonlit snows I trudge, half-crippled by the slashed tendon in my heel, each step a battle of will against my own mutinous foot. I crash through the thick spruce forests like a dragon in delirium, leaving a crooked swath of toppled and splintered trees to mark my hobbling trail, and I tramp over the frozen fens, where my lurching feet break through the permafrost to press ponds deep into the steaming mud; when I cross the tiny granges where peasants graze their goats and swine, the stone fences erupt beneath my lame foot, and as I lumber by the manors of highborn earls, even the lofty keeps tremble with the fear that I will stumble against them. Thus does Lanaxis the Chosen pass, not with the great strides of an ancient and mighty titan, but with the scuttling limp of a vile, ragged beggar.

This taste of mortality I could have done without.

Understand, it is not the pain I speak of—hardly so! after three thousand years of the Twilight Vale's cold numbness, *any* sensation is a welcome one—rather, it is the *idea* of the pain that offends me. To be injured by a mortal—by a mere firbolg runt!—it is an affront almost more than I can bear. Is it not enough that I have forsaken the Twilight Vale? Cruel Ones, I have sacrificed eternity for the glory of Ostoria. Why must you insult me as well?

*"Damned fool! We told you where to look. . . ."*

*". . . you must do it, my darling; do it for me. . . ."*

*". . . now! You will kneel before your betters or I'll have your . . ."*

Ah . . . you wish to humble me. My hubris was my downfall—and the ruin of Ostoria. I must learn humility before I may ask forgiveness, and until *I* am redeemed, the empire of giants will not rise again.

Very well, I shall endure your burden; though it be a thousand times heavier than this tower I carry, I shall bear it without complaint. You have chosen well, for I was firstborn of Annam the All Father, and my long eternity of cold contemplation has made me naught but stronger.

\* \* \* \* \*

Brianna sat braced in the splayed sill of a second-story arrow loop, holding a crimson ash leaf in her hand and uttering the mystic syllables of her spell. Kaedlaw, tied to her stomach in a makeshift sling, fidgeted and growled, clearly unhappy with the scratchy bundle into which he had been stuffed. Avner was on the floor above, with the five guards who had been in the tower when Lanaxis pulled it from the ground.

Brianna finished her incantation, and the ash leaf vanished in a puff of pink smoke. A long blade of scarlet flame shot through the arrow loop to slash across Lanaxis's breast. The fiery tongue did not burn the titan so much as sear away the dusky gloom clinging to his person.

The queen angled the flame toward Lanaxis's face. He instinctively raised one hand to cover his eyes, leaving the tower to swing free and nearly dislodge Brianna from her perch. A series of booms echoed through the ceiling as several men tumbled across the floor above, then the titan lowered his hand to catch his slipping burden.

Brianna raked her flame over Lanaxis's jaw and up toward his eyes. The fire caused no actual harm to his flesh, but merely burned away his purple murk to expose the pale, aged skin beneath. The titan lowered his eyelids and tried to twist away from the fiery blade's advance, but he could not turn far enough to keep the queen from combing the crimson shaft across the corner of his eye. The lid turned instantly white and baggy.

The clatter of firing crossbows echoed down the chimney, then a trio of dark shafts streaked toward Lanaxis's face. One bolt caught him in the purple murk beneath his jaw and passed harmlessly through his body. The second lodged itself in his wrinkled cheek, causing no greater injury than a splinter would cause a man. The final bolt struck home, catching the corner of the titan's eyelid and sinking clear to the butt.

Amazingly enough, Lanaxis did not roar or bellow or thunder his pain. He let out a long, exasperated sigh, which blustered over the tower like a gusting blizzard. Then he carefully stooped over to let his burden slide gently to the ground.

Brianna slipped out of her arrow loop. She heard her soldiers' boots reverberating across the floor above. The clack of two firing crossbows echoed down the chimney, followed by Avner's command, "Reloadreloadrelo—jump!"

In the next instant, a deafening clatter sounded from the floor above. The entire tower shook. Fragments of stone fell past the arrow loop, and Brianna knew the titan was demolishing the third story. A man wailed in agony, and a second and a third, their voices fading as their bodies plummeted groundward. Another crash and more screams followed, then something fell into the chimney, muffling the terrible sounds.

The tower stopped shaking.

Kaedlaw fell silent and motionless, but Brianna could feel his breath, damp and cold, beneath her cloak. She thrust her hand into her satchel and fumbled through spell components, hoping to come across one that would spark a workable escape plan.

An enormous fingernail appeared in an arrow loop, then pulled away a section of wall larger than a door. Lanaxis's eyes appeared in the opening, one lid still pinned shut by the crossbow bolt. The milky pupil of the other slowly searched the room. In desperation, Brianna pulled a glass rod from her satchel and pointed it at her captor. The motion caught the titan's attention, and his gaze locked on her.

"You have already made me dispose of my nephew's servants." Lanaxis's rumbling voice seemed to reverberate from the walls themselves. "Do not force me to destroy his mother as well."

Brianna lowered her hands. She had guessed correctly about the titan's defenses—once a bright light burned away his murky armor, he could be injured by normal weapons—but she knew better than to think she could utter her incantation faster than he could pull his head away.

"Waiting *would* be a wise decision. A dead mother will be of little use to my nephew." Lanaxis pulled his eyes away from the window, then held an enormous hand beneath it. "Now toss out your bag. If you test me again, I fear the gods shall be disappointed in my humility."

Brianna did as Lanaxis ordered. Her satchel fell into a palm crease and disappeared from sight, then the titan pulled his hand away from the chamber.

"What do want with my son?" she demanded. "Why do you keep calling him your nephew?"

"That should be obvious," Lanaxis replied. "He was fathered by my brother—the ettin."

"You're wrong!" Brianna wrapped her arms around her baby. "Kaedlaw isn't your spy's child. Kaedlaw looks like Tavis."

"The one you call Kaedlaw looks like Tavis." The titan's milky eye appeared before the opening. "It's the other child I want—the child whose face you refuse to see."

Brianna's heart suddenly felt as heavy as lead. "A child can't have two faces!"

"We see what we expect to see," Lanaxis said. "You see your husband's child. I see my brother's. They are both there."

Brianna felt a snake of ice slithering through her intestines. The titan's explanation accounted for too much: the secret Avner had refused to tell her, why her own husband and the firbolgs kept insisting that the child was ugly, and—most importantly—the strange visage she herself had glimpsed in the silver mines.

Brianna stepped forward and pulled Kaedlaw from the sling on her belly, but the thing she lifted into the light could not have been her son. He had a fat, round head with bloated pink cheeks and a short pug nose. Beneath his jaw hung two rolls of double chin, and in his brown eyes there sparkled an intelligence as malicious as it was precocious.

When the child twisted his blubbery red lips into an impish smile and let out a low, brutal cackle, Brianna's hands turned to liquid.

She did not mean to drop him.

# ✦11✦

# The Cold Marches

Avner dropped through the demolished damper throat into the second-story fireplace, his body at once numb and anguished from the untold hours he had spent wedged in the sooty flue. His legs felt dead and cold, his back ached, and every heartbeat filled his head with such a throbbing he feared his skull would split. His hair was matted into a helmet of frozen blood, and he could feel a deep gash running along his crown—presumably put there by the small boulder around which he had found himself folded upon awakening.

The tower reeled with the titan's lurching stride. The sway pitched Avner out of the fireplace and sent him tumbling across the listing chamber. By the time he smashed into the far wall, his head was swimming so fast he half-expected his throbbing brains to slither from his ears like eels. The young scout rolled onto his back and barely braced his feet against the floor before Lanaxis took his next step.

The ashen blush of first light seeped through the ragged remains of an arrow loop, filling the chamber with a drab, pale glow. Such an eerie stillness hung in the air that Avner thought Brianna had moved to some other part of the tower. The impression was reinforced when he saw her fur cloak lying abandoned next to him, along with several discarded capes. He snatched up the clothes and began to rummage through them, searching for any clue as to why they had been tossed aside.

After pulling a striking flint, a candle stub, and a handful of coins from the cloak's pocket, the young scout felt the hair rise on the back of his neck. With his heart rising into his throat, he put the clothes aside and peered into the chamber's dark recesses.

Brianna sat halfway up the adjacent wall, braced in the shadowy, cockeyed ledge where the entry foyer protruded into the room. She wore nothing but a light shift more appropriate to her well-heated bedchambers than the battered tower's drafty confines. Her son lay naked and still between her feet. Though the queen's gaze remained fixed on Avner, her eyes were as glassy and vacant as a dead woman's.

"In the name of Hiatea, no!" He could think of only one thing that would plunge the queen into such a state. "Don't let him be dead!"

Avner snatched the clothes and scuttled to the foyer, then climbed up beside Brianna. She was shivering violently, and her flesh had the pale, blotchy appearance of someone profoundly chilled. Though her gaze followed his movements, she did not speak or otherwise react.

The young scout steadied himself on her shoulder, then leaned over her leg to look at the child.

Avner did not know whether to be relieved or repulsed. Kaedlaw's chest pulsed with rapid, shallow breaths, but his skin had turned pale blue, and his pupils were dilated. His face was that of the ugly child: fat and round, with a double chin, pug nose, and brown eyes sparkling with dark ire.

Avner braced himself with his head next to the queen's feet, then reached around her legs and pulled Kaedlaw into his arms. He slipped the frigid baby under his own cloak and held the child for a long time, hardly able to believe Brianna would let her own son freeze. Something had snapped inside her mind. If he had crawled out of the chimney later than he did, the infant would have frozen to death, and perhaps the queen, as well. As it was, Kaedlaw showed no sign of warming. His skin remained as clammy and cold as it had when the scout found him.

Avner pressed the baby into Brianna's arms. "You must feed Kaedlaw, Majesty. Your milk will warm him and give him strength to fight the cold."

Brianna's eyes remained blank, but she accepted the child and cradled him in her arms. Avner draped her fur cloak around her shivering shoulders.

The queen shrugged it off, then placed her son between her feet and pulled his swaddling away. She did not look at Avner or acknowledge that he was by her side.

"Brianna, you don't know what you're doing!" Avner protested. "You can't let your own son freeze!"

When the young scout reached for the child again, Brianna's hand grabbed him by the collar. Her vacant eyes drifted to his face.

"L-Leave us alone."

Avner shook his head. "I helped this child into the world. I won't let you kill him."

"That is n-not your ch-choice."

Brianna jerked his collar, and Avner found himself flying off the foyer alcove. However despondent she was, the queen's strength remained as incredible as ever. The scout sailed halfway across the room before slamming into the floor, then he tumbled down the oak planks to smash against the wall.

He tried to gather himself up immediately. Every moment carried Kaedlaw closer to death, but there were a hundred forge hammers battering inside Avner's skull. When he stood, the pounding grew to thunderous proportions, and such a wave of nausea rolled over him that he fell back to his knees.

A heap of cloaks sailed off the foyer alcove and landed on Avner's back, knocking him to his belly.

"You knew!"

Avner crawled from beneath the cloaks and saw the queen, still on the alcove, glaring down at him. Her eyes had paled from their normal violet to a fiery silver.

"That's what you wouldn't t-tell me!" Despite her anger, Brianna was so cold she could not keep from stuttering.

"I saw Kaedlaw's second face, if that's what you mean." The pounding in Avner's head was subsiding. "And I also know you're making a terrible mistake, Majesty. You can't kill the ettin's child without killing your husband's."

"Then I must k-kill us all," Brianna replied. "The oath I swore as q-queen is not so different than the one Tavis swore as first d-defender. I must guard Hartsvale at any p-price."

"Against what?" Avner scoffed. "An infant?"

"Infants do not have secret f-faces," Brianna said. "This is a fiend's spawn, and I will have n-none of it!"

Brianna grabbed her son from between her feet and raised him over her shoulder, as though she were going to hurl him at Avner.

"No, Majesty!" Avner jumped up to catch the child, his shoulder slamming against the wall as the tower rocked. "I forbid this!"

Brianna's face clouded with fury, but, without appearing to realize what she was doing, she lowered the child. "You *what?*"

"I forbid you," Avner repeated calmly. Regardless of her oath, Brianna did not want to kill her son—or the infant would be dead by now. To save Kaedlaw, the young scout had only to keep her distracted until he found an excuse to spare the child. He reached inside his cloak and withdrew his sling. "I won't allow you to kill your son."

Brianna's eyes widened. "You would assault your q-queen?"

"To save her from herself, milady." The young scout plucked a fist-sized stone off the floor and slipped it into his sling's pocket. "Now, feed your baby—or I'll knock you senseless and do it myself."

"What of your s-scout's oath?" Brianna demanded. "You vowed to defend and *obey* me!"

"What of your oaths, milady?" Avner shot back. "As a priestess of Hiatea, didn't you vow to protect and nurture all the children of your kingdom?"

Brianna's face blanched, and Avner knew he had found the excuse he needed.

"Kaedlaw is dif-f-ferent." This time, it was not the cold that caused the queen's voice to quiver.

"Why?" Avner demanded. "Because he has two faces?"

"Because he is evil!"

Avner raised his brow. "Really? How do you know that? Has Hiatea sent you a sign?"

"No, but G-Galg-gadayle—"

"Galgadayle is no priestess of Hiatea," Avner insisted. "And even if he's right, who says that makes Kaedlaw evil? Maybe Hiatea *wants* your son to be king of giants. Which oath should you honor then—the one you swore to your people, or the one you swore to your goddess?"

"Hiatea would never f-force me to make such a d-decision."

"But she *would* ask you to murder your own child?"

Avner scoffed. "The goddess of parental love?"

Brianna shrank away as though Avner had struck her. She closed her eyes and screwed her face into an anguished grimace, then remained silent for many moments. Finally, she laid Kaedlaw in her lap and looked up.

"Throw m-me your water," she said. "I let mine f-freeze solid."

Avner took his waterskin from beneath his robe and tossed it up, then gathered the cloaks and made his way across the rocking tower. By the time he clambered up onto the alcove, the queen had taken the flaming spear amulet from her neck and dipped it into his waterskin. The liquid inside was bubbling and steaming from the heat of Hiatea's blessing. Kaedlaw's eyes were closed, and his skin was as blue as a tourmaline. Only the sporadic rise and fall of his chest indicated he was still alive.

"Open a c-cut on his arm." Brianna motioned Avner to lay the cloaks aside.

The young scout hesitated to obey. He had seen the queen heal the injured often enough to know what she was doing. When she poured the blessed water on the cut, it would cleanse the infant's blood of wicked thoughts and emotions. If the child was truly evil, the process would cause an endless black froth to erupt from the wound.

"What are you w-waiting for, Avner?" Brianna demanded. "Are you afraid of Hiatea's j-judgment?"

"Only for myself, Majesty." Avner pulled his antler-hilted skinning knife and drew the blade across the infant's forearm.

A thin line of blood welled up beneath the steel, and Brianna poured the bubbling water onto her son's arm. The blue flesh turned rosy pink. Kaedlaw's eyes opened wide, and he let out a pained growl that rumbled through the chamber like a bear's roar. A single bubble rose in the center of the cut.

It was white as snow.

"Hiatea, forgive me!" The queen snatched the child into her arms. "He's pure! He's as innocent as any newborn!"

Brianna lowered her collar over her shoulder, then held her son to her breast. The feel of his icy flesh filled her with a guilty burden heavy enough to crush the titan's heart. Kaedlaw reluctantly began to nurse, and Avner covered them both with the cloaks he had brought up.

"Avner, I'm grateful," Brianna said. The first silver rays of dawn were beginning to stream into the tower. "Your impertinence prevented me from committing a grievous sin against Hiatea—and it spared me more anguish than I could bear."

"Then he's going to be all right?"

"Thanks to you." Kaedlaw was already suckling eagerly at her warm milk. "And I would ask you to make a new oath to me—one you won't break this time."

"I didn't break the last one!" Avner objected. "At least not much."

"I doubt Tavis would agree," Brianna replied. "But he wasn't here, and you were right to stop me. Now I ask you to pledge that you'll always protect Kaedlaw—against anyone who would harm him."

"Brianna, I've already made that vow."

"I mean the lord high scout in particular," Brianna clarified. "If we can't convince Tavis to ignore Galgadayle's prophecy, can you kill the man who raised you?"

Avner bit his lip and looked away. "If it comes to a fight, I doubt Tavis will be the one who dies—but I'll give him a good battle. I can promise that much."

"Thank you. I'll need you at my side," Brianna said. "I hope I'm not making traitors of us both. If Kaedlaw grows up to lead the giants, we're committing a terrible crime against our kingdom."

Avner shrugged. "Crime is a relative thing. Besides, the time hasn't come to give up. My guess is that Hiatea wants us to escape, especially when you consider the kind of uncle Lanaxis would make."

Brianna grimaced at the thought, then glanced at the pale rays streaming through the shattered arrow loop.

"I think Lanaxis will stop when it gets light, but he'll be ready for an escape," she said. "We can't expect to succeed."

"You're right, we can't escape." Avner smiled. "But he might accidentally leave us behind—if he doesn't realize we've slipped away."

"And how are we going to do that?" Brianna demanded. "After your escape attempt at Wynn Castle, Lanaxis must know about the sally port."

Avner nodded. "He saw me climbing back into it."

"There aren't any other secret doors in this tower."

"But there might be a thief's gate," said Avner.

"A thief's gate?"

"On the first floor, in the bottom of the chimney," the youth explained. "The water collects down there and rots the mortar. I used to sneak into buildings all over Stagwick by scraping the mortar out and pulling a big stone loose."

Brianna scowled at this idea. "I'm hardly small enough to climb down through the chimney."

"Sure you are. In a tower like this, the chimney is huge—well, big enough anyway," he explained. "It's squeezing through the damper throat that can be tight—but Lanaxis has already solved that problem for us. The throat is smashed to pieces. You can practically walk into the flue."

Brianna eyed the battered fireplace on the high side of the room. The lintel was four feet above the hearth.

"I think I'll have to crawl," she said. "What can I do to help you?"

"Do you have any way to dissolve mortar?"

Brianna shook her head. "Not without my spell satchel," she said. "And even then, not quietly."

Avner grimaced. "Then I'll have to scrape it out." He fingered the antler hilt of his skinning knife. "I'm glad Tavis won't be here to see how I treat his gifts."

"I'm sure he would understand." Brianna motioned toward the fireplace. "You'd better get busy. After the titan stops, I'll feign an escape. It won't work, but Lanaxis will get suspicious if I don't try."

"Good—but be careful."

Avner scrambled up the floor and climbed into the fireplace. He hoisted himself past the smoke shelf, then entered the flue and started his descent to the first floor. Once he had disappeared, Brianna tore a woolen cloak into strips and began to braid it into a rope. Kaedlaw was suckling hungrily now, and she could not help wincing at his enthusiasm. The blue tint had vanished from his skin, which now felt warm and pleasant against hers, but his head remained plump and ugly. The queen could not help wishing that it was Kaedlaw's other face she saw.

Brianna was still making her rope when Lanaxis stopped and kicked his heel into the frozen ground. The strike sent such a jolt through the floor that the queen's teeth clacked together. A few moments later, the shocks ceased and her stomach suddenly rose into her throat. A weary groan reverberated from the tower foundations, then the building tipped toward the fireplace and steadied itself.

Brianna stuffed her half-finished rope beneath her cloak and went across the room to the smashed arrow loop. The air outside was so crisp it sparkled and so cold it stung like a wyvern's breath. At the base of the tower lay a short expanse of virgin snow, gleaming blue in the pale morning light. At the edge of the field rose an enormous drift, the stubs of three battered chimneys poking above the wind-crusted surface. Dozens of smaller mounds lay beyond the largest hillock, some with smaller chimneys or splintered beams showing above the snow. Beyond the buried village rose the black wall of a dense conifer forest, where the barbed tips of spearhead spruce and bloody tamarack scraped at the cloudless belly of a violet sky. In the center of the wood, the sun was poking its yellow crown above the horizon, kindling embers of golden fire in a small crescent of dark boughs.

Brianna placed their location somewhere near Hartsvale's northern border, for the forest was typical of the groves in the Cold Marches. The village itself was certainly one of the many manors that had fallen earlier this year when a tribe of frost giants had slipped across the frontier and gone on a month-long rampage.

A long boom, deeper and louder than any sound Brianna had ever heard, rose from the other side of the tower. Stones began to rattle in the walls. The snow lifted off the field outside, whirling around the building in a whistling white funnel. Kaedlaw howled in protest, but the queen could not hear him. She merely felt his body quivering with the effort.

Brianna rushed across the chamber and peered through an arrow loop, where she found her view blocked by Lanaxis's gloom-shrouded form. As the sun rose behind the tower, a tide of yellow light slowly crept down his robe. The purple murk rose from the cloth like steam, exposing the dingy, tattered linen that lay beneath. Though she could not see past the loop's upper sill to examine the titan's face, one hand dangled within her view. The skin was slack and wrinkled, and covered with scaly liver spots the size of platters.

Lanaxis fell to his knees beside the queen's tower, and the floor jumped so hard that Brianna nearly fell. She found herself staring at the titan's profile. His white-bearded chin was tipped up, with his mouth open and bellowing at the sky. His eyelid, still pinned shut by a crossbow quarrel, was baggy and wrinkled. The crow's-feet at the corner of his eye were as deep as planting furrows, and all that remained of his hair was a sparse fringe of coarse gray strands.

As the growing daylight swam over his body, Lanaxis dropped his head and fell silent. At first, Brianna thought the pain of his first sunrise in three thousand years had caused the howl, but then the titan's voice came crashing down as though it had echoed off the sky itself.

"Sons of Vilmos, I summon thee!" it boomed. "Answer the call of your ancient uncle, I command it!"

A southerly wind came howling out of the still air and tore across the field, driving before it a blinding wall of snow. The pounding gale hammered the foyer door against its jamb. Tongues of ice whipped through the arrow loops, lashing at Brianna like the strands of a torturer's flail. Distant peals of thunder erupted in the south. The tower shuddered so violently that it would have toppled had Lanaxis not thrust out a hand to hold it steady.

Brianna pulled up her hood and fastened her cloak tight, then retreated across the chamber to look through the arrow loop Lanaxis had shattered the night before. A line of snow clouds had appeared on the southern horizon. They were racing northward so fast it looked as though the gods were drawing a curtain across the sky. Inside the churning mass flashed a constant flicker of silver lightning, and the howling wind carried a musty, rainlike scent.

Storm giants.

It had been centuries since their last visit to Hartsvale, but Brianna knew the signs well enough. As a young girl, she had listened in heartbroken captivation to the tales of their gloomy visits, when rivers spilled over with tears and mountains thundered with grief. Simon, her father's high priest, had once told her they were the noblest of all giants, but also the most dangerous because even their huge hearts could not contain all of their ancient sorrows.

With a makeshift sling, Brianna fastened Kaedlaw to her chest, then tied her rope to one of the crossbar brackets on the foyer doorjamb. She opened the door and ran the line across the small hall to the gaping hole that had once connected the queen's tower to its stair turret. She dropped the end over the side. The wind caught it and whipped the long cord against the tower wall.

Brianna sat down and dangled her legs over the door-jamb, then took the homemade rope in hand. The clouds already covered half the sky, and the thunder was so loud she felt it in her bones. In the dark forest, the trees either bowed to the wind or snapped. Great white plumes of snow billowed off the drifts where the village lay buried, and the field below was concealed beneath a raging ground blizzard. The queen hoped Lanaxis would catch her soon, for she did not relish the thought of struggling through a thunder-snow with a heavy baby tied to her chest.

Brianna slipped off the doorsill and slid down the rope. The distant village and forest vanished behind a curtain of wind-driven snow. When the titan did not immediately recapture her, she uttered a prayer beseeching Hiatea's protection and struck out in the approximate direction of the hamlet. The snow was so deep she sank to her hips, and she had to swim more than wade to make progress through the powdery stuff. Her face

quickly went as numb as a rock, and her breath came in
gasping wheezes. The queen struggled onward. For
Avner's plan to work, she had to convince Lanaxis this
was her only hope. She would not accomplish that by
turning back.

It took only a few minutes for the tower to vanish
behind the driving snow. For a while, Brianna kept her
bearings by traveling parallel to the advancing line of
clouds, but it was not long before they had drawn a
formless gray shroud across the entire sky. The thunder
grew deafening, and graupel—hard pellets of rain quick-
frozen into snow—hammered down on the ground. Silvery flashes of lightning danced all around the field. The
queen struggled blindly onward, cringing in terror and
shivering with bone-aching cold, praying Lanaxis would
catch her soon.

The thought occurred to Brianna that perhaps dawn
had weakened the titan more than she knew. Certainly,
after thousands of years of constant twilight, full daylight
would be excruciatingly painful. But the queen saw no
reason it would paralyze or cripple her captor. Even after
the sun had seared away his gloomy cloak, Lanaxis's
ancient body had looked healthy enough to hobble after
her.

The wind stopped as suddenly as it had started. A
pearly white cloud separated from the gray mass
above and slowly descended, still pounding the field
with a torrent of graupel. The dark forest appeared
through the storm, its skyline jagged and irregular
with broken trees. The village lay off to the left, the
leeward sides of the demolished manor and several
huts now stripped of snow. Hundreds of birds large
and small were streaming over the ruins into the field,
filling the air with a cacophony of screeches and
squawks and blood-chilling shrieks. The storm giants
would arrive soon; according to the legends, the birds

189

were their harbingers.

From behind Brianna came the muffled crunch of compacting snow. She felt the powdery stuff settling around her hips, then suddenly found herself standing in Lanaxis's hand. As he lifted her into the air, the queen had to grab his thumb to keep from sliding off his slick palm. The titan twisted his wrist around so that she found herself staring up his sloping nose into his single good eye.

"Insolent child!" The words flew from his cavernous mouth on a dank, warm wind. "You would risk my nephew's life in a thunder-snow?"

The pearly white cloud descending from above settled over their heads, filling the air with a cold fog so thick Brianna could barely see her captor's face. The birds arrived in the same instant, their screeching silhouettes streaking through the thick mist like black ghosts. There were many different species—eagles, owls, warblers, even a condor—all cackling or hooting or chirping in melancholy voices.

Brianna watched the display for a moment, then remembered herself and tore her gaze away. She glanced over the edge of Lanaxis's hand and slid toward the brink as though she intended to jump.

The titan's fingers tightened around her legs. "I cannot believe you would be so stupid."

A cold knot formed in Brianna's stomach, and she wondered if she had overplayed her ploy. "Better to die for freedom than live in captivity."

"Kaedlaw *is* free!" The titan's bellow would have blasted Brianna from his palm had she not been holding his thumb. "He is emperor of Ostoria. No one can be more free."

"If that were so, you would let us go," Brianna said. "Let me raise him in his own home."

"So the filthy giant-kin can slay him?" The white cloud

was lifting, and Brianna could see the titan's desiccated lips curled in derision. "Or do you think your puny citadel can stand against their hordes until he reaches manhood?"

"Why not?" she demanded. "So far, we have held your giants at bay easily enough."

Lanaxis shook his head. "The gods have decreed Twilight his new home. They have chosen me to raise him, to mold him into a wise and powerful emperor."

"They gave him to me first," Brianna countered. "I am his mother, or have you forgotten?"

"You?" Lanaxis's breath had turned as sharp and caustic as brimstone. "You are no more to him than a nursemaid. Once he is weaned, he will be done with you."

A searing anger swelled inside Brianna. She suddenly felt her dagger hilt in her hand and saw no reason to restrain herself.

If Lanaxis felt the blade slash his thumb, he showed no sign. He merely turned toward the queen's tower, where six pale figures stood waiting, barely visible through the thinning fog. They were large even by the standards of giants—taller than her battered tower—but they seemed mere children compared to the immense titan. Brianna judged that even the biggest would rise no higher than her captor's chest, and it would have taken all of their number to match his bulk.

As Lanaxis neared the tower, Brianna's view of the giants improved. All were clean-shaven, with unkempt, blue-black hair cascading over their shoulders. They had solemn, handsomely chiseled faces with gloomy silver eyes, and wan violet skin so pale it was nearly gray. Their simple tunics were belted at their waists, clean but rumpled. Each warrior wore a king's ransom in silver jewelry, all of it black with tarnish.

The birds were swarming the giants, circling their heads or roosting on their shoulders, sometimes perching on their belts or the pommels of their huge two-handed swords. Save for the constant flutter of wings, the entire flock had fallen as silent as a snowfall. Their eyes were fixed on Brianna and her captor, giving the queen the uneasy feeling that while there was a bird overhead, she would never be out of a storm giant's sight.

When the titan reached the tower, the six newcomers knelt in the snow and bowed their heads. The air smelled musty and old, and Brianna's joints began to throb with a cold, damp ache.

"You have called, aged uncle, and we six have answered," said one giant. He did not look up, and his voice sounded as dismal and languid as a dying man's. "How may we serve?"

Lanaxis regarded the giants with a cold eye. "You may start by standing, Anastes," the titan rumbled. "I have summoned you here to amend the wrong committed by your ancient paramount."

The storm giants turned the color of snow and looked up with uncomprehending eyes. The birds left their shoulders, filling the air with a melancholy din of chirping and trilling. Peals of the thunder rumbled down from the sky, and the graupel sounded like a drum chorus as it hammered the exposed planks of the tower's third-story floor.

"Stand I say!" Lanaxis ordered. "I did not call you here to brood."

The giants obeyed, but the wind picked up, and the graupel fell harder than ever.

"Forgive our feelings, ancient uncle. Your news comes as a great shock—as much as we welcome it." Anastes's voice sounded anything but happy. "At a time like this, it is difficult for us to control our emotions."

"Vilmos had no trouble." Lanaxis cast an impatient glance skyward, then lowered his hand to display Brianna. "Beneath her cloak, this queen carries the new

emperor of Ostoria. You will guard her while I sleep—
and if you allow anything to become of him—or her—I
shall give you reason to storm for centuries."

Lanaxis stooped down and thrust Brianna into the second-story foyer. When she retreated through the door,
she found the room filled with flitting birds. From the
chimney flue came a faint scratching sound, which she
at first attributed to the birds, but quickly realized was
more likely Avner scratching at the mortar in the fireplace below.

Brianna went to a corner and chased a bevy of siskins
off the floor, then sat down and opened her cloak to
check on Kaedlaw. His face remained round and ugly,
but his skin was pink, and the sparkle had returned to
his brown eyes. He raised one of his chubby hands
toward the queen's breast. She lifted him to suckle.
Nothing came out, and he growled.

Brianna cringed at his gravelly voice, then switched
him to the other side. "You're a hungry one, aren't you?"

From across the chamber came Anastes's melancholy
voice. "A baby giant does need plenty of milk."

Brianna's heart jumped into her throat. The noises in
the chimney suddenly sounded dangerously loud, and
she had to struggle to keep her gaze from straying
toward the fireplace. She looked instead toward the shattered arrow loop, where Anastes's sad eyes were staring
into the room. It seemed unlikely he would hear the
faint scratching of Avner's knife, especially over the hissing wind and the fluttering birds. Still, the queen did not
know how keen the giant's ears were, or what he might
learn from his pets within the chamber.

Brianna pulled up her cloak to shield Kaedlaw and
her partially exposed breast. "If you'll excuse me, I'm
nursing."

"I'm truly sorry for the intrusion." Anastes made no
move to look away. "And if you'll forgive me for express-

193

ing my concerns, I must say a tiny thing like you will never keep a baby giant fed."

"Lanaxis thinks I'll make a fine nursemaid." Although the scratching had grown no louder, it filled Brianna's ears like a trumpet blare. "He seems to believe that's all a mother is good for."

"I suppose that's what comes of being born to a mountain." Anastes was referring to the legend that Lanaxis and his brothers had been born of the mountain goddess Othea. "When one crawls from the birthing cave fully mature and immortal, how can one fathom the soothing balm of a mother's love?"

"Perhaps you'd better teach him," Brianna suggested. "Or your new emperor will grow up as warped as your titan."

A doleful look came to Anastes's silver eyes. "Would that I could, but we storm giants have already brought misery enough to the world. By trying to change what is destined to be, we can only make things worse."

"How convenient for you."

Anastes's face darkened to sullen blue. The thunder outside growled plaintively, and a flurry of birds flashed past his face. The sulking storm giant looked away, turning his enormous ear to the window.

The queen's stomach knotted with alarm. She rose and paced across the floor, holding her son to her shoulder as though she were burping him. Kaedlaw immediately growled his protest, filling the chamber with such a rumble that the birds fluttered off their roosts. Even Brianna could no longer hear the scratching in the fireplace.

Anastes turned back to the chamber. "Poor child. The pain of life is so new to him."

"Perhaps he is cold," rumbled a second storm giant. "We could strike a fire."

"No!" Brianna spun around to find a huge gray eye

peering through the arrow loop behind her. A pair of brown falcons were roosting on the sill, their cocked heads turned toward the giant. "The chimney's blocked. We'd choke on the smoke."

"That's a small matter to fix," offered another giant, this one peering through an arrow loop by the chimney. "I'll have the flue clear in an instant."

"I don't want a fire!" Brianna insisted. She doubted the smoke would trouble Avner in the bottom of the chimney, but she didn't want a giant dropping a stone on the young scout. Besides, the queen suspected she would find it difficult enough to crawl into a flue that was cold. "I'll only have to put it out when Lanaxis lifts the tower, and even then I'll have embers flying all over."

Anastes knitted his brows, but did not argue. "Is there *anything* we can do to make you more comfortable?"

"What I really need is to eat." It was the truth, but Brianna also hoped to keep the storm giants busy. "If you want to help, bring me some fresh rye bread, goat's cheese, and a warm meatcake."

"There's a pair of moose in the fen beyond that forest," rumbled one of the giants. "Wouldn't they be enough for you?"

Brianna shot an impatient scowl at Anastes. "Do you see my cooks here? Or perhaps you expect me to eat raw moose?"

"Nikol and Ramos can cook them for you," offered the giant.

"Very well," Brianna sighed. "But my moose must be slow-roasted on a spit, and cooked through. Of course, I shall need wine to wash it down, a honeycomb to sweeten the flavor, and a bowl of pottage to settle my stomach."

Anastes paled. "You have demanding tastes, milady."

"You're the one who suggested moose," Brianna

reminded him. "I'd be just as happy with my first request—but if that's too much trouble, perhaps you could keep the milk flowing for your new emperor by feeding me finches and falcons."

Anastes winced. "No, of course not! We wouldn't think of such a thing!"

He was speaking more to the birds than to Brianna, but that did not keep the queen's unwanted guests from leaving the chamber in a squawking flurry. Clearly, the creatures understood more than she would have liked.

Kaedlaw let out an enormous burp and stopped growling. Brianna continued to pace, sliding her feet across the floor to mask the sound of Avner's work.

"Well?" she demanded. "What shall it be?"

"We will cook the moose," Anastes sighed. His head rose out of view, then his muffled voice reverberated across the third-story floor. "Nikol and Ramos, you roast the moose. Sebastion, you and Patma find some wine and vegetables for the queen's pottage. Eusebius, see if the thrushes can guide you to a beehive."

The giants did not rush off to do their paramount's bidding.

"Before we go, I would like to behold our new emperor," said one. "Perhaps we are not worthy of the honor, but it is truly my heart's desire to lay eyes on him at least this once."

Brianna started to pull Kaedlaw from beneath her cloak, then thought wiser of it. She might make better use of this boon later.

"The emperor is resting now."

The storm giants sighed, and a chain of frigid drafts twirled through the chamber. Somewhere above the tower, half-a-dozen hawks voiced a string of forlorn *tseers*. The wind picked up and whistled past the arrow loops, spinning flurries of graupel into the room, and, save for Anastes, all of Brianna's captors lumbered off to gather the food she had demanded.

"You are right to deny us, of course." Anastes looked away, and a peal of long, soft thunder rumbled across the sky. "It is wrong for us even to hope we might lay eyes on one so sublime."

"And why is that, Anastes?" Brianna was at once sympathetic and impatient with the giant's self-pity. She went to the shattered arrow loop and stopped there. "What ancient wrong did Lanaxis call you to amend? No deed can be terrible enough to condemn an entire race to such suffering."

The storm giant lifted his chin and fixed an enormous, woe-filled eye on Brianna. "I fear you are wrong, milady." His lips trembled with shame. "Our race is to blame for all the misery and suffering on Toril."

Behind Anastes, forks of lightning lanced down from the gray snow clouds, stabbing at the ground and spewing great plumes of hissing steam into the sky. The birds screeched as though they were dying. The graupel battered the giant's shoulders so fiercely he grimaced.

"That's a heavy burden to claim," Brianna observed. "Are you certain it belongs to your race alone?"

"Oh, yes. There can be no doubt." Anastes's voice was growing louder and more pained with each syllable he spoke, once again raising the storm outside to blizzard proportions. "We are the ones who plunged the world into chaos and war. We are the ones who slew Ostoria's divine ruler, Hartkiller, and drove Annam the All Father from Toril forever!"

The howling winds buffeted the tower so harshly that Brianna had to brace her arm against the wall. "I see!" she shouted. "But did you ever consider that your ancestor might have done other races a favor? Perhaps they had no wish to be ruled by giants."

Anastes looked aghast, and the storm lulled. "How can you say that?" he demanded. "You, a descendant of Hartkiller!"

"I'm more human than giant," Brianna reminded him. "I'm glad to rule Hartsvale instead of the giants, and the humans are happy to have me."

Anastes shook his head in disbelief. "Then you are as foolish as your people," he declared. "Annam decreed that the giants would rule Toril, not for our sakes, but for the welfare and harmony of all races. By killing Hartkiller, we defied the All Father's will. We destroyed Ostoria."

"Now you're the one who's being foolish," Brianna countered. "My runecaster has translated the histories written by the stone giants. I know who destroyed Ostoria, and it wasn't your ancestor. It was Lanaxis."

Anastes's face went as white as the snow. The birds on his shoulders took flight, and the storm grew so quiet that even the graupel seemed to hang frozen in the sky. The scratching of Avner's knife hissed loudly in the queen's ears.

Brianna pinched her son. Kaedlaw responded admirably, filling the chamber with a low, angry growl.

"You mustn't say such things about Lanaxis," Anastes warned. "Never!"

"Why not?" Brianna demanded. "Must I tell *you* the legend? Annam the All Father wanted true giants—his progeny—to rule Toril. But faithless Othea spawned children by many different gods, and she wanted all her offspring to share the world. That's why she helped one of her lovers unleash the glacier that would one day wipe Ostoria from the land."

"I know the history of my own people!"

"Then think about it." Brianna was beginning to hope she could make an ally of the storm giant. When men consumed by false guilt learned the truth, they often turned against those who had abused their emotions. "After Othea forbade Lanaxis from destroying the glacier, he poisoned her, and that made him a murderer. What did he become when he allowed his brother kings to drink the same poison?"

"He loved Ostoria!"

"Lanaxis would not be the only fool to destroy what he loves most," Brianna replied. "Nor the only one to go mad after he realized what he did."

Kaedlaw fell silent. Though Brianna could still hear the faint scratching of Avner's knife, she did nothing to cover the sound. Anastes was lost in thought, and it seemed a worthwhile risk to let him think in peace.

At length, the birds returned to the storm giant's shoulders, and the wind howled as mournfully as before.

"We still bear the blame for Hartkiller's death." Anastes sounded almost relieved. "Lanaxis did not murder *him*."

"By then, Ostoria was already lost," Brianna said. "Your race has been blaming itself for a tragedy the gods set in motion. By trying to right things now, you'll be making a mistake even more terrible than the one for which you have blamed yourselves all these centuries."

The giant's silver eyes grew thoughtful, and he looked away. Once again the winds quieted, the graupel fell more slowly, and the birds deserted their roosts—then a muffled clatter echoed out of the fireplace.

Anastes's head snapped back toward the tower. Brianna braced herself for a tempestuous display of temper, but the storm remained calm.

"How do you know?" demanded Anastes. If he had heard the clatter, he paid it no heed. "What makes you certain Lanaxis is wrong to restore Ostoria?"

Brianna breathed no sigh of relief. She pulled her son from beneath her cloak and said, "I know because I have seen the face of your new emperor."

Another clatter sounded from the fireplace, this one too loud to miss. Brianna turned Kaedlaw toward the shattered arrow loop and thrust his hideous visage toward the storm giant.

Anastes's silver eyes opened wide, and he grimaced with revulsion. "There is nothing I can do." He looked away from the tower. "What will be will be—the matter is entirely out of my hands."

# ☙ 12 ☙
# Surprise Attack

The birds would be a problem, Tavis knew. The birds and the cold. He had never seen so many birds, and he had never been so cold. He felt sick with cold. His clothes were frozen stiff with his own sweat, and his thoughts bumped through his mind like icebergs. The weather was not particularly frigid, but, as Munairoe had warned, the high scout's system had been weakened by too much magic. After last night's long run, his body lacked the stamina to keep itself warm, and now he would have to deal with the birds. There were thousands and thousands, from warm lands and cold, representing every species Tavis knew and a hundred he didn't.

On the icy winds above wheeled a dozen glacier vultures, their black heads and blue-tinged wings all that showed through the dusky snowstorm. A clan of dervish owls sat perched on the battered rim of the queen's tower, their huge golden eyes tracing every movement of the strange blue pheasants below. On the shoulders of the storm giants, kestrels roosted with sparrows, harriers with siskins, hawks with crows; only the egg-stealing skunkbirds sat apart, their white-striped bodies tangled like bats amidst the giants' windblown hair. There was even a pair of condors waddling around the roasting fire, snatching slabs of moose off the spits when the cooks looked the other way.

Tavis was studying the scene from atop a thirty-foot knoll, where he and the three giant-kin chieftains lay belly-down in a deep blanket of wet graupel. The 'kin army was behind them, quietly gathering at the base of a long, gradual slope. Ahead of them, the hill descended in a steep, rocky scarp to the snow-covered meadow of an abandoned farm village.

In the center of the meadow, a low, snow-mantled drumlin spewed plumes of white steam into the air and occasionally stirred in its sleep: the titan lying blanketed beneath a thick jacket of snow. The queen's tower stood nearby, with a storm giant kneeling beside it so he could peer into the second-floor chamber. At the west end of the field was the roasting fire, where two giants were tending a like number of spitted moose. At the opposite end of the meadow, two more were rummaging through the debris of the demolished village. The sixth giant was in the forest beyond the hamlet, his location marked by trembling treetops and a halo of circling birds.

The fomorian chieftain, Ror, shifted in the snow at Tavis's side. "What we do now?" he whispered. "Them storm giants don't let us kill baby, no."

"Ror, we're here to recover Kaedlaw, not kill him." As he spoke, Orisino cast a sidelong glance in Tavis's direction to make certain the high scout was listening. "What happens after that is up to Tavis."

The fomorian's froggish face winced, and he said, "Right. Ror mean *rescue* kid."

The high scout paid the exchange little attention. He knew better than to think either chieftain would keep his word, but Raeyadfourne had pledged the Meadowhome firbolgs to let Tavis decide Kaedlaw's fate. When the time came, that promise would go far toward countering the treachery of the verbeegs and fomorians.

"How shall we do it?" Raeyadfourne cast an uneasy glance toward the sinking sun. "We don't have much light left, and I don't fancy fighting storm giants after dusk."

"Titan sleeping. Kill first, him," suggested Ror. "Then storm giants leave, them."

"That's absurd, Ror," said Orisino. "How will you kill that titan?"

It was Raeyadfourne who answered. "We wounded him last night, and many of our axes still bear Basil's rune marks." The chieftain squinted at the titan for a moment, then reluctantly shook his head. "But Lanaxis is no fool. Even Tavis couldn't get within a hundred paces of him without being seen. One way or another, we're going to have fight the storm giants first. I say we attack as soon as our warriors are ready."

Raeyadfourne craned his neck to look down the back side of the hill. Tavis and the others did likewise. The firbolgs stood at the base of the gentle slope, clouds of white vapor spewing from their panting mouths. The short-legged verbeegs had gathered at the western end of the hill. They were leaning on their spears or kneeling in the snow, their ribs heaving as they gasped for breath. The fomorians, hindered by their deformities, were still scuttling or limping or slinking over to the eastern end of the hill, where they were collapsing in the shelter of a small spruce copse. Two companies of human footmen were also rushing northward at their best pace, but they would not arrive in time for the battle.

After studying the exhausted warriors for a moment, Tavis looked back to the meadow. "The f-firbolgs will ch-charge the t-titan," he said. "I'll sn-sneak into the t-tower to get B-Brianna and the ch-child."

The three chieftains all raised their brows at the sound of Tavis's stuttering. A predatory grin crept across Orisino's broad mouth.

"You sound . . . chilly." The verbeeg glanced at Ror, then observed, "Strange; it doesn't feel that cold to me."

"That's enough," growled Raeyadfourne. "You know well enough why he's cold. I doubt you'd make the same sacrifice for someone you loved."

"Fortunately, verbeegs aren't foolish enough to indulge such emotions."

Tavis shot the verbeeg a warning glance.

"I'm w-warm enough to n-nock my bow." The high scout glared at Orisino until the verbeeg looked away, then shifted his gaze to the western end of the field. He pointed to the storm giants at the roasting fire. "The v-verbeegs will attack those t-two. Ror and his f-fomorians will take the p-pair in the village."

Ror scowled, then looked beyond the village into the forest. "Ror see three giants—one in wood. Firbolgs go to village, them. Fomorians sneak up on tower, us."

Tavis shook his head. "There won't be any sneaking during this battle. Even fomorians can't—"

The sound of wings broke overhead. The high scout rolled onto his back and saw two glacier vultures swooping low over the knoll. In an eyeblink, the birds were past and diving toward the firbolgs at the base of the slope.

Tavis pushed himself down behind the hill crest, pulling his bow off his shoulder as he slid.

The vultures reached the bottom of the slope and beat their wings, one turning toward the verbeegs and the other toward the fomorians. By the time Tavis had nocked his first arrow, both birds were rounding the corners of the hill. Most of the warriors below showed no sign of noticing the creatures, and none made any move to down them.

Tavis returned his unfired arrow to his quiver and scrambled back to the summit. The vultures were racing across the field toward the queen's tower. They flew straight to the giant kneeling there and landed on his shoulder, then began cackling and groaning into his cavernous ear.

"I think we've been spotted," Tavis growled. "Damn birds!"

"To your tribes!" Raeyadfourne rose to his feet. "We'll follow Tavis's plan."

Ror shook his head emphatically. "Ror like ambush better—"

"Do it, Ror!" snapped Orisino. "There's no time to argue."

Orisino stood and bounded down the slope. Ror scowled after the verbeeg a moment, then reluctantly hefted his great bulk and waddled toward his own tribe. Tavis fixed his attention on the queen's tower and remained on the hilltop, aching to the bone with weariness and cold. The battle was off to a bad start. Without the confusion of a surprise attack, it would be difficult to sneak past the giants to the tower, much less steal away with Brianna and her child.

After listening to the vulture's report, the storm giant rose to his full height, two full heads taller than the queen's tower, and peered up the rocky scarp toward Tavis's hiding place. The birds cackled into his ears again, and the giant looked toward the west end of the hill. He raised a hand and pointed in the verbeegs' direction.

"Nikol and Ramos, there are verbeegs there." The storm giant's voice blustered across the field like a howling wind. "See to them."

The two cooks looked first toward their leader, then toward the hill. They abandoned the spitted moose to the condors and started forward, drawing their enormous two-handed swords. The weapons were twenty feet long, with hawk-sized nicks on the blade edges and blemishes of orange rust on the flats.

The vultures continued to cackle in the leader's ears. He turned to the other side of the field, where the two searchers had stopped their explorations. He gestured at the eastern end of the hill.

"Fomorians are gathering there," he rumbled. "Call Eusebius from the wood. They are for him."

One of the searchers took an owl off his shoulder and sent it into the forest. The other called, "What of us, Anastes?"

Anastes pointed toward the center of the hill. "Firbolgs for you, Sebastion, and for Patma as well."

Sebastion and Patma nodded grimly, then drew their swords and angled across the field toward the center of the hill. Anastes pulled his own weapon and positioned himself squarely between the queen's tower and the giant-kin, precluding any possibility of anyone slipping past his fellows during the confusion.

Tavis cursed the giant's wisdom. It addition to protecting the tower, the storm giant was shielding Lanaxis from the firbolgs. The high scout shifted his gaze to the titan's slumbering form, wondering how much of a factor the ancient colossus would play in the coming battle. The mere fact that he had stopped suggested his power was diminished in daylight, but there was no way for Tavis to guess to what extent. It seemed too much to hope the titan would be rendered completely helpless.

The high scout glanced over his shoulder and saw his 'kin allies still struggling to organize their warriors.

"Q-Quickly! The giants are c-coming after *us*!" Tavis began to shiver, more with cold, he thought, than fear. "Two for the v-verbeegs, two for the firbolgs, and one f-for the fomorians."

The chieftains boomed their commands even louder. The verbeegs slipped around the corner and the firbolgs started up the slope at a trot, but the fomorians continued to mull about with no sense of direction.

A cacophony of bird calls erupted over the field, and stinging pellets of graupel began to pelt Tavis. The high scout looked back toward the heath and saw the first four giants already moving into attack positions. The fifth, Eusebius, was just emerging from the forest and starting toward the fomorians. Anastes remained in front of the queen's tower. All six giants were hidden from the thighs down by a curtain of blowing snow, and they had thick clouds of birds whirling over their heads.

Tavis reluctantly pulled a runearrow from his quiver. By drawing attention to himself early in the battle, he was making it more difficult to reach Brianna. But he could not allow the storm giants to carry the fight to the hill's back. Unless the combat occurred in the meadow below, he would have no chance at all of reaching the queen's tower.

Tavis nocked his runearrow and rose, aiming at the giant who had been addressed as Sebastion. The high scout had to take a moment to steady his arms, for the icy wind had chilled him to the point of trembling. Peals of thunder rumbled across the sky, so loud that his ears throbbed and his knees ached to buckle.

Sebastion stepped onto the hill, with Patma close behind. Tavis had to angle his arrow only slightly downward to set the tip on his target's breast. He emptied his lungs, then drew his bowstring and loosed the shaft.

A flurry of screeching falcons streaked down from the sky and struck at the arrow as though it were a lark. One of the birds snatched the missile from the air, then banked away over the field. Sebastion climbed a step higher, and Tavis had to crane his neck to look into the giant's eyes.

"Damn birds!" The high scout's cold-numbed fingers fumbled for another runearrow.

Sebastion raised his sword to strike. Tavis found a shaft and pulled it from his quiver, nocking and firing in one smooth motion. This time, the target was so close that there was no chance for the falcons to snatch the arrow. It flashed through the whirling birds and lodged itself deep in the giant's breast.

Sebastion did not even wince. He simply squinted at Tavis and started to bring his sword down.

"esiwsilisaB!" Tavis cried.

A ray of sapphire light lanced from the wound. Sebastion's chin dropped, and the strength left his swing. The giant's chest opened across its entire width. His arms flew out to the sides and sent his great sword spinning through the sky, and his body folded around his mangled torso. He pitched over backward and disappeared into the blowing snow at the bottom of the scarp. A tremendous boom rolled across the meadow, and the hill bucked so hard that it bounced Tavis into the air.

The high scout came down on his side and felt the air rush from his lungs. Blowing snow blocked his view of everything around him, save for the whirling birds above and Patma's head rising over the crest of the knoll. Tavis did not wait for his breath to return, or even for the pain of his fall to register. He pushed off with all fours and leapt to his feet, facing the back of the hill.

Raeyadfourne's tribe was rushing up the gentle slope, concealed from the waist down by a blustering white curtain. Bolts of lightning skipped through their midst like dancers, hurling firbolgs and shattered stone in all directions. The air smelled of charred earth, seared flesh, and rain, and not even the howling wind could cover the cries of the wounded.

Tavis spun around to find Patma's face glaring at him. The giant's thin lips twisted into an angry snarl, his silver eyes flashed like lightning, and his sword came arcing down out of the sky. The high scout dived away.

A terrible screech sounded behind him; then the entire hill shuddered beneath the impact of the giant's huge weapon. Tavis hit the cold ground rolling and came up on his feet. In his freezing fingers he held a runearrow he did not remember drawing. He turned around and found himself standing beside an enormous steel blade buried deep in the knoll's stony summit. The birds were as thick as fog around him, and their angry cries drowned out even the rumbling of the thunder.

Patma jerked his sword free, leaving a smoking crevice where the blade had struck. Tavis fumbled his runearrow onto his bowstring and pointed it at his attacker.

The piercing shriek of a tarn hawk stabbed Tavis's ear. Something sharp slammed into his shoulder and dug in. His bowstring slipped from his fingers, and the runearrow arced harmlessly over the hill crest. He toppled onto his side, then slid across the icy ground, wings beating madly about his head, talons tearing at his shoulder.

Tavis twisted onto his back and brought Mountain Crusher up, hooking the end around the bird's neck. Its head came down instantly, the beak darting at his eyes. The high scout turned aside, then cried out as the raptor's powerful mandibles tore into his cheek. He reached up blindly and, when he felt the creature's nape in his cold grasp, gave a sharp twist. The hawk squawked briefly and fell limp, shrouding the scout's face beneath its feathery wings.

"Damn birds!" Tavis pushed the creature off his head. "Surtr's flames t-take you all!"

Tavis leapt up and faced the hill crest, expecting to feel a huge sword biting through his shivering midriff at any moment. Instead, he saw Patma's rust-flecked blade sweeping along the ridge, spraying a cone of hail at the charging firbolgs. So fierce was the icy stream that it swept the burly warriors off their feet and hurled them, bloody and groaning, back down the slope. Even those

209

who eluded the hail were not spared. A fan of silvery sleet trailed from the back edge of the weapon, coating everything it touched beneath a suffocating mantle of blue ice.

Knowing better than to waste another runearrow, Tavis nocked a normal shaft and fired at the giant's eyes. A swarm of birds streaked to intercept the missile, startling Patma and temporarily blocking his view. A gray harrier caught the shaft in its breast and careened out of the bevy, and the hail stream veered from its targets.

That instant was all Munairoe needed. The shaman's voice rang out from the rear of the firbolg ranks, and a crackling tongue of flame arced up the slope to strike Patma's sword. The crimson streak sizzled up the weapon's length. The hail and sleet gave way to a hissing geyser of white steam, then the blade shattered, spraying jagged shards of hot steel in all directions.

A pattern of bloody stains blossomed across Patma's white shift, and a dozen firbolgs clutched at their faces and went down. Something hissed past Tavis's head. He reached up and discovered blood trickling down his neck. His ear had been sliced open by a steel shard he had not even seen.

Several of Raeyadfourne's warriors thundered past Tavis, hurling themselves off the hill crest at Patma. Their axes struck his chest with a series of wet-sounding thuds. The storm giant blasted the ridge with a ferocious bellow of pain. He toppled out of sight with three firbolg axes lodged in his chest, the warriors still dangling from the handles. All four combatants tumbled down the rocky scarp in a clamorous maelstrom of crashing bodies and shouting voices.

Raeyadfourne rushed past with the rest of the Meadowhome firbolgs, and Basil stopped at Tavis's side.

"Look at you! You're covered in blood again," the runecaster panted. "You can't take much of this.

Munairoe said—"

"I know what M-Munairoe sssaid," the high scout stuttered. "But Brianna's d-down there."

Tavis charged over the summit in time to see the Meadowhome firbolgs swarming Patma. Only the storm giant's wildly flailing limbs were visible, for he had fallen beneath the veil of wind-driven snow at the base of the scarp. The high scout bounded down the rocky face, stealing glances at the rest of the battlefield as he bounced between outcroppings.

At the eastern end of the meadow, the furtive fomorians were nowhere in sight. But the giant Eusebius was swinging his blade back and forth through the ground blizzard, flinging gore in all directions. At the western end of the field, the battle looked to be bloody on both sides. One of the storm giants had fallen to his knees with several verbeeg spears in his midriff, but the other was standing his ground against Orisino's orderly ranks, cleaving through his foes' waists two and three at a time.

By the time Tavis reached the bottom of the scarp, Patma's limbs had disappeared beneath the ground blizzard. A thick cloud of birds wheeled over the body, crying mournful songs and raking at the firbolgs' heads. The high scout skirted the fringe of the crowd. He was just tall enough to see over the curtain of blowing snow. Directly ahead, Anastes remained at his station in front of the queen's tower. The storm giant's eyes were melancholy and resigned, but he held his rust-flecked sword in one hand and a crackling ball of lightning in the other.

As Tavis started toward the center of the meadow, the snow suddenly avalanched from the flanks of the little drumlin behind the queen's tower. A long aquiline nose emerged from beneath the white blanket, followed by a wiry, square-cropped beard and the rest of Lanaxis's head. His crown sat upon his pate, cocked forward and lopsided, with a few wisps of coarse white hair poking out from beneath the band. His face was shriveled and white with age. A crossbow bolt had pinned shut one of his haggard eyes, which was now inflamed and oozing infection.

The titan gathered his feet beneath him and stood, voicing a deep, soul-drained groan that made him seem as old and weary as the mountains.

Raeyadfourne caught up to Tavis. "Wait! We need to regroup!" he yelled. "We cannot—"

"*I* can! Take your tribe and go!" Tavis shoved Raeyadfourne toward the eastern side of the tower. "Circle around there—and if you reach Brianna first, remember your promise!"

Tavis circled in the opposite direction, plowing through waist-deep snow at his best sprint. He happened upon Sebastion's corpse and scrambled onto the body, startling hundreds of birds from their roosts. Seven quick paces took him the cadaver's length. When he jumped back into the deep snow, the birds followed, assailing him with angry screeches and raking talons.

A deafening volley of thunder rolled across the field. Tavis glanced eastward. Anastes stood no more fifty paces away, looming above the ground blizzard like Stronmaus himself. The storm giant was hurling lightning bolts down upon the firbolgs' heads and shoulders, the only parts of the Meadowhome warriors that showed above the whistling curtain of snow.

Tavis turned directly toward the queen's tower. Lanaxis stood beside the battered structure, peering over the top to survey the battlefield. The high scout continued to rush forward, unconcerned about being seen. The titan's good eye was looking the other direction.

Tavis had closed to within twenty paces of the tower when a black spire eagle swooped low over his head and turned toward the titan. The bird voiced its shrill cry, drawing Lanaxis's attention at once. The titan's gaze lingered a moment on the reeling birds above the high scout's head, then seemed to pierce the feathery cloud and fall directly on Tavis's face.

He stopped and drew a runearrow from his quiver. The titan simply looked away, then knelt in the snow and wrapped his arms around the queen's tower.

Tavis nocked his arrow. The spire eagle appeared before his face, talons extended to strike. The scout leapt sideways and loosed his shaft, then tumbled backward as the raptor slammed into his shoulder.

"esiwsi—"

The eagle sank its beak into Tavis's gullet, and they dropped into the snow together. The high scout released his bow and twisted toward his attacker, at the same time drawing his belt dagger. The raptor tore a hunk of flesh from Tavis's neck. He drove his knife deep into the bird's feathery breast, drawing a startled squawk and a last, feeble peck at his face.

"Damn damn damn birds!"

Tavis leapt up and turned toward the center of the meadow. Lanaxis had already risen to his full height and was cradling the queen's tower in the crook of his elbow. The runearrow was lodged in the shoulder of the same arm, but if the titan noticed it, he showed no sign. He was already limping away from the battle.

Tavis started to utter the command word that would detonate the runearrow, then realized how far the building would drop if he blew the arm off. A cold, sick ache more painful than any wound filled his body, for he knew better than to think his wife and child would emerge alive from the rubble. He stood motionless in the snow, torn between the futile impulse to stumble after them and the wiser decision to turn back and help his allies regroup.

Basil's hand grasped his shoulder. "You're as mad as Memnor!" the runecaster puffed. "Attacking the titan alone!"

"He's weak during the day," Tavis croaked. The effort of speaking pained his savaged throat, but he barely noticed. "I almost had him."

Basil cocked an eyebrow. "I'd say you're lucky you didn't." The verbeeg retrieved Tavis's bow from beside the dead spire eagle. "But we have other problems at the moment. Ror has betrayed us all."

The runecaster pointed Mountain Crusher across the blowing snow, toward the eastern end of the meadow. It took Tavis a moment to find what concerned Basil, then he saw them: a long line of hulking shapes in the forest beyond the village, slipping through the trees as quietly as thieves. In the lead was a massive figure with a potbelly and spindly legs.

"Ror!" Tavis exclaimed. "He's chasing Lanaxis!"

"And leaving the firbolgs to the storm giants," Basil said. "Look."

Tavis turned his gaze back across the field. Raeyadfourne and his warriors were forming ranks to charge Anastes in mass, completely oblivious to the huge figure rising over the hilltop behind them.

It was Eusebius.

Tavis grabbed his bow and plowed through the snow, shouting and gesturing as he ran. The thundering storm drowned out his voice, and the Meadowhome warriors were too intent on their charge to notice his waving arms. Balls of lightning filled Eusebius's hands. He began to hurl the bolts into firbolg's rear ranks, but they were too determined to notice the attack from behind.

Raeyadfourne himself led the first rank into the fray, flinging his axe into Anastes's midriff. The storm giant bellowed and stumbled, then his great sword came down, reducing the chieftain and three more warriors to a crimson spray.

Behind the firbolg column, Eusebius hurled his last

lightning bolt, then drew his sword and descended the scarp in two strides.

Tavis drew a common arrow from his quiver. He had one more runearrow left, but he could not use it without also detonating the one in Lanaxis's shoulder. He stopped and nocked the shaft.

Eusebius stepped away from the hill and was upon his quarry. Tavis fired his arrow, aiming low so that it would skim the heads of the last two ranks of Meadowhome warriors. A flurry of birds flashed down to intercept the shaft, but the bustle caused several firbolgs to duck and look over their shoulders.

Eusebius's sword came down, slicing through the last rank from one end to the other.

An alarmed cry rose from those who had seen the attack, and the rear ranks slowly wheeled around to face their menace. Munairoe's voice briefly lifted above the clamor, beseeching the aid of the fire spirits. A fountain of molten rock erupted beneath Eusebius, drawing a long and agonized wail.

With his legs still flaming, Eusebius stepped out of the fiery column and swung his mighty sword. Munairoe fell with five warriors at his back. Then Eusebius and Anastes, each as bloody and battered as the other, hacked their way toward one another, hewing firbolgs as though they were harvesting hay.

Tavis nocked another shaft, then heard Basil's heavy breath at his back. The high scout turned to his panting friend and presented the tip of his arrow to the runecaster.

"I need magic!" Tavis said. "Something to keep the birds off!"

"No time . . . for anything powerful." Basil pulled a runebrush from his cloak and traced a quick pattern on the arrowhead.

A tremendous crash shook the field, and Tavis glanced

back to see a shroud of birds settling over Eusebius's fallen body. Anastes stumbled another step forward and brought his sword down, cleaving his comrade's killer down the center. The last three firbolgs, Galgadayle among them, buried their axes in the storm giant's leg. His knee buckled with a loud crackle, then he dropped into the snow with a long, mournful groan.

"Done!" Basil reported.

Tavis brought his bow around and fired. The arrow streaked away, a great plume of red smoke roiling from its tip. The birds dived after the missile and disappeared into the crimson cloud, then emerged on the other side disoriented and hardly able to fly. The shaft reached Anastes unimpeded. He twitched slightly as it planted itself in his ribs, then struck a glancing blow off the heads of Galgadayle's companions. Both firbolgs collapsed with crushed skulls.

Basil yelled an arcane command word, and a spout of green flame shot from Anastes's arrow wound. The storm giant roared in surprise and glanced down to look at the hole.

Galgadayle stepped forward to attack, throwing all his weight into the blow. The seer's axe bit deep, splitting the giant's chest cleanly down the sternum.

As if by instinct, Anastes's hand rose and closed around the seer. A long rasping gurgle sounded from the storm giant's throat, then the howling wind fell silent and the blowing snow settled over the meadow.

Tavis drew his bowstring with no conscious memory of having nocked the arrow between his fingers. It was not the runearrow.

"Stop!" Tavis's voice cracked as though he were lying. He could probably finish the storm giant with a common arrow, but not quickly enough to save Galgadayle. "Let that warrior go!"

Anastes looked at Tavis, his face grave with the

unfathomable weight of his race's ancient remorse. For several moments, they stared at each other more in pity than menace or anger.

Finally, Tavis lowered Mountain Crusher and took the arrow off his bowstring. "The battle is done," Tavis said. "I see no more sense in killing."

"Nor I. What will be will be."

The storm giant lowered his hand and released Galgadayle, then closed his eyes. A warm, wailing wind rose out of the south. The air pulsed with the beat of a hundred thousand wings and the sky dimmed beneath a myriad of feathers.

Anastes gasped, "The matter is entirely out of my hands."

# ❖13❖
## Cuthbert Pass

Brianna cringed as Avner pushed against the loose stone. The young scout sat on the smoke shelf just above the fireplace damper, using his feet to shove the heavy block out of its niche in the chimney wall. He had already scraped the mortar from the joints, but the block moved slowly, grinding against the stones around it and filling the murky chamber with a loud, harsh grating.

"Quietly!" Brianna urged.

"We don't have time to be quiet," Avner retorted. "Whatever Lanaxis is doing, I'll wager it has to do with twilight. He'll be on his way again as soon as dark falls, and us with him if we're still here."

It was late afternoon, the day of the battle between the giant-kin and the storm giants. Brianna had crawled down the chimney into the tower's first-floor chamber, where all manner of weapons had been knocked from their racks and scattered across the floor during the rough journey northward. The room's only outlet, aside from the chimney flue, was a doorway that had once opened into the internal passages of Wynn Keep's thick walls. Now, the portal was covered by a twinkling curtain of purple gloom, as were the sally port, the arrow loops on the second floor, and all of the tower's other exits. Lanaxis had used his magic to draw the dark screens over the openings shortly before twilight, when he had suddenly stopped and set the tower down. Brianna and Avner had no way to look outside and so did not know where their captor was presently. But a minute earlier they had felt the floor shuddering, presumably as the titan walked away.

The grating in the fireplace ceased, and the stone fell free with a muffled clack. A brief rustle sounded in the flue as Avner rearranged himself, then a puff of icy wind rolled out of the fireplace. The young scout stuck his head down beneath the lintel.

"Now's the time, Brianna." As Avner spoke, little black clouds billowed from his soot-packed beard. "I'd say we still have twenty minutes before dark."

Brianna passed Avner a waterskin filled with her milk and a rope they had found in the room's debris. Then she pressed her lips to Kaedlaw's brow and held them there for a long time.

At last, Avner said, "Majesty, I'm not fond of this plan of yours, but if it's going to work, we'd better be on our way."

Brianna nodded, then looked into Kaedlaw's round face. "Good luck, my son. I love you—both of you." With tears in her eyes, she passed the child to Avner, then touched the young scout's soot-covered face. "And arrow's speed to you, my defender. Watch over my child."

"With my life," Avner assured her. "I'll see you at Wind Keep."

"Don't wait. That's not my purpose."

"I know," the young scout replied. "But you'll fool him. Hiatea will help you."

Avner withdrew onto the smoke shelf, pulling Kaedlaw out of the queen's sight.

Brianna tried to stop crying for a moment, then gave

up and went to the side of the fireplace. She removed a rock from the mouth of a tin ewer and thrust her hand inside, grabbing a terrified rat Avner had caught for her. The rodent tried to bite her and squirm free as she pulled it from the pitcher, but the queen had it by the back of the neck. It was helpless in her grasp. She removed Hiatea's amulet from her neck and took a tress of Kaedlaw's coarse hair from her pocket, then pressed them both to the creature's chest.

"Valorous Hiatea, take mercy on your humble servant," Brianna beseeched. "Grant this lowly creature the aspect of my beloved son, that mad Lanaxis may have a prince worthy of his mad plans."

The tip of the silver spear glowed red and the flames began to dance, singeing the fur from the helpless rat's chest. The creature let out a shrill squeal and writhed wildly, but Brianna's grasp remained secure. She uttered the mystic syllables of her spell. The rodent grew calm, tranquilized by the goddess's magic. A flickering yellow fire spread over the beast's body, burning away the fur and revealing skin as pink and tender as a baby's.

The rat began to grow, its narrow face broadening into the round, double-chinned visage of her son. The muzzle receded to form Kaedlaw's flat, rather swinish nose, the long fangs shrank into a mouthful of snaggled incisors, and the lips grew puffy and as red as blood. As the rodent's size increased, its body softened and thickened. Its claws retracted to become toenails and fingernails, its gaunt limbs changed into an infant's chubby arms and legs, and almost before she knew it, the struggling creature in her arms appeared to be her son. Only the eyes gave away the truth; the black pupils were almost as large as the irises, and so full of fear that the queen felt sorry for the confused beast.

Brianna swaddled her decoy in a pair of woolen cloaks, wrapping him tightly so that he could not squirm, then crawled into the fireplace. The breeze hissing down the flue smelled of spruce and pine, and its frigid bite felt good against her skin. The queen pushed her shoulders through the damper throat, and a pale, wintry light shone through a square hole in the back of the chimney. She laid the rat-child on the smoke shelf and hoisted herself up, then retrieved him and sat down, pushing her feet through the opening. A mountain stream outside gurgled softly under its ice, and trees rustled in the wind, but she heard no sound to suggest that the titan waited nearby. Clutching her burden to her chest, she squirmed through the passage and dropped into the cold snow.

Brianna found herself next to a moonlit ribbon of ice that snaked its way through a broad, round-bottomed canyon. A blanket of gangly conifers covered the valley bed, but the forest grew steadily thinner as it crept up the steep walls of the dale. A short distance downstream, the frozen creek abruptly became an icefall and dropped away into nothingness, with only sky and the distant Baronies of Wind beyond. The queen saw no sign of the rope Avner had taken, which was good. It meant he had already reached the bottom of the waterfall and retrieved his rappelling line. By now, he would be well on his way toward the canyon mouth and the shelter of Wind Keep.

Brianna turned to inspect her own route. The flat expanse of a snow-covered tarn lay fifty paces upstream. Beyond the frozen lake, the dale's craggy headwall rose a thousand feet to the narrow saddle of Cuthbert Pass, where the slender silhouette of Gap Tower was barely visibly in the afternoon light. At its crown flickered the orange speck of a signal fire, a sure sign that the garrison had observed Lanaxis's approach. The queen saw no sign of the titan himself.

Brianna clutched the rat-child close to her breast and started up the canyon.

\* \* \* \* \*

On the last sun-tipped peak I stand, the savage winds whistling across the ashen sky, cold twilight flooding the purple valleys below. In the distant west, a golden crescent sinks behind endless ranks of sawtooth mountains, shooting effulgent rays across the heavens to stab, like daggers, far, far into my wounds.

There was a time when warmth and light caused me no pain, and well do I remember it. Thinking of those days does me no good now, yet I will stay longer—in memory of what once was, and to honor what will come again.

She will run; of course she will. I could lodge the tower in the granite heart of this mountain, and still Brianna would run. The queen is, after all, a daughter of Hartkiller's line, and it will take time to tame her. She must learn for herself the futility of defiance; only then can she embrace the glory of what she has spawned.

I have grown old today, immeasurably ancient and more feeble than I would admit. Perhaps my strength will return with the darkness, or perhaps the ebbing light will leave me even weaker. I do not know; how could I? This is the first sunset I have seen in three thousand years. Perhaps nothing will happen, perhaps I will shrivel into a withered husk, vulnerable to even a mortal's dagger; it will be safer to find the answer alone.

So I wait, if not enjoying the feel of the sun on my face, then at least savoring the memory of a forgotten joy. I watch the yellow beams as they trickle between the teeth of the distant mountains. One-by-one, the golden rays sink away. Twilight rises higher in the valleys, and the last bead of golden sunlight settles below the jagged horizon. A familiar dullness laps at my feet, like the frigid waters of a sea too salty to freeze, and the pain fades from my crippled heel. A blush of evening gloom creeps over my legs, rich and deep as the last moment of dusk, and beneath this cold murk my shriveled skin grows supple and young again. As the purple tide rises higher, it laves the aches from my bones; the arrow floats from my shoulder, the iron quarrel sinks from my eye, and the strength flows back into my body. I am well again. I am Lanaxis the Chosen One, the Titan of Twilight.

A cold, tingling energy seeps into my body. I step forward into the purple gloom, with aught but a thousand feet of frigid void below, and stretch my hands to my sides. I plummet a hundred feet through the darkness, and shadowy layers of feathers sprout along my arms. I fall another hundred feet, and an umbral tail fans at the base of my spine. My legs become a pair of sticklike silhouettes, my toes the talons of a great raptor. Two hundred feet more, and my lips stretch into a hooked beak. The winds swell beneath me. My umbral wings beat the air, and I rise into the night. I feel as light as a cloud.

At last, the shadowroc is free! I climb higher and soar as I have only dreamed of soaring. The mountains below become dark ruffles of stone streaked by the creamy, writhing snakes of moonlit glaciers. Baronies and fiefs pass like clouds beneath my breast, and the stars above twinkle and wink at me, beckoning. If I had time, I could fly to them, but already the sun has sunk too far below the horizon. Purple twilight is fast yielding to night, and with its dying light shall go my umbral wings.

I wheel and dive. All the northlands spread beneath me, from the sparkling sands of the desert Anauroch to the Coldwood's black tangle. I sail over valley after valley, crossing aretes and ridges and whole lines of mountains, until I spy a fleck of orange light flickering in the saddle of Cuthbert Pass: the signal blaze at Gap Tower. I swing toward the flame, wondering what fires they will light this time, and soar up the canyon.

In the forest below, dark shapes glide along the edges of the snowy leas and slip quick from the shadow of one tree to the next. They are hulking, disfigured masses, but they move with a slow, silent grace that belies their brutal temper. The fomorians have arrived sooner than I thought, but it hardly matters. Already I see the queen's tower listing atop the frozen waterfall.

My eyes, as keen as those of any raptor, spy the queen. She stands halfway up the headwall, her ribs heaving, my nephew bundled in her arms. Brianna watches me soar up the valley, then turns and races along the trail to a nearby cliff. She raises the child above her head, as though she expects me to believe she would actually hurl him to his death.

Now will I tame her. I swing my talons forward and voice my woeful screech. So loud and so shrill is the cry that it blasts the snow from the mountainsides and shakes the canyon with rumbling avalanches.

\* \* \* \* \*

Avner was wondering if the last of the fomorians had passed when the shadowroc's screech broke over the canyon. Even inside his hiding place, a boulder heap near the bottom of an avalanche chute, the cry was the loudest, sharpest noise he had ever heard. It made his ears ache and his head throb, and so he did not immediately hear the rumbling. The stones around him began to tremble; wisps of powdery dust fell past his nose. Then came the roaring: a low, muffled, basal murmur at the base of his skull. No one who had experienced that soft growl would ever forget it.

With Kaedlaw fastened tight to his chest, Avner leapt

from his hiding place and rushed toward the gully wall. He had dug enough victims from avalanches to know that any risk—even being caught by fomorians—was better than being trapped beneath hundreds of tons of snow.

Avner reached the craggy wall in three steps. The cliff was shaking and clattering with the force of the approaching cataclysm. He refused to look toward it; to do so would waste a precious second and petrify him with fear. He grabbed a spear of rock and pulled himself up. Kaedlaw's head banged against the stone, but if the child complained, the scout could not hear it. The avalanche was closer and larger now; the mountain was groaning beneath its fury. The rumble sounded like thunder.

Avner grasped the edge of a massive granite flake. Something cracked in the base of the slab, and it tilted toward the gully. He pulled harder and scrambled up the sheet in two steps. It began to tip faster. The scout stood on top, clutching a rocky spine that ran along the rim of the gulch.

The avalanche arrived with a mighty boom, spraying billowing white clouds high into the air. A wall of loose snow slammed into Avner's side. He swung his legs up, hooking a foot over the gulch rim, then hoisted himself onto a windswept ledge of dry granite. He rolled onto his side, panting and quivering with fear as he stared into the raging white river that had nearly carried him away.

Avner never saw the fomorian who speared him. A sharp blow struck his side, then a huge blade slipped between his ribs. His entire torso erupted with cold fire. Blood filled his mouth, and a deep voice yelled, "I got one, me!"

Avner hooked an arm around the shank of the spear and jerked it toward the gulch, at the same time kicking backward with a heel. His foot slammed into a huge ankle, and he felt the body at the other end of the shaft toppling forward.

"Hey—arrgh!"

The fomorian tripped over Avner's legs and fell into the thundering avalanche, jerking the spear from the scout's body.

A gout of warm blood shot from Avner's mouth, then a strange, gurgling rasp filled his throat. His limbs began to ache terribly, but he was too shocked to realize he was banging them against the ground until the avalanche passed and he heard them clattering against the stones.

Avner forced himself to hold still. Kaedlaw felt warm against his breast, but the cold fire inside his chest was seeping through the rest of his body, down through his bowels into his legs, up through his shoulders into his arms. Blood kept filling his mouth, and he had no more healing potions. He had used the last of those—it couldn't have been only the day before yesterday—in the Silver Gorge. He was going to die.

Damn his luck! He had thought he would do better for the queen's son; at least make it to Wind Keep.

Avner still heard a bellowing voice. The sound was coming from lower down the slope: another enemy. The young scout braced his hands on the mountainside and pushed himself into a seated position. He could see the fomorian now, a pear-shaped shadow down at timberline.

Avner coughed up a mouthful of bright blood, then summoned the courage to look at his wound. It was as big around as his fist, and deeper than he wanted to know. With every breath, a froth of brilliant red blood came bubbling out of the hole. There would be no sewing this wound shut.

Avner pulled his dagger and cut Kaedlaw free, then laid the baby on the lee side of a boulder. The young scout choked on a mouthful of blood, reminded himself to spit, and unbuckled his sword belt.

"There, Awn see him!" yelled a fomorian. "Maybe kid, too!"

Awn was so close that Avner could hear the stones clattering beneath the hunter's feet.

"Give me strength, Hiatea," Avner gasped. "For Kaedlaw."

Without removing his sword from its scabbard, the scout used it to push himself to his feet. Awn was less than twenty paces down the mountainside, his eyes fixed on the ground beneath his feet as he clambered up the ridge. A dozen more misshapened silhouettes were a fair distance below at timberline, and beyond them the forest was swimming with shadows.

Avner glanced at Kaedlaw. "Too many," he gasped. "Just too many."

Leaving Kaedlaw behind, Avner hobbled down the hill to the largest boulder he could find. He shoved the tip of his sword scabbard beneath the uphill side, turning it edge-on so the blade would not snap as he pried at the rock. He let the whole of his weight fall on the pommel. The ridge was steep enough that the stone did not need much encouragement. It tipped forward and went bounding down the slope.

The boulder did not strike Awn, nor did it unleash a landslide, as was Avner's desperate plan. It simply bounced fifty paces down the mountainside, sending a crashing boom across the canyon each time it hit, and sailed into the avalanche gully.

Awn stopped and looked up. "Stop, you!" he said. "Awn hurt you good, him!"

Avner hacked up a mouthful of bright, frothy blood, then staggered over to the next boulder. The fire had left his body, and now he felt only cold. There was such a rushing in his ears that he could barely hear Kaedlaw's growling, and his vision was fast narrowing into a black tunnel. He slipped the tip of his sword under the rock and collapsed over the end.

The stone rolled away. It hopped once, then bounced toward Awn. The malformed warrior cried out, not yelling but whimpering, and the last thing Avner saw were the fomorian's arms rising to catch the bounding boulder.

\* \* \* \* \*

The shadowroc's monstrous talons sank a dozen feet into the mountainside. Again, the gloomy wings beat the air, blowing Brianna and her rat-child against the slope. The enormous bird backed away. His shadowy claws tore huge masses of stone from the trail, leaving the queen trapped between two gaping chasms. He circled off to release his burden, and untold tons of rock and earth plummeted through the frozen surface of the tarn below.

Brianna gathered herself up and raised the decoy over her head, determined not to allow the shadowroc's deafening screech to stun or disorient her again. She ran to the chasm and waited until the immense bird turned back toward her, then raised the rat-child over her head.

That was when the first bellowing giant-kin voices began to reverberate up the canyon. Brianna faltered, worried for Avner and Kaedlaw, and the shadowroc dipped a wing to turn toward the sound. The queen let out a loud, mournful wail to draw the bird's attention, then hurled her burden into the chasm.

The rat-child shrieked in terror, then thumped off the rocks below and fell silent. The shadowroc folded his wings and dived, giving voice to a watery screech that did no more than send a shiver down Brianna's spine. She sank to her knees and buried her face in her hands, wailing in what she hoped would be a convincing imitation of grief.

More bellowing echoed up the canyon, followed by the boom of tumbling boulders. Brianna resisted the temptation to look down the valley. The crashing was caused by giant-kin trying to dig their fellows from the avalanches unleashed by the shadowroc's screech. It had to be.

After his dive, the shadowroc did not pluck Brianna from the trail, did not screech at the loss of his nephew. He remained silent, and the clatter of falling rocks continued to reverberate up the canyon. Finally, the queen opened her hands.

The shadowroc was not in the chasm. In his place stood Lanaxis, once again fully cloaked in robes of purple gloom and holding a blood-soaked mass of pulp and rags in one hand. His damson eyes were turned down the canyon, and Brianna saw no sign of either despair or anger on the profile of his murky face.

The titan tossed aside the rat-child's pulverized body, then turned to Brianna. "Enough of this nonsense," he rumbled. "Your son has need of us."

Lanaxis plucked Brianna from the trail, then descended the slope. It took him less than a dozen strides to pass the tarn and reach the top of the waterfall. Not far down the canyon, dozens of twisted silhouettes were clambering up a ridge, and Brianna heard her son's voice growling in the wind. There were no other sounds: no more clattering boulders or bellowing echoes, no clanging steel, no hint that Avner was anywhere near.

"They have killed your servant."

Brianna let a groan slip past her lips and felt warm tears streaming down her face.

Lanaxis made no move to descend the waterfall. "What do you wish me to do?"

"What?" Brianna gasped. "Can't you save my son?"

The titan nodded. "There is still time. The fomorians have not reached him yet. But I cannot save your son from you. A child needs his mother, or so I have heard."

"Save Kaedlaw!" Brianna ordered. "Kill the fomorians!"

"Then there will be no more of your willfulness?" Lanaxis pronounced. "You accept his destiny?"

Brianna had no idea where her son was, but the fomorians were already well above timberline. Assuming Avner had been trying to circle around them, she doubted the young scout would have climbed much higher than that.

"I want Kaedlaw to live," the queen replied.

"So do I—but it will take both of us to accomplish that," Lanaxis insisted. "There can be no more escape attempts."

Brianna looked toward the distant figures of the climbing fomorians, then swallowed once. "There's no other safe place to go. I am done with escaping."

"Then let it be so."

Lanaxis's words kindled a cold tingle deep within Brianna's core. The sensation seeped up through her stomach and into her heart, and she knew that she was as bound to her word as any firbolg was to his.

Lanaxis muttered a few syllables in the ancient language of his magic, then took a long deep breath and spewed it down the canyon. A howling cloud of purple murk shot from his mouth and billowed over the fomorians, sweeping their disfigured silhouettes off the ridge and hurling them into the ravine beyond. The titan jumped down from the waterfall as easily as a man would leap off a meadow fence. He walked calmly down the valley, his steps booming off the walls, the bedrock cracking beneath his immense weight. He waded through the debris of an avalanche fan and climbed the ridge, sending the warped shadows of a dozen fomorians scuttling back into the thin forest.

Lanaxis set Brianna near Avner's fallen body. "Gather up your son. I will see to our enemies."

The queen had no trouble finding her growling son. He lay on the lee side of a boulder, swaddled in blood-soaked wool. Brianna unwrapped the child and found him cold and hungry, but otherwise uninjured. She bundled him up and turned down the slope.

Lanaxis was standing at timberline, glaring into the trees. As Brianna climbed down to Avner, the titan plucked a spruce out of the ground, then tossed it over the forest. Embers of violet fire danced among the boughs; then the tree burst into amethyst flame and shattered into a thousand blazing splinters. Wherever the slivers fell, geysers of purple fire shot high into the sky. All that lay beneath their light erupted into damson flame.

Holding Kaedlaw beneath her arm, Brianna knelt beside Avner's body. The young scout lay facedown in a pool of frothy blood, with his sheathed sword beneath his body. The tip lay over a hollow where a boulder had once rested.

"No one could have done better, Avner—not even Tavis." Brianna's voice broke as she said the words. The queen touched the young scout's neck, checking for a pulse that was not there. "I wish I could repay your courage, but even Hiatea's magic cannot bring the dead back to life."

\* \* \* \* \*

Avner's spirit lingered with his body long after the titan took the queen and left, until long after his flesh had frozen as solid as the stones it lay upon. He did not stay because duty demanded it—he had never been much for such folly and certainly did not feel bound by it

231

now. Nor did he stay because unfinished business tied him to the world—he had died valiantly, and an honorable death always cuts such fetters.

He stayed for vengeance. The fomorians had started to scream almost as soon as Lanaxis set the forest alight, and the agony in their voices had been music to Avner's dead ears. They had continued to wail all through the night, some of them until long after the last tree had burned. Even now, the dead scout—he had lived more of his life as a thief, really, but he had died as a scout, and he wanted to be remembered that way—even now, with the gray dawn light revealing the charred and barren landscape of the canyon, he could still hear a few of them moaning. Avner would always remember Lanaxis kindly for this favor, at least.

But the dead scout knew that he must soon forsake even this final pleasure. Already, he could feel the pale sunlight scorching his gossamer spirit, burning away the last airy threads by which he clung to his lifeless body. The time was fast approaching when he would have to let go and begin that terrifying journey every spirit makes alone. Avner saw no reason to wait. He loosened his hold, and his ethereal substance started to sink.

Then he heard a familiar voice coming up the ridge. Avner grabbed hold of his body—with what, he was not exactly sure—and held tight.

"Up here!" The voice belonged to Tavis Burdun, the firbolg who had changed him from a thief to a scout. "They came this way!"

"I'm coming Tav—" The speaker suddenly fell silent. Avner recognized this voice as his friend Basil's. "Stronmaus save me! What is that there?"

"Avner."

A pair of large, hot hands—they felt as fiery as forge irons—slipped between the young scout and his body, then lifted the remains off the ground. Avner struggled to stay, but there was nothing for him to hold to and he began to sink.

"Now will you listen to me?" Though Basil was screaming, his voice was fading fast. "Now will you use Sky Cleaver?"

Avner did not hear the answer, for he had already settled into the emptiness between the stones.

# ✦14✦
## Split Mountain

Tavis skirted a monolith the size of a castle tower, then clambered up another as large as an entire keep. He and Galgadayle were following Basil through the swarthy depths of Annam's Hallway, an icy gorge running straight as a lance through the heart of Split Mountain. A thousand feet of jumbled talus boulders, some as enormous as hills, covered the canyon's floor. Its sheer granite walls soared more than a mile upward, narrowing into a pair of jagged, needle-tipped peaks that could have been mirror-images of each other. According to Basil, Annam the All Father had created the chasm a hundred centuries earlier, when, exasperated with Othea's faithlessness, he had hurled Sky Cleaver into the mountain.

The runecaster stopped atop a monolith, then slipped his divining rod from his belt and held it before him. The glowing tip bent downward at nearly a right angle.

"We've found it!"

"Not so loud!" Tavis urged. Though Orisino and the verbeegs still trailed a hundred paces behind, the high scout did not want his friend's elated voice to carry to their ears. The last thing he needed was to let Orisino hear about Sky Cleaver. Tavis stopped next to Basil. "Put your rod away."

On the other side of the monolith, a boulder-lined pit corkscrewed a hundred feet down into the talus stones. The deep-worn channel of an ancient trail spiraled along the shaft's jagged walls, jumping from one listing monolith to another like some sort of cockeyed fomorian staircase. At the bottom of the hole, the track slipped beneath a stone as large as Keep Hartwick and vanished into the crooked maw of a dark, yawning grotto.

"I thought Sky Cleaver was a lost weapon," Tavis said. Although he still felt the cold, the scout was well-enough rested that it no longer made him stutter. "How come it has a guardian? Lost weapons don't have guardians."

Basil shrugged. "The stone giant histories don't describe any guardians."

Tavis gave the runecaster a sidelong glance. "Have you read *anywhere* that the axe is guarded?" he asked. "Saying yes won't stop me from trying."

Basil met his gaze squarely. "I've told you all I know." The runecaster showed no irritation at Tavis's mistrust. "This is for Avner. I wouldn't hold back."

Tavis accepted the reassurance with a nod. Avner had been half grandson, half accomplice to Basil. The runecaster would never lie on the youth's name.

"Well, *someone* lives down there," Tavis said.

"And he must be as old as the mountains," added Galgadayle. Though it had been two days since the storm giant battle, the seer remained hunched over in pain. Despite the death of his own shaman, he refused to allow Orisino's healer to mend his cracked ribs. "To wear a trail that deep into solid granite must have taken ten centuries."

"At least ten centuries, but the path was not made by a single walker," Tavis said. "The steps are too erratic. Everything from verbeegs to cloud giants has lived down there."

Galgadayle raised a brow. "Then the axe can't be here. Someone would have claimed it by now."

"If they knew how to free it—which isn't possible," said Basil. "It took *me* three years and two new languages to learn the secret, and even I wouldn't have succeeded without the library at Castle Hartwick."

"That still doesn't explain the trail," Tavis said. "If whoever's down there can't retrieve the axe, why do they stay here?"

"Because a mortal doesn't possess a weapon of the gods," Galgadayle answered. "It possesses him. This is a bad idea, my friends. By recovering Sky Cleaver, we may do more harm than letting the titan keep the queen and her child."

"I'm still going after it." Tavis spoke softly, for he heard Orisino and the verbeegs clattering toward their location. "It's the only way I can kill Lanaxis."

"And after the titan is dead? What will you do then?" Galgadayle also spoke more quietly. "If you lack the strength to slay Brianna's child, you have only unleashed two scourges on the world."

"Perhaps not," Basil countered. "The titan's death will certainly alter Kaedlaw's future."

"You cannot change a person's destiny," Galgadayle warned. "You can only kill him before he fulfills it."

"If you're right, we'll know soon enough," Basil said. "Sky Cleaver can cut to the heart of the matter. After that, Tavis will do the right thing."

"Assuming he can recognize it," Galgadayle replied. "Sky Cleaver's power will be a bright and shining thing. Even Tavis's eyes may be dazzled by the glare."

"Then you and Basil will help me see." Tavis glanced over his shoulder at the approaching verbeegs. "And now we will discuss the matter no more."

The three companions turned to await the exhausted verbeegs, who were laboriously pushing and pulling each other over the massive talus boulders. Only twenty-five of their number had survived the battle with the storm giants, and many of those suffered from wounds their shaman had not yet healed. Still, with the fomorians strewn in ashes over Cuthbert Pass and the firbolgs annihilated, even two dozen warriors were sufficient to give Orisino command of the war party. Tavis had tried to win back control by waiting for the two companies of royal footmen trailing them since the storm giant battle, but the crafty verbeeg chieftain had ordered his followers to keep moving, objecting that humans would only slow the company down.

Leaving his warriors to assemble at the bottom of the monolith, Orisino climbed to Tavis's side. "What's . . . this?" he panted, peering into the pit. "The Twilight Vale?"

"Does that hole look titan-sized to you?" Basil scoffed. "But it might be a shortcut through the talus field. Tavis will see, then come back for us."

Orisino's eyes flashed with suspicion. "Why don't we all go together?"

Basil gestured at the pit. "Look at those steps. If the passage happens to be full of giants, or it's a den instead of a shortcut, we'll save a lot of trouble by letting Tavis scout ahead."

Orisino considered the explanation, then said, "It sounds reasonable, but I want Tavis to say it."

"I don't have anything to add," the high scout replied.

"All the more reason to hear it from your mouth," Orisino insisted. At the base of the boulder, his huffing warriors were straining to hear the conversation. "Tell me this is a shortcut."

"I don't know that it is," Tavis replied. "But if it's full of giants, we all have a better chance of reaching the gorge's far end if I'm alone."

Orisino narrowed his eyes. "I don't know who you

hope to fool, but it won't be me! You're not going alone."

"Fine," said Basil. "You go with him. The rest of us will wait here until you two return."

Tavis shot the runecaster an angry glance. "He'll be in the way!"

"Perhaps, but Orisino's suspicion is understandable," said Galgadayle. "Take him along. It's the only way to assure him you aren't trying to desert us."

"The two of you will make less noise than the entire war party." Basil glanced at the exhausted verbeegs gathered below. "And I'm ready to collapse as it is. The last thing I want is to follow you into some cavern, then find we've wasted our effort and retrace our steps."

This brought a hearty murmur of agreement from the verbeegs, and even Orisino looked as though he were having second thoughts.

Tavis turned to Orisino. "You'd better keep those flat feet of yours quiet," he growled. "And I won't wait for you."

"You won't have to," Orisino sneered. "You're not so strong anymore—or have you forgotten the price you paid for Munairoe's healing?"

"I've strength enough to take care of myself," Tavis replied. "It's you I can't defend."

"I never thought you'd bother," replied Orisino. "I certainly wouldn't for you."

Orisino went off to gather a few things to eat and a torch to light his way. Tavis simply asked Basil to paint a rune of light on the blade his dagger. While he waited for his friend to finish, the high scout peered into the shaft, studying the spiraling trail and its awkward steps. It did not take him long to decide that it would be safer, and faster, not to trust the cockeyed staircase. He removed a short length of white rope from his satchel and dangled it over the shaft.

"suordnowsilisaB."

A silver spider climbed from the cord's end and dropped into the pit, trailing a single filament of white silk. The strand began to sparkle and grow steadily larger in diameter, becoming as thick and sturdy as any rope. Tavis waited until he could see several feet of line lying loose on the shaft floor, then looped his end of the cord around a small boulder and tied it off with a secure anchoring knot.

Without waiting for Orisino to return, the high scout straddled the rope. He wrapped it around one hip and over the opposite shoulder, running the line parallel to his bow. He sat over the edge of the pit and rappelled down with slow, easy strides. As he touched bottom, the sweet, stale odor of old age wafted from the cavern mouth behind him. He kept a careful watch over his shoulder, but the grotto itself remained as silent and still as a crypt.

Tavis untangled himself, then took a few minutes to examine the area. The floor was covered with six inches of glassy ice, so clear that he could see a pair of yard-long bootprints frozen in the mud underneath. The tracks had been old and weatherworn even before freezing. They revealed little now, save that the giant who had left them was not very large and seldom left the grotto. There was no sign that anyone else lived in the cave, and that troubled the high scout. Only ettins were solitary by nature, and the two-headed giants seldom viewed visitors as anything but a convenient meal.

A loud rattle sounded from the rim of the pit, then Galgadayle cried out, "Watch yourself!"

Tavis looked up, expecting to find a stone plummeting toward him. Instead, he saw several stones. Close behind came Orisino's gangly figure, bouncing down the wall in great, barely controlled arcs. The verbeeg was clearly an inexperienced mountaineer. In addition to wrapping himself into the rappelling line backward, he was trying to slow himself by squeezing the rope with his guide hand, while his braking hand clutched at the cliff in a frantic effort to keep himself upright.

Tavis retreated into the cavern, then grimaced as first the stones, then the verbeeg crashed to the bottom of the icy pit.

"So much for being quiet!"

"Karontor take this rope!" Orisino sat up and hurled the tangled line at the wall. "It did nothing to stop me from falling!"

"It did too much," Tavis retorted. "If it hadn't slowed you down, I wouldn't need to worry about all the witless things you're bound to do inside the cavern."

Without waiting to see if Orisino could hoist his battered frame off the ice, Tavis drew his glowing dagger and started into the cave.

The place was a confusing web of dark, jagged voids that shot off in all directions, with the sharp corners and broken edges of huge talus boulders jutting into the passages from every angle. In the distance, curtains of wayward sunbeams hung across the skewed corridors, like gray tapestries concealing the private halls of some madman's castle. If not for the deep grooves of the ancient giant trail, the high scout would have been as lost as a child in a fen. Within the area lit by his glowing dagger alone, he saw at least fifty corridors, and off each of those there would be fifty more.

Unlike true caverns, whose depths were kept above freezing by the mountain's warm heart, this jumbled maze of angles and corners was as frigid as a glacial crevasse. The cold air seeped down from above like drizzle down a chimney, riming the granite with hoarfrost and leaving the listing, sloping path as slick and treacherous as a ribbon of frozen stream. Tavis moved slowly and carefully, leaving his sword sheathed and Mountain Crusher on his shoulder, never taking a step without first finding a secure hold for his free hand. In this tangle of monoliths, any fall could be a fatal one, shooting the victim down the jagged mouth of an impossibly deep pit, or lodging him forever between a pair of granite boulders.

Orisino came up behind the high scout, clattering and groaning as he struggled to maintain his footing on the icy trail. The verbeeg had not bothered to light his torch, which left him both hands to maintain his balance. This was just as well. If the verbeeg happened to fall and injure himself, Tavis would feel compelled to offer help. Until the chieftain actually violated their agreement, the law demanded that he be treated as an ally, and allies did not leave wounded comrades to die in cold caverns.

"Be quiet, fool," Tavis growled. "The giant will hear you coming a thousand paces away."

"It hardly—ahhhh!" Orisino clutched Tavis's arm, nearly falling and sending them both off the edge of a monolith. The verbeeg regained his balance, then said, "We can't use this shortcut. We'd lose half our warriors on this ice."

Tavis disengaged himself from the chieftain's grasp. "You go back if you want. The trail may dry out up ahead."

"Dry out? This whole place is one . . . big . . ." Orisino let his sentence trail off, then his voice grew sly. "What are you looking for? It's no shortcut."

The high scout did not reply. He continued forward, finally stopping at the head of a steep chute where one boulder stood against another. The corner between their two faces formed a long, angular ravine that descended into inky darkness beyond Tavis's light. Some ancient giant had cut a series of huge, zigzagging stairs down the trough, but the frost-rimed treads were spaced at eight-foot intervals. Anyone as small as Tavis or Orisino would have to jump from one icy platform to the next.

The only alternative was to climb down the center, using the seam between the monoliths for fingerholds. If either of the 'kin slipped, there was no telling how far they would fall.

"We'd better get our rope," Orisino suggested.

Tavis did not bother to remind the chieftain of the line's true ownership. Verbeegs considered private property an uncivilized and archaic concept, claiming instead that all things belonged to all people.

"If you want my rope, you fetch it," Tavis said.

"And I suppose you'll wait here until I return?" the verbeeg scoffed. "You go down first. I'll watch how you do it."

The wily chieftain was proving more difficult to scare off than Tavis had expected. The high scout sighed in exasperation. "If I don't want you falling on me, I'd better teach you how to do this."

Tavis passed his glowing dagger to the verbeeg, then removed his gloves and demonstrated how a person could support himself by jamming his fist into a narrow crack, such as that between the two boulders. Though the concept was simple, the art itself was full of nuances. Depending upon the width of the seam and the climber's position, the fingers had to be folded into all manner of different configurations to lock the hand securely in place. Orisino paid careful attention, and was quickly able to run through the standard positions.

"You can twist your boots against the sides of the seam to wedge them in place, but don't trust any footholds on the walls themselves," Tavis cautioned. "The stone is too slick. Stay in the crack and you won't have trouble."

The high scout retrieved his glowing dagger and slipped the handle between his teeth, then lay on his belly and swung his legs over the chute. He wedged a foot into the crack and climbed down a short distance to wait for Orisino. The verbeeg reluctantly dangled his toes over the edge, kicking blindly at the crevice and grunting in frustration. For a time, Tavis thought his unwelcome companion would turn back, but the chieftain finally locked a boot into the crack and started to creep downward. After that, it did not take long for the verbeeg to gain his confidence, and soon the two 'kin were moving at a steady pace.

The stones grew colder as they descended. After a few minutes, Tavis's bare hands felt so numb that he had difficulty feeling his handholds. It was impossible to tell how far they had come, or how far they still had to go. There was nothing but darkness below, with shadowy boulders and jagged, murk-filled passages advancing on them from all sides. In the bewildering array of gray corners and gloomy hollows, only the faithful tug of gravity prevented Tavis from losing his bearings and becoming completely disoriented.

A startled shriek broke from Orisino's mouth and skipped through the crooked labyrinth in all directions, nearly concealing the clatter of the chieftain's boots slipping free of their holds. Tavis pulled himself tight against the rock and twisted his hands and feet into the crack, locking himself in place. He gritted his teeth against the coming impact and silently cursed his companion's clumsiness. Despite the frosty walls, the chute was no more difficult to descend than a ladder; as long as a climber kept a hand and foot lodged in the crevice at all times, falling was next to impossible.

Orisino did not land on him.

"Tavis, did you feel that?" The verbeeg's voice was shrill with panic.

Tavis looked up and saw his companion dangling by a single arm, the soles of his hobnailed boots scant inches away. The chieftain was looking over his shoulder into a lopsided triangle of empty air.

The high scout freed one hand to take the dagger from his mouth. "The only thing I felt was you—almost knocking us *both* to our deaths. What's wrong?"

Orisino gestured at the dark triangle. "Something pushed me! I felt a gust of warm air—a giant's breath, maybe—then something big reached out of there and tried to push me off!"

Tavis raised his glowing dagger, illuminating the mouth of the dark passage Orisino had indicated. The high scout could not see far, but it was readily apparent that while a giant's arm might squeeze through the hole, not even a verbeeg could actually crawl into it.

"I don't see anything now," the high scout said. "Maybe it was a bat."

"It pushed me, like a hand!" Orisino insisted. "I'm not imagining this."

"I didn't say you were," Tavis replied. "But we can't do much about it now."

The high scout returned his dagger handle to his mouth and continued downward. Orisino kicked his feet back into the crevice, then drew his own knife and followed. Their descent slowed significantly. Not only did the verbeeg insist upon keeping one hand free to hold his weapon, he spent more time peering into dark crannies than he did searching for handholds. Even then, he continued to cry out at random intervals, claiming that he smelled a foul odor or felt a gust of hot breath. Tavis never shared any of these sensations, nor did he hear the slightest clatter or flutter to suggest something was stalking them.

The high scout had finally decided his companion was imagining things when a sharp crack sounded above. A loud, clattering rumble reverberated down the chute, and the walls shuddered beneath the power of a tumbling boulder. Tavis pulled the dagger from his mouth and held it out over the trough, illuminating a pair of frost-rimed steps on the walls below.

"Jump!"

Knowing Orisino would leap for the closest step, the high scout jumped toward the one on the opposite wall. With the rumble reverberating ever louder in his ears, he dropped through eight feet of darkness and hit above the stair he wanted to reach. He turned his face toward the stone, scratching at the cold granite with his dagger and numb fingers.

A crack sounded from the center of the chute. The gray blur of a boulder bounced past his shoulder, with Orisino's shrieking figure sliding down the trough close behind.

The stone vanished beneath the high scout's face and chest, then he slammed onto the front half of the stair he had tried to reach. He flailed at the icy shelf with both hands.

A tremendous crash reverberated in the bottom of the chute.

Tavis's glowing dagger caught in a crack and brought his fall to an abrupt halt. He glimpsed the blade bending under the sudden strain, then a sharp *ping* echoed through the cavern. Basil's light rune abruptly faded, and the scout slipped.

Tavis released the hilt and grabbed for the broken blade. He felt a strange, painless sensation as the edge sliced into his numb palm, but he stopped sliding. He slipped the fingers of his free hand into the same crack where the blade had caught, then pulled himself onto the step.

A booming voice, deep but wavering with age, echoed down the chute. "You 'live, stupid thieves?"

Tavis did not respond, nor did Orisino—whether due to wisdom or injury, the high scout did not know.

"Answer Snad, stupid thieves!" quavered the giant. "You dead, or what?"

The dull-witted questions and low, booming voice left little doubt that Snad was a hill giant—but he was hardly an ordinary one. Though hill giants were clumsy and no more able to see in the dark than firbolgs, there had not been so much as a rustle or a glimmer of torchlight as this one slipped into place for his ambush.

" 'Kay, stupid thieves! Snad comin' down," the giant warned. "Better be dead when he gets there!"

Tavis cupped a hand to his ear and craned his neck to look up the chute. There was not the slightest rustle, nor the faintest gleam of light. For all the high scout could tell, Snad was a mere voice in the dark—a resentful voice.

Tavis crawled to the edge of his step, then lay on his belly and stretched his bleeding hand along the face of the dark granite. He barely managed to reach the center of the chute and slip three cold fingertips into the narrow crevice. The high scout pulled himself toward the opposite wall, at once swinging his legs off the stair and reaching for the fissure with his good hand.

The soles of his boots landed on the far side of the trough, slipped on the hoarfrost, and shot out from beneath him. Tavis started down the chute, then caught the crevice with his second hand and jammed a fist inside. The craggy stone scraped away long ribbons of skin, driving the numbness from his flesh, but the hand held. He brought himself to a halt.

Tavis resumed his descent, moving as quickly as he dared in the darkness. He had no idea whether Snad was descending the chute above or coming via another passage, but he suspected it would not be long before the hill giant arrived. Before then, the high scout wanted to have Orisino's torch lit and be well down the trail.

A dozen steps later, the sole of Tavis's boot came down on the jagged corner of a small boulder. He lowered himself onto the rock, then slipped down its side to something that felt like a jumbled platform of firewood. With a series of brittle cracks, his weight settled onto the sticks.

The sharp point of a sword poked Tavis in the short ribs. The scout leaned away from the tip and thrust a leg out, aiming a rear stomping kick just below the weapon. His boot sank into something soft. The breath left his attacker's lungs with a muffled *whumpf*, then a 'kin-sized body slammed into a monolith and slumped to the floor. A series of receding clangs echoed through the cavern as the ambusher's weapon skittered down an unseen slope.

Orisino simultaneously groaned and wheezed for breath. "Tavis . . . why'd . . . you do that?"

"Why did you stick a sword in my back?"

"I didn't mean . . . any harm." Aside from his lack of wind, Orisino sounded healthy enough. "I thought you were the giant."

"He'll be here soon enough," Tavis replied. "Give me your torch."

When Tavis reached down, the verbeeg grabbed the proffered hand and used it to pull himself up. "I don't think a torch is smart. It'll lead the giant straight to us."

"He'll find us anyway." Tavis reached around the verbeeg and pulled the torch from his belt. "Until he does, we need to see where we're going."

Tavis removed his tinderbox from his satchel and knelt on the floor, spreading a mound of tinder before him. He found his flint and steel and fumbled with them until his numb fingers struck a fire. As the flames flickered to life, the high scout was surprised to see that the floor was covered not by sticks, but by a yellow tangle of bones.

"It appears we're not Snad's first victims," Orisino said.

"We're not victims yet."

Tavis touched the torch to the tinder, which was already burning out, and blew gently on the flames until the oil-soaked head caught fire. The brand's broader circle of light revealed thousands of bones. A few were fresh enough to have bits of withered hide clinging to their surfaces, but most were naked and almost petrified with age. A few were so gray and soft that they would powder at the slightest touch. They came in all sizes and shapes, from tibias no thicker than arrows to ribs as long as the floor planks of Keep Hartwick. Giants and 'kin were represented in equal proportions among the skulls scattered through the tangle, as were humans, elves, and other small races.

Tavis led them away from the bones, following the well-worn trail along a contorted route of corners and doglegs that took them ever downward. They heard no more of Snad until his splintered voice echoed through the stones above their heads.

"Snad the One! Not you, stupid thieves!" The giant's voice sounded more imploring than angry. "Come back now, or Snad—"

The rest was too garbled to make out.

"The giant's moving!" Orisino whispered.

"True, but at least he seems to be behind us." Tavis passed the torch to Orisino, then pulled Mountain Crusher off his shoulder. "Assuming you'll lead for a while, I'll be ready when he catches up."

Orisino looked dubious, but turned down the path. Tavis kept pace easily, even with his bow in hand, and stopped often to study the murky passages around them. Once a warm draft wafted out of a side passage. The high scout fired an arrow into the breeze on the off chance Snad had caused it; the shaft clattered against an unseen rock. Their pursuer remained a mere voice in the dark.

They continued to descend, slipping and sliding over

the frosty stones, until at last they traversed the face of a long monolith and came to a fork in the trail. One route turned sharply to the right, while the other zigzagged down a small shaft. The ruts descending the shaft looked about twice as deep as those in the horizontal passage.

Orisino passed the torch to Tavis and sat on the edge of the pit. "I'm going to need both hands for this climb." He glanced at the scout, then added, "That is, unless you're so mad that you really are looking for a shortcut."

When Tavis did not reply, a crafty smile crossed Orisino's lips. "I thought as much."

The chieftain climbed down to the limit of the torch-light, where he sat upon a huge, well-worn step to wait for Tavis. The high scout dropped the brand to the ver-beeg, then slipped his bow over his shoulder and climbed down to the same place. They had to repeat the process only twice more before Orisino reached the bottom of the shaft.

"I think we're almost there." The verbeeg turned to peer down a dark, diamond-shaped passage. "The floor in there is solid bedrock, and I can see—"

A large stone flew out of the side passage and struck a glancing blow off Orisino's brow. The chieftain's head snapped back, flinging blood across the walls, and he collapsed in a crumpled heap. His eyes remained open and vacant, focused somewhere in the darkness high above Tavis's head.

"Snad warn stupid thief!" rumbled the giant's quaver-ing voice. "Snad the One!"

Tavis dropped the torch into the pit, then descended to a ledge above the diamond-shaped passage. He pulled Mountain Crusher from his shoulder and started to nock his last runearrow, then thought better and selected a normal one. He had killed plenty of hill giants with regular arrows, and it would be wiser to save his magic for a more desperate situation.

"Go back, stupid firbolg thief!" cried Snad. "Snad keeper of Great Axe, not Tavis Burdun!"

"How do you know my name?" Tavis slipped out of his cloak.

"Snad know," Snad replied. "Axe have Snad."

Tavis raised his brow at the choice of words, then nocked his arrow. He tossed his dark cloak into the pit.

A large rock sailed out of the passage. The stone caught the cape in midair and carried it across the shaft, where it bounced off the wall and came down on Orisino's arm. The verbeeg's fingers flinched, but Tavis had no time to consider what that meant. He dropped onto the pit floor with his bowstring drawn and his arrow pointed into the diamond-shaped tunnel.

Tavis could not quite grasp what he saw. At the end of the corridor, the darkness changed from soot-black to a silvery hue that was neither glow nor gloom. Standing before this strange ether was the shadowy skeleton of a hill giant. It was as though Tavis and Orisino had descended through the talus boulders into the realm of the dead.

"Stupid tricks not fool Snad!"

The dark skeleton twisted toward the wall, stretching his arms out to grab another stone. Tavis drew Mountain Crusher and aimed at Snad's midsection. Normally, he would have tried for the heart, but he doubted that strategy would kill a skeleton. His only chance of a swift victory was to shatter the spine.

Snad pulled his boulder from the wall. Tavis forced himself to wait, struggling to keep his arms from trembling. Once, he could hold a true aim and a taut bow for minutes, but now he was too weak for that. As Munairoe had warned, his strength was failing.

The skeleton turned, exposing the dark line of his spine. Tavis let the arrow fly, but he could feel by his trembling hands that his aim was not true. He stepped away from the passage mouth, already reaching for his last runearrow—then Snad bellowed. A muffled bang echoed down the corridor as the giant dropped his boulder.

Tavis peered around the corner, half-expecting to be knocked as senseless as Orisino. Instead, he saw his foe turning away, hunched over and holding the bones of one hand to his midsection. The arrow hung in the emptiness where Snad's stomach should have been, a foot short of the spine.

Tavis's jaw fell. He was looking not at a living skeleton, but at the skeleton inside a living giant.

He traded his runearrow for a normal one, then nocked and fired again. The shaft caught its target between the shoulder blades. Snad roared and tumbled into the room beyond. If his body crashed to the ground, there were no shuddering stones or thunderous booms to betray that fact. The giant simply dropped into the eerie gray murk and vanished.

A pair of flat feet slapped the shaft floor behind Tavis. He spun and saw Orisino already upon him. The verbeeg's eyes were mad with battle lust, and he held the torch in his upraised hand. Tavis brought his bow up to block, at the same time reaching for his sword.

Orisino brushed past without attacking. "What's wrong with you?" he shouted, racing down the corridor. "Hurry up, or we'll be on the wrong end of our axe!"

The scout started down the passage, feeling rather foolish. From the verbeeg's perspective, there was no reason to argue over the axe. After they recovered it, the weapon would belong to him as much as it did to Tavis.

A loud wail broke from the far end of the passage, then a fierce gale tore through the narrow corridor, extinguishing Orisino's torch and hurling him back into Tavis. Both 'kin lost their footing and went tumbling down the corridor, bouncing from one jagged wall to the other.

Tavis covered his head with his free hand and used the other to keep a firm grasp on his bow. He lost contact with Orisino, then his arm was nearly jerked from its socket as Mountain Crusher caught on something. He held fast and dragged himself out of the scouring wind into a small cranny alongside the passage.

"Tavis?" Orisino's voice was barely audible over the wind, but it came from someplace ahead. "What's happening?"

Tavis cupped his hands to his mouth. "The axe's magic!" Basil had said the weapon could control weather. "Are you hurt?"

"Can't understand you," came the reply. "Come forward."

Though Tavis had long ago learned the wisdom of pushing his arrows into a cork pad fastened in his quiver, he took the precaution of checking his supply. He had lost half-a-dozen shafts, but the runearrow remained in place. The high scout pushed it deeper into the cork, then squirmed into the passage and crawled. He stayed flat on his belly and kept his eyes pinched shut against the blowing ice and sand. Every now and then he risked raising his head to peer forward, and eventually he found himself a mere arm's length from the strange pearly hue at the end of the passage.

Though Tavis could see only the top half of the chamber, it looked as vast as a castle bailey. The ceiling was formed by the haphazard vaulting of a dozen huge monoliths, which had fallen together like the steepled fingers of two gnarled hands. Ribbons of snow and ice were whistling around the room and whirling down upon him with bone-battering force.

"Orisino?" Tavis could not tell whether the verbeeg was waiting at the tunnel mouth, for the interior of the passage remained black as soot to the very edge of the vast chamber. "Are you here?"

The wind was roaring so loudly that Tavis barely heard his own voice. He repeated the question, then finally crawled to the brink of the gray room.

Ahead lay a craggy funnel littered with the petrified bones and abandoned possessions of hundreds—if not thousands—of dead giants and 'kin. Upon every ledge lay heaps of frost-rimed armor and curving spines; from every rock spur dangled rotting haversacks and yellowing pelvises; against every crag leaned tarnished shields and smirking skulls. At the heart of this gruesome mess, in a small space kept meticulously clear of clutter, stood Snad's skeletal form.

In the light of the chamber, it became apparent that the giant's flesh had not fallen away. Rather, it had grown almost transparent. Tavis could see the heads of his two arrows lodged deep inside his foe's torso, yet he could also make out the ghostlike contours of an ancient and withered face. Snad looked to be at least four hundred years old.

The giant was touching the heft of an enormous hand axe whose blade was buried deep in a granite cleft. The eight-foot handle angled up from the floor at a steep incline, so that the pommel hung within easy reach of Snad's long arms. The entire shaft was made of ivory, and wondrously carved with scenes of godly might. The huge head, fashioned from obsidian as black as a mountain's heart, was bound to the handle with golden twine.

A lump of awe formed in Tavis's throat. Without realizing it, he slipped from his hiding place and started down the slope. Even without Basil's description, the scout would have recognized the glorious weapon below as Sky Cleaver, the lost hand axe of Mighty Annam, and he had to have it.

Tavis soon realized he was not the only one who

coveted the axe. Orisino huddled in the bones at the edge of Sky Cleaver's small clearing, and his eyes were fixed on the prize. The verbeeg grabbed a spear from the rubble and began slowly pacing back and forth beyond the hill giant's reach. As the scout approached, he heard the two talking.

"You're being selfish and stingy, Snad," Orisino said. "All I want to do is touch it."

"No! Snad the One, not stupid verbeeg." The hill giant's voice was quavering more than it had been a few moments earlier. Snad shot a scowl up at Tavis, then added, "And not stupid Tavis Burdun, either!"

Orisino cast a jealous glance at Tavis, then slipped away from the safety of his bone pile. "You can't even pull it out of the ground, Snad! Let me try!"

"Snad the One!"

"You're not!" the verbeeg yelled. "You've had centuries to pull it free!"

"Liar!" Snad slipped around to place himself between the axe and Orisino. "Snad only find axe last winter—after he kill old Kwasid."

The name brought Tavis to a halt. Not many years before, he had known a fire giant by that name. But Kwasid had been an athletic young fire dancer—hardly someone that even a dull-witted hill giant would call old.

"And how old are you Snad?" Tavis yelled down.

"Still plenty young to be the One." Snad kept his eye fixed on Orisino. "Fifty summers."

Tavis gasped. At fifty, a hill giant was barely an adult. The high scout began to consider the wisdom of turning back while he still had the strength—then Orisino leapt for the axe's ivory handle.

Tavis's reservations vanished as suddenly as they had appeared. He found his runearrow in his hand, nocked and ready to fire, and in his heart there burned a fierce desire such as he had not known since his wedding night.

Tavis aimed at Orisino's heart.

Snad's ancient foot lashed out and caught the verbeeg in the chest. The chieftain crashed back into the bones from which he had crawled, and Tavis switched targets without thinking. The runearrow caught Snad squarely in the ribs.

"esiwsilisaB!" Tavis yelled.

Nothing happened, except that Snad reached up and snapped the shaft off at the head.

"Stupid firbolg magic can't hurt the One!" Snad chortled. He cast a suspicious glance at Orisino's motionless form, then stepped away from the axe to finish what he had started. "Kill verbeeg dead this time—then kill Tavis Burdun."

"esiwsilisaB!" Tavis repeated.

A resounding crack shook the cavern, then a brilliant blue light flared inside Snad's translucent body and scattered his dark bones in every direction.

The rumble had not even faded before Orisino was on his feet and charging the axe. The ivory hilt was nearly as long as the verbeeg was tall, but that did not stop him from wrapping both arms around the shaft. He braced his feet on the floor and tried to pull it free.

"Come to me!" Orisino cast a nervous glance in Tavis's direction, then stooped beneath the motionless handle and pushed against it with his shoulders. "By Karontor, I shall have you!"

"Wrong god."

Tavis dropped Mountain Crusher and stretched both hands toward the axe. Then, speaking the ancient syllables that Basil had made him repeat a thousand times in the last two days, the high scout called Sky Cleaver to him:

*"In the name of Skoraeus Stonebones, Your Maker, O Sky Cleaver, do I summon you into the service of my*

*hand.*"

With a groan as ancient as Toril itself, the mighty axe pulled its dark blade from the cleft and rose into the air. Orisino leapt up and snatched the ivory handle with both arms. The axe shook him off as a dragon shakes off a mountain lion, then floated into the scout's waiting arms. The weapon stood as tall as its new owner, with a head as big as his chest. It was so heavy that the mere act of swinging it would drain the last ounce of Tavis's strength, but he did not care.

Sky Cleaver belonged to him.

# ❖ 15 ❖
# The Bleak Plain

Tavis sat upon a moonlit drumlin, staring down at the narrow rift as though he could force it open through will alone. The crevice ran northward across the frozen plain for nearly a thousand paces, ending beneath a cloud-scratching wall of ice that could only be the Endless Ice Sea itself. Nowhere along its entire length was the fissure as wide as a dagger blade, yet the titan's trail stopped here at the near end, beneath a lonely, ice-caked inselberg that Basil had dubbed Othea Tor. Somehow, Lanaxis had descended into that narrow cleft, and with him he had taken Brianna.

The high scout would have her back, and it did not matter that a titan had locked her away in a prison of solid bedrock. Tavis was the One Wielder, and he would have whatever he wanted. With Sky Cleaver in his hand, there was no enemy he could not slay, no riddle he could not solve, no evil he could not conquer. He could do whatever he wished, have anything he wanted—anything, that is, except what he needed most: sleep.

Tavis had lost count of the days it had taken to cross this frozen waste, but it had been more nights than that since he had rested. He trembled almost constantly with exhaustion, and he moved about in a waking stupor that would long ago have given way to deep sleep, save for Sky Cleaver. It was not that the axe gave him strength—though perhaps it provided more than he knew—but that Tavis did not dare close his eyes. The verbeegs watched him constantly, their thieving gazes riveted on his weary eyelids, waiting for him to nod off so they could steal his axe. They were watching now, gathered below in the still, cold air, sitting on their haunches and staring at him with the gluttonous patience of vultures.

Tavis knew better than to think he could send them away. They came with Sky Cleaver. They would do anything he commanded—march across barren snows, jump into dark abysses, fight ancient titans—but never would they leave him. They would always flock to the One Wielder, as ready to serve as to usurp. Six of the boldest had tried already and died for their trouble; more would follow tonight. He could feel their thirst building.

Tavis hoped one would be Orisino. The verbeeg had actually touched the ivory handle, and he had heard the ancient words of command. Like the One Wielder himself, Orisino had not slept since Split Mountain, and his eyes never left the axe's sable head. His lips often twisted into strange configurations, forming the half-remembered syllables of the ancient words of command. Sooner or later, the chieftain would try for the weapon. Then Tavis could kill him, but not until then.

The crunching of boots on ice sounded behind the One Wielder. He laid Sky Cleaver at his feet and jumped up, straddling the mighty axe and pulling his sword from its scabbard. Sky Cleaver was much too awkward and heavy for Tavis to heft in battle, and so far he had been forced to defend it with bow and blade.

"Easy, Tavis," urged Galgadayle. The seer stopped a cautious distance away and turned up his palms to show that his hands were empty. "I didn't come to steal your axe."

Galgadayle looked as haggard as Tavis felt. The seer's beard was caked so thick with ice that his cheeks sagged beneath the weight, making the circles beneath his eyes seem even darker and deeper. The cold had long ago turned his flesh as white as the moonlight, and the tip of his nose had lost several layers of frozen skin.

Tavis sheathed his sword. He picked up Sky Cleaver, resting the pommel in the snow and the obsidian blade against his shoulder.

"Come closer, my friend. I didn't mean to frighten you." Tavis glanced around the base of the drumlin, where his verbeegs sat waiting on the milky snowpack. "But I must be vigilant. Orisino is waiting to steal my axe. They all are."

Galgadayle's face twitched with some emotion destined to remain hidden beneath his frozen flesh. "You belong more to that axe than it does to you. It would have been better for us all if you had died in the cavern and left Sky Cleaver unfound."

"How can you say that?" The One Wielder was aghast. "Think of all I can do! Drive the giants from the northlands! Unite the 'kin under one law!"

"What if our brothers have no wish to live under the law?"

The question left Tavis confused and blank-minded, for it had never occurred to him to think of what they might want. He considered the matter for a moment, then decided there would be no need to compel the obedience of the verbeegs and fomorians.

"They will live under the law. Uniting will make them strong, and the only way to unite is to live under the law."

Galgadayle shook his head. "The law is the firbolg way. Fomorians do not understand it, and verbeegs only twist it to their own ends—this journey has taught me that much."

"Then they will follow *me*," Tavis insisted. "With the giant-kin behind me, I can drive evil from all Toril!"

"How?" Galgadayle scoffed. "You can barely lift Sky Cleaver, much less wield the weapon."

Tavis stepped closer to the seer, carrying the axe with both hands. "I could if I were only a little larger."

Galgadayle's eyes grew as round as saucers. "What are you saying?"

"I'm as much a firbolg as you or any of Meadowhome's warriors," Tavis replied. "You could show me how to change size."

"No." Galgadayle raised his hands as though to push the scout away. "If the gods wanted the evil chased from Toril, they would do it themselves."

"Why do you think they gave me Sky Cleaver?" Tavis was growing more exhilarated by the moment. It was all becoming so clear to him. "Why, of all the thousands of warriors who found their way down to the axe, was I the only one who could pull it free?"

"That had nothing to do with the gods," Galgadayle growled. "If Basil hadn't taught you the magic words, you'd still be down there fighting with Orisino."

"But I'm not," Tavis retorted. "The gods sent Basil to me so I'd know the magic words."

Galgadayle stepped close enough to grab Tavis's arm. "Listen to this madness spilling from your mouth! It's the axe speaking!"

"What does it matter who's speaking?" Tavis spun the seer around. He pointed past the looming shoulder of Othea Tor, toward the unseen mountains beneath the frozen horizon. "Think of it—a world without evil! Is that madness, from my mouth or Sky Cleaver's?"

Galgadayle's gaze did not falter. "Yes, if you think such a world can be won by might of arms." His voice calmed. "Tell me Tavis, before you strike someone down, who will decide he is evil, you or the axe?"

"I will!" Tavis's voice broke, making the statement sound more like a horse's whinny than an honest claim. "I mean, I *summoned* Sky Cleaver. It serves . . ."

When his voice continued to squeal like rusty winch gears, Tavis dropped the axe into the snow. He let his sentence die and stepped away from the weapon, glaring at the thing as though it had suddenly come alive and cut off his arm.

Galgadayle's eyes filled with sadness. "You retrieved Sky Cleaver to rescue your wife, and to . . ." The seer paused to choose his next words carefully. "And to prevent Lanaxis from turning her son against his mother's realm. If you have forgotten that, you would do better to discard the axe and attack the titan with your bare hands."

Tavis's eyes remained locked on Sky Cleaver. It seemed to him that a shimmering mist of darkness was rising off the obsidian blade and slowly spreading across the snow in his direction. He glanced at Galgadayle, but saw no sign that the firbolg also saw the ebon fog.

Tavis shook his head. "Even if I could cast it off, it's too late." This time, his voice did not crack as he spoke. He slowly turned to study the verbeegs gathered below. Save for Orisino, who continued to sit on his haunches with his lips moving, they had all risen and taken a single step up the drumlin. Tavis bent down and retrieved the axe. "I have taken Sky Cleaver in hand, and now I must use it."

"May Hiatea have pity on us."

Tavis fixed his gaze on the seer. "Help me," he pleaded. "Help me do what I came for. If I can't wield this weapon, it will wield me."

"And after you have freed your queen?" Galgadayle pointed at Sky Cleaver. "Who will you turn it against after the titan?"

"I have no idea," Tavis answered honestly. "But I do know this: only Brianna can give me strength to make that choice wisely. Otherwise, it will be Sky Cleaver that decides."

The seer closed his eyes and nodded. "I'll help you," he whispered. "But first, let me call Basil. We must find our way into Twilight, and he knows more about the place than anyone."

Tavis clutched Sky Cleaver more tightly to his breast and glanced down the slope. The runecaster stood a short distance away from the other verbeegs, his thick brows arched expectantly.

"Call Basil," Tavis said. "But stay between him and the axe. With his magic, he is more dangerous than any of Orisino's warriors, and the temptation will be great for him. I think Sky Cleaver's draw is stronger than even he realized."

"I have no doubt about that." Galgadayle cast a wary glance at the axe. "I have sworn not to touch the weapon, and all that vow has earned for me is the constant temptation to break my oath."

The seer nodded to the runecaster, who quickly ascended the drumlin. Like Galgadayle, Basil looked half-frozen and entirely exhausted. His eyes were pinched and bloodshot from his constant battle with snow blindness. His beard had become a single great icicle, and most of his face had turned white with frostbite. If there was no healer available when he thawed, the runecaster would lose both of his ears. The drooping appendages were as stiff and translucent as ice.

Basil stopped a dozen feet away and kept his eyes on the snow. "Thank you for letting me come up."

"There's no need to thank me." Tavis struggled to focus his thoughts on the friendship he and the runecaster shared. "We want the same thing."

Basil smiled, and his gaze flickered to Sky Cleaver.

"I'm glad to hear you say that."

"I'm not talking about the axe," Tavis warned. "And let's not pretend that it means nothing to you. I know you're tempted to steal it—"

"Borrow!"

"It doesn't matter," Tavis said. "Sky Cleaver's hold is just as strong on me as it is on you. I couldn't lend it to you any more than I could lend you my heart."

Basil bit his lip and looked away. "I know that."

"Good, then we have things well in hand." Galgadayle slipped between Tavis and Basil. "Now, how do you suggest we go about entering the Twilight Vale?"

Basil stepped around the seer and moved to the front of the drumlin, where he could peer down at the narrow rift. "The stone giant histories say little about the Twilight Vale itself." He apparently did not notice as Galgadayle once again slipped between him and the axe. "But there's no need for concern. If all else fails, we can use Sky Cleaver to 'cut to the heart of the matter', as the stone giants describe it."

"We?" Tavis demanded.

"I mean *you*," Basil sighed. "But I wouldn't advise doing so lightly. From what you described of the previous wielder's condition, calling upon Sky Cleaver's powers carries a heavy price."

Tavis cringed at his memory of Snad's translucent flesh. "I hope you're saying there's another way into the vale."

"I have several ideas, yes," Basil replied. "But before I can say which is correct, we must examine the signs and see how each one fits our theories."

The runecaster motioned for his companions to follow and started to plow down the snowy slope toward the southern end of the rift. Tavis laid his heavy burden over his shoulder, then, using one hand to balance it there, drew his sword and followed. The descent was treacherous. Tavis was so cold and weary that he found it difficult to keep his footing on the snowy slope, especially with Sky Cleaver's unwieldy bulk pulling him off-balance. By the time he caught up to Basil and Galgadayle, he was panting and sticking his sword into the snow like an alpenstock.

Orisino trudged up to join the trio. "Have you found the way in?" the chieftain asked. "Are we going after the titan?"

Tavis cast a warning glare at the verbeeg. "Not yet. I'll call you when we're ready—but stay away from me until then."

"As you wish." A sly grin crept across Orisino's lips, and he bowed deeply, but did not back away. "I have no wish to trouble you—provided we make a bargain."

"I've no interest in bartering with you," Tavis sneered.

"Not even if it allows you to sleep?" Orisino countered. "I will promise not to take Sky Cleaver as long as you live."

"Why would you make such a promise?" Galgadayle interposed himself between Tavis and the verbeeg.

"Obviously, because I don't think Tavis will live very long," the verbeeg retorted. "Even if he doesn't destroy himself like Snad and all the other Ones, the titan will do it for him. All I ask is that he teach me the calling command, so that I may retrieve the axe after he's dead."

"Tavis, he won't wait," Basil warned. "You can't trust him."

"I wouldn't make the bargain even if I could." Tavis kept his eyes fixed on Orisino. "Whether I'm dead or alive, I certainly wouldn't want a verbeeg to be the One Wielder."

"I suppose that's wise," sighed Basil.

Orisino was not so accepting. "Have it as you will, fool!" Despite his anger, the verbeeg backed away as he spoke. "The axe shall be mine in the end, and it makes no difference to me if I have it sooner rather than later."

Tavis pushed past Galgadayle, pressing the tip of his sword to Orisino's throat. "My thanks for the warning," the high scout hissed. "It's a courtesy I wouldn't have expected from you, and I shall repay it with a warning of my own: if you come within ten paces of me again, I shall take you at your word."

Tavis stepped away, then turned and followed Basil toward Othea Tor. The mount towered more than two hundred feet above—hardly as high as the ice wall at the other end of the crevice, yet somehow more looming, more *imposing*. Even beneath the thick mantle of ice, it was not difficult to see why Basil insisted the inselberg was the lifeless body of the ancient Mother Queen. The crag resembled the figure of a fleshy woman kneeling deep in the snow, with her haunches resting on her heels. Her thighs were two snow-capped knolls that led up to the rounded slopes of her rolling stomach, her bosom was a pair of stony buttresses, and her arms were steep aretes that curved down sharply from her massive shoulders. An ice-draped boulder hung tipping out over the goddess's chest, resembling a rather flat-faced head with deep, shadowy hollows for a mouth, nostrils, and eyes.

Basil stopped at the base of the tor, where a small, deep-shadowed crater lay at the southern end of the rift. Beyond the basin, a chain of smaller depressions—the titan's snow-filled footprints—advanced from around the corner of Othea Tor. Despite the clear night and bright moon, it was difficult to tell much more about the site. Since Lanaxis had passed through, several storms had battered the area, blanketing the entire site beneath three feet of fresh snow. Tavis had been waiting for dawn's light to make his careful inspection and learn the secret of his quarry's escape.

Apparently, Basil saw no reason to wait. He gathered a

handful of snow and packed it into a tight sphere, then removed an awl from his cloak and carefully traced one of his magic symbols on the surface. The ball's surface turned icy and hard. In the heart of the orb, a shimmering glow sparked to life and rapidly brightened. The runecaster waited until the light had grown painfully brilliant, then tossed it into the sky above the crater. As the globe reached the top of its arc, he pointed a crooked finger at it and commanded, "Stay."

The ball stopped in midflight and hung motionless, casting a dazzling silver radiance over the face of Othea Tor, the surrounding drumlins, and the crater at their feet. Tavis could now see that the small basin was about fifteen feet deep, with the indistinct outline of a buried firecircle in the center. Flanking the fire-scar were a pair of ten-foot terraces where the titan had placed his feet, and on the rim above was broad depression where his rump had rested.

"The titan stopped and made camp." Tavis glanced back to make sure Orisino and the other verbeegs were keeping their distance, then sheathed his sword and climbed over the rim into the crater. "He was waiting."

"That rules out one of my most troublesome theories." Basil started down the slope after Tavis. "If Lanaxis stopped to wait here, his magic isn't what opens the rift—or holds it closed."

Galgadayle had to scramble to catch up. "What were they waiting for?"

"Lanaxis's punishment was to live forever in the twilight of Othea's shadow," Basil explained. "So it seems probable that the rift opens at twilight. That would be the only time it could open without allowing the sun to pour in."

Tavis reached the bottom of the crater and scraped the snow away from the fire-scar, then pulled a half-burned torch from beside the stump.

"That can't be, Basil," he said. "If they were waiting for the sun to go *down*, they wouldn't have needed this."

The high scout tossed the torch to the runecaster.

Basil caught the stave. "Oh, dear."

"Perhaps it stays open only during twilight," Galgadayle suggested. "If they arrived during the night after twilight, then they would have had to wait until the next evening."

Tavis scraped more snow away from the fire circle, then pointed to the charred stubs of a dozen thick logs. "When was the last time you saw a tree?"

The seer shrugged. "A tenday ago?"

"So Lanaxis carried this wood across the Bleak Plain," Tavis said. "He planned to arrive after dark."

"Which would imply the vale opens at dawn," Basil said. "But that makes no sense for a place of perpetual twilight."

"Maybe it does."

Tavis climbed the crater wall, using Sky Cleaver's shaft as a walking stick. When he reached the rim, he found Orisino and the other verbeegs cautiously stealing forward to look into the basin. The scout cast a warning glare at the chieftain, then fixed his gaze on the ground and started to count the number of paces between them.

Orisino gave him a sneering smile and slowly backed away.

When Basil and Galgadayle climbed out of the crater, Tavis asked, "Can you move that light over the rift, Basil?"

"Of course." The runecaster pointed a finger at the glowing sphere and whispered, "Move."

Basil swung his crooked digit toward the rift, and the silvery snowball drifted into place. Tavis went to the end of the crevice and knelt in the snow, sighting down the entire length of the fissure. As he suspected, the snowpack sloped away from the dark line ever so gently.

"The snow is higher along the rift," Tavis reported. "The sun never shines on it, so it melts more slowly."

"Yes—now I see!"

In his excitement, Basil tried to approach Tavis and collided with Galgadayle, who, as he had promised, remained between the scout and the runecaster. Basil scowled briefly, then seemed to realize what was going on and backed away.

He continued his explanation without complaint: "As she was dying, Othea told Lanaxis, 'Already I have laid my curse upon you. . . . Can you not feel my shadow? When I leave here, it shall remain behind.' "

"And there can be no shadow without the sun," surmised Galgadayle.

"Exactly," Basil said. "The vale opens in the morning, when Othea's shadow first touches it. It doesn't close until evening, when the dusk shadows take the place of the goddess's. That way, the valley always remains in shadow; it never knows the light of day, or the dark of night."

"So it's always in twilight," Tavis surmised.

"Yes . . . precisely." Basil's tone was absentminded. He turned toward Othea Tor, at the same time swinging his glowing snowball toward the goddess's head. "I wonder . . ."

The runecaster let his sentence trail off and said nothing more, lost deep in thought.

"You wonder what, Basil?" Tavis asked.

The old verbeeg smiled broadly. Then, speaking to himself as though the others were not there, he uttered, "By Stronmaus, I think it might work!"

"What, Basil?" Tavis stepped toward the runecaster, only to find Galgadayle scowling down at him. He remembered himself and clutched the axe more tightly, then peered around the seer's flank. "What might work?"

The runecaster smiled broadly. "What do you suppose

would happen if tomorrow after the vale opens, you used Sky Cleaver to split Othea Tor down the center?" Without awaiting a reply, he answered his own question, "The vale would have its first sunrise in thousands of years!"

"Or it would close instantly," Tavis countered. "I'd never reach Brianna."

"That's a possibility, of course, but I don't think so." Despite his assertion, Basil appeared far from certain. "The key must be different shadows; once Othea's shadow opens the vale, it'll stay open until dusk. Then it will close and, assuming we have cleaved the tor correctly, it will never open again."

Tavis shook his head resolutely. "If you're wrong, Brianna will be trapped forever."

"He can't be wrong!" Galgadayle sounded as excited as Basil. "As I recall, the titan is no friend of sunlight."

Tavis backed away, raising Sky Cleaver and holding it between them. "What else would you say?" he snapped. "Nothing would please you more than to see the rift slam shut forever, with Kaedlaw and Brianna trapped inside."

Galgadayle's hurt showed even through his frozen flesh. "Before we became friends, perhaps—but not now. No one hopes that my vision can be changed more strongly than I do. And, more importantly, I know how much you need Brianna. If you cannot control Sky Cleaver, what Kaedlaw wreaks on the world will pale by comparison to the evil you unleash."

More than anything, Tavis wanted to hear Galgadayle's voice break, to hear the telltale squeal of a lie and know that the seer was trying to manipulate him. But Galgadayle's voice remained steady and deep. The scout could only conclude that it was Sky Cleaver, not the firbolg, trying to manipulate him, to undermine the only power in the world that could save the One Wielder from himself: his true friends.

Tavis lowered his axe. "If you think that's best. All I ask is that you do everything you can to be certain of yourselves."

Basil's glance drifted to the axe, and a hungry gleam came into his ancient eyes. "If you want to be certain, we could use Sky Cleaver's power."

Tavis shook his head. "No, there are some things better left to the judgment of friends." The high scout turned away from Basil's shining snowball and studied the stars until he found the Midnight Circle, high overhead. "We have about six hours until dawn, Galgadayle. Is that enough time for me to learn how to change sizes?"

"It should be plenty, even with the disadvantages of your upbringing," the seer replied. "I have taught the technique to children in six minutes."

Tavis glanced back toward the verbeegs. They were standing twenty paces down the rift, near the drumlin upon which the high scout had been sitting earlier. Their hungry eyes were locked on Sky Cleaver's dark blade, and Orisino's cold-burned lips were silently moving to the half-remembered syllables of the axe's ancient summoning call.

Tavis looked back to Galgadayle. "Now's as good a time as any to teach me, as long I won't be impaired."

"You might feel a little dizzy as you grow larger." The seer glanced toward the verbeegs. "But I doubt Orisino or his warriors will dare approach when they realize you're big enough to swing Sky Cleaver. I suggest you lay aside anything you don't want to grow with you. Whatever you're touching when you start the process will grow larger along with you."

Tavis glanced down at Sky Cleaver. Something inside whispered not to set the weapon aside, that Galgadayle was only trying to trick him and steal it.

The high scout dropped the axe at his feet. "I'm ready."

The seer glanced at the weapon, then nodded and smiled. "I believe you are," he said. "Now, changing sizes is basically a breathing exercise. You start by exhaling slowly, then draw a deep breath and hold it."

Tavis filled his lungs with icy air.

"Look inward and see yourself growing larger," the seer instructed. "Sometimes it helps to close one's eyes, but that's not necessary—especially if it's going to make you worry about what you're not holding."

Tavis closed his eyes.

"Good," Galgadayle said. "Exhale again, but don't open your mouth. Blow the air out of your lungs into the rest of your body, and you'll start to grow."

Tavis tried to do as the seer instructed, but the air came rushing out his nose.

"That's okay," Galgadayle said. "You're not really blowing yourself up—it's only one way to visualize the change. Try again, and push your tongue back to block your throat. It'll help you seal off not only the air passage, but the energy channels as well."

Tavis took another frigid breath, held it, and pushed his tongue to the back of his throat. He tried to exhale. He felt a terrible pressure inside his chest, and it seemed his sternum would crack under the strain. An instant later, the force simply melted away. His torso felt strangely hollow, then his entire body swelled up, not with air, but with muscle and bone. The One Wielder heard Basil's voice, and something dark and sinister whispered that the runecaster might be calling Sky Cleaver.

Tavis put the thought out of his mind and drew another breath.

"Good. You've grown half-a-foot already," Galgadayle reported. "Continue as long as you can. Your body will know when you can't take any more."

Tavis expelled the breath and felt himself swell, then inhaled again. He continued for many minutes, never opening his eyes, growing larger and stronger with each lungful of icy air. Soon, his head began to spin, as Galgadayle had warned it would, and his muscles started to burn with weariness.

"By Stronmaus!" Basil hissed.

"How are you feeling, Tavis?" Galgadayle asked.

"Dizzy," the high scout replied. "Weak."

Tavis gulped down another lungful of frigid air.

"Perhaps you should stop," Galgadayle suggested. "Given your condition and lack of sleep, it might be best not to press matters."

Tavis expelled the breath into his body, and again felt his chest grow hollow. "One more time," he gasped. "When I face Lanaxis, I want . . . to . . . be . . ."

A whistling roar filled the scout's ears, replacing his own voice. He felt himself falling. It seemed to take forever before his face met the ground, and then he heard a strange choking sound: himself, trying to breath snow as fine as flour. A pair of tiny hands, no larger than those of a child, grasped his shoulder and laboriously rolled him over. Another hand, no larger than the first, slipped between his lips and cleared his breathing passage.

"Tavis!" It was Basil's voice, but much more tinny and high-pitched than normal. "Are you all right?"

"He'll be fine." Galgadayle's voice also sounded sharp and high. "He needs to sleep. I should have known that as tired and feeble as he is, he wouldn't have the strength to—"

Galgadayle suddenly stopped speaking, and Basil hissed, "What's that?"

Tavis opened his eyes and saw the faces of his two friends, barely half their normal size. They were looking away from him, back toward the drumlin where the verbeegs were waiting. Then the One Wielder heard it, Orisino's shrill voice calling out to Sky Cleaver in the ancient language of its divine maker:

*"In the name of—"*

Tavis sat up, his hands flailing about for the axe, but finding only snow.

*"—Skoraeus Stonebones, Your Maker, O Sky Cleaver—"*

"Enough of that. Move!" hissed Basil.

The runecaster pointed at the shimmering silver snowball that still hovered over the fissure, then swung his finger down at Orisino's distant figure.

*"—do I summon you in—"*

The snowball crashed over Orisino's head, ending the intonation in midword. The silver sphere shattered into a thousand pieces and spilled its shimmering radiance over the chieftain, who immediately fell motionless. His flesh turned as glossy and hard as ice, then he toppled onto his side and did not move.

"That will keep him quiet," Basil chuckled. "At least until he thaws out—which could be quite some time."

Tavis continued to thrash about in the snow. "My . . . axe," he gasped. "Sky Cleaver!"

Galgadayle grabbed the high scout's wrist and guided his hand through the snow. Tavis felt a familiar handle in his palm. Though the shaft was much smaller than he remembered, the One Wielder could feel the energy of Orisino's half-completed call coursing through the ancient ivory. He pulled the weapon to his breast and collapsed back into the snow, his weariness descending upon him like a flight of starving wyverns.

"That's right, Tavis. Sleep." Galgadayle's whispering voice was fading fast. "Rest. Let your friends watch over you until dawn."

# ✦ 16 ✦
# Titan's Vale

Tavis stood on the summit of Othea Tor, watching a veil of flaxen sunlight cascade down the Endless Ice Sea's looming face. As the sun behind him rose higher, the curtain fell faster, until it was descending so swiftly that when the sallow light finally reached bottom, it splashed out onto the bleak snows and spread across the entire empty plain in the span of a single expectant breath. Othea's shadow did not fall over the rift so much as appear along its length all at once, and suddenly the high scout found himself staring into the purple bowels of a deep, gloomy abyss. He could hardly comprehend what had happened. There had been no earthquake, no plume of billowing darkness, nor even a thunderous rumble to proclaim the opening of the fissure. The vale had simply appeared, as though it had been there all along and required only the goddess's umbral touch to reveal itself.

The abyss was shaped exactly like Othea's shadow: a long, narrow triangle that stretched from the base of the tor to the foot of the Endless Ice Sea. Its walls were as sheer and black as slate, descending more than a hundred feet before they vanished into the swarthy murk that filled the bottom of the chasm. In the center of this gloom hung the silhouette of a palace roof, supported by nothing that Tavis could see except viscous shadow. The structure appeared to be a harmonious balance of three symmetrical wings arranged around a central cupola, but it was impossible to tell more. The rest of the building remained a dusky, half-sensed enigma, as nebulous and obscure as the vale itself.

Tavis turned away from the palace and started down the back of the rugged tor, occasionally stumbling over a crag as he struggled with the length of his new stride. That morning, he had awakened refreshed and famished and not quite the size of a hill giant, as he had discovered when he reached for his rucksack with a hand as large as a buckler. Only after devouring all of his food, and much of Galgadayle's as well, had he paused to inspect his new body. He had found legs as thick as spruce trunks and arms as big as putlogs, and a chest so large a cooper could have bent cask hoops across it. Though the scout stood a full head taller than any firbolg he had ever seen, Galgadayle had not been particularly surprised. The ability to change sizes was primarily a matter of spirit, the seer had explained, and anyone who intended to battle a titan certainly had an ample supply of that.

At the bottom of the tor, Tavis found the verbeeg warriors lingering a safe distance away, their hungry eyes fixed, as always, on Sky Cleaver's obsidian head. After witnessing Orisino's fate, they had grown temporarily more cautious. Their attitude would change the instant they had a chance to steal the weapon, of course, but their current wariness had allowed the One Wielder a few hours of rest. He now felt stronger and more clear-headed than he had since Wynn Castle.

Tavis stepped over to Basil and Galgadayle, who were huddled together at the center of the tor. Over their shoulders, he could see a labyrinthine diagram of glowing green strokes that the runecaster had traced on the mountainside. The scout had seen enough runes to realize this was not one. Rather, the lines seemed to be a chart of the mount's fracture zones and stress points. He waited in silence while his friends discussed internal forces and cleavage planes, then Basil selected another runebrush from his cloak and traced a single red line down the spine of the mount.

When he finished, the runecaster stepped back and gestured at the red line. "That's where you should strike, Tavis," he said. "Did the rift open? I didn't hear anything."

"It opened, but not like we expected," Tavis answered. "When Othea's shadow fell over it, the vale just appeared."

"Appeared?" Galgadayle echoed.

Tavis nodded. "Like the shadow *is* the Twilight Vale."

"Oh, dear!" gasped Basil. "We can't destroy Othea Tor without destroying her shadow!"

"And destroying her shadow would close the vale?" surmised Galgadayle.

Basil shook his head. "Worse. If Othea's shadow *is* the vale, then, by definition, eliminating the shadow wouldn't close the valley—it would eliminate it."

"And what happens to those inside?" Tavis asked.

The runecaster set his ice-crusted jaw in determination. "I don't know, but we've already lost Avner," he said. "I won't take chances with Brianna."

"Even if you're right, destroying the shadow shouldn't hurt her, or the child," Galgadayle said. "It would be like opening the drapes in dark room. The sun will illuminate what's inside."

"Assuming they still have an independent existence, of course—but there's only one way to be certain." Basil pointed at the axe in Tavis's hands. "Perhaps you'd better use Sky Cleaver."

The One Wielder nodded. "I think I will."

Tavis stooped down to gently push his companions aside, then raised Sky Cleaver over his head. The mighty hand axe was still too large for him to wield one-handed, but he was now large enough to swing it with both arms.

"That's not what I meant!" Basil slipped between Tavis and the mount. "Cleave our quandary, not the tor!"

"Isn't cleaving a prime power, whether it's substance or circumstance?" Tavis asked.

Basil had explained that the axe possessed two kinds of magical power. The most potent was the ability to *cleave* anything, be it a material object like a mountain, or a circumstance like ignorance. The weapon's lesser ability was the capacity to *defend* the wielder from most kinds of harm.

Unfortunately, Sky Cleaver's magic carried a heavy price. After hearing the high scout describe Snad's ancient and translucent body, Basil and Galgadayle had deduced that the weapon's magic was too powerful for mortals. *Cleaving* burned away the bonds that connected the One Wielder to the physical world, until they finally grew too weak to bind his spirit to his bones. *Defending* was more insidious. The axe invoked this magic on its own, filling the bearer's body with powerful energies that aged him far beyond his years. Accordingly, the three companions had decided Tavis would use the axe's powers as little as possible, and even then only when the damage to the titan would balance the harm to the One Wielder.

After a thoughtful silence, Basil said, "Cleaving is a prime power, but it would be wise to use it now. If Brianna and Kaedlaw are eliminated with Othea's shadow—"

"They won't be." Tavis motioned for the runecaster to step aside. "You said yourself they'd be all right if they still exist apart from Twilight."

Basil refused to move. "I hesitate to bring this up, but I *have* made one or two mistakes in my life."

"Not this time," Tavis said. "If daylight didn't destroy Lanaxis, then *he* exists apart from twilight. Why would Brianna and Kaedlaw be any different?"

"Besides, it's safer to trust our own judgment than to rely on Sky Cleaver's power," Galgadayle pointed out. They had already discussed how fast the axe's magic destroyed its wielders and decided they could not even guess. "For all we know, Tavis could turn as transparent as Snad when he cleaves the answer you want, and vanish entirely when he cleaves the mountain. Then where would Brianna be?"

Basil reluctantly nodded. "It would be better for her to disappear with Othea's shadow." He stepped away from the tor and flourished a hand at the red line he had traced down the spine. "Swing away, my friend."

Tavis brought Sky Cleaver down, whispering, as Basil had taught him, the ancient word for *cleave*. A stinging fire erupted in the bones of his hands and rushed through his arms to spread into the rest of his body. The axe struck with a sharp crackle, slicing clear through the rock to the icy plain below. A loud, sonorous sigh rose from the other side of the mount, and a gust of wind went rustling across the plain toward the distant glacier. A crack appeared at the base of the tor, then ran up the spine to the summit.

Nothing else happened, save that Tavis stumbled away from the mount, his breath hissing through his clenched teeth. He pulled up his cloak sleeve. His skin was sparkling like a fresh powder snow and had turned as white and lustrous as polished silver, but it still seemed fairly opaque. From the looks of his flesh, he guessed that he would be able to use the cleaving power five or six more times before turning into a ghost. The high scout stepped forward, raising Sky Cleaver to strike again.

There was no need. The spine of the tor suddenly turned to talus and cascaded down toward Tavis. As the scout turned to flee, an eerie chill rose from Sky Cleaver's heft and engulfed his body. A boulder came bouncing at his head, then inexplicably rose and sailed past without striking him. The rest of the landslide scattered around his flanks and arced over his head. Tavis looked at his arm again and found the flesh hanging more loosely than he remembered, and etched with lines that had not been there before.

A low, rumbling groan rose from deep within the tor. The two halves of the mount slumped away from each other, and the rockslide came to an abrupt halt as the boulders fell into the cleft instead of tumbling down the slope. The rent continued to open, and Tavis gasped at what he saw emerging from the murky abyss beyond: the palace whose roof he had glimpsed earlier.

Clouds of purple gloom were rising off the walls like a ground fog in the dawn sun, and Tavis could see that the monumental structure was larger than all of Castle Hartwick. The entrance portico alone was as spacious as the inner bailey, while each of the colonnaded side wings could have held the entire keep beneath its roof.

"Bleak Palace," whispered Basil, coming up behind the high scout. "He must have rebuilt it for Brianna."

\* \* \* \* \*

They come at dawn. Of course.

How the sunlight scratches my eyes! like scouring hot sand after thirty centuries of cool, purple-shadowed snow. My skin, it does burn beneath the fiery light; in my joints there flares such a sweltering ache I swear my marrow will boil. Thus does Lanaxis the Chosen, Maker of Emperors, greet golden dawn: racked with fever, so weak and anguished that he would lie upon the stone floor next to mighty Kaedlaw and roar his pain.

But I cannot set such an example. My young charge is just beginning to understand why I bring him here when he groans, to lie alone upon the throne hall's cold floor. Emperors must not cry. That is the first lesson, and if I wail my grief, how will he learn?

Through the antechamber echoes the *tick tick* of the Emperor Mother's feet, then her tiny figure scurries out from among the column pediments. What a trifling thing she is. If my palace had vermin, even they would dwarf her.

Brianna crosses the floor at a dead run and snatches the child into her arms. She knows better. I have forbidden her to hold him when he is crying, but the sun has made her rebellious. The light strengthens her as much as it weakens me, and she delights too much in that.

"Put the emperor down. He has not stopped crying."

Brianna raises her face toward the golden rays streaming through the cupola and clutches Kaedlaw closer to her breast. "I have been praying to Hiatea," she says, as though that should exempt her from my commands. "I will take my son to see the dawn."

"After he stops crying."

I flick my hand in her direction. The Emperor Mother falls to the floor and drops her son on the cold stones, for she is bound to my will by the power of the oath she swore. She promised not to escape, and disobedience is nothing if not fleeing. The child howls, and Brianna stretches a hand toward him. She does not touch him; she cannot reach him until he is silent.

I rise from my throne and walk toward the exit. "I will go and see to the fools who have caused this dawn."

The antechamber is more comfortable than my throne hall, for there are no windows here, and only the dimmest light filters in from outside. But as I pass down the great colonnade, the glow grows steadily brighter. A headache throbs behind my eyes, and my legs tremble with weakness. By the time I reach the foyer, the glare is so brilliant that it seems as though I am walking into the flaming forge of Surtr himself.

I step onto the portico where in ancient times my brothers and I would stand to greet the dawn, long before men and their ilk ruled Toril. Now, I hardly dare to peek at the light upon the stones, and only from the shade of a pillar larger than I. My palace stands upon a jetty of sunlit rock, its sides flanked by a chevron of abyssal shadow that points toward the sundered figure of Othea's stone body. It almost seems she is giving birth still; the two halves of her craggy figure have fallen wide apart, creating a broad cleft that is filled with the crowning orb of the blinding yellow sun.

Silhouetted against the shimmering disk stands a figure the size of a hill giant. Something is familiar about his shape, but it is the axe that keeps me staring into the searing dawn. The obsidian head swallows light as dragons swallow gold, and even half-blinded, I see every figure carved into the ivory handle: Stronmaus smashing moons with his mighty hammer, Hiatea thrusting her flaming spear into the heart of the fifty-headed hydra, Iallanis joining the hands of Memnor and Karontor in brotherly love.

Sky Cleaver!

It cannot be. No mortal can wield my father's hand axe; its magic would destroy *me*. Yet, I would know the weapon anywhere; it is impossible to mistake Sky Cleaver. What are you doing to me?

*"As you wish. But don't expect me to condone your treachery. . . ."*

*". . . slice you open and feed your entrails to my swine, and there's nothing you can do . . ."*

*". . . last time! No more, my husband. Away, away with*

*you forever. . . .”*

Do you wish me to fail?

No matter. Even you cannot stop mighty Lanaxis, for I have allies of my own. I turn and point to the drumlins where my poisoned brothers have lain these three thousand years.

“Arise, my brothers!” I call. “Arise, cowards! You who in life would not defy faithless Othea, arise now and serve the Mother Queen again, in her death and yours!”

First one, then two, and a moment later many low groans echo across the barren plain. The drumlins crack like eggs as the bejeweled fingers of my dead brothers push up through the snow. Their hands are not skeletal, but emaciated and black, as flesh becomes when it has been frozen for three thousand years. One after another, their heads pop from their snowy cocoons and look toward me. Tufts of ropy hair protrude from beneath their dirt-crusted crowns. Their faces are as withered and dark as their hands, with yellow teeth showing through their ripped lips and puckered eyes that hang from the sockets like shriveled apples.

I point at Othea’s cleaved body. “Take vengeance for the sundering of our mother,” I command. “Go and punish the one who has defiled her legacy!”

My brothers rise and obey. They are no match for Sky Cleaver, of course, but I suspect neither is the bearer. And even if he is, the delay works to my advantage. The day is not long in the north country, and twilight shall return soon enough.

\* \* \* \* \*

One by one, the dead giants climbed from their scattered drumlins and stumbled toward the sundered tor, their golden crowns and bejeweled rings too rimed with dirt to sparkle in the morning sun. There were more than a dozen of the kings, one for each true giant race that had ever walked Toril. When the world was young, they had been immortal monarchs, born of gods and destined to rule their progeny as long as Ostoria endured. Now they were mindless zombies, called back from a restless sleep by the same brother who had poisoned them.

Tavis did not fear so much as pity them the indignity of this second betrayal. Despite their shriveled flesh and the grotesque disfigurements wrought by so many centuries of lying frozen beneath the plain's barren soil, Tavis recognized many of them from ancient stone giant tales.

The tallest, wrapped in a cloak of the whitest linen, would be Nicias, dynast of the cloud giants. Behind him was red-bearded Masud, khan of the fire giants, his dark armor glimmering through even the thick layers of dirt and ice crusting the steel. Next were Vilmos, paramount of the storm giants; Ottar, jarl of the frost giants; Ruk, chief of the hill giants; Obadai, sage of the stone giants; and several others, among them the progenitors of some races that had not been seen in the Ice Spires since before Hartsvale was a kingdom. In their black and withered hands, all the monarchs clutched ancient weapons of splendor and power.

"Hiatea watch over us!" Galgadayle was standing with Tavis and Basil between Othea's sundered halves, looking over the verbeegs toward the drumlins south of the tor. "We're doomed!"

"Yes, we are," agreed Basil. He was looking in the opposite direction, toward Bleak Palace's looming mass. "By the time we finish with those cadavers, twilight will be upon us."

Tavis said nothing. He knew better than to think he could defeat all of the dead giant kings, even with Sky Cleaver in his hand. The weapon's defenses would age him to dust long before he could strike half of them down. Still, the titan had been appallingly haughty to call his own victims to his defense, and there was always a way to use an enemy's arrogance against him.

A cry of fear went up from the verbeegs. Tavis glanced back. The giant kings had stopped well short of the tor, and now they were raising their weapons over their heads.

"Grab hold of me!" Tavis hefted Sky Cleaver. He had no idea whether the axe would protect his friends, but he hoped that if they were close enough to him, the attacks would also be deflected around them. "Don't let go."

Nicias whirled his pearly morningstar over his head, spraying a cloud of boiling white vapor toward the sundered tor. In the same instant, Vilmos brought his sword down on the plain, Ruk smashed his ebony club into his own palm, Masud pointed his flaming spear at Tavis's chest, and a dozen different kinds of cataclysm struck the tor. The air turned as foul and thick as arsenic; sheets of lightning swept across the plain to crackle and dance off Othea's battered stones; great rifts opened in the ground, and earthquakes pummeled the mount; fire gusted through the cleft like wind, reducing everything it touched to ashes and smoke.

Through it all, Tavis stood motionless, watching in gape-mouthed awe as Toril herself groaned and wailed in complaint. A savage, biting cold rose from Sky Cleaver's handle and hovered about his body. He felt his skin wrinkling and folding over his flesh, his shoulders stooping beneath the weight of years not yet gone, his bones aching with rheumatism he had not earned. Yet no lightning touched him, no fire scoured him, no poison seeped into his breath; with the world itself ending around him, he did not fall.

At last, the cataclysms ceased, and all that lay between

the giant kings and Tavis had vanished. The icy plain
had become a torn and churned wasteland, with no sign
of the verbeegs or anything else that had cowered there.
Except for the stones beneath his feet, Othea Tor herself
had crumbled to dust and blown away. Even her abyssal
shadow had vanished, save for a single purple shaft at
the base of the boulder upon which he stood. And there,
lying at Tavis's feet and clinging to his legs like frightened children, were Basil and Galgadayle. The eyes of
both 'kin were white with shock, their expressions as
void as the ground around them, their mouths gasping
for air.

Seeing that their foe still stood, the giant kings lowered their weapons and started across the wasteland.
Where their magic had failed, their strength would not.

"Your brother has made fools of you!" Tavis called. He
gently freed his legs and turned to face Bleak Palace,
which still stood proud and tall behind Ottar, the frost
giant, and Obadai, the stone giant. "He murdered your
mother, he poisoned you, and now he has summoned
you from your rest to serve his foul purpose."

The giant kings continued to approach, their shriveled
eyes vacant and blank.

Tavis fixed his gaze on Lanaxis, who was peering out
from the portico's shadowy depths. He pointed Sky
Cleaver's head at the titan's dark figure.

"No!" Lanaxis's voice echoed out of the colonnade,
trembling and quivering with fear. "I forbid it!"

"See what the titan has made of his immortal brothers!" Tavis cried. "Cleave!"

A stinging fire erupted inside the One Wielder's
hands and rushed up his arms into his body. Ottar
stopped, then Obadai, Vilmos, and the others. Their
shriveled eyes sparkled with glimmers of reason, and
one by one they turned to face Bleak Palace.

Lanaxis's looming figure strode forward through the

shadowy portico. As he neared the entrance, he hunched over and scuttled sideways, presenting his shoulder to the sun and shielding his face behind his dingy cloak. He looked more ancient than ever, with a bald pate protruding through his golden crown and a back as hunched as a fomorian's. He waved a gnarled hand at the giant-kings.

"I release you!" His voice was brittle with age. "Return to your graves!"

The giant-kings raised their weapons as they had done when they attacked Tavis. One of Lanaxis's eyes opened wide, then the titan abruptly drew himself to his full height and turned to meet his brothers head-on.

Tavis leapt off his boulder and left his dazed companions behind. He sprinted across the broken ground, praying that the angry zombies would not destroy Bleak Palace before he rescued Brianna and Kaedlaw.

He needn't have worried. As the giant-kings released their cyclone, Lanaxis retreated into his portico and called out the incantation to some spell so ancient and powerful that Tavis felt the air draw tight and crackle with faerie lightning. A shimmering silver curtain fell over the portico, and the zombies' cataclysms ricocheted off the screen like stone-tipped arrows off steel armor.

Tavis stopped running and crouched on the ground, watching in awestricken wonder as rivers of flame and seas of lightning broke over Bleak Palace. The plain itself was melting around the portico, filling the air with billowing clouds of gray steam. Lanaxis's citadel did not even quiver beneath the attacks. The giant-kings continued to press forward, persevering in their assaults until at last they reached the building's entrance.

The cataclysms faded as suddenly as they had begun. Tavis rose and started running again, but he was still a hundred paces from the entrance. Nicias whirled his pearly morningstar and swung it against the shimmering screen Lanaxis had raised. The magical curtain vanished with a blinding flash and a deafening crackle, then an entire corner of the portico crashed down upon the cloud giant's head.

Nicias fell beneath the avalanche, his huge body broken beyond recognition. The other giant-kings rushed through the opening he had created. Lanaxis stepped forward to meet his zombies, swinging a great sword as tall as gate tower. A thunderous tumult erupted from within the colonnade. Ruk came crashing out of the side wall, his body severed in two. Next fell Masud, who perished beneath untold tons of stone when he knocked a pillar from its foundations. The slaughter continued; Obadai, then Vilmos, and the rest, the portico crashing down around their heads, battering the plain so severely that crevices and rifts shot out hundreds of paces in all directions.

By the time Tavis danced around the pools of melted stone and reached the bottom of what had once been the palace's entrance, the giant kings had all fallen. Lanaxis stood amid the ruins of his portico, leaning on his great sword and huffing gusts of searing wind across the plain. As far as the One Wielder could tell, the titan had suffered no injuries. The zombies were shattered beyond recognition; bits of their blackened flesh hung across toppled pillars, shards of their broken bones lay scattered through the rubble, and pools of their blood boiled in the cratered floor.

Tavis dragged himself up the great stairs as though he were climbing a cliff, his lungs burning with exertion and his muscles aching with fatigue. The stones jumped beneath his body as the titan pounded down the shattered colonnade to meet him. The scout tried to climb faster, but his aged body simply would not move as quickly as he wanted to. His liver-spotted skin had turned slightly translucent with his last use of the cleaving power, and he did not know whether to attribute his quivering muscles to his racing age or to the general weakness he had suffered since Wynn Castle. It did not matter; the battle would be over soon enough, and as long as he had the axe, Lanaxis could not harm him.

When Tavis clambered atop the last stair, he found himself staring at the titan's ancient knee. He raised Sky Cleaver to attack. Lanaxis backed out of range, stepping over a toppled pillar as thick as Tavis was tall.

"You have done well, but Sky Cleaver is not for mortals," the titan rumbled. "I shall take my father's axe."

"Never!" Tavis could not tell whether concern for Brianna or love of Sky Cleaver inspired his anger, but at least he was sure of its target. "I am the One Wielder!"

Tavis charged, leaping onto a column pedestal and from there to the toppled pillar over which Lanaxis had retreated. This time, the titan did not withdraw. He lowered his hand and called to Sky Cleaver in the same ancient language that Basil had taught Tavis.

*"In the name of Skoraeus Stonebones, Your Maker—"*

Tavis felt Sky Cleaver's handle slipping. "No!" The One Wielder's fury became a fiery red curtain, so brilliant and hot he could barely see. He began his own chant. *"In the name of Skoraeus Stonebones—"*

*"—O Sky Cleaver—"* boomed Lanaxis.

So fierce was the titan's angry voice that it knocked Tavis backward off the pillar. He felt a cold surge rise from the axe's handle, then landed on his feet amidst the jumbled rubble. Sky Cleaver slipped another inch through his fingers.

*"—Your Maker—!"* Tavis yelled, but he could tell that his voice was no match—and never would be—for the titan's.

*"—do I summon you into the service—"*

Tavis grasped the shaft with all his strength and leapt

toward the titan. "Cleave!"

"—*of my hand,*" Lanaxis finished.

A fiery surge of pain shot through the One Wielder's body, then he felt himself being pulled through the air as Sky Cleaver answered the titan's call.

Tavis held on to the axe's ivory handle with all his strength. He slammed into Lanaxis's palm, and the titan's fingers closed to crush him. Another wave of cold energy surged from the axe handle. The scout found himself falling, holding on to Sky Cleaver by no more than its pommel.

It was enough. The blade bit Lanaxis's leg above the knee, then sliced through the great limb as cleanly as it had cleaved Othea Tor. A thundering cry of pain pealed across the steam-shrouded skies, then Tavis dropped, once more cushioned by Sky Cleaver's defenses, onto the bloody, rubble-strewn floor.

Lanaxis tumbled from the portico and slammed into the shattered ground below. The entire building bucked beneath the force of his fall, bringing the remains of the colonnade tumbling down about Tavis's head. Another cold surge rose from Sky Cleaver's shaft. Two pillars smashed down beside the One Wielder, then a section of entablature landed across them. Tavis found himself buried in a sheltering cave of rubble, sitting in a pond of the titan's hot blood.

The portico continued to shake and tremble for several moments, until at last all of the massive debris had finally fallen. Even before the quake subsided, Tavis was already working to dig his way out, pushing cornices and capitals away as fast as his exhausted body would allow. He had no idea how old he had grown in the past few moments, but the wheezing that he heard in his ears did not sound as if it came from the chest of a young firbolg.

At last, Tavis reached the surface and clambered over

the rubble to the front of the portico. To his surprise, he did not find Lanaxis waiting to attack, or even lying helpless at the foot of the palace stairs. Instead, a river of blood led across the broken plain to the single boulder that was all that remained of Othea Tor. There was no sign of the titan himself, but Basil and Galgadayle were kneeling atop the stone, staring down at its purple shadow with their faces twisted into expressions of utter astonishment.

# ►17◄
# Bleak Palace

The battle roar continued to ring in Brianna's ears long after the portico had come crashing down, so she did not hear the scuttling boots until the walker had already crossed most of the fume-choked antechamber. The steps were ponderous and slow, not loud enough to be the titan's, but too heavy to be man or 'kin.

Brianna slipped off the plinth where she had been sitting and rushed to place herself between the entrance and Kaedlaw, who remained wailing upon the floor. She did not try to take her child into her arms. It would have been easier to grab a cloud. No matter how closely she approached before kneeling beside her son, the queen always found herself beyond arm's length. She removed Hiatea's talisman from her neck and pulled a sliver of broken mirror from her cloak pocket, determined that if she could not touch the child, neither would anyone else.

While the battle raged outside, Brianna had stayed in the throne hall with Kaedlaw, so she could only guess who, or what, was coming after her son now. By the sound of his shuffling gait, he was large, patient, and either wounded or exhausted—possibly both. He also had to be someone of incredible power; no one else could have survived the harrowing battle that had shaken Bleak Palace for the last ten minutes. The queen half-expected to see a god's avatar stepping out of the fumes to claim her son.

It hardly mattered to Brianna. She would attack, and without fear. The queen had long since worried herself into such an emotional frenzy that she could no longer feel anything except a seething, mindless anger: at Lanaxis for leaving her unable to defend her child, at Tavis for failing to stop the titan at Wynn Castle, and, most of all, at herself for drinking a spy's drug and allowing an ettin to get a child on her. Whoever was coming did not realize it, but he was doing her a favor. She would fight him to the end. She could no longer bear to watch her child suffer, and death was the only escape left to either of them.

A large, stooped shape shambled into the smoky doorway, the silhouette of a great axe clutched in his hands. Brianna silently called upon her goddess's magic and felt the talisman growing warm. When she uttered her spell incantation, the sliver vanished. A silvery light flashed from her hand and bounced off the throne room walls, returning in the form of a thousand long, gleaming needles. The queen pointed at the gray figure, and the silvery darts hissed toward him in a deadly stream.

A weary groan rose from the newcomer's throat. The torrent of needles suddenly parted and tinkled off the floor around him, changing into harmless sparkles of light. Brianna cursed and reached for her knife.

"Brianna?"

The voice was a reasonable imitation of Tavis's, save that it quivered like an old man's and was far too deep. She hurled her dagger at the doorway. The weapon flew as level and true as any throwing blade, for she had enchanted it with a feather from the shadowroc's wing.

Again, the stranger groaned. The knife veered off

course and shattered against an unseen pillar. The fellow let the axe head drop to the floor, and he leaned on the heft.

"Stop that." He sounded even older than before. "I can't stand more of this."

Brianna pulled a ball of candle wax from her pocket. "Imposter!"

"That was Julien, not me." The stranger shuffled into the hall, moving with the weary steps of an old man. "And what he did doesn't matter. Remember what I said when he claimed to have gotten a child on you? It's still true today: 'I believe you. I always have.'"

Brianna returned the wax ball to her pocket. "Tavis? It's really you?"

"None other," replied the ancient voice. "I'm sorry I took so long, milady."

The newcomer—Tavis—stepped out of the smoke, revealing a beardless, elderly firbolg who would have stood as tall as a small hill giant, if not for the hunch in his back. His hair had turned as silver as a coin, a blue haze hung over the pupils of his ice-colored eyes, and his wrinkled skin was so thin and translucent that Brianna could see through it to the stringy muscles beneath. In his liver-spotted hands, he held a huge axe with an obsidian head and a wondrously decorated ivory shaft.

Tavis squinted around the room for a moment, then finally seemed to find Brianna. He smiled. "I hope you can do something about my eyes." He shuffled toward her. "Fighting Lanaxis is hard enough when I can see."

"Tavis!" Brianna screamed again. She couldn't quite believe he had really come, or comprehend what she was seeing. "Has it really been so long? How can it have taken you a lifetime to find me? Kaedlaw has aged only a month!"

The high scout glanced down at himself, then chuckled grimly, almost madly. "It *has* been a lifetime—but not the way you mean. My age is Sky Cleaver's doing."

Tavis raised the great axe in his hands, and a wave of heated nausea rushed over Brianna. She had experienced such feelings before. They were premonitions sent by her goddess to warn her of some terrible danger, but the sensations had never been this strong.

The queen backed away. "Don't come any closer."

The high scout frowned, but stopped. "What's wrong?"

"You tell me," Brianna said. "Put that axe down."

Tavis's eyes narrowed. "What for?" He did not lower the weapon. "It's mine. I won't let you steal it."

Brianna slipped her hand into her pocket and rolled the wax between her fingers, suspecting it would do her no good even if she had to use it.

"You don't sound like Tavis Burdun," she said. "The lord high scout would never disobey his queen's order."

An angry light flashed in Tavis's eyes. "As you command, milady." He laboriously stooped down to place the axe at his feet. "But I must warn you, Sky Cleaver's hold on me is great. If you try to steal it, I—"

"Steal it!" Brianna scoffed. She was beginning to understand her premonitions of danger. It was not her husband that was dangerous, but the weapon's hold over him. "What would I want with an axe so large I could not pick it up?"

Tavis's gaze remained suspicious for only a moment, then he blushed in shame. "Forgive me, Brianna. It seems my heart is not as pure as yours."

Brianna shook her head, relieved. "We both know that can't be. It's just that I'm more accustomed to dark temptations."

The queen had almost decided it was safe to embrace her husband when she heard the distant clamor of more 'kin clambering across the rubble-strewn portico. She positioned herself between her wailing son and the doorway, clutching her goddess's talisman in one hand and dipping the other into her cloak pocket.

"Valorous Hiatea—"

"There's no need for that." Tavis raised a silencing hand. "That would be Basil and Galgadayle. They won't harm Kaedlaw."

"How can you say that?" Brianna demanded. "Galgadayle wants him dead!"

"Perhaps, but he's pledged not to kill the child himself."

"What? He would never make such a pledge, unless you . . ." A chill crept down Brianna's spine. "And what did *you* promise, Tavis?"

"We can decide what to do about Kaedlaw's destiny later, after we've had time to think," the high scout replied, in the same breath both answering and avoiding the queen's question. "At the moment, we'd better prepare ourselves. I only wounded Lanaxis, and twilight is not so far away."

The *slap, slap* of Basil's flat feet rang off the walls of the antechamber, with the thud of Galgadayle's boots close behind. Tavis's baggy eyes grew narrow and wary, and he stooped over to retrieve Sky Cleaver. An instant later, the two 'kin raced into the throne room. They appeared as battered and exhausted as the high scout, if much younger.

Basil threw his arms wide and rushed Brianna. "Majesty, you're well!"

The queen started to back away, saying, "Stay where you—"

Basil gathered her up and embraced her for a long moment. Finally, he seemed to hear Kaedlaw's wail and put her down, then knelt beside the child. His heavy lips cracked a delicate grin, and his ice-crusted eyebrows slowly formed an awestruck arch.

"What a handsome child!" he exclaimed. "He looks

just like his father!"

Brianna felt someone peering over her shoulder and glanced back to find Galgadayle standing behind her. Though the seer remained silent, the disdainful sneer beneath his beard made it clear that he wondered which father Basil meant. The queen found the differing reactions of the two 'kin surprising. Kaedlaw might look as handsome as Tavis one moment and as sinister as the ettin the next, but she had never seen both faces at the same time.

Basil turned to the queen. "Far be it from me to criticize, but I thought only verbeegs let crying infants lie. Don't human mothers comfort their children?"

"Don't you think I've tried?" Brianna was filled with such a sense of shame that she could barely whisper the admission. She knew that the affliction was no fault of hers, but that did not prevent her from feeling like a failure. "I can't do it."

"You don't have to keep him quiet," Galgadayle said. "I doubt Lanaxis can hear him anyway. But we really must hurry if we are to leave this place."

Brianna whirled on the seer, her frustration and fear pouring from her mouth in a tempest of angry words. "Why, so Tavis can commit your murder for you?"

The queen had no defense left except her rage. Her magic would not work against her husband, and she could not best a trio of giant-kin—even 'kin as old as these three—with her bare hands.

She cast an accusatory glare at Tavis. "If you have come to keep your vow, do it now, Husband!"

Tavis's cloudy eyes turned as soft as water. "I *have* come to keep my vow," he allowed. "But not by killing you or Kaedlaw."

"Tavis, must I remind you of our agreement?" Galgadayle demanded. "You promised—"

"I *know* what I promised!" The high scout's head

swiveled toward the seer, anger flashing like lightning behind his cloudy eyes. When Galgadayle voiced no more objections, Tavis exhaled slowly, then stepped over to Brianna. "Milady, do you trust me?"

Brianna started to ask what he meant, but then she heard Avner's voice ringing inside her head: 'Tavis will see what you see. . . . It's your only hope.' The young scout had spoken those words less than a day before his death, but the queen seemed to hear him now more clearly than ever. Whatever her husband intended to do, it would be the right thing. It simply was not in his nature to do anything else.

Brianna nodded. "Yes, Tavis. I trust you completely."

The high scout stroked her cheek with a huge, wrinkled finger, then stepped around her and knelt beside Kaedlaw. He scooped the child up in his palm and studied him for a moment, a broad smile creeping across his cracked lips.

Kaedlaw's wails began to subside, and Tavis said, "You're right, Basil. He is handsome—and he has my eyes."

Galgadayle brushed past Brianna to peer at the infant. "I don't see that, not at all," the seer said. "To me, he's as ugly as a troll. Use the axe."

Now that Kaedlaw was growing quiet, his face had once again assumed a handsome and loving aspect in Brianna's eyes. Her deepest instincts urged her to leap forward and snatch her child from Tavis's palm. She desperately wanted to know the truth about her son and just as desperately wanted to remain ignorant. It was the conflict between those two emotions more than her willpower that kept her standing fast as her husband covered her helpless child with the flat of Sky Cleaver's obsidian blade.

Tavis spoke a word in the same ancient tongue the titan used to cast spells. He grimaced with pain, and the last of the color faded from his pale skin. Even his muscles turned partially translucent, so that beneath the stringy cords of sinew, Brianna could see the yellow outlines of bone and the more nebulous shapes of internal organs.

Kaedlaw's growls gave way to a muffled chortling.

The high scout took Sky Cleaver's blade away. In his palm lay a rather plain-looking baby, neither as handsome as Tavis, nor as hideous as the ettin. The infant had a rather cherubic face with pudgy jowls, rosy cheeks, and twinkling eyes as gray as steel. Brianna could see her husband's influence in the child's straight nose and even features, while the ettin's could be seen in the cleft chin and dark, curly hair.

"He's not handsome any more!" Basil gasped. "He just looks normal!"

Tavis's smile broadened. "He's always looked that way," he said. "But we couldn't see it."

Galgadayle frowned. "What? I know what I saw before. It was as plain—"

"Of course it was!" interrupted Basil, growing more excited by the moment. "Kaedlaw is no different than any child. We see in him what we expect to see—isn't that what the axe showed you?"

"More or less," Tavis answered. "Like any child, Kaedlaw has the capacity for both good and evil. How we rear him will decide which comes to dominate."

"That is the more," said Galgadayle. "What is the less?"

Tavis cast an uneasy glance at Brianna, and the queen felt a cold dread seeping into her heart. She began to fear that Galgadayle's prophecy had been right, after all. Whether Kaedlaw grew up good or evil, he would lead the giants against the rest of the northlands.

When her husband still did not speak, Brianna said, "Tell me."

Tavis took a deep breath. "Kaedlaw has two fathers," he said. "I'm sorry, milady. Please forgive me for allowing it."

Brianna hardly heard the apology. She felt no need of one, and there were other, more pressing matters on her mind. The queen took a tentative step toward her son.

"What of his future?"

Tavis shrugged. "No one can say. It's impossible to tell the future—at least Kaedlaw's."

Galgadayle shook his head violently. "What of my dreams?" he demanded. "You're lying!"

Brianna swept Kaedlaw from Tavis's hand, then whirled on the seer. "Don't be ridiculous." She was almost laughing. "Firbolgs can't lie!"

"Then what of my dreams?" the seer demanded. "They have always come true!"

"Have they really?" Basil's tone was more one of curiosity than debate. "Has anything ever happened *exactly* as you saw it?"

"Of course!" the seer replied. "A landslide swept Orisino's village away, just as I dreamed."

"In your dream, what happened to Orisino's tribe?"

"They were buried."

Basil smirked. "Obviously, your dream was inaccurate. We both know you warned Orisino in time to save his tribe."

Galgadayle furrowed his brow.

"The same thing happened with the fomorians, I presume," the runecaster continued. "You dreamed they would drown, then saved the entire tribe by warning Ror of their danger."

The seer's face grew almost as pale as Tavis's, then he fell on his knees before Brianna. "By the gods, I have made a terrible mistake!" he cried. "How can I earn your forgiveness?"

There was a time when Brianna would have turned

the firbolg away in contempt, perhaps even struck him, but the joy she felt now was more powerful than any fear he had ever inspired. She could not condemn the seer for what had been an act of conscience—and ultimately one of kindness and concern as well.

Brianna took Galgadayle's hand and urged him to his feet. "There's nothing to forgive. You may have frightened me half to death in the silver mines, but it was better that you were chasing us than the fire giants—and they would not have been so kind to their prisoners," she said. "Fate has a way of pursuing its own course; all you or I can do is follow our consciences and hope for the best."

"You are more generous than I deserve," Galgadayle replied. "But I thank you."

Basil cleared his throat. "Now that all's forgiven, perhaps we should turn our thoughts to leaving before Lanaxis comes back. As bad as he's wounded, I doubt the titan has given up."

Brianna felt her joy changing to hot tears. "That's what I was trying to tell you earlier! I can't leave the palace. The titan's magic is too strong!"

"By my brush!" Basil gasped. "That's what he meant!"

"What?" Tavis asked. "He said something?"

"As he was slipping down the hole into Twilight," Galgadayle confirmed. "I believe it was, 'This is not done, not done at all.'"

"It doesn't matter," Tavis said. "I can cleave even the titan's magic."

"But I can already see your bones!" Basil objected. "At most, you can use the axe twice before it destroys you—perhaps only once."

"I'll have to take that chance," Tavis said. "And if I fade, Galgadayle can . . . he can always . . ."

"What's wrong?" Brianna asked.

Tavis stepped toward the seer and raised his axe menacingly. Galgadayle wisely lowered his gaze and retreated.

"He can't have Sky Cleaver!" Tavis shouted. "I'll never give it up! I'm the One Wielder!"

"Of course you are," the queen replied. She stepped back and motioned for Basil to do the same. "We all know that."

This seemed to calm Tavis, and they all stood in silence, considering their options.

At last, Brianna said, "Running won't do us any good. One way or another, we're going to end this thing tonight."

Tavis shook his head. "We'll lose. I can't beat Lanaxis—and the rest of you can't even touch him."

"Don't worry about your sight," Brianna said. "The goddess still favors me. I can repair your eyes, at least."

"My eyes aren't the problem!"

Brianna frowned. "What's wrong? I know your concern can't be for yourself."

"Oh, I'm frightened enough for myself." Though Tavis's skin was so transparent that it was difficult to tell his expression, he seemed unable to raise his cloudy gaze from the floor. "But my first concern is still for you and Kaedlaw. I'm just not strong enough to best Lanaxis."

"Perhaps you could go into Twilight and slay him while he rests," suggested Galgadayle.

"He'll expect that," Brianna said. "Besides, the only time I've ever seen him rest was when he got caught in daylight. Twilight restores his strength."

"Then it's better to wait for him here," Basil said.

Tavis clutched the axe to his chest. "He'll steal it from me!"

"Steal it?" asked Galgadayle. "If Lanaxis gets close enough to grab it—"

"Not grab—call," Tavis said. "How do you expect me

301

to outshout a titan? He almost stole it before!"

"That makes no sense," said Basil. "The bond between Sky Cleaver and its wielder is an emotional one. Even Lanaxis shouldn't be able to call it simply by shouting."

"Of course he should!" Brianna said. "Lanaxis is mad with power-lust. Tavis's anger is no match for that."

Galgadayle sighed heavily. "Then we are finished."

Brianna shook her head. "Perhaps not. There are plenty of emotions mightier than power-lust." She turned to Tavis. "When Lanaxis tries to call Sky Cleaver away, fight him with a stronger emotion. Call it back with compassion in your heart, and you will win."

Basil shook his head. "That won't work. How can Tavis fight while he's trying to be compassionate?" the runecaster demanded. "He'll never kill the titan that way!"

Brianna let her eyes drop to her son's cherubic face. "Of course not, Basil." She kissed Kaedlaw on the brow. "We can't defeat Lanaxis by killing him."

\* \* \* \* \*

Fools. Watch this.

\* \* \* \* \*

A gloomy hand appeared first, as they knew it would, rising from the pit as the ashen afternoon darkened into twilight. Tavis stood on the boulder, Sky Cleaver in hand, with Basil and Galgadayle to either side of him. Brianna, unable to leave Bleak Palace, stood beside Kaedlaw at the end of the demolished portico.

Waiting was the hardest part. The queen's plan called for the One Wielder to attack last, but he wanted nothing more than to leap now and finish the battle. They had made their plans and completed all their preparations. He felt as though the combat had been fought already and they were only awaiting news of the victor.

The arm climbed slowly, filling the pit so completely that it seemed to drag the edges of the hole up with it. The limb continued to rise until it loomed above the boulder to twice Tavis's height, then tipped toward Bleak Palace and lay flat as a fallen tower. The hand wedged its fingers into the broken plain and pulled. An enormous, gloom-cloaked shoulder appeared in the hole.

"Now, Galgadayle!" Tavis urged. "Before he can call to Sky Cleaver."

The seer stepped forward and threw a glowing dagger. The blade sank deep into the titan's flesh, illuminating his shoulder in a brilliant halo of light.

If Lanaxis felt the weapon's sting, he showed no sign.

Basil attacked next, rushing forward with a javelin-sized knife stolen from the palace kitchen. For once, his flat feet made no sound as they slapped the ground, for he had painted runes of silence upon his boots. The runecaster lowered his weapon as though it were a lance and drove the point deep into the titan's clavicle.

Basil's legs were still pumping when the tenebrous arm abruptly dissolved into wisps of purple murk. He plunged forward. The verbeeg's mouth opened in a silent scream. He flailed his arms, dropping his weapon into the dark pit where the titan's shoulder had been a moment earlier.

Tavis leapt off the boulder and grabbed Basil's arm, pulling him away from the hole before he followed his knife into what remained of the Twilight Vale.

"It was an illusion!" Galgadayle continued to stare into the pit as he spoke.

"Then he'll be returning from someplace else." Tavis spun toward Bleak Palace, expecting to see the titan's looming figure charging across the demolished portico.

There was only Brianna, standing at the edge of the lowest step, with twilight rising around her like a ground fog. Tavis turned slowly and saw the purple gloom seeping up all across the plain.

No, not across the entire plain. To the east, a blanket of damson light was falling from the sky to cover the ashen snows. Twilight did not rise from the ground, not on a tableland as vast as the Bleak Plain.

"Watch yourselves!" the high scout yelled. "He's coming up under—"

Four purple talons burst from the ground and seized Tavis, crushing his arms to his sides. Sky Cleaver popped free and tumbled away. The shadowroc's foot closed only tightly enough to hold the high scout motionless, as though the bird thought he still had the axe and feared squeezing too tightly would trigger the weapon's defenses.

The shadowroc was emerging upside down. As its enormous breast rose from the plain, both Sky Cleaver and Basil tumbled off. The runecaster hit first, with the axe's enormous heft falling across his chest.

The verbeeg's baggy eyes grew as round as plates. His thick-lipped mouth fell open, and he glanced up at Tavis. When he found the high scout still locked helplessly in the raptor's enormous claw, he raised his sagacious eyebrows in apology. He looked away and wrapped both arms around Sky Cleaver's ivory handle.

Tavis felt the syllables of the axe's ancient summons rise spontaneously in his chest, but he could not force so many strange words past his trammeled ribs. An unreasoning panic welled up inside him, not because he was caught in the titan's grasp, but because he had lost Sky Cleaver.

As the shadowroc's enormous wings and tail rose from beneath the plain, Basil rolled onto his stomach and covered Sky Cleaver. The runecaster murmured something, then he began to pale—hair, flesh, even his clothes.

A shrill screech erupted from the shadowroc's throat as it broke completely free of the ground. Tavis felt himself whirl. The enormous bird rolled off its back, and then the air throbbed beneath the force of its great wings. Basil's figure, already as translucent as alabaster and still paling, began to recede. The raptor beat its wings again. The plain spread out beneath Tavis like a milky-blue sea. In the center lay a dark island of shattered ground, the ruins of Bleak Palace.

There was nothing above save the shadowroc's umbral torso, a ceiling of purple feathers as vast as a cloud. Every few seconds, the bird's distant wingtips dipped below its gloomy abdomen, lifting them ever higher into the sky. Perhaps twenty paces away, the sticklike stump of a severed leg dangled beneath the fan of a monstrous tail.

Tavis began to work his pinned arms back and forth. Though it required only a few moments to free an arm, by the time he succeeded the shadowroc had carried him so high he could have looked down on the moon. The immensity of Bleak Palace was a mere dot in the milky snows below. He could look across the Endless Ice Sea to where it spilled off the northern edge of the world, and in the opposite direction he saw the dark valleys of Hartsvale lying beyond the white teeth of the Ice Spires North.

The shadowroc leveled off. Tavis wrapped his free arm around a talon toe and jerked back as hard as he could. There was a muffled crack, and the bird opened its claw. The high scout dangled for an instant, then pulled himself up to wrap his free arm around the raptor's ankle. He shimmied up the tarsus as fast as he could, trying to reach the jungle of feathers overhead.

The shadowroc's ebony beak darted back beneath its

breast, a blue tongue fluttering in its gaping maw.

Tavis grabbed a handful of feather vanes and pulled himself into the dark thicket that covered the bird's meaty thigh, barely escaping the hooked mandible that came scraping across the tarsus below.

Suddenly, the high scout's legs began to rise, as though floating, and his entire body followed, straining away from the shadowroc's thigh. The vast expanse of the Endless Ice Sea flashed past his eyes, then the starlit sky, the jagged Ice Spires, and finally the creamy snows of the Bleak Plain. Tavis pulled himself deeper into the feathers and held on for his life, trying to keep from being thrown clear as the raptor tumbled. Again, the Ice Sea flickered past, followed so quickly by the stars and distant mountains that the sky and ground blurred into a kaleidoscope.

The shadowroc pulled a beakful of feathers from its thigh and tossed them to the wind. Tavis could not tell how far the bird had already fallen, but he felt certain those hooked mandibles would find him long before the raptor crashed itself into the ground. Nor could he climb to a safer hiding place. It was all he could do to keep from being flung off the tumbling creature. He realized now why the titan had attacked in this form. As long as they were in the air, Lanaxis was the master; even if the high scout had been holding Sky Cleaver, he could not have killed his foe without sending himself plummeting toward the wasteland below.

For the next several seconds, the shadowroc struggled against the force of its wild fall to bring its beak to bear. Then, with the ground so close that Tavis could see his friends standing on Bleak Palace's shattered portico, the raptor's beak closed around the feathers to which he was clinging.

Tavis thrust one hand into a nostril. The air inside was as bitter and cold as ice. He grabbed hold of a jagged edge and clung tight as the shadowroc flicked its head to rip the feathers from its thigh. The high scout felt his feet swing around and sink into the soft tissue of the bird's eye. It squawked in shock, then whipped its head in the opposite direction. Tavis slammed against the side of its beak and reached over the top, sticking his hand into the other nostril.

"Try to get rid of me now!"

The high scout had barely growled the challenge before he floated into the air, remaining connected to the beak only by the strength of his trembling old hands. The shadowroc's enormous wings spread out to both sides of its body. The bird swept low over the ground, and the kaleidoscope of their long, tumbling fall abruptly gave way to the milky snows of the Bleak Plain.

They glided toward Lanaxis's palace, flying no higher than the cupola. Basil was standing on the portico, supporting his ancient frame on Sky Cleaver's heft. Already, the runecaster's organs and most of his bones showed through his transparent skin.

"Throw it, Basil!" The cry was not so much a command as a prayer, for not even Basil had believed he would have the strength to part with Sky Cleaver once he touched it. "Now!"

As they passed by, Tavis kept his gaze fixed on the palace. To his amazement, Basil grasped Sky Cleaver's heft and began to spin like a hammer-hurler. The shadowroc dipped a wing and wheeled around. Tavis lost sight of the verbeeg, then felt a sudden rush of wind as Lanaxis drew a deep breath through the cavernous bird nostrils.

The high scout whipped his head back around in time to see Basil releasing the axe. In the same instant, the shadowroc voiced the terrible screech Brianna had warned them about. An anguished ringing erupted in Tavis's ears, and his entire body stung from the powerful vibrations that reverberated through the bird's beak. The cry swept Basil from his feet and hurled him across the portico into Galgadayle and Brianna.

Sky Cleaver dropped toward the ground.

Tavis pulled one hand from the shadowroc's nostril and stretched it toward the axe. *"In the name of Skoreaus Stonebones, Your Maker—"* The high scout's ears were ringing so painfully he could not be certain he was uttering the syllables correctly, but the axe began to rise into the air. *"O Sky Cleaver, do I summon you—"*

The shadowroc screeched again, and wheeled around so violently that Tavis slammed against the side of its head. As they turned, the high scout glimpsed the axe sailing after them. He finished the last part of the command, unable to hear his own words:

*"Into the service of my hand."*

Sky Cleaver flew to Tavis, turning its heft toward his outstretched palm. The shadowroc flapped its wings madly. Once more the vibrations of its deafening screech racked the high scout's body; then he felt the axe's ivory handle in his palm.

The bird flung its head wildly, trying to throw its passenger away before he could strike. Tavis glimpsed the moonlit snows a thousand feet below. He knew Sky Cleaver would save him even if he destroyed the shadowroc, but Brianna had warned him against thinking he could kill the titan so easily. He would have to defeat Lanaxis another way.

Tavis waited and hung on, more for his son's sake than his own. When at last he felt himself bouncing toward the shadowroc's face, he struck not with the edge of the axe blade, but with the flat.

"Cleave!" he commanded. "Sunder this madness!"

Tavis could never speak of what happened next, not even to Brianna. He remembered a wind that shined like light and a radiance that boomed like thunder. He stood on the whirling emptiness between the stars, with the titan kneeling at his side, head bowed toward a majestic figure that resembled the smell of freshly cut spruce and the sizzle of lightning and the howl of a lonely wind sweeping over an endless glacier. A voice like oak coursed through the high scout's body and, he supposed, through Lanaxis's as well.

"I can return, but why?" demanded the majestic figure. "You poisoned your brothers. You destroyed Ostoria. You cannot raise it again."

"But the voices, Father!" Lanaxis seemed as young as the day he had walked from Othea's birthing caves, with a strapping lean body, curly brown hair, and a brow unfurrowed by centuries of worry. Only his eyes, as deep and sad as twilight, betrayed his timeless remorse. "I have listened to them—I have studied them—for decades of centuries. You want me to rebuild Ostoria. The message is clear!"

"Message? There is no message! The time of giants has passed without notice on Toril, and that is your doing. The voices are punishment, nothing more."

A sob of boundless anguish rose from Lanaxis's throat. "No, Father!"

"Your punishment is not eternal, Lanaxis." The god's voice had grown so hard that it scraped along Tavis's bones like a rasp. "After all, you are a mortal now."

Lanaxis gave a cry, then suddenly dropped through the whirling emptiness and vanished from sight. The high scout prepared himself to follow, but instead felt Annam's voice, as supple as a chamois brushing over his skin.

"You have something of mine," the god said. "Return it, and I shall return what is yours."

Tavis held Sky Cleaver out at arm's length. "Take your axe, please. It has no place on Toril."

"That shall be for you to decide," Annam replied. "I

know you mortals. It is easy enough for you to behave when you are frightened, but you do tend to change your minds at the last moment."

Tavis felt himself sinking through the emptiness. He tried to toss Sky Cleaver toward the god, but the ivory handle would not leave his palms.

"Wait! How do I—"

He emerged above the Bleak Plain, with Lanaxis's palace below. He was in exactly the same place as when he had cleaved the titan's madness, but the shadowroc was no longer there. Tavis clutched Sky Cleaver to his breast, waiting for the familiar cold tingle that would mean the weapon was saving him.

The high scout continued to fall, the cold wind whistling past his ears ever faster. He started to cry out for the weapon to work its magic, then remembered Annam's comment about mortals. He drew his arm back and tossed the axe into the sky.

"Take it!"

Tavis never saw what happened to Sky Cleaver. He had hardly released the handle before the shadowroc swooped down between them, obscuring his view of the weapon. The bird's powerful claw closed around his body, bringing his fall to an abrupt end.

The great raptor wheeled on its wingtip and dived toward Bleak Palace, where Brianna and the two 'kin still stood on the ruined portico, staring into the sky. For a moment, Tavis thought the bird actually meant to rescue him. Then its claw bore down, squeezing the air from his lungs. His bones began to pop and groan under the terrible pressure, and he felt a talon slip between his ribs.

The shadowroc swooped low over the palace cupola, then beat the air with its great wings. It came to a near stop over the shattered portico and started to drop, sending Brianna and the others scrambling for weapons and cover. Then, just when the high scout thought his captor meant to land, the bird beat its wings again. Its claw opened, dropping Tavis on the rubble-strewn portico.

Brianna was on him almost before the pain. "Where does it hurt? Can you feel . . ." The queen's mouth fell open, and she gasped, "In the name of Hiatea!"

Tavis peered to the suddenly empty sky. He pushed himself upright, expecting to feel the anguish of some gruesome injury. Instead, he seemed amazingly well, save for a few bruises from his fall and the talon wound in his torso. The high scout raised his hand and saw that not only had his flesh returned to its normal ruddy complexion, it was no longer wrinkled or spotted with age.

"You're young again!" Brianna cried.

"For the most part, anyway." Galgadayle stepped over to the scout's side and fingered a lock of gray hair. "I doubt this will ever be bronze again."

"I'll settle for gray." Tavis stood up and looked from Brianna's empty arms to Galgadayle's. "Now where's my son?"

"Be patient," growled Basil. "We're coming."

The runecaster sounded older and more tired than ever. Tavis turned to see a disconcerting figure tottering toward him. Unlike the high scout, Basil had not recovered from Sky Cleaver's effects. His face was a mask of yellow bone set with moving eyes and a few translucent strings of muscle. The runecaster's body was worse; it looked as though he had somehow survived being flayed by fomorian hunters.

Basil passed Kaedlaw into Tavis's arms. "What happened to Sky Cleaver?"

"I gave it back . . . I'm sorry."

The verbeeg looked down at his translucent body, then shrugged. "It's not your fault. Even knowing the cost, I'd do the same again. I had to know."

"What?" Brianna stepped to Tavis's side and took his hand. "What did you have to know?"

Basil's mouth twisted into an ecstatic, if particularly gruesome, smile. "Everything," he answered. "Everything that matters."

An uneasy chill ran down Tavis's spine, though he could not say whether it was because of the runecaster's reply or the eerie keen he heard building across the plain. The high scout turned to face the noise. He saw the shadowroc's silhouette wheel high in the sky, then dive toward the western horizon. The screech arrived a moment later. At such a distance, it was hardly powerful enough to knock anyone off his feet, but the skirl set their ears to ringing and caused Kaedlaw to start crying.

"Ssssshh." Brianna stood on her toes, holding Tavis's arm while she comforted their son. "The titan can't hurt you. Your father's here."

# Epilogue

I soar upon the ashen winds of dusk, a restless shadow in the eternal eventide, a hunter always chasing and never catching. The sun lies just below the horizon, sinking as fast as I fly, forever retreating, forever calling me onward. Below passes Toril, the world the giants should have ruled: swarthy deserts behind gloom-shrouded mountains that loom over twinkling cities standing upon the shores of glimmering seas strewn with islands as numerous as stars, an endless procession of savage lands and forbidden realms and lost kingdoms, a vast, exquisite reward for a crime as dark as the night.

Now and again, I see the ones who did this to me, standing upon the parapets of their brittle castle, holding my nephew in their arms and teaching him to be a frail human king. Often I swoop low over their heads and cry a greeting, shaking the loose stones from the crenelations and blasting the guards from their feet. This frightens the groveling humans, I know, but never Kaedlaw. He has begun to walk now, and in the summers he often sneaks onto the keep roof and waits for my umbral wings to appear in the dusk sky. When I screech, he claps his hands with glee and chortles madly until his father the firbolg rushes out to gather him up.

There was no reason to save Tavis, I know. Do not ask me to explain. Perhaps I was repaying him; he struck with compassion when he could have slain, and I suppose that creates a bond of sorts.

*"If that's what you believe, then it's true. . . ."*

Or perhaps it was Sky Cleaver's doing; Tavis was the One Wielder, after all, and I was as bound by Annam's will then as I am now.

*". . . to be free? Stop crying, now you are . . ."*

It was my own mortality, then. I didn't know this before I left the Vale—how could I?—but there is a bond between all things that die, and in the firbolg's passing I saw reflections of my own.

*". . . sound like a sop. Talk like that . . ."*

Say what you will, whoever you are! I have learned better than to listen to your voices.